Jackson Speed at the High Tide

♦

by

Robert R. Peecher Jr.

Jackson Speed at the High Tide

Cover Illustration by Alex McArdell

For information, the author may be contacted at:

PO BOX 967; Watkinsville, GA; 30677

or at robertpeecher.com

This books is a work of historical fiction. While some characters represented in this book are actual people and some of the events represented in this book took place, these are fictionalized accounts of those people and those events.

Copyright © 2015 MoonCalf Press/Robert Peecher

All rights reserved.

ISBN: 1514377683
ISBN-13: 978-1514377680

For Jean,

Always for Jean,
Who walked these hills with me.
And for our sons,
Harrison, Nathan and Robert,
Who made the charge with us.

ACKNOWLEDGEMENTS

I owe a tremendous amount of gratitude to author and historian Glenn Tucker whose research into the Battle of Gettysburg I relied on extensively for the writing of this book. His book "High Tide at Gettysburg" changed perceptions about the battle but also went a long way to changing perceptions about how history should be told. Tucker has always been one of my favorite Civil War historians, and it was a joy to find myself so heavily immersed in "High Tide." The title of this book is intended as a tribute to Tucker. I hope it is one he would appreciate.

So, too, do I owe debt to Shelby Foote, another fine Civil War historian, whose work helped to inspire Jackson Speed. Jackson Speed's very existence came about because I happened to be reading Shelby Foote's "Civil War: A Narrative" at the same time I was re-reading George MacDonald Fraser's "Flashman." So it is that Jackson Speed is the odd convergence of Foote and Fraser.

I also feel compelled to thank Jim Tate, who led me around the Gettysburg battlefield and whose grandfather was there at that time.

Also, the artist Dale Gallon, whose painting "The 20th Maine and the 15th Alabama" (a print of which hangs in my office) has come to provide me with daily inspiration.

I also want to thank Alex McArdell who illustrated the cover of "Jackson Speed at the High Tide." Perhaps it is true that you cannot judge a book by its cover, but people will certainly get an excellent first impression of "Jackson Speed at the High Tide"!

My father instilled in me at a young age a love of history. Dr. Bob Wilson, formerly a history professor at Georgia College & State University in Milledgeville, convinced me that history was not just interesting but also fun. I am grateful to both of them for creating in me this obsession with history.

I am also appreciative to Jean Peecher, India Powell, Arthur Wayne Glowka and Ken Sawyer who offer encouragement.

CONTENTS

Introduction	i	Chapter 14	156
Chapter 1	1	Chapter 15	172
Chapter 2	8	Chapter 16	184
Chapter 3	22	Chapter 17	199
Chapter 4	34	Chapter 18	207
Chapter 5	47	Chapter 19	218
Chapter 6	55	Chapter 20	228
Chapter 7	72	Chapter 21	238
Chapter 8	93	Chapter 22	247
Chapter 9	106	Chapter 23	265
Chapter 10	121	Epilogue	271
Chapter 11	133	End Note	276
Chapter 12	136	Footnotes	279
Chapter 13	151	Map	302

The Jackson Speed Memoirs

Volume IV

June and July, 1863

♦

Edited & Arranged by

Robert R. Peecher Jr.

INTRODUCTION

With the passing of time, the name "Jackson Speed" has become less familiar to the American public than it was during the mid- to late-1800s. Certainly, however, those armchair historians who spend time studying 19th Century American history will be familiar with Jackson Speed (1830 – 1922).

"The Hero of El Teneria" in the Mexican-American War, a Pinkerton agent who saved the life of the 16th president, Jackson Speed was honored by both Abraham Lincoln and Robert E. Lee for the services he provided to their respective sides during the American Civil War. Speed was a Texas Ranger and rode with the infamous Regulators in the Lincoln County War.

Over the years, however, Speed has largely been relegated to the position of a historical footnote.

While researching another project, I happened upon a letter written by Speed's granddaughter in 1906, and in that letter she reported that Speed was "furiously laboring at his memoirs."

Intrigued at the prospect of finding the musings from one of the 19th Century's most colorful adventurers, I began contacting Speed's known descendants in the hopes of finding the unpublished memoirs.

When I did find them, and secured from his descendants permission to edit and publish them, I was dismayed by what I'd discovered.

The man who received a battlefield promotion from Jefferson Davis and received the Congressional Medal of Honor at Gettysburg and was toasted for his bravery by Theodore Roosevelt turned out to be a confessed coward, an adulterer and, quite possibly, the luckiest scoundrel to ever charge into battle.

As editor of his memoirs, I make no judgment on the character of the man. His proximity to great men during the great moments of our nation's history make his memoirs an invaluable historical resource, and in editing the first four volumes of the Jackson Speed Memoirs I have found that Speed often provides the last word on historical mysteries.

I have endeavored to provide footnotes to help put Speed's very personal recollections into a historical context wherever I felt it was necessary, and I have divided Speed's massive memoirs into chapters and volumes to make them more easily digestible to the modern reader. I am releasing the memoirs in the order in which they were written rather than a chronological order of his life. The current volume, Volume IV, takes up a very short period of time from mid-June, 1863 to the first few days of July 1863.

Volume III of the Jackson Speed Memoirs includes the period of time I titled "Jackson Speed on the Orange Turnpike" – his exploits during the winter of 1863 and his involvement in the Battle of Chancellorsville.

To provide context for the current volume for readers who might have skipped Volume III, I offer a brief synopsis of the previous volume.

During the winter of 1863, while serving in Richmond, Va., as a liaison for General James Longstreet, Speed took up residence with a Union spy by the name of Jenny Rakestraw. When Rakestraw determined that she no longer wanted to stay in Richmond spying for the Union, Speed helped her cross the Rappahannock River and get north where she intended to return home. Before leaving, Rakestraw handed Speed a slip of paper with the name of her hometown and encouraged him to come visit her if he had the opportunity.

Readers and students of history will know that while at the Rappahannock assisting Rakestraw, Speed was caught up in the Battle of Chancellorsville. Speed was at the front of Stonewall Jackson's famous flanking charge that routed O.O. Howard's corps of the Army of the Potomac.

In the days following that battle, Speed was summoned to Confederate President Jefferson Davis's office in Richmond. There, President Davis sent Speed on a mission as a spy into the north. Once he was safely across enemy lines, Speed decided to abandon his duty as a Confederate spy and flee the war. His intention was to desert both armies and go to New York where his brother-in-law operated a furniture factory.

However, Speed's lustfulness got the better of him, and on his way to New York he decided to visit Jenny Rakestraw. Retrieving the slip of paper from his hatband, Speed read the name of the Pennsylvania town where Rakestraw lived: "Gettysburg."

The current volume, Volume IV of the Jackson Speed Memoirs, picks up immediately where Volume III left off.

As always, it has been a distinct pleasure to serve as the editor of Jackson Speed's memoirs, and I am grateful for the opportunity.

Robert Peecher Jr.
Editor

CHAPTER 1

Editor's Note: "Old Peter is dead ..." Thus begins the third volume of the Jackson Speed Memoirs. The writing of Volumes III and IV of the Jackson Speed memoirs appears to have begun the day Jackson Speed learned of the death of his old general from the Confederacy, James Longstreet. Volume IV of the Jackson Speed Memoirs, the current volume, picks up immediately where Volume III left off. Readers who have not yet read Volume III, Jackson Speed on the Orange Turnpike, will need to know that after the Confederacy's success at the Battle of Chancellorsville in May of 1863, Speed had accepted a mission from Confederate President Jefferson Davis to sneak across the Rappahannock and serve as a Confederate spy. Not long after crossing the river with another Confederate spy, Harrison, Speed ran into a Union cavalry troop and a brief battle ensued from which Speed fled. Determined to abandon the war entirely, Speed intended to go to New York where – with his wife's brother – he had set up a furniture factory before the start of the war. But upon further reflection, Speed decided to make a stop in Pennsylvania before going on to New York to see the Union spy Jenny Rakestraw with whom he'd had a several months-long affair in Richmond earlier in the year. And so his memoirs continue ...

So that was how it was that I came to desert my way into the biggest battle of the war. The thought of Jenny Rakestraw's luscious blonde hair, green eyes and cherry-red nipples led me to remember that scrap of paper with the name of the town where I could find her. I fetched it from my hatband, unfolded it and read the name of the town: Gettysburg. I'd never heard of it before, and there was no reason why I should have. Gettysburg was a farming community and they made buggies there. You'll know enough about the battle to realize that several roads led into Gettysburg – most of 'em famous now for the armies that marched along 'em or charged over 'em – and at the time of the battle they were bringing in additional railroad lines, so I suppose it is correct to say that Gettysburg was on the precipice of becoming an important place. But in June of '63, I couldn't know how important.

After abandoning my fellow Confederate spy to whatever fate he could work out for hisself, I continued my ride north and east. I was too afraid to stop, and by my second day of traveling, I was mostly walking along beside my horse to spare him. We were both exhausted and spent, and it was owing to nothing more than good fortune that I did not cross paths with any more Yankee cavalry, for I was in such a state of weariness that bluffing my way past 'em would have been too much to ask of me.

I purposefully avoided towns, riding or walking the horse through fields or along the edge of woods rather than along roads so that I might not happen across any more Yankees. I had rations for three days in my saddlebags, and that was enough to keep me going except for my lack of sleep. But I was too frightened to stop for any length of time. I could not allow myself to be caught, and the only way to be sure that I wasn't caught was by keeping my eyes open.

But eventually my exhaustion was such that it forced me to seek shelter for a night. I found it in a tavern near Taylorstown. There, for the first time, I was able to get my bearings and determine where I was. Still in Virginia, I'd ridden north of Washington D.C. and was near the Maryland border.

Here, so close to Washington and the Union, I found the couple who owned the tavern sympathetic to my blue uniform, even though I was still in a secesh state. Over the years I've forgotten their names, though I can remember their faces quite clearly. They were an elderly couple, and when I first met them they struck me as a sad pair. They were still mourning the loss of a son who had been killed in Union blue at Antietam, which was not far to the north.

The man was mostly bald, with a few wisps of white hair here and there. His face was cracked with deep wrinkles. His hands were big and calloused, and I suspected he had spent a fair part of his life working a farm somewhere. He was thin, and whatever strength there had been in his arms was now gone. His wife was short and round, and she wore her gray hair in a bun. She wore a plain blue dress, I remember, and she had a white apron tied around her. She walked with a noticeable discomfort from arthritis in her knees.

I was the only guest in the tavern that evening, and the old man ate his supper with me at a table. I recall we had potato soup with onions and carrots, and I'll tell you that after two days of hardtack and jerky it was a good and decent meal.

"I rode out to the battlefield with a wagon to find my son's body," the old man told me over supper. "Were you there, at Antietam?"

Well, I'd been there – hadn't I? But I was on the Sharpsburg Ridge, looking down on Burnside's Bridge, wearing Confederate gray and firing my pistol into a mass of blue.

"I came across the bridge with Burnside," I told the old man.

He thought about it for a moment. "No," he said thoughtfully. "No, my son was under General Hooker, and I found his body in a cornfield."

"Aye, that would have been on the other side of the battle," I said.

Talking about his son, the old man had tears welling up in his eyes. I was seeking to escape the war as best I could, and I did not care to hear the old man reminisce about his dead son and have to endure with him the recollections of what this war had taken from him. I was tired and irritable, and I've always believed that it served no purpose to dwell on another man's sorrows. I'd seen plenty of death over the past two years – corpses blown to bits by canister, men run through or shot, men weeping for their mothers or their wives or their children as they lay dying – and I learned long ago that the way you survive is to never get too interested in another man's suffering. If you start to pay attention to other's sorrows, you're liable to get careless of avoiding your own. The old man's sadness was as much as he could bear, and I did not have the strength nor the desire to help him with it.

"Do you have other children?" I asked, seeking to change the subject.

"Our youngest son is fighting with the Rebel States," the old man said, wiping the tears from his eyes and taking a gruffer tone. "But we do not speak of him. We have two daughters, also, who are both married to Union men. One is with General Hooker at the Rappahannock, the other is out west with General Grant.

"But the boy killed at Antietam was our first born, and he didn't betray his country and his family by joining with the Rebel States," the old man said, returning to his dead son. "He has a wife and two sons who now depend upon us. But we're old, and what will become of her and my grandsons?"

"The war is a terrible thing, sir," I told him.

He looked up from his potato soup. "The seceshes are a terrible thing," he said. At that, the old man stood up and excused himself and went off to bed.

I'd not seen much of this side of it. Even during my days in Richmond, if there were parents or wives of dead soldiers, you didn't see them about, mourning and thinking of the dead. The affect the war had on families and civilians wasn't something anyone cared to think on much at the front. For the most part, the boys soon to face battle enjoyed the moments between battles with games, songs, dancing and camaraderie. That's as it had to be. Any day, the army could be on the march, and the next day you could be shot dead. So you didn't think much about the hardships of your family at home.

In her letters, my Eliza wrote about our two young sons. James was now eleven, and young Drew was already a toddler and I'd never even seen him. James was the man of the house, she reported, forever marching around with a stick he used as either a sword or a rifle and wearing a too-big gray coat given to him by a neighbor who had come home wounded. If there were hardships, Eliza seldom mentioned them. Oh, she'd complain about the price of this or that and how there were some necessaries that could not be found, but Lord knows we had the money to pay the prices, and she found a way to do without what did not exist. She mentioned from time to time people we knew who had been killed or wounded or gone missing in battles, but there was little emotion in any of it.

But this old couple put a face on the misery at home for me. One son dead, another disowned.

I finished my soup and then finished off what the old man had left in his bowl, and then I went to bed myself. It was fatigue that had convinced me to stop for the night in this tavern, and I was near to nodding off into my soup by the time I rose from the table.

I undressed myself, tossing my Yankee uniform onto a chair in the room, but once in bed I found I had trouble falling asleep. My slumber was disturbed with, not dreams, but images flashing through my mind of Eliza and myself as an old couple, waiting to hear news of our sons Jamie and Drew off to fight in the war. We were elderly and sad, and I found these images troubled my sleep, and I tossed and turned for the longest time.

I believe I was getting homesick for Eliza. For all my travels and adventures in other women's beds, it's a fact that Eliza remained one of my two or three favorites. And I'd enjoyed being with young Jamie so much when he was just a little boy. Spending time with my young'n, throwing balls, riding off across the countryside with him perched in front of me in my saddle, and even reading stories to him, these were fine pursuits. And I was missing my son. And the other boy, the one who was conceived in New York in November of '60; I'd never laid eyes on him. He wouldn't even know his Pa when I finally returned home.

Aye, if I'd been south of the Rappahannock this night, I believe in the morning I would have turned south and found my way back to Georgia.

But I wasn't south of the Rappahannock, and the comfort I sought was to be found to the north in Gettysburg, Pennsylvania.

When I rose with the sun the next morning, I found that the woman had come into my room at some point and gathered up my clothes. She brushed the dust off my coat and pants, and had me looking like a proper Yankee officer. I ate a meager breakfast of bread and broth, and I fetched that slip of paper from my hatband.

"Ever hear of Gettysburg, Pennsylvania?" I asked the old man.

He nodded. "They make buggies there," he said. "Is that where you're bound?"

"Aye," I said. "Official business for the Union."

"This road 'ere," he said, pointing out the window, "will take you north to Frederick. From Frederick, you'll go through Emmitsburg and then you'll be near to Gettysburg."

I thanked the couple for their kindnesses and paid them for the room and the meals. Before I left, though, I had a word with the old man. I don't know what it was that overcame me. It was none of my business. But I suppose it was thinking on my own sons that made me say something. As I saddled my horse and prepared to ride out, it was just me and the old man out there in his barn, and I said to him: "Your other son, the one fighting for the Confederacy. If he ever comes home, you should welcome him home and forgive him."

The old man's face wrinkled even more, and I thought he was going to curse me.

"It is the Rebel states that has caused all this misery!" he exclaimed. "How could I forgive him?"

"He's your son," I said. "You just forgive him. And be glad he's survived it."

The old man stared at me, and I shrugged my shoulders. "Of course, he mightn't survive, so then it won't matter a bit. But if he does, your remaining years will be the better for it if ye welcome the boy home."

"How can a Union officer recommend forgiveness?" the man questioned me, but I noticed the harshness to his tone was softening. It was almost as if he was giving me the opportunity to give him permission to forgive.

"Look 'ere," I said to him. "When this war is over and the Union is victorious," – I was, after all, wearing Union blue as I spoke – "the only way our country comes back together is through forgiveness. Ain't that right? We welcome home the seceding states when the time comes. Prodigal son and whatnot. And so we should within our families, too. I ain't telling you what to do, but if it was me, I'd write my boy and tell him when this terrible thing is done and dusted, he should come home and see his ma."

The old man stared for a moment, and I saw tears leaking from the corners of his eyes and flowing like rivers through the cracks in his face. And then the old bastard grabbed me bodily and pulled me into a bear hug. I patted him on the back and broke free just as quick as I could. Then I climbed into my saddle and rode north on the road he'd pointed out to me.

I couldn't tell you what came of that old man and his wife, for I never went back through there again. I've wondered from time to time, though, if he did take my advice to heart and if there was a reunion between parents and prodigal son.

Likely as not, though, the boy caught a Yankee bullet in the chest and was buried in an unmarked grave on some battlefield where his pa would never find him.

CHAPTER 2

The afternoon when I first rode up the Emmitsburg Road into Gettysburg, Pennsylvania, could not have been a prettier, more delightful afternoon.

The sun was shining, there was a pleasant breeze blowing, flowers were blooming, corn and hay were growing in the surrounding fields, and if there was a war on you wouldn't have known it. I felt a certain contentment, an ease of spirit that can only be described in a single word: Peace. I believed at last I had escaped this miserable war after two years of constant danger, constant death and constant destruction.

I'd survived Manassas and Shiloh; I'd nearly been hung at Richmond, but survived that too. I'd survived the Seven Days. I'd been at Antietam and Fredericksburg and had led the charge on Hooker's flank at Chancellorsville. Now I was free and clear of both armies, well in the rear of the Union lines, and riding along the Emmitsburg Road, as I looked about me, I was convinced that whatever further horrors this war could devise, I would be away from all harm.

Even so, riding along the road I foresaw everything that would take place in less than a month.

To my left was Seminary Ridge. On my right were the towering hills, first Round Top and then Little Round Top, which leveled out into Cemetery Ridge. Between the two ridges lay a valley about a mile wide. As I emerged from Pitzer's Woods, I saw the peach orchard. I saw the hay field where Pickett would make his charge. I saw the swale and the rise where the boys in gray – me along with them – would dash for the umbrella shaped tree.

And as I rode along, in early June, I saw as clear in my mind's eye as I would on July 2 and July 3, two armies facing each other on those two ridges, firing cannon back and forth at each other.

At one point, I even turned in my saddle and looked back at Round Top. I envisioned a flanking maneuver going through that peach orchard and up the side of the big hill.

Before Bobby Lee or George Meade ever set foot in Gettysburg, I saw their two armies facing each other.

It was no premonition on my part. After two years of war, and particularly the past several months serving on Longstreet's staff, I'd reached a point where everywhere I looked I could envision armies positioning themselves for good and better ground. Every time I saw a hill of any size, I envisioned an army occupying that hill and another army trying to get up it.

But I'll say this: In all my travels and all the thousands of times I've looked at terrain and imagined armies occupying that terrain and jockeying for position, I have never once seen a field that I thought was more perfectly suited to be a site for a battle. If God had ever laid hill beside hill, rock upon rock, or scattered tree beside tree and thought to hisself, "Here is where men will fight," this was surely the place. Oh, I've heard of Megiddo, and though I ain't never seen it, I am convinced it is no better suited for war than Gettysburg.

That first day, riding into Gettysburg, the thought struck me as clearly as any thought ever had: "If Longstreet were here, he'd pick that eastern ridge and let the Yankees come at him all day long."

Well, you'll know as well as I do who it was occupying the eastern ridge, and you'll know how it turned out.

But those thoughts did not dissuade me from my intentions. As I said, I didn't see a hill without thinking about how I would hold it with Old Peter's First Corps, and so I had no reason to think that these particular hills would be occupied with something other than imaginary soldiers in three weeks or that I would be in among 'em, praying for my life.

Since crossing into Pennsylvania I had twice come across the local Home Guard out patrolling the countryside. On both instances, they rode to me to make conversation, mostly wanting news of whether or not the Rebels were coming. It was worth noting, I thought, that neither time did the local militia inquire as to what I was about or where I was going, and I never even had to produce my forged passport. The only concern they had was for the Rebel army and whether or not Bobby Lee was coming along presently.

The Home Guard was also not at all impressive. Mostly it consisted of men whose portly stature was an abuse to the overburdened animals on which they were mounted. If not men of vast stature, the Home Guard consisted of children who did not have the strength to raise and fire a musket and so carried none.

In the towns, it was the same thing, although something closer to panic among the citizenry at my appearance. I did not ride more than a few blocks into a town before I was being accosted by self-appointed delegations of citizenry eager to know if my arrival was an indication that they should ship their valuables north and hide their good horses in the hills. They were all skittish that Bobby Lee was coming to get them.

At every opportunity, I eased their minds that I was merely on leave and there was no army following me, though they would find out differently soon enough.

As I neared the town, passing by a farmhouse on my right, I was confronted by a boy who looked to be about six-years-old. He had appointed himself as the local Home Guard and somewhere had acquired an army issue forage cap. It fit him poorly so that he had to elevate his nose to point toward the sky to be able to see from underneath the brim of the hat. He was armed with a stick that he brandished at me like a sword.

He had propped himself on the top rail of a fence, but as I neared him, sword pointing at me, he leapt from his perch and stood facing me in the middle of the road.

"Ho there!" he called to me, but seeing my uniform his eyes lit up. "Are you with the army?" he asked, dropping his stick to his side.

"I am," I said. "And who are you?"

"I am Fred Thorn," he said. "I am captain of the Pennsylvania Voluntary Cavalry." He pointed his stick to the fence post where he'd been seated as I rode toward him. "That's my fine mount."

"And what is the Pennsylvania Voluntary Cavalry doing today?" I asked.

"Laying in ambush for the Rebel army," Fred Thorn said.

"Well, I've not seen them on their way here, and I've been as far south as Virginia, so I suspect you should run along and get some supper before resuming your ambush."

"Ye've been in Virginia?" he asked, his eyes still wide with awe.

"'Course I have," I told him. "Where else would a Union major be?"

"Well what are you doing here?" he asked wisely. If this was Gettysburg's Home Guard, the town seemed better protected than all other towns I'd ridden through. Here was a Home Guard who knew his business, questioning passersby not about the position of the Rebel army but about their own intentions.

"I'm on leave currently," I told him. "I've come to Gettysburg to visit a friend of mine. Perhaps you know her. The name's Jenny Rakestraw."

"I know Miss Rakestraw," he said. "She was away, but she come back a few weeks ago."

"Do you know where she lives?" I asked.

"I don't know which house is hers, but she lives somewhere near the Diamond 'cause I always see her there."

I was hopeful that I'd find Jenny quick once I was in town. I didn't want to be about asking a lot of people for directions and drawing any kind of suspicion. I knew that an overactive Home Guard or a local sheriff was as likely as not to arrest me as a spy – with or without a passport – and I hoped to avoid anything such as that. This encounter with young Fred Thorn boosted my confidence that I might be successful in finding Jenny before the day was out.

"Well, Captain Thorn, I'm also going to need a bed to sleep in," I said.

"I'm sure you could stay in our house. My pa is away with his regiment."

"Well, that's kind of you, but I was thinking more along the lines of a hotel. Do you know of one?"

"There's the Globe Inn," he said, but he seemed to be thinking about it. "My grampapa says they's sympthizers, but I know both Mr. Wills and his son, and they's nice folks for symp-thizers."

"And where is the Globe?" I asked him.

He turned to face the town, still north of us. "Go up yonder into the town, and when you get to the Diamond it's off that way down a street," he said, indicating to the right with the point of his stick. He then turned back to me. "What's it like in Virginia?" he asked.

"Oh, there's lots of Rebels all over the state," I said. "But there's lots of Federals, too. And mostly we just sit and look at the Rebels across the river from where we are, and they look back at us, and every once in a while they shoot at us or we shoot at them."

"You ever shot one?" he asked.

"Well, I'm a major, so I don't shoot so much as I point to the spot where I want other men to shoot."

This deflated his enthusiasm quite a bit, and he frowned disappointment at meeting a Federal officer who could not lay claim to having killed any Rebels. "Where's your father's regiment?" I asked.

"They're in Virginia, too," he said.

"Well, maybe by now your daddy's shot a Rebel," I offered.

Young Fred Thorn's enthusiasm returned at that. "I sure hope so!" he said.

"Well, get on to your supper, or back to your ambush or whatever you intend to do," I said. "I appreciate your help quite a bit, Captain Thorn. You've been very kind. And if you happen to see Jenny Rakestraw before I find her, please don't tell her I've asked about her – I'd like it to be a surprise."

"Yes sir!" he said, and he saluted and then he climbed back on his "fine mount" and commenced to ambushing the Rebels and swinging his sword this way and that.

I rode on into town along the wide street, and I was struck by the complete absence of any sort of evidence that there was a war on. The homes and businesses were clean and orderly. Men and women were in the streets, going about their business. I saw carts loaded with goods and there were plenty of men – even fighting age men – carrying boxes and bags of goods out of stores. Gettysburg appeared wholly untouched by the war. The homes and businesses were all neat and well kept. The men and women were all dressed in decent clothes.

You'd have not seen a scene like it in any Southern town that I knew. In the South, war had touched every town and every home. In the South, there was such a lack of goods that commerce had come to an almost complete standstill as everything had gone into the war effort. Women were making clothes from curtains and rugs. Houses were stripped of every item that might become useful – didn't Eliza write to me of the campaigns to get farm bells to melt down for bullets? It seemed, too, that every Southern family had sent a son or more to the war, and families stripped their homes of anything that might provide comfort to their sons.

If I'd ever thought that the Confederacy would survive the war, I knew as I rode through Gettysburg that it could not. The South was all spent out. But the Yankees – a mere three or four days from the front – were living life as if there was no war. Aye, certainly they had sent some number of their men off to face the Rebel yell, and surely they were worried that word would come that the Confederates were across the Potomac and marching in their direction, but there was no want nor sacrifice. You'll know, too, that Gettysburg's colleges were full of fighting-age men who were studying rather than serving at war.

The Union had plenty – plenty of supplies, plenty of food, plenty of guns and bullets, and plenty more men who could still enter the army. The South would never be able to keep up.

But, winners and losers in the war were of little or no consequence to me. So long as I survived the thing, I did not care which side won. My life was decent enough as a citizen of the United States, and except for the bullets coming at me, I suspected I'd get along just fine as a citizen of the Confederacy. What I wanted was the thing settled and done so that I might go on about my business of living without every general and president on either side of the thing trying to get me killed.

Following young Captain Thorn's directions, I presently found myself at the town square, referred to by the locals as the Diamond. I took a road leading off to my right – the direction young Captain Thorn had indicated with his stick, and two or three doors down was the Globe Inn. I slid down off my horse, grateful for a moment to stretch my legs, and tied the horse to the post out front. Then I went into the Inn.

There were a couple of long tables, long enough to fit twenty people to a side, in the dining room and over to my left was the bar where I first met John Wills who, with his father, was the proprietor of the Globe Inn. The younger Wills was standing behind the bar, and he kept his eye on me when I entered the hotel. I would guess he would have been about twenty-five years old, not much more than that, certainly. He was of average height and slim and wore no whiskers on his face. His eyes were active, taking in every detail of the goings-on in his establishment. The tables were neither one full, but as it was late in the afternoon there were several people seated at both tables. I scanned them quickly to make certain no Union officers who might be curious about me were seated in the dining room, and then I went to the bar.

"I'd like to get a room for the night," I told the proprietor. "And a meal. I suspect I'll be staying at least a couple of days."

"A meal is thirty-five cents," he responded. He wasn't hostile, nor would I even say that he was cold, but there was certainly something in his manner that made me feel I was not particularly welcome. "A drink of whiskey is five cents. A room is seventy-five cents."

"I'll have the whiskey and the meal now," I said, and I opened up my wallet to pay him for the meal and the room up front.

"On leave, are you?" he asked, and though I'd put cash on the bar, I still detected a stiffness in his voice. At first, I decided to write it off to Yankee mannerisms, but then I remembered Captain Thorn's warning that Mr. Wills and his son were "sympthizers." Jenny later confirmed for me that the Globe Inn was the local headquarters of the Democratic Party and father and son Wills might have been more sympathetic to me if I'd showed up in butternut.

"I am," I said. "I was hoping to locate a young lady by the name of Jenny Rakestraw who I understand lives here in Gettysburg. We've met a couple of times and are on friendly terms."

"She doesn't live far from here," Wills said. "I can send somebody for her, if you'd like." It was a kind enough offer, but it was made without friendliness.

"That would be ideal," I said. I have a habit, when greeted with rudeness, to respond with even more than my usual charm. And now I smiled brilliantly at Mr. Wills and – without thinking about what I was doing – allowed a little extra Southern to flow into my accent. "Just tell her that her favorite captain has arrived in town and would very much like to have her join him for dinner."

Wills looked at me curiously. "You're a major," he said, indicating my uniform.

Confronted with my own slip, I was caught me off guard for a moment, but I recovered quick enough to avoid suspicion. "Oh, aye," I said, "but I was just a captain when we last saw each other."

He said nothing for a moment, eying me doubtfully. I cursed myself for not being more careful. I'd allowed the pleasantness of Gettysburg, that lack of evidence that there was a war on, to lull me into being careless. I'd slipped Southern into my accent and had forgotten my own rank. "Should I wait your meal, then?" he asked.

I drained the glass of whisky he'd poured for me and pushed the glass back over to him. "Do that, and I'll have another drink while I wait."

Wills poured another glass of whiskey for me, and I seated myself at the end of one of the long tables away from the other patrons. Wills called a teenaged boy over and said something to him, and the boy left out the front door.

I sat at the table spinning my glass of whiskey and watching it for a bit, and then I absent-mindedly looked around at the Globe's other guests. Seated at the opposite end of the same table where I was sitting, farthest away from the door, was a group of four men. They were all in their mid-thirties, and to a man they all had the hard look of war on their faces. They were dressed in civilian clothes, but I could see it plainly that these men had recently been in battle. There were no crutches, no bandaged faces or empty sleeves that might suggest they had received wounds in battle that had sent them home. I studied them for a moment, wondering what circumstances had these four men who were bore the look of warriors sitting in Gettysburg in civilian clothing.

They were all huddled together in conversation, but one of them glanced in my direction. I smiled and nodded to him, but then I realized that there was a look of shock and recognition on his face. The man knew me, and I knew him! He was on Jubal Early's staff. We'd seen each other around camps and at the balls held in Richmond for staff officers. The damned fool kept his staring and gawking, but I quickly looked back at my whiskey as if I'd not recognized him.

It unnerved me to no end to see a staff officer from the Army of Northern Virginia in Gettysburg. I'd heard nothing to suggest that the army had crossed the Potomac. But for these four men – assuming all four were Rebels – to be so far north it had to mean that the army was on the move. Were they scouting? And if so, did that mean the army was coming here, to Gettysburg?

I glanced back over at them and was relieved to see that Early's staff officer was no longer staring at me with his mouth agape. And if Wills the proprietor knew who his other clients were, no wonder he was acting the way he was toward a man in Union blue.

I turned over in my mind whether I should flee the place or not, and I was nearly convinced of doing just that when the hotel door opened behind me. I turned in my seat and saw the teenage boy returning, and behind him was Jenny Rakestraw.

She was as beautiful as ever, with her flowing blonde hair and green eyes. She was wearing a plain sort of dress that did too much to hide her other natural assets, but when her eyes landed on me her face split into the sort of smile that can erase all the horrible, awful memories of recent days.

"Oh, Jackson, I was hoping it would be you," she said, and the tone of her voice convinced me that surely she was hoping it would be me.

I stood to face her, and she came directly to me, wrapping her arms around me and putting her lips against my cheek.

"I could not understand how you could possibly have gotten into Gettysburg," she whispered against the side of my face, "but I suppose as a Federal officer you can get anywhere you like up around here."

I stepped back to look at her and gave her my best Speedy grin. "Why, Miss Jenny, I swear that there are no obstacles that could prevent me from finding my way to you. I do hope you do not mind my sudden appearance, but finding myself near Gettysburg I decided that I could not resist your kind offer."

"Oh, I don't mind at all Major Speed," she said, and the gleam in her eye showed her amusement that her Rebel captain was now a Yankee major.

"Then would you care to join me for dinner?" I asked.

"I would be delighted," she said.

I resumed my seat and Jenny took the seat across from me. As we sat down, I nodded deliberately toward Early's staff officer and his group, and Jenny glanced down the table at them.

Jenny Rakestraw was the sort of girl who could capture a room's attention any time, but she had certainly done that now. Early's staff officer and the others had all watched her come in and they'd watched us all during our reunion. Now, though, they'd fallen back to talking among themselves in their huddle.

"Do you know those men?" I asked Jenny, leaning toward her and speaking at a whisper.

"I do not," she said.

"I believe I recognize one of them as one of Jubal Early's staff officers."

Jenny, who knew her business as a spy, did not look back at them. "What would they be doing in Gettysburg?" she asked.

"I was just wondering that myself. Could this town possibly be a target for Lee's army?"

Jenny thought for a moment about that, but then she shook her head. "I do not see why it would be," she said. "They might pass through here on the way to Harrisburg or even Philadelphia. But there is nothing here that would present a target for the army."

"Perhaps Early has sent scouts on to Harrisburg and these men are just passing through," I whispered, "but it's damned unnerving to find them here. I was all but ready to forget about the war."

"Is that why you're here – to forget about the war?" Jenny asked.

"I'm done with the thing," I told her. "I've left it behind me and intend to stay north until it's over."

Jenny smiled brightly, and I knew that she was thinking my intention was to stay in Gettysburg with her.

Presently the proprietor walked over to us carrying two plates of food. "Mr. Wills," Jenny said. "This is my dear friend Jackson Speed."

"I'm John Wills," he said, setting the plates in front of us. "Major Speed says he'll be staying with us for a day or two."

"Oh, I do hope it will be longer than that," Jenny said.

"It may well be," I remarked.

After we ate I went out to see that my horse was in good hands at the livery, and Jenny went up to my room on the second floor of the Globe to wait for me. It was when I walked outside that Jubal Early's staff officer followed me outside.

"I didn't expect to see a fellow Confederate here in Gettysburg," he said, catching me by the arm.

"I wasn't sure if you recognized me," I said.

He introduced himself, but over the years I've forgotten his name. [1]

"I assume, despite your uniform, that you and I are on a similar mission," he said.

"Aye, that seems about right. General Longstreet sent me north some days ago," I said.

"General Early sent me and my companions," the man said.

I looked up and down the street to see if we'd attracted any attention, and my heart stopped when I realized John Wills was standing at the front window of the Globe watching us.

"Well, I'd best be on about my mission, and you with yourn," I suggested. The staff officer nodded agreement and went back into the hotel.

I think in that moment Wills deduced that he had two Confederates dining in his hotel, though, for from then on he treated me a good bit kinder.

I bathed that night, washing away the dried sweat, dust and stench of having ridden from Virginia to Pennsylvania, and Jenny spent the night at the hotel with me.

After that, we spent the next few days leisurely. Another sign that the North was little discomfited by the war came when I went out on my second day in Gettysburg to buy civilian clothes. Oh, certainly, there wasn't the selection I might have found prior to the war, but shirts were plentiful, I found britches that fit well enough and even bought a decent looking brown suit. I was most pleased to get a new pair of shoes, and you'll know well enough that I wasn't the only Southerner who came to Gettysburg for new shoes.

Jenny's home was a couple of blocks north of the Diamond on Carlisle Street, not far from the Globe Inn, and just north of the impressive edifice of the Gettysburg Railroad Passenger Depot. After a couple of days at the Globe, I took up residence with her. Jenny spread the word among neighbors that I was a wounded Union officer, a friend of her family's and that I was convalescing in Gettysburg under her care. If they cared to accept this explanation or suspected that we were sharing a bed was no matter to Jenny, and therefore it was no matter to me. She was an independent and brave woman, and the raised noses of suspicious neighbors were far below her concern.

To their credit, a delegation of the local Home Guard – old men armed mostly with pitchforks and axes and rusty old muskets – visited me at Jenny's home a day or two after I'd moved in. They were led by Bob Bell, who soon enough would form up a company of volunteer cavalry from among the men of Gettysburg. They wanted my expertise as a Union officer in drilling their men, and once or twice I remember riding out to a field with them to teach them how to form up and charge. They were, as I recall, a disorderly bunch of Dutchmen and Scotch-Irish who refused to be taught a thing, argued amongst themselves and – when the war actually came to their front stoops – were among the first in town to seek shelter beyond the Susquehanna. [2]

Jenny's father had died a number of years prior to the war, her mother had died in '59. Her father had been a lawyer and a judge of some note in the area, and they had left her a large, two-story brick home in the heart of the city. His lawyer's office had been in one of the front rooms of the house, but it was now converted to a pleasant parlor. Jenny and I spent a fair amount of time in this room with the windows open to allow a pleasant breeze to come in off the street.

I have vivid and wonderful memories from those days in mid-June, 1863, of living on Carlisle Street. The road was wide and tree lined, and being so near to the Diamond there was often activity outside that drew our interest and provided diversions of all sorts. Her father had a good library, and I found a number of books that took my interest during those days.

When I think of setting up house with Jenny there on Carlisle Street, I find in my memory that I was very fond of her and could have been plenty content to have spent the remainder of my days there with her. I have loved a couple of women – Eliza, of course, and Kate Cherry rank highest among them all – but there were others of whom I was very fond. Weenonah, my Cherokee wife who was Stand Watie's niece. Weenonah was a good wife for the short time we were together. That Apache girl, too, who sewed my scalp back on. She was more protective of me than any other woman I've ever known and was as faithful and loyal as a puppy. The Spanish woman in Cerralvo who nursed me back to health after those rancheros tried to drag me to my death during the Mexican war. And Jenny Rakestraw. She was a lovely young woman who enjoyed laughing and playing, and when I think back on my contentedness at being with her on Carlisle Street in Gettysburg I can't help but feel very fond toward her.

They were pleasant days we spent together, no doubt about it.

On a couple of days when the weather was fine we rode north of town and picnicked. We took many strolls through the town, with Jenny pointing out to me the places of interest in her hometown. She walked me out to the Lutheran Seminary, and we strolled along a path through Pitzer's Wood where I would soon see Old Peter bow his head in defeat. Jenny and I had taken so many strolls about town, that after just a few days in Gettysburg I knew the place as well as I knew my own hometown back in Georgia.

The fact is, these pleasant strolls about probably saved my life.

The walks around town, sitting together and reading in the parlor with a pleasant breeze coming through the open windows, it was all wonderful stuff. But I'd be a liar if I said my fondest memories of Jenny were anything other than those afternoons and evenings spent with my right hand clasped on one of her round teats and a hard nipple pinched firmly between finger and thumb. There is no doubt about it, the finest diversion I discovered from the horrors of war was having Jenny Rakestraw's nimble body pinned below my own.

CHAPTER 3

But the horrors of war were determined to seek me out.

"Jackson, there's some trouble outside," Jenny said, shaking me awake. I was asleep in her bedroom, and it took me a moment to get my bearings.

A candle flickered on the night table beside the bed, providing enough light that I could see real fear in Jenny's face.

"What is it?" I asked.

"Something is going on outside," she said in a hushed, hurried tone. "I do not know what it is."

I could hear it, too. Off in the distance, down the street, there was a great rumbling of noise. We'd been sleeping with the windows on both sides of the house open as it allowed a decent breeze to come through the house, and on this particular night there was a coolness to the breeze that hinted that rain would be coming soon.

I pulled the sheet off me and stepped into on my trousers. I pulled the suspenders up over my shoulders. My belt and holster with my Colt Revolver were hanging from a rocking chair in a corner of the bedroom, and I walked over and grabbed the belt and slung it over my right shoulder. Next I sat in the rocking chair and pulled my boots up over my feet.

Jenny was wearing a cotton nightdress, and she pulled a robe on over that. She slid her feet into a pair of sandals and together we walked downstairs and out to the front porch of the house where we could see a crowd gathered several blocks south on Carlisle Street.

I buckled my belt and holster at my waist, and, shirtless, walked toward the crowd with Jenny beside me.

As we neared them, a fellow from the mob turned and sprinted toward us. Jenny recognized him and called to him: "Alexander Buehler! Where are you going and what is happening?" she demanded. [3]

"I'm going to warn my father," Alexander said, already breathless from his short run. "The Rebels are south of the town and they are burning as they come!"

Jenny looked at me, and in the dim light I could see that she wore a look of honest fear. "Could it be?" she asked me in a hushed voice.

I was doubtful, and I told her so. "Bobby Lee ain't burning nothing," I told her. "And if the Army of Northern Virginia is south of town, we'd have seen Jeb Stuart ride through here two days ago."

All the same, I slid my Colt out of its holster and felt with my fingertips to be certain there were balls in each of the chambers of the revolver. I had a pocketful of percussion caps in my britches.

We continued forward to the crowd and pushed our way in among them. And there we saw what had started the ruckus: Off in the distance, well south of town, we could see a fire glowing. It was so far off in the distance, maybe as many as a dozen miles, that it had to be a fire of some consequence for us to see it.

"What's that way?" I asked of Jenny, but a man standing near by answered me: "That must be Emmitsburg," he said. "The Rebels are burning Emmitsburg!"

And at his words, a general call went out among the crowd. They were getting themselves all worked up again.

"Home Guard!" someone shouted. "All men of the Home Guard, gather your weapons and your horses! Our town and our state are now in need! Form up south of town!"

Presently, the mob began to disperse, some rushing off to get their pitchforks and plow horses, others to load wagons with their personal valuables and try to get to the Susquehanna before Johnny Reb could catch them.

If for a moment I thought it was the Army of Northern Virginia burning Maryland villages, I'd have been in the lead division of the army of Gettysburg civilians fleeing north. But I was so convinced that this was not Bobby Lee, that I told Jenny I was going to ride out with the Home Guard.

"What if it is the Rebels?" she asked.

"Then you'll see me back here before you see the rest of the Home Guard," I laughed. "But it ain't them. If Lee was going to burn towns, he wouldn't do it in Maryland anyhow. But I am curious what's going on there, and so if ye don't mind I'm going to ride south with the Home Guard and see what's what."

Jenny, who was not given to over-excitement anyway, took her cue from my confidence.

"Well, I'm going back to bed. Don't wake me when you get back," she said.

I went to the livery behind The Globe where I was keeping my horse – the liveries all over town had just become the most popular places in Gettysburg – and saddled my horse, and I then rode back to Jenny's home to collect a shirt and coat, but not my Yankee coat. I could not be more confident that it would not be Bobby Lee's army the Home Guard and I would encounter south of town, but on the smallest of possibilities that I was wrong, there was no way I would don the Union blue and risk being captured as a Federal officer.

Within just a few minutes of leaving the mob, I was riding south of town where the Home Guard were forming up with their pitchforks and rusty muskets. There were a great deal fewer of them prepared to ride south to face the advancing Rebel hoard than there had been when we were doing drills north of town. Most of those missing were loading valuables onto wagons and preparing to race for Harrisburg.

"Not much of a company to face the Rebels," one among them remarked.

Without more comment, the dozen or so of us who were gathered together set off south down the Emmitsburg Road.

As we rode, the fire before us continued to burn brightly off in the distance. When we'd covered five miles or more, we could see well enough to know that half the town of Emmitsburg was ablaze, and I will grant you that I had some nervous moments at seeing that sight. I did not believe that Bobby Lee would allow his army to burn out civilians, and there was no sound of guns or battle that would suggest a fight. Nevertheless, a burning village in wartime is always a dangerous sign and could mean anything.

But about that time, when we found ourselves halfway to Emmitsburg, it became obvious that the fire was dwindling some, and the nearer we got, the more the fire went down.

About a mile from Emmitsburg, that's when we came across a rider coming north. One of our lead men hallooed to him and we all reined up.

"What's happening in Emmitsburg?" one of our men asked the rider.

"Fire!" he exclaimed.

"Well, we can see that," another Gettysburg Home Guard man said.

"There must be 30 houses burned!" the man said. "Families left homeless!"

"What started the fire?" another man from our company asked. "Is it the Rebs?"

The Emmitsburg man was still talking – "Everything's so dry, the bucket brigade had no ability to douse the flames or stop the spread of the fire" – but when our man from the Home Guard asked about the Southern army, the Emmitsburg man looked perplexed.

"Is it who?" he asked us.

"The Rebels, son," I said, riding to the front of the group so that I was up closer to the Emmitsburg man. "Is it the Army of Northern Virginia burning Emmitsburg families out of their homes, or what has happened in town?"

"Oh, no," he said. "It ain't Rebels. We think old Mister Wertzel got inebriated and knocked over a candle. But everything's so dry, it took no time for the fire to spread all over town!"

"And where are you off to?" I asked the man.

"I'm riding to the Bowden farm up north of here to see if they can take in some of the refugees. At least thirty families are left homeless!"

And with that, the man rode on north.

Now I cast my gaze back south to Emmitsburg, not much more than a mile away, and saw that the flames – though not gone – seemed to be well down and well under control. If this boy was correct and thirty homes had burned, then likely as not there was no tender left to feed the flames.

"Well, we can ride down there and see if they need help putting out the flames," I said, "or we can go home and report that there ain't no Rebels around Emmitsburg."

One of the elderly men of our Home Guard snorted. "I wonder if there's anyone left in town to report to, or if they all skeedaddled. Where is Shiverly? Where is Marks? I know I saw them out of bed this night, and I saw Marks at the livery! Did they take some other road to Emmitsburg that I am unaware of, or did they take a road to Harrisburg? Home Guard, indeed!"

And with that, the old man turned and began riding at a leisurely pace back toward Gettysburg. All the others in our company also began to ride back north, and so I figured it wasn't part of our responsibilities to be putting out Emmitsburg fires, and I followed along behind them, well pleased with myself that I'd been correct that there was no threat from the Army of Northern Virginia. [4]

That was my first and only actual service of rushing into battle with the Gettysburg Home Guard. Had it been a more dangerous bit of service, they'd have had to fend for themselves without me.

However, this was only the first in a series of events that should have served as warning enough that the war was not done with me, no matter whether I was done with the war.

The following event came on the very next afternoon.

I remember that I slept late due to my being out all night with the Home Guard, and it was not until around noon that Jenny woke me.

There was a light drizzle coming down, and the day was very gray with clouds.

"If we'd gotten this rain yesterday, perhaps some of the houses in Emmitsburg might have been saved," Jenny remarked.

We'd taken up seats in the rocking chairs on her front porch where we were both reading books. I remember clearly that Jenny was reading Uncle Tom's Cabin, for the thought went through my mind that my dear Eliza would have been less horrified that I was, on a nightly basis, violating the vows of our marriage with Jenny Rakestraw than she would have been to learn that it was a staunch abolitionist I was getting belly to belly with. Eliza would have been disappointed that I was cavorting with "Yankee trash." What I was reading I cannot recall, and that should tell you something about the quality of the work.

"It was quite a fire," I said back, not taking my eyes from the page. Rocking slightly in my chair, I was beginning to doze, and Jenny's remark had stirred me back awake.

"My heart is sick for those poor families with no home," she said.

"Oh, well, there's worse that could happen to them. If it truly had been Bobby Lee coming north and burning as he went, they'd have found out how much worse."

"Do you think the Rebels will burn towns?" Jenny asked me, and I noticed that she'd put her book down in her lap.

"Naw," I told her. "Lee don't make war like that. He'd be mortified if he thought one of his soldiers so much as failed to tip his hat and say 'mornin' ma'am' to a woman. No, Bobby Lee ain't burning towns. He'll come north so that people know he can. His men'll take everything they can get, but they'll pay for it with Confederate scrip."

"Which is worthless," Jenny noted.

"That ain't the point, though," I said. "The point is, they're paying for it with something. No Yankee will be able to complain that the Army of Northern Virginia treated them roughly. 'Cept until Bobby Lee meets up with Hooker, and then there'll be some rough treatment."

"You don't think the Union can beat the Confederacy?"

Well, I was at the Place of Peace, wasn't I? I knew a Federal army could beat a Southern army, for I'd seen it firsthand. [5]

"Oh, undoubtedly the Union could beat the Confederacy, and if I were betting on the affair I would say that in the end the Union will win its victory over the Confederacy. But will Fighting Joe Hooker beat Bobby Lee? Not anytime soon. Lee's men will go anywhere and do anything he asks them to do. The Union will only win because it has more men and material than the Confederacy. Every victory Lee scores comes at too high a cost. The Yankees can keep producing soldiers until the Confederacy runs out of bullets, and that's how Lincoln will win."

"Train's coming," Jenny remarked, and I heard it too, in the distance, on its way into town.

"Besides, I talked to Old Peter before I left to come north. He told me plain that he was opposed to invading the north, but that Lee conceded that whenever they met Hooker, Lee would be willing to fight a defensive battle. That's where James Longstreet can't be beat. No general in the Union can beat Longstreet when his back is anchored and the Federals are coming at him."

"What about Grant?" Jenny asked.

"Oh, Sam Grant's out west, and as long as the Union capitol remains in the east, Sam Grant don't matter. He'll take Vicksburg before long, but the war is being fought here in the east, and this is where it'll be won."

Well, I was right, wasn't I?

"I believe I'm going to get my umbrella and walk down to the depot to see if there is any news aboard," Jenny said. "Would you care to join me?"

"You're not piqued that I've said your Yankees can't beat Lee, are you?" I asked, teasing her a little as I set down my book.

"No, Jackson, I think you're right in everything you've said. The northern armies have been poorly led, and it scares me to think of what General Lee will accomplish north of the Mason Dixon Line when the best we have is Joe Hooker to stop him." As if to add emphasis to what she'd said, Jenny tossed her book down on a table and stood up from her rocking chair, and there was an air of disgust about her. "I will never know how that man got such a nickname!" [6]

I put my book down as well and stood up and stretched. Being up half the night and with the drizzle coming down all afternoon, I was finding it hard to stay awake. But I decided a walk down to the train station would be a worthwhile diversion.

Jenny found an umbrella inside, and we huddled together under the thing as we walked the couple of blocks down to the station, though the rain was not coming down so hard at the moment that shelter was even necessary.

The train had arrived from the south just as we were getting to the depot, and there was the usual activity as a few people exited the train, although it seemed to me that this particular train was more crowded than I would have expected. As I looked along the rows of cars, I realized that every passenger car was positively stuffed with people, and few seemed interested in debarking.

But two men stepped off the train onto the covered platform of the depot in front of where we were standing. They were both professional looking me, clean and wearing good suits, and one had an expensive looking watch in his hand. I suspected right away they were both bank officials, though I had no other evidence than their clothes and their bearing to suggest this. The two men were obviously in conversation with each other.

"We're not nearly far enough north," one of the men remarked.

The one with his watch in his hand nodded agreement. "The Rebels will be here in less than a week," he said.

"We should press beyond the Susquehanna," the first man said.

"Yes, but I dare say Harrisburg is not safe. We should be farther north than that."

I'd heard all this, and I stepped forward now. "What's that you say about the Rebels?" I asked. "Here in a week?"

The man with the watch looked up at me. "Yes. That's right."

Then raising his voice so that anyone nearby might hear him over the other sounds on the platform, he said very clearly, "The Rebel army is across the Potomac!"

It was routine in Gettysburg in those days for a couple of dozen people, sometimes more, to drop what they were doing and stroll down to the depot anytime they heard the train coming. Everyone was hungry for news. So it was that there were a handful of Gettysburg citizens on the platform already when the man spoke up. Now they all stepped forward.

"What's that?" one man called to them. "Did you say the Rebels are beyond the Potomac?"

"Yes, that's correct," the man with the watch announced, and now that he saw he had an audience forming, he cleared his throat so that he might put on a proper show. "We've come up from Hagerstown today, and the word has spread from Williamsport that the main body of the Confederate army has effected a crossing there. The Rebels will be in Pennsylvania in a week, perhaps less." [7]

A local woman standing nearby us gasped audibly and put a gloved hand over her gaping mouth. A young boy cried out, "I've got to tell my pa!" and leapt from the platform and began running south down Carlisle Street.

"Did you see the Rebels?" I asked.

The man looked affronted that I would even question the veracity of his news. "Well no," he said. "I'm a Union man, and as soon as I heard that the Rebels were over the river, I and my clerk felt it was most prudent for us to move north at once. But there is no doubting whether or not my information is accurate. It came from a Williamsport man who was also fleeing the Rebels." The man paused and looked at me very intensely, "And he did see them!"

This was proof enough for most of the other Gettysburg residents on the platform with us, for they all immediately began talking in hushed and breathless tones.

"What of the Union army?" I asked. "Where is Hooker?"

The Hagerstown man shook his head in obvious disappointment.

"Hooker is no where to be found. I have heard it said that he has not even moved from his encampment on the Rappahannock."

I caught Jenny looking at me, and I could see real concern on her face, but I just smiled and winked at her.

Word spread quickly that a man who had news of the Confederate army's movements was at the depot, and now others from the town were coming up to the platform to hear what he had to say, and he started his story over. Only this time he added in a few embellishments to avoid questions on the back end: "I have word from an eyewitness from Williamsport that the main body of the Rebel army is across the Potomac and marching this way while General Hooker remains encamped at the Rappahannock!"

As he continued with his story, I took Jenny by the elbow and led her away from the growing crowd.

"What do you think?" she asked me. Jenny was a bright girl who understood troops and movements of armies better than most men, and she was not easily startled. But I could tell that she was anxious at the news that Bobby Lee was coming north.

"It may be true what he says," I told her, "but there's no reason to believe that the army will move through Gettysburg. If you look at a map, I think it's more likely that they will move along the west side of the mountains and up to Harrisburg. They'll capture Harrisburg and then I would guess they would either move on Philadelphia or perhaps Washington D.C. itself."

"But that would put them very near Gettysburg," she said.

"Oh, aye, but they won't come to Gettysburg in force," I said. "We may see some cavalry, but I've been studying maps of the area and it makes no sense that Lee would turn east and come through Gettysburg. He'll move along in the valley, up through Chambersburg. The valley is like a natural roadway straight to Harrisburg. Why, when he could capture the capital of a Yankee state, would Lee ever come to a tiny town like this where all they do is make buggies?"

Jenny nodded, seeing the logic in my argument, but then she said something that set my belly to rumbling.

"But Lee's movements won't be determined solely by Lee," she said. "At some point Hooker must leave his camp facing Fredericksburg. And when he does, he will march in such a way that he is always between Lee's army and Washington, D.C."

"Yes, that's right," I agreed.

"So that may very well put Hooker marching through Gettysburg," Jenny said. "And at some point, Lee will turn and fight. Might not that happen here?"

Well, I had no answer for this, and it was proof that I was right that Jenny knew her stuff when it came to war, for this was exactly how it happened.

Throughout those days, though, there were always rumors floating about. A day or two after the Emmitsburg fire, the Pennsylvania governor sent an alert throughout the state that the Army of Northern Virginia was invading, and he called for militias to form. Several men and a fair few number of the local college students answered that call, though I remember the word around town was that the president of the college vehemently argued that the students should return to their studies. [8]

But I remained unconcerned during these days. It is inexplicable, looking back on it now, that I should have been so confident that the war was done with me and that I ignored the daily warnings that Bobby Lee and his army were on the march with an intention of dragging me back into the thing.

When I think back over the course of my life, I can tell you that I always had a good nose for sniffing danger, and I was always lickety-split to skedaddle when I smelled trouble in the air. But there were times when I failed utterly to catch a whiff of the warnings, and as a result landed myself in no end of troubles. And I blame those times, each and every one, on Ashley Franks. Had she not tempted me with her peach cobbler when I was just a pup, young and impressionable, I believe I would have always and forever been three steps ahead of danger. But she gave me a taste of the fairer sex that often and repeatedly throughout my life corrupted my sense of self-preservation and blunted my ambitions for survival.

I was happy and content living here in this quaint Pennsylvania town with Jenny Rakestraw. She was a lovely diversion from the horrors I'd so long experienced in battles from Tennessee to Virginia, and the war seemed a distant thing, like the kings of Europe or the chaparral of Mexico. And I found that when I considered leaving the comfort of Jenny's bosom, it was easier to convince myself that Bobby Lee and Fighting Joe and the rest of them would go and do their fighting somewhere other than here.

I was also something of a local celebrity. A couple of different rumors spread about me, one that I was on leave, another that I was recuperating from a wound, so that I had a bit of mystery about me. Everyone in town knew I was a Yankee officer, or believed I was at any rate, and they were always deferring to me on issues of importance regarding the war. With the town council constantly packing up their valuables and riding north to Harrisburg at any rumor of danger, I'd become for many a local leader in the Gettysburg community.

To keep everything peaceful and calm among the populace, I stayed pretty cool and stuck to my contention that Bobby Lee would swing well west of Gettysburg and attack Harrisburg and that we in this town had nothing to fear. I had most folks believing it – except for the panicky bunch who left town every couple of days only to return when rumors were proved to be untrue.

And then Pettigrew came looking for shoes, and my comfort was disrupted and the town of Gettysburg forever altered.

CHAPTER 4

"The Rebels are at Cashtown!" Jenny said, rushing into the house. I was seated on her couch in the parlor, half dozing while reading from an issue of *Harper's Weekly* about Pemberton's woes out west. I remember very clearly it was a Friday, sometime maybe just before noon. [9]

She was breathless and panicked. "It's no rumor this time, Jackson! It's true!"

For days we'd heard that the Rebels were on the move through the hills to the west and even in Chambersburg. Just a few days before, refugees from towns south and west came flooding into Gettysburg in an almost ceaseless river. Mostly it was darkies fearing capture and enslavement, carrying all their valuables in handcarts or on their backs, but it was also bankers and merchants in wagons loaded with money and valuables. Sincerely, an enterprising highway robber could have set himself up quite well in the last week or two of June, 1863, if he'd established an ambush on the roads leading north out of Gettysburg. Had my gold mines in California not already made me a wealthy man, I'd have finished out the War of Northern Aggression the richest man in the country.

I rose from the couch, for beyond Jenny I could see a mass of activity through the open door. Jenny was in a state of extreme distress, she was pale beneath cheeks flushed from running.

"Oh, Jack, you must flee! The town council and all other men are leaving even now! Every man is either leaving town or going to join the militia!"

Sure enough, looking out at the street I saw a commotion commencing. Word had reached Carlisle Street, and many men were rushing up and down the roadway, either on horseback or in buggies or on foot. Some were rushing to pack up their valuables and skedaddle, others were running home to get a gun and go to join the militia.

For a moment, I was nearly caught up in her panic. Cashtown was not more than five miles to the west, much nearer than I expected the Rebels would ever be. But it was likely only Stuart and the cavalry out harassing the villages.

Besides, if Bobby Lee was this close, I did not think much of the idea of flight. I'd been with the Army of Northern Virginia long enough to know that if Lee's army was just a few miles to the west that Jeb Stuart would be closer than that. [10]

"Cavalry will round up all those boys fleeing east," I said, watching the chaotic activity outside in the street. Wives were kissing their husbands goodbye, small children were crying and waving to their fathers; boys were running to try to keep up with those who were already making their departure.

"But surely you cannot stay?" Jenny asked me. She was still breathing hard; when she'd heard the news she had run home to tell me. I couldn't help but give a glance at her heaving breasts.

"Aye, I'll stay," I said. If I'd had a moment's thought of fleeing, those heaving breasts erased that forever from my mind. I was in no hurry to give up my time with Jenny Rakestraw.

"But Jackson, what if you're caught here?"

I'd already thought the thing over several times. For the past few days there had been rumors enough of Confederates nearby. But I knew that Bobby Lee's army wasn't coming through Pennsylvania to rape and pillage and murder. Those boys would be on their best behavior, just as if they were tourists on a holiday. Lee's intention was to seduce the Yankee war opposition into pressuring Lincoln to give the thing up. Rape and murder, theft and vandalism, behavior such as that would in no way accomplish his goals. Even more to the point, Bobby Lee wasn't that sort of man, and as a result, his army wasn't that sort of army.

If the Rebels did come through Gettysburg – and even then, with boys in butternut just five miles off, I wasn't convinced they would – I believed my best chance was to be in Gettysburg. In the worst of situations, I'd be arrested, and at that point I would have the arresting officer put me in front of Maj. Sorrel who would sort the whole thing out. I'd explain to Sorrel I was attempting to rejoin the army as Old Pete had told me to, and the thing would be settled that easy. The worst that would happen would be I'd be back with the army.

Most likely, though, I would go unmolested. Those boys in butternut were more in fear of defying Lee's orders than they would be interested in harassing me.

But if I fled, then I would likely as not have to face the cavalry that would be scouting out to Lee's east. And the cavalry, even under orders to proceed politely, would be far more likely to shoot a mounted man in flight and then try to determine if they'd done the correct thing. And if I did flee, I'd be in among all these others who were dashing off to the east and hoping to get across the Susquehanna. They were all bound for Harrisburg or someplace near there, and it made much more sense to me that if Bobby Lee's cannons were going to open fire on a city, it would be Harrisburg and not Gettysburg. Gettysburg had nothing Lee wanted, and there was no reason to think my fellow Southerners would be doing anything more than passing through.

I explained all this to Jenny and her heaving breasts.

"I have no money, no valuables that they want. They have no reason to take an interest in me at all," I said. "We should be more concerned with burying your silver and other valuables under the cellar floor than we are with me trying to escape."

Jenny, smart girl that she was, saw the reason in my thinking and agreed with me. The redness that had flushed her cheeks dissipated, her breathing calmed, and the rising and falling of her breasts, disappointingly, subsided.

We walked out to the front porch of her home and watched the activity outside for some time. All the men were too excited or too afraid to give any thought to me, and not one of them asked why I wasn't packing my bags and heading north with the rest of 'em.

Down the street we saw some of the older men of the town closing the shutters of their homes and locking themselves inside. They would not flee, but they would not make themselves an inviting target for looters, either. Even now, sitting on Jenny's front porch and watching the activity around town, I was still unconvinced the Rebels would be entering Gettysburg. The night previously we'd seen the singular sight of the Rebel campfires burning several miles west toward Chambersburg. The Confederates were camped there in strength, but I still did not believe they would linger. Not with Harrisburg so near and such an inviting target. If Lee could put a Yankee capital under siege, he might not need Washington D.C. at all. Imagine the outcry for peace should an occupation army from the South be in control of the capital of Pennsylvania!

And now from the porch we could hear a smattering of musket fire out to the west. Whatever battle was taking place out there, it didn't seem to me to be much of a fight. Having been at some of the bloodiest, most hotly contested fights of the war, I knew the difference between a small skirmish and a pitched battle. This was the volunteer infantry, the 26th Pennsylvania Militia, I think they called themselves. A company of the 26th had been formed up in Gettysburg just a few days before, and among these men were some of the local college students the school's president had encouraged to stick to their books. [11]

Well, no doubt they were getting quite the lesson this afternoon.

Jenny's house faced to the east, and it was difficult with the house in the way to hear much of what was going on or get a sense for how near it was.

"I'm going to walk down to the Diamond and maybe stroll out to the edge of town to see what I can see," I told Jenny, but just as I said this a rider thundered up to the edge of the porch and reined in his horse. Though he was covered in dust and had that strange ghostly look on his face some men get in battle, I recognized him right away as Major Bell of the local volunteer cavalry.

"Sir, I believe the arrival of the Rebels is imminent," he shouted at me, and I noted there was a bit of panic in his voice. "I am ordering my men to make their own way across the Susquehanna and report to me in Columbia! If events determine that I am not there, then they should report to me at Harrisburg. I would strongly recommend, Major Speed, that you join us! Surely we will have business soon enough, and I would like to know that we can depend upon you and your expertise when it comes!"

Well, here was one thing I did not expect, though I suppose I should have known it was coming. Major Bell had seen me around town enough to know that there was no physical injury to prevent me from joining the militia. I had to think pretty quick to give him a plausible explanation for why they could not count on me to join them.

"Major Bell," I said, "when you meet Bobby Lee's army – whether it is at Columbia or at Harrisburg or in Philadelphia – the worst that will happen is that you will be forced into surrendering your command. At that point, the Confederates will parole you, and you may all return to your wives and children here in Gettysburg, and you can be confident that you have done your duty. And good on you for doing it! But when you surrender and it is discovered that among your men is a regular army officer, I will be held as a prisoner of war. I can assure you, Major Bell, President Lincoln hisself thinks more highly of my potential worthiness to the Federal Cause than being taken as a prisoner of war with a gang of militia."

Bell looked at me for a moment, and I'm certain a debate was raging inside him as to whether or not President Lincoln had ever had any thought of me.

"Lincoln?" he asked me.

"Lincoln, hisself," I confirmed.

Major Bell now called to his horse and turned the beast back south to ride to the Diamond where the rest of his militia were forming up to flee the town. If Bell suspected cowardice he did not have time to argue the point, though I'll note that it was I who was staying put in the face of the Confederacy and he who was speeding in its opposite direction.

"Oh, Jackson, I sometimes wonder if ye've ever uttered an honest word in all your life," Jenny said, laughing at my speech and the look of consternation Bell had on his face as he rode off.

I watched Bell ride back to the Diamond, and turn a corner. At that moment, a Gettysburg man who I recognized as living a few doors down and across Carlisle Street came galloping up from the Diamond. He rode his horse right up the front steps of his home, and on the porch he dismounted, opened his front door and led the horse into the house.

It seemed an odd thing to me, and I was just about to step off the porch to walk toward the Diamond when I heard a sound that is enough to put a quake in the bravest of men's hearts. I'd heard that sound enough and knew well what it would portend.

B'God it was the Rebel Yell being lifted up, and I swear it sounded as if they were already within the streets of the town!

Even by the time of Gettysburg I'd heard the Rebel Yell coming at me more times than I cared to remember, and certainly during the course of the war I'd heard it when it made my stomach turn summersaults worse than that day at Gettysburg, but all the same I spun round on Jenny's porch like I'd been gut shot.

"Inside," I told her, and whatever calm assurances I'd given her or myself in the previous days now evaporated. "They're in the town!"

Jenny didn't need telling twice, and in two strides we were both in the house and bolting the door behind us. In moments, we saw them through the windows, absolutely covered in dust, and galloping north through the middle of Carlisle Street yelling and firing pistols and carbines into the air. I don't suppose more than a couple dozen cavalrymen rode past, but they wheeled around and headed back south toward the Diamond from which they'd come, so that for a few moments the street seemed full of yelling Rebels. [12]

Jenny and I raced up the steps to the top level of her home, and from the windows there we were able to see all that was taking place all the way to the Diamond and beyond. First the cavalry rode this way and that through the town's streets, yelling and firing off their arms to put an absolute fright to anyone in the town. By now the streets were empty except for the Confederates riding about the place hollering and firing their guns.

Just behind the cavalry – who were all still riding through the town and putting the fright to Gettysburg's citizenry as it huddled for safety inside homes – came the infantry. I was more than a little surprised to find the infantry so close on the heels of the cavalry, but there was no mistaking what was coming because from the vicinity of the Diamond I could hear a band playing Dixie, and presently the band came into view as it formed up in the Diamond and continue to play Southern tunes.

When the infantry entered the town, many people who had watched the spectacle of the cavalry from their porches now feared that if their doors were open the infantry would view that as an invitation and rush in to take valuables. So presently we saw the few people on Carlisle Street brave enough to watch the cavalry hurry inside.

From our vantage point we could see the infantry coming in on three roads, and it seemed no time before the streets were crowded with Confederates. Though they'd eaten better in the past several weeks than they had throughout the campaign, they were to a man little more than scarecrow ragamuffins, and what they had of clothing was covered in the same dust that also covered their hands, faces and hair so that they looked like an army of dust soldiers.

Presently, though, I saw play out one of the most bizarre scenes I've seen in war, and I'm told it happened over and over as the Confederates entered one town or the next on their invasion of Pennsylvania.

Perhaps it was the influence of the band performing in the Diamond. Maybe it was simply the gentlemanly manners of our Southern boys, clad in dust and rags though they were. But whatever it was, slowly people began to come out of their homes. Most dared not leave their porches or stoops, but the people of Gettysburg seemed intent on getting a better look at the Southern army. And the infantry boys loved the attention. From our perch on the third floor of Jenny's home we saw the first few people coming out of the houses, and rather than rush in and steal the silverware, the Confederate boys ambled about and made small talk. I think a fair number of them were glad to have the opportunity to show off their wit to the Yankee women.

Now curiosity got to me. "Let's go out and see what's up."

"Is that a good idea?" she asked. "It's one thing for women and children to go out and talk to the Rebs, but will they let you go unmolested?"

"I think I'll be fine," I said. Not only was I fine standing on Jenny's front porch as the Rebels walked by, I even descended the steps and walked up and down Carlisle Street, milling about with the troops and picking up tidbits of information as I went.

I'll give you a bit of advice: If ever you find that your hometown is being invaded by an army, and if you have the choice, let me recommend to you the Army of Northern Virginia led by one General Bobby Lee. You'll find that as an invading army, they are the most agreeable visitors you could hope to find. Another word of advice: again, if you have the choice, make sure it ain't Tecumseh Sherman coming to visit.

I won't say that here and there they didn't do some rotten things – vandalism and theft was the worst of it – but on the whole I thought Bobby Lee's army behaved themselves quite admirably. Those who might have been inclined to do worse to the women had fellow Confederates keeping a pretty sharp eye on them.

Mostly the soldiers ambled through the town. I think they were intent on putting up a good show for the citizenry – as the cavalry had done – because soon enough Jube Early would be riding into town making demands for cash. In groups or sometimes in ones and twos, the Rebels engaged the women and men who were now almost universally coming out of their homes. Some shopped in stores if they could find one that hadn't been bolted shut. Many stopped by one of the city's hotels or restaurants for a drink of whiskey, or two or three drinks. I saw for myself a small group of Southern privates bust into a sweets shop, roust out the owner and then pay him in Confederate bills for all they took.

I witnessed one rebel private who had clearly got hold of some liquor stumble into a yard where another private was sitting on the front steps. The boy on the steps had asked for food, and the woman of the house had gone inside to get him some. Having seen the woman moments ago, before she'd turned to go back into the house, the drunken private said something pretty rough about what he intended to do to the "Yankee bitch."

The private on the steps had calm air about him that told me even though he was still quite young, he'd seen plenty of the war. As I recall, he was picking at his fingernails with a knife, or maybe he was whittling a stick. Either way, he didn't look up from his business. But he said pretty clear and loudly, "You do it, and I'll report you."

Whatever warnings were issued among the men to behave themselves must have carried with them the promise of swift and merciless punishment, for the threat of being reported was all it took for the drunken private. He did an about-face and fell back in with the rest of the marchers, muttering to himself but making no other objection.

I was at my ease walking among them in civilian clothes, and not a one of them paid me any mind. Nevertheless, with an invading army in the streets and whiskey available on every block, I decided I didn't need to linger too long on the street, so I returned to Jenny's house where I found her on the front porch giving bread and butter to a group of soldiers.

"Cavorting with the enemy now?" I asked her as they wandered off.

Jenny shrugged. "They looked hungry," she said, "and they're causing no harm. It's not as if they're stealing or burning or killing. Most of them are just boys, anyway."

Well, those she called boys were not much younger than Jenny herself, but her work as a spy had turned her into an old soul. Of course, these boys in the infantry had souls old enough, too.

It should say something of how Johnny Reb behaved that as Early's army passed through Gettysburg, some searching houses and others demanding bread and butter, that I felt at ease enough to lounge on Jenny's front porch with her, rocking in a chair. Lee's army was in high spirits, and the worst I saw from any of them was gentle teasing.

"How come you ain't fighting fer the Yankees?" one of them asked me, stopping at the white fence in front of Jenny's house. Jenny and I were presently engaged in rocking in her chairs and watching the soldiers pass. He was a young man, probably around twenty years old, and he wore a hat with no crown, a pair of pants with a hole in one knee and a white shirt so grimy with road dirt you'd have thought it was butternut brown. A couple of his buddies – one of them wearing a hat with no brim, a thing I will not forget for between them they had one good hat for two heads – stopped with him, grinning like buffoons as the Reb questioned me.

"Wounded at Antietam," I told him.

"Antietam, eh?" he called back, thoughtful like. "I was at Antietam. May be I'm the one that did it?"

I grinned back at him. "Could be," I said, adopting his thoughtful attitude. "I was wounded when a jackass kicked me and broke my leg. You look very much like the fellow."

His buffoon friends guffawed all the louder now, slapping my inquisitor on the back. "Haha! You do look like a jackass, Mose," one of them said.

Young Moses, without a quick enough wit to find retort, accepted his besting pretty well and laughed along with his friends. He stood at the fence for a moment longer, searching for some sort of response. In the end, he grinned widely, shook his head and said, "Well don't ye get behind me or I'll kick ye again." And with that Moses and his friends continued on their way.

Those boys were in high spirits. I do not think that any of them even realized it was possible that they would not have Philadelphia or Washington D.C. within the week. I think they all just accepted as fact that wherever Bobby Lee wanted them to go they would win another victory. [13]

Presently we heard thunder off in the distance, and for a moment Jenny and me and every Southerner in sight stopped and turned our ears to the sound. I feel certain every one of us had the same thought, wondering if it was the boom of cannon we heard. But another, nearer, crack of thunder answered our question, and soon an afternoon shower came up and dumped a pretty hard downpour on us.

The Southern boys paid the rain no mind. Some of them pulled from their haversacks carpets with holes cut out of the middle that they pulled over their heads and wore as ponchos, creating a bizarre scene of color in the downpour. Others simply got soaked. And about that time that deceitful, no-account Jube Early rode into the Diamond and demanded the town's authorities report to him.

Word passed up and down the street with the soldiers calling for the mayor or the councilmen, and finally we heard them passing word back that someone said they'd all skedaddled.

I didn't witness it, though I know that someone was found to whom Early could make a list of demands for cash and foodstuffs and other supplies for the army. At some point, whether it was there in those days at Gettysburg or if I read it in the years after the war, I learned that Early did not receive the cash, but he did get some bacon and flour. [14]

The Rebels camped outside the city, though throughout the night there were plenty of them in town drinking whiskey and burning railroad cars loaded with goods of one kind or another. I saw for myself that John Wills, proprietor of the Globe Inn, was allowed to unload several boxes of whiskey before the cars were set to fire.

The next morning they were gone just like that. Oh, surely, they'd left a fair amount of destruction in their path, having burned the railroad cars and a number of railroad bridges near town. They tore up the tracks and tore down the telegraph lines. But most of the citizens of Gettysburg would probably have been well pleased with their lot in life if that had been all of the war that had touched them.

Jenny and I slept well, even knowing the Rebels were encamped at the edge of town, for I was convinced they'd had their fill of Gettysburg and would be moving on rapidly to some more important location.

Jube Early set off at dawn for York to the east where he was a threat to Harrisburg, Philadelphia or even Washington, D.C. I continued to believe that Lee intended to mass his troops at Harrisburg. While Early swung east and then north to Harrisburg, the remainder of Lee's troops, I expected, planned to continue northeast through the mountains to the west of Gettysburg and advance on

Harrisburg from that position.

"It was chance and chance alone that they came through here at all," I told Jenny that morning as we breakfasted on toast and jam and bacon. "They were not interested in Gettysburg or her citizens, but only in the roads running through Gettysburg and where those roads would take them."

"Oh, I suppose you're right," she said. "It's funny, but I would imagine for two years the biggest fear anyone in this town ever had was that the Rebel army would come marching into town, just as they did yesterday. But there was so very little to it, that I imagine now the entire town must feel silly for all its anxiety. All anybody got out of the secesh visit was a good story to tell their grandchildren one day."

"That's right," I said. "Bobby Lee ain't interested in harassing civilians. That ain't his style. Unless Joe Hooker is fool enough to bring his army to Gettysburg, I think we've seen the last of the war. Oh, it might be that a courier rides through town from time to time, or maybe a unit of cavalry will come charging through going from one place to another, but I guess that'll be the extent of it." [15]

Throughout the day there were rumors that the Rebels would come back, and late in the afternoon we heard that the lead elements of the Army of the Potomac would be in Gettysburg by nightfall, but none of that proved true, and other than the alarm and worry of the citizenry, it was a peaceful Saturday that I spent in leisure with Jenny.

What I did not understand clearly, because no one in the Army of Northern Virginia was inclined to bother with keeping me informed of troop movements – and wouldn't have known where to find me should they be so inclined – was just how completely surrounded we were in Gettysburg.

The Confederates had made a huge semicircle stretching from Chambersburg to our west north toward Harrisburg – indeed, there were elements of the army as far north as Carlisle – and curving back east to York and Wrightsville.

The militia at Wrightsville had burned the bridge – we heard this rumor that proved to be true on Sunday, June 29. The flames had spread from the bridge into Wrightsville itself where Confederate soldiers became part of the fire brigade and assisted in extinguishing the flames before the entire village could be consumed. But by burning the bridge at Wrightsville, the militia there had succeeded in preventing Early from crossing the Susquehanna.

What I also did not know was that Hooker's army – of course by now it had become Meade's army – was moving straight north like an arrow intending to pierce the center of Lee's semicircle. The battle might have taken place at Harrisburg or at Carlisle. It might have taken place at York or Hanover. But on that Sunday, Lee sent orders out calling for his army to return to him, telling them to mass at Gettysburg or Cashtown. And the Union army, arrow straight, was pointing directly at Gettysburg so that it was increasingly becoming impossible the two armies would not clash in that place.

Had I known any of this, even just a piece here or there, I believe I'd have been able to determine what was going to happen. But I was confident that Lee's army had come and gone. Oh, certainly, we still saw the campfires out in the mountains to the west and knew there was a sizeable force still in our vicinity, but I was convinced that he had enough troops at or near Harrisburg that the entire army would soon be upon that place. Harrisburg, after all, was a military target. Gettysburg was just a pleasant little village where I was enjoying getting belly-to-belly with Jenny Rakestraw.

And if I'd been able to determine what was going to happen, of course I'd have mounted my horse and ridden hard for safer environs. At that point, I might even have fled to Washington, D.C.

But I was ignorant of all of this. I can only shake my head in constant amazement that I hadn't deduced what was coming, but – as I've noted – Miss Rakestraw was an ever-present distraction to me.

CHAPTER 5

I suppose it was about ten o'clock in the morning on Sunday, because Jenny and I were on our way to morning worship, when from the south of town there was an explosion of cheering and enough other commotion that we – along with the rest of the town – abandoned any notion of church and instead wandered to see what was up.

Presently, John Buford and his cavalry rode into view, and all those around us let out a great hoorah for the Union men. Girls began singing to them, and the women of Gettysburg opened their doors and offered the men sandwiches and bottles of water and cakes. Buford came up from the south, and in spite of the generosity the citizens were showing, he didn't linger long. His cavalry, which I estimated at two brigades, rode off to the east in the direction of York.

And now, for the first time, I began to grow concerned for my safety.

The day after seeing Buford off, Monday, I suppose it was, Jenny and I went to the Diamond where others were gathering. With the telegraph wires down and the tracks destroyed, little information was now coming into Gettysburg, though someone had acquired a newspaper with a story claiming that Hooker had been relieved by Meade.

"If Buford is the advance of the Army of the Potomac," I told Jenny and others who were gathered with us at the Diamond, "then it's quite possible that the entire army will be coming up through Gettysburg. If Lee determines the army is advancing in this direction, he might order his men to meet the Yankees here."

This sent a horrified gasp through the gathered crowd, and I can tell you I was more than a little horrified, too.

Because everyone in the village seemed to know that I was a Union officer, they continued to look to me as an authority on what was happening, though in truth I knew little more than any of them. The town officials who fled when Jube Early came to town were all still gone, and I suppose I might have been the highest ranking official in the town at this point.

One man in particular was keen to hear every word I had to say. Dr. Jacobs, some kind of professor at the college, was forever at my elbow during these final days of June. He was a tall, thin man, quite a bit older than me though with a full head of black hair. He wore closely trimmed muttonchops and had a long nose, and close-set eyes, and everything from his appearance to his mannerisms suggested that he was an academic. Though I doubted he would have lasted a week encamped with an army and not an hour in battle, he was exuberant in his interest of all things military and seemed to be calculating all possible outcomes with every word I spoke.

"Are you suggesting then that the battle will take place here in Gettysburg?" he asked, and I noted there was perverse excitement in his tone. His son Henry, who looked to me plenty old enough to be wearing the Union blue, was constantly at his side. [16]

"Oh, aye, it could," I said, praying in my mind that it would not.

"Should we run?" some other nervous fellow asked. "Should we flee the town?"

Now this was a question I'd been chewing on over and over ever since I saw John Buford's dour face come riding into town on Sunday morning, disrupting church services and causing my belly to turn in a most uncomfortable manner. And I gave 'em the conclusion that I'd arrived at each time I thought on it.

"This entire countryside is overrun with cavalry from both armies as well as Confederate infantry," I said. "It won't make a difference which side it is, if they catch ye out on the road on a good horse, the best thing that can happen to you is they'll confiscate your horse. More likely than not, they'll arrest ye as a spy and you can spend the rest of the war in a prison camp somewhere trying to explain how you were just trying to get out of the way before the guns started going off. If ye make to flee, they'll shoot ye dead. The time to run has come and passed. The best thing we can hope for is that Bobby Lee don't know the Army of the Potomac is coming this way and he's still planning to march into Harrisburg. If that's the case, Gettysburg will remain unmolested and the battle will be north of here."

"But what if he does know that the Union army is on its way north through Gettysburg?" Jacobs asked, and I believe I know what answer this madman wanted.

"Then Lee will mass his army somewhere right around here," I said. "He'll find some high ground and he'll sit and wait. And when the Army of the Potomac comes at 'im, he'll destroy that army."

"You can't mean it!" a woman shouted, as if I'd just committed treason.

"Meade ain't the fighter Bobby Lee is," I said. "I have information that Lee has vowed to fight a defensive battle, and there's no man better than Lee's lieutenant James Longstreet at fighting a defensive battle."

"But if you are right and the Army of the Potomac is destroyed, what will happen then?" the woman asked, her voice quavering.

"Then Bobby Lee will do whatever he wants. He'll take Harrisburg if he likes. Or Philadelphia. Or both. And then, I imagine, he'll cast his gaze on Washington, D.C., and if he wants, he'll set up the headquarters of the Army of Northern Virginia on the lawn of the White House."

Oh, it was a fine speech, and I suppose I laid it on a little thick for the fun of seeing all them Yankee women swoon. After all, when you're as great a coward as I am and your belly is doing summersaults and your ass is farting fear, not much makes you feel better than seeing everyone around you in a worse state than you're in.

"How can a Union officer have so little confidence in the Union army?" some man asked, and I could tell by his tone he was accusing me. "Are you suggesting our men are not just as good as their men?"

I knew I needed to placate them a bit, now. "It is no lack of confidence in the Union men," I said. "But I've been in too many battles and seen how the Southerners fight when they're on good ground. Now, if Meade could gain the high ground and entice Lee to attack him, maybe things would be different. But Lee ain't likely to take that kind of bait."

There was a good bit of grumbling about this, but no one who'd read the reports from the previous battles could argue much with what I had to say, particularly not after the Union disaster at Fredericksburg seven months prior or the Chancellorsville fiasco just two months ago.

The rumors we heard that afternoon put Meade just a few miles south of Gettysburg.

"If that's accurate, Meade will arrive here tomorrow and be gone by Wednesday evening. Surely if there is a battle it will take place north of here," Jenny said. There was good sense in what she said, but I wasn't certain that either of us found it to be a convincing argument. With each passing hour, it seemed more and more likely that we were going to find ourselves in the midst of a pitched battle between the two armies.

Monday night, the campfires to our west were as numerous as ever in the mountains near Chambersburg. Lee's main body did not seem to be moving, and everyone – me and Jenny especially – understood that his lack of movement most likely meant he was calling his forward elements back to him rather than moving up to meet them. And if Meade was truly just a few miles south of Gettysburg, then a battle was imminent. We had seen nothing of Meade all through the day, which meant that Jenny's prediction that he would pass through Gettysburg by Wednesday was now done.

That evening, huddled in her parlor with Dr. Jacobs and a few others who had followed us back to Jenny's home for a late supper, I took out a map and an oil lamp.

"Here," I said, putting my finger on Cashtown. "If all the information we have heard today is true, I believe in two days, or maybe three, there will be a battle fought here. Lee will put his back against South Mountain or in the hills west of Cashtown. Meade will advance through Gettysburg, with his lead elements coming up tomorrow. And the two armies will meet at Cashtown or just west of Cashtown."

"That is only eight miles from here!" Dr. Jacobs exclaimed.

"Aye," I said. "We'll hear every shot that's fired."

Jacobs and son Henry both looked overjoyed at the prospect that the battle might be so near. You can imagine my own thoughts on the issue.

When our guests departed, Jenny and I retired for the night, and I believe the desperation of our present circumstances added to the passion we felt for each other. Later, with our heads resting on a pillow and both of us unable to sleep for the thoughts in our minds, Jenny said, "If the battle is at Cashtown, Gettysburg will certainly be enveloped by it. If forced to retreat, the Union army will come through here, and the Confederates will pursue. If the Union army stops here and attempts to make a stand, the Confederates will surely shell the city."

"If it comes to that, we will stay in the cellar," I told her. "We'll be safe enough there."

"Even if the Federals are not forced into a retreat, we will be in the rear of their lines. The wounded will be brought here."

Prior to serving as a Yankee spy, Jenny had been a nurse. She didn't talk much about it, but I knew from what she'd said to me in the past that it had been a horrifying experience for her. I'd seen the hospitals set up in the rear of battles, the piles of arms and legs, the screaming from men who had no chloroform as sawbones operated on them. No soldier who had ever witnessed one of these hospitals wanted to find hisself in one. "Lord, if they shoot me, let it be a clean shot that ends me right away." That's the prayer the soldiers who'd visited a hospital prayed. Jenny, too, was equally haunted by what she'd seen as a nurse.

"Likely enough," I said.

"It is too much, Jackson," Jenny said. "We both came here to be free of the war, and now the war has followed us here."

"Oh, aye, it might pass us by yet," I said, though there was not much hope in the words.

"I don't know that I can bear it," Jenny said. "It is too awful to see the wounded. The amputated arms and legs. The suffering. I hear the screams in my dreams, Jack." Her voice trailed off and she was silent for a moment. Then she spoke again, "You know, before I went to Richmond I volunteered as a nurse.

"I was at a field hospital in the rear at Manassas," she said. "When I close my eyes, even now, I can see it all again in my mind, as clear as if it was there in front of me. I was determined that I should serve the cause that I believed in, but I could not do it as a nurse. So that was how I became a spy. An officer at Manassas, a wounded man in whom I had confided, introduced me to a Scotchman who was running spies for the Union. That was how I came to be in Richmond working as a spy."

"A Scotchman?" I asked. "Wasn't Allan Pinkerton, was it?"

Jenny looked at me severely.

"How would you know that?" she asked.

"Oh, well, I've done a fair bit of work for Pinkerton, meself," I told her. "That makes you and I old cohorts, and we didn't even know it!"

"You spied for the Union?" Jenny asked, and her voice was incredulous.

"Oh, I've done a bit of everything," I told her. "I did some work for Pinkerton in Baltimore before the war and he and Lincoln both pressed me into service when the war came. I worked for the Federals up until Shiloh, and at that point I found it necessary to shift my allegiances."

"Lincoln?" Jenny asked. "Are you saying President Lincoln personally pressed you into spying for the Union?" There was a ring of laughter to her voice, and I was glad to hear it.

"Oh, aye," I said. "Lincoln and I go way back, too. Back before he was much more than a backcountry lawyer. Him and Pinkerton both worked pretty hard on me, and for a time I was reporting information to McClellan hisself."

Jenny laughed out loud at me. "Oh, Jackson, you really do have no allegiances to anyone other than yourself, do you?"

"Oh, I like you well enough, Miss Jenny," I told her.

"We are living in the worst of times," Jenny said. "Everything, everywhere, is sorrow and misery, and still you can make me laugh. I think that is why I love you so."

But she stopped laughing as quickly as she started, and the mirth was gone from her voice again. "Should we run, Jackson? Should we flee now before this terrible thing comes down upon us?"

I thought about it. God knows, I'd done nothing but think about it for the past couple of days.

"We've seen nothing of Jeb Stuart," I said. "He must surely be somewhere to the east. Even if we could get past Early's infantry without being arrested, we must surely run into Stuart at some point. I cannot imagine that any good would come from leaving here at this moment. Perhaps, if it appears that the battle is going to take place at Cashtown or somewhere to our west, we might try to flee then, with the Army of the Potomac between us and Lee. But for now, we just have to hope that Lee comes no closer to Gettysburg than he is now."

At this time, my chin whiskers had grown considerably, and so I leaned over and tickled Jenny's bare breasts with my whiskers. "Whatever comes, we'll be just fine," I told her, hoping to reassure her. I don't know that I believed it myself, but presently – tickling one of those red nipples with my whiskers and giving the other a good look over – I was more interested in getting her in a frame of mind where she might be interested in another go.

"If the thing comes, we'll be two steps ahead of it, I promise ye that."

I've found in the course of my life that if madmen have you surrounded and are determined to get you in at the death and there's no opportunity for flight, the best thing for it is to find a lovely lass and get to grips with her as frequently as possible. You never know, when two armies are about to wage war right outside your front door, when it might be your last chance.

Fortunately for me, in those late days of June, 1863, I had a willing and able accomplice in Jenny Rakestraw.

CHAPTER 6

It was Henry Jacobs pounding on the front door the morning of Tuesday, June 30, that woke us bright and early.

"What the devil is it, Henry?" I asked, rubbing my eyes at him after opening the door.

"Father's asked that I come and fetch you," Henry said. "He has something to show you that he believes you will want to see for yourself!"

"Not now, Henry," I said. "Run along and tell your father I'll be glad to see him after I've had some coffee. I was up late last night and am still not fully awake."

"Up late last night?" Henry asked, the little busybody. "But Major Speed, we left out of here still early in the evening! You should be plenty well rested."

How a man of eighteen or nineteen years can be such a naïve fool is beyond me, but there you have it. No doubt it comes from being reared by a professional educator. Why, if we were back in Milledgeville, a nod and a wink would have told an unschooled boy of ten what was what, but here this one who should have been as well educated as any man in town failed to deduce why, when living in the home of a gorgeous young creature like Jenny Rakestraw, I might not have retired directly to my slumber when our guests left the previous evening.

"Hmphf," I scoffed at his ignorance.

"Well, Major Speed, I really do think you should come along, coffee or not," Henry urged. "Father was insistent, and I believe myself that you will want to see what he has to show you. Besides, we've got coffee at home!"

I'd put on trousers and shirt to answer the door, but I made Henry stand outside while I went back in put on my boots. I also buckled on my belt and holster and checked to be sure my Colt revolver was still loaded. By doing so, as I'll tell you presently, I delayed the opening of the battle for a day and quite possibly caused the South to lose the Battle of Gettysburg. Had it not been for me, Pettigrew, looking for shoes, would have been in Gettysburg on June 30, well in advance of Meade. Buford likely would have been unable to hold Pettigrew in check long enough for Meade to advance, and quite possibly the Confederates would have secured the heights south of town in time to fight the defensive battle Longstreet wanted. It's all pure speculation, of course, for who knows how it might have all turned out. But at any rate, had it not been for me, the battle surely would have begun a day earlier with vastly different distributions of forces.

Henry did not seem to appreciate that I intended his remaining outside as a gesture of my annoyance, for he was bouncing from one foot to the other, eager for me to join him, when I came back out. [17]

I followed Henry back to his home where I found his father waiting for me in the front hall.

"Dr. Jacobs, Henry says you've got something worthwhile for me to see," I said. I noticed in his hand he held a rather large spyglass.

"I do indeed!" Jacobs said. "I think you'll find this fascinating! Come with me, up here to our garret window and see this uncommon sight!"

At that, Jacobs turned and bounced up the steps with Henry bouncing behind him, and I at a pace more in keeping with my lack of coffee.

"Say, Henry," I said, "didn't you say there was coffee about?"

Henry's face dropped. Whatever it was his father wished for me to see, Henry was clearly excited about seeing it, too.

In a crestfallen tone, the boy mumbled, "Yes. I'll get you some."

"Ah, that would be fantastic," I told him. "And don't spare the sugar!"

We reached the third floor of the home, and Jacobs beckoned me to a west-facing window. He held out the telescope to me.

"It's a good telescope," he said. "We use it at the university for astronomical viewing, and I think you'll find it's stronger than those you military men use in the field. Point it west, and tell me if you are not thrilled by what you see!"

Thrilled wasn't the word for it. My guts exploded. My God, looking through his telescope I could see their faces as if they were standing just across the street! The Confederate army was on the move, and they were coming directly into Gettysburg.

On a ridge I could see clearly several Confederate officers on horseback, and they were pointing down to the village – for that matter they seemed to be pointing directly at me. Beyond them, though they were mostly shielded from view, I could see enough of a line of infantry to understand that the army was coming at us in strength.

"Almost surely the two armies will meet here in Gettysburg," Jacobs said, and I swear the man was licking his lips in anticipation. Perhaps I could be more generous toward Doctor Jacobs. He'd not seen anything of it. He didn't know how bad it was going to be. And to someone ignorant of the horrors of the thing, a rousing battle with lots of infantry and cannon and horses trotting about probably sounded like quite the lovely diversion. But good Lord, the man was a college professor and he should have known enough about the world to know that a line of Southern infantry marching toward you with Yankees near enough cannot be a good thing.

I took the glass away from my eye and tried to gauge how far off they actually were. The men were at a halt now, and they did not seem to be in a hurry. But they were near enough that hurry or not they'd be on us before the morning was out.

"B'God they'll be in the town before noon!" I said.

Jacobs took the glass from me and looked through the window at them.

"If you look beyond those men on the crest of the hill," Jacobs said, "you can see infantry and artillery. They are descending on us in strength."

I was consumed in my thoughts. I had convinced myself that the coming battle would take place west of town, over at Cashtown or even as far away as South Mountain below Chambersburg. That was where the Confederates were, and surely Lee and Longstreet would wait for Meade to come at them there. My personal safety was completely dependent upon the battle being in one of those places and not here on top of us. I might put on a brave face for Jenny, but the idea of enduring a shelling in her cellar unnerved me to no end. Suddenly before me I could see Fredericksburg after the shelling the Yankees had given her: Shattered buildings with nothing left standing but a single wall and a pile of rubble. I remembered the desolate and distraught faces of the refugees as they fled the city. Oh, my Lord, but I had no desire to die in Jenny Rakestraw's cellar as her entire house fell in on top of us!

It was Henry coming up the stairs with coffee cup and saucer rattling that shook me back to consciousness.

"I must go!" I said to the two Jacobs men.

"But your coffee?" Henry said, holding it out to me.

"Not now," I said. Then I paused. "Did you find sugar for it?"

"I did," he answered.

I snatched the cup from the saucer and tested it against my lips. It wasn't too hot, so I drank it down in several gulps. Henry stood staring, eyes agape, with the saucer still held out in front of him. I drained the last of the coffee, put the cup back on the proffered saucer and patted the boy on the head.

"Where are you going?" Doctor Jacobs asked.

"I've got to try to do something to keep those damned Rebels out of town!"

And do ye know, by the time I returned to the village they were calling me the Savior of Gettysburg? In my absence, young Henry must have gone door to door telling all the citizenry of how the Yankee major had gone out to face the entire Rebel army armed only with a Colt revolver and a look of steely determination. The look was actually sheer panic, but Henry was too naïve to understand what he was seeing.

I suppose if I'd been successful in delaying Pettigrew longer, the sobriquet would have stuck and in addition to being the Hero of El Teneria I'd have also been the Savior of Gettysburg. But when the battle commenced the next day, most of the citizens forgot how I'd dashed off to save them all from the destruction of war.

I raced down the stairs and out of the house and paused for just a moment as I debated my next move. Down the street I saw a local farmer mounted on his farm horse. The horse wasn't good for much other than carrying its owner into town, but it was the best I could do. I ran to the farmer.

"Ho there!" I said. I recognized the man from having been around the past few days. He'd been engaged in some of our open conversations about the events taking place around Gettysburg. I was relying that, like many of the others in town, he viewed me as something of a local authority. "Do you know me?"

He was an aged man, perhaps in his sixties, and he wore trousers, a dirty shirt, suspenders and a hat. I tried to recall his name but could not.

"I know ye," he said, and he gave me a skeptical look.

"I'm an officer in the Yankee – I mean, the Federal army," I said.

"Uh-huh," the geezer responded.

"The Rebs are marching into town, even as we speak," I said. "They're coming down the Chambersburg Pike! I've got to get out there and try to get them back."

"Uh-huh," the old man responded, still with a skeptical look.

"B'God man, I'm asking you for your horse! Loan it to me!"

"Ain't much good if ye're trying to outrun the Rebel cavalry," he said. "She's just an old farm horse."

"I'm not trying to outrun them," I said. "I'm trying to turn them back."

"By yerself?" he asked, and I did not think he could wrinkle his face any more than he already had, but now he outdid himself.

"Yes! Dammit, man, I need your horse!"

The man chewed his bottom lip for an interminable time, but at last he handed the reins over to me.

"Ye'll have to bring 'er back," he said.

"Yes, I'll do that."

"I live out on the Chambersburg Road," he said. "My name's John Burns. I'm trusting you, on your word of honor, to bring 'er back and that ye're not gonna rush off and try to escape on m'horse."

"Yes, yes," I said, hurrying him out of the saddle. "John Burns. Chambersburg Road. I'll bring your horse back to you," I said. [18]

I mounted the old man's horse and started west, though I did not go by the Chambersburg Pike. I was not a hundred paces outside of the city when, from behind me, I heard a massive uproar, and when I turned to look back at the city I saw Union cavalry riding into town from the south. It was Buford's advance guard, who'd been through town two days prior and ridden off east. Now Buford was coming up the Taneytown Road at a gallop with two full brigades of cavalry.

I kicked my horse into a faster pace and rode out across the fields leading to the west, south of the Seminary and through the woods. Behind me, the lead elements of Buford's cavalry were riding out west of town, and I knew for certain they were setting up an ambush for the advancing Confederates.

I advanced some distance over a couple of ridges and across a small creek and then found a path that would lead me back north toward the Confederate column. The whole way I was putting my thoughts together for how I might convince the Confederates to turn back. Buford's appearance in town behind me would either serve my purposes perfectly or would lead to disaster.

Luck was on my side, for as I cleared the woods I discovered the path I was on had led me directly into the flank of the Confederate column. Immediately I found myself surrounded by dust covered, ragged looking Southern boys.

"Halt there!" one of them said, advancing on me with his bayonet pointing up at me. "Cain't ye see ye're riding right into the Army of Northern Virginia? Are ye trying to get yerself kilt?"

I raised up both my hands, dropping the reins, and gave the boys my best Speedy grin. "I'd like to talk to your commanding officer," I told him. "What company is this?"

"We're the 47th North Carolina," said one of the others, also with pointing bayonet.

I tried to recall who was in command of the 47th North Carolina, but I wasn't even sure which Corps the company belonged to. I only knew for sure they weren't part of Longstreet's First Corps.

"Who's your commanding officer?" I asked.

"Colonel Fairbault," the first one said.

"Dammit, don't tell 'im that!" the second one said.

"Why not?" the first one asked.

"Cause he's a spy. He's gettin' information on us!"

"I ain't no spy," I told them, cool like with my hands still in the air. "Since when do spies ride right into the flank of an advancing column? But I need to see Colonel Fairbault. It's deadly serious that you get me to him right now."

Neither of them looked particularly convinced, and I was starting to worry these two buffoons might simply arrest me and pass me back to the rear of the column and my plan would not only be unsuccessful but I might be caught with the column as Buford's cavalry came upon them.

Desperate times call for desperate measures, no doubt about that, and I was beginning to panic in my desperation. It was foolish enough, but I gave it a gamble.

As the two men bickered with each other, neither one nor the other paying much attention to me, I resolved that I would offer them some evidence of my loyalty.

In a flash, I dropped my right hand to my holster, wrapped my fist around the Colt revolver and drew my weapon before either of them could react. With the barrel of the revolver I parried away one of the bayonets, and then I pointed the revolver directly into the face of the other man.

"Look 'ere," I said. "I ain't no spy. But I do have information for your colonel, and it cannot wait while you two bicker with each other about what I am or what I am not. The fact is, I've got half a mind to shoot you in the face" – and at this I thrust my revolver toward the one in a threatening manner – "just to convince your friend here to take me to the colonel."

Now I cooled my temper a bit, and I holstered my revolver. "But instead, I'm showing you that if I wanted to kill you, ye'd be dead now. That should be evidence enough that I'm your friend and not your enemy, and so I'm asking you in friendship to take me to your colonel."

Neither of them had expected this sort of behavior, and it seemed to have been enough to convince them. Had I not had that revolver on me and been able to force the issue, I believe the three of us would still be there to this day debating whether or not I was friend or foe.

"A'right," one of them said. "C'mon with ye then and we'll let the colonel decide if ye're a Yankee spy or not."

"Excellent decision," I said.

I dismounted and walked the horse along the column, which presently was at a standstill. These boys, just as Early's had been when they'd come through town four days ago, were in high spirits. They were all standing around, laughing and drinking from their canteens and leaning against their guns, and there was nothing about them that would have left you with the conclusion that soon enough they'd all be dead or wounded or defeated. The 47th North Carolina, for instance, was decimated on the first day of the battle. I didn't know it as I passed them by, and they didn't know it either, but in twenty-four hours these carefree boys would make a charge that would leave the bulk of them shattered in the fields just west of town.

Like Early's command, most of them couldn't put together a decent suit of clothes if they all combined what they were wearing.

Their coats were worn thin, I don't believe a man I passed had cloth covering his knees for their trousers were full of holes, and a fair number of them were barefooted. I've never seen an army that didn't complain in the best of times, but Lee's men were all in high spirits, and I believe for most of them there was no place they'd have rather been.

At the head of the column we found the colonel.

"Colonel, sir, this man 'ere rode up outta the woods just now, says he needs to see you," the private told him.

Fairbault, whom I did not know, looked me up and down and took in my horse.

"That's a good revolver for a man with such a poor horse," he said at length.

"Listen here, colonel," I said, and having prepared my speech in my mind ahead of time, I dove right into what I had to say: "I've got some information for you and you're just going to have to trust me. My name's Jackson Speed, I'm a captain on General Longstreet's staff. A month ago he sent me north to do some scouting. I've not yet returned to his command, but when I saw you this morning riding into town I knew I must get here to warn you. The Yankees are in Gettysburg in force, and there's more coming up from the south. I don't doubt but that the entire Army of the Potomac will be upon the town before sundown. Unless your intention is to become engaged in a full battle with a hundred thousand Federals right here on this spot, you must halt this column and turn it back to Cashtown or South Mountain.

"The fact is, if you go much farther along this road, you will walk straight into an ambush. There's Yankee cavalry just up there," I said, and I pointed east toward Gettysburg.

Fairbault seemed a bright sort of fellow to me, and he didn't speak at first as he considered my warning.

"How can I know you're telling the truth?" he asked at length.

I cast about in my mind for some answer. I had nothing that would identify me as a Confederate officer.

"Who's your commander," I asked. "Perhaps I know him."

"General Pettigrew," Fairbault answered.

Ah now, here was another stroke of luck. I knew Pettigrew from being around Lee's headquarters. He would know me by sight and by name.

"You can take me to him," I said.

Fairbault shook his head. "General Pettigrew is still back of the column, and I've already sent a messenger back to him. I'm not taking you back there with the town under our noses."

I frowned my frustration at him, but then another thought occurred to me. "I'm a Knight of the Golden Circle, Milledgeville, Georgia Chapter. Surely a North Carolina colonel is a fellow Knight?" I asked.

Fairbault cut his eyes at me. "Prove you're a Knight," he said.

And so I gave him the secret handshake known to the Knights of the Golden Circle from one end of the country to the next. Fairbault knew the handshake, too, and both of us started laughing.

"All right," he said grinning all over. I suppose it was relief at meeting an old fellow, but suddenly Fairbault's suspicious manner gave way to extreme friendliness. "Order the men to take cover!" he said to one of his staff, and presently the entire column began to spread out into the woods and behind trees. As they did, Fairbault and I walked to the tree line. He then opened up, telling me all the secrets of the army he could think to tell. Lucky for him, I wasn't a Yankee spy.

"We're part of Heth's Division of the Third Corps. When Jubal Early came through Gettysburg a couple of days ago, he sent word back to General Heth that there was some quantity of shoes in the town. Having come through the column, I'm certain you noticed our need for shoes. So last night, General Heth ordered General Pettigrew to come into town to requisition the shoes."

"Aye," I said. "Shoes and trousers. But I doubt ye'll find 'em in Gettysburg. The merchants all shipped their goods over the Susquehanna the first they knew you boys were in Pennsylvania."

"Well, I'll send a messenger back to Pettigrew with your information. Should I arrange an escort to take you back to General Longstreet in Chambersburg?"

"Naw," I said. "I'm obliged to you, but I ain't done with my work yet. I'll rejoin Old Peter soon enough, but not today."

And at that, I mounted my horse and told Fairbault I'd just ride back down the Chambersburg Pike into town. [19]

It was a damned fool thing to do, for I'd not cleared a hundred yards when I realized that in the tree line to my left and right there were dismounted cavalry laying in ambush for the Confederates. It was Buford's advance guard that had come into Gettysburg as I was leaving. Again, though, luck was with me for a jumpy cavalryman might have shot me dead, but they must have figured me for a local farmer and I was able to ride past them unmolested. Not long after I passed, though, I heard a smattering of musket fire and was left to assume that Buford's cavalry could not wait to spring their trap and had fired off a few shots at the head of Pettigrew's column.

I was about three miles from town when I left Fairbault, and I'd now come halfway back to Gettysburg when I saw riding toward me a lone man. He looked to be a civilian, and I'd have probably paid him no mind except that as he got closer there was something familiar about him. As we approached each other, I studied the rider and felt certain I knew him, and then I realized that I recognized the horse as well.

B'God it was Longstreet's spy, Harrison!

The last I'd seen him we were both fighting for our lives, and I had fled and left him to his fate, so I wasn't sure how he would receive me.

I pulled up on my reins as he drew even with me, and Harrison stopped his horse as well.

"I figured you was dead," Harrison said, eyeing me.

"Aye, I nearly was," I said. "I'm sure glad to see you made it through unscathed."

"The Union cavalry is coming in the town up ahead," Harrison said. "Meade's army ain't far behind, either. Looks like there's going to be a lot of dead Yanks in the next day or two."

"The Yankee cavalry is back behind me, too," I said. "I heard some shots a bit ago. You might not want to continue forward."

"I've got information to pass along," Harrison said. "I'll take my chances. General Longstreet asked about you when I returned to his command in Chambersburg two days ago. I told him what happened at the Spotted Tavern and that I didn't know how you came out of it. Have you had any communication with him?"

This was tricky business. Though I fully intended to not see Old Peter again so long as this war continued, I also knew enough that fate can be a fickle mistress, and so I did not want Longstreet to conclude that I had in fact deserted from his army.

"I've loose ends to tie up," I said. "General Longstreet will see me before the battle commences, but there is good I can still do for our cause before I rejoin his command."

Harrison stared at me for a moment, spit off to the side of the road, and then drew up his reins. "Well, good luck to you, then. Haw!" he shouted, and his horse broke into a trot.

As I topped McPherson's Ridge on my way back into town, I had a clear view of Gettysburg and the Taneytown Road to the south. There I saw the remainder of Buford's two brigades in a long column stretching as far down the road as I could see.

It was relief I felt at the sight of that blue column, for I was convinced that with my warning, and the information from Harrison, Pettigrew would turn back and rejoin the rest of the army at Cashtown. Lee, with the knowledge that Meade was coming up, would establish a defensive line at Cashtown, or perhaps he'd put his back against South Mountain. Meade would be obliged to attack the Confederates there, and I would be well away from danger in Gettysburg.

Whatever the outcome, I knew that I would soon have to abandon Jenny Rakestraw and her pleasant village. I had identified myself as one of Longstreet's officers, and I'd been spotted by Harrison, who knew me. My presence in Gettysburg would soon be known by Old Peter, and he would be expecting me to rejoin him presently.

No, as much as I was enjoying life here, Gettysburg had just become an uncomfortable place for me. I decided in that moment that I would wait it out a day or two to see what was going to happen with the two armies, and then I would have to take my chances and try to escape to the northeast.

As I rode back into town, I considered whether or not I might take Jenny with me, for she was an excellent companion, but in the end I rejected the idea. I was still worried about Jeb Stuart, for I believed he must surely be somewhere to the east, and if I did get caught in a chase with Confederate cavalry I did not need a woman to slow me down.

On the Chambersburg Road I found an old man who was missing an eye and inquired if he could point me in the direction of John Burns' house.

"Isn't that John's horse ye're on?" he asked, squinting at the horse with his one good eye.

"It is," I said. "I'm looking to return the horse."

"Aren't you that Union officer that's been staying at the Rakestraw home?" he asked.

"I am," I said.

"Do you think the battle's going to be fought here?" he asked.

"No," I said firmly, trying to convince myself as much as this one-eyed geezer. "The fight's going to be back toward Cashtown. Maybe over at South Mountain. Lee's main body is still too far away, and Meade is nearly to town."

"You going to join in the fight?" he asked.

"I might. Can you tell me where John Burns lives?"

"You're sitting in front of his house," the geezer said, pointing over my shoulder at a large clapboard home with a leaning porch that badly needed whitewashing.

"John Burns!" the old man yelled at the house. "That Union officer is out here and says he wants to return your horse!"

A moment later, Burns himself appeared at the door. I dismounted and tied the horse to the post propping up his leaning porch.

"Did ye turn them Rebels back?" Burns asked me.

"I think I did," I told him.

I started to walk back toward the Diamond – just three blocks away – but as I started to cross Washington Street – which south of town was called the Taneytown Road – it occurred to me that I might visit Doctor Jacobs again and look out his window to be certain Pettigrew's column had heeded my warning. As I turned down the street, I realized that just a few blocks south and riding at a walk toward me was the remainder of Buford's column, coming up to join their comrades laying in ambush.

All up and down Washington Street, women and girls and boys were gathering to wave handkerchiefs to the advancing Union cavalry. Some of the girls nearby started up a song as the head of the column advanced toward us. Others had baskets of sandwiches or slices of pie or pieces of cake and bottles of water that they were handing to the cavalrymen as they passed.

I studied the faces of the Yankee cavalrymen as they came near. Some of them smiled at the girls and women. Some joined in the singing. But in their eyes was blazing determination. Here and there a staff officer would peel off from the main body on one mission or another. Almost before they were in town, Buford had orders printed up and passed around that prohibited the sale of spirits while his cavalry was there.

Near the head of the column I saw the dour faced Buford, who wore a thick blonde moustache and seemed to forever be looking through squinting eyes. He had a square jaw. I do not think the man had ever smiled in his life, and I can only assume he made it a practice of shooting those who laughed in his presence, for his entire staff and most of his command seemed just as dour as he was.

They were a serious bunch, those Yankee cavalrymen. At the time

I believed the contrast between them and Pettigrew's command – where the infantrymen were at their ease and joking and laughing – was evidence of the confidence the Southerner had in his previous and future success as opposed to the acceptance the Yankee had in his past and future failure. But knowing now how the battle turned out, I can't help but wonder if the Yanks' features weren't giving away their determination to reverse those past defeats in defense of their homeland.

I made my way through the crowd lining Washington Street down to Doctor Jacobs' home. I had to cross the street, and I stood waiting for some time for a break in the column of cavalry so that I could dash between them to Jacobs' house. The door was open and Henry and one of Jacobs' daughters were both standing at the door watching the column.

"Is your father upstairs still?" I asked.

"He is!" Henry said, and his manner betrayed his excitement. "Isn't this the most exciting event you've ever witnessed?"

"It is not," I said. "I've seen these men, or men like 'em, at the charge. Now that's something for you to see if you want excitement."

This pleased Henry to no end, and he called up the steps for me, "Father! Major Speed has returned!"

I took the steps two at a time.

"Ah, Major Speed," Jacobs said as I hit the landing. "If you would like to see a most singular event, come here and have a look. Below us, the Union cavalry. And beyond, the Southern infantry encamped among the Blue Ridge mountains. The tide of war, at this hour, is halted under our very eyes!"

I took the glass and looked first to the mountains off to the west. Indeed, wherever there was a clearing I could see smoke from campfires. I could even see men cooking or going about other camp chores. The telescope was so strong, that I believed if I had squinted a bit harder maybe I could even recognize some of my old friends. I took Jacobs' telescope away from my eye and looked down at Buford's passing column. One was at its ease and one was riding into battle. Still, as unconcerned as Lee's army appeared in the mountains, I knew that Meade had better hurry up from the south or Buford would be in trouble.

Now I looked out the Chambersburg Pike for evidence that Pettigrew's command had taken to heart my warnings.

Indeed, they were pulling back, slowly and reluctantly, and making their way back toward Cashtown. This was just exactly where I wanted them to be. Now, so long as Meade didn't dillydally, the point on the map that would be in contention must be Cashtown or west of there. If Meade came up in strength and was quick about it, he might force Pettigrew back. That would work to Lee's advantage, though. Allow Pettigrew to fight a halting battle, retreating slowly to the main army. And there, another 10 or 15 miles west of Cashtown, Longstreet would be well ready for Meade and the Army of the Potomac. Thinking back on the slaughter at Fredericksburg, I almost felt sorry for the Federals.

"I believe with this fine telescope of yours, you will have an excellent opportunity tomorrow, or maybe the next day, to watch the next great battle in our national struggle," I told Jacobs. "You keep your eye on those mountains yonder and you will have quite a show."

I handed him back the telescope and made to leave, satisfied at what I'd seen.

"You'll come back tomorrow and watch with us?" Doctor Jacobs asked, too excited to contain himself.

"Oh, aye," I said, "unless it turns out that I join my brothers in the Union Army and have a view closer than this one!"

Jacobs, becoming misty-eyed, patted me on the back and told me it was men like me who would save our Union and rid us of the scourge of slavery, and I told him he was quite probably right.

Buford's cavalry was still in town when I exited Doctor Jacobs' house. Some of his men were scattering north and west of the town to bivouac for the night, others were sharing their liquor with Gettysburg's citizens who had been forbidden from selling the stuff by Buford's order so that the only way to get a decent drink that night was to buy it off a cavalryman.

It seemed on the afternoon of June 30 that everything had come up well for me. I'd ridden west of the town, given the secret handshake and warned the Rebels to about-face and they'd heeded the warning. Buford's men were camping out on the outskirts of town. I'd have rather they move on out toward Cashtown, but it was enough that Gettysburg was now inside the Federal lines.

I knew that I must make my escape soon, but my actions would have to be dictated by the movements of the armies. I was nervous about Stuart's cavalry that I'd still not seen anything of, but I felt taking my chances with Stuart was better than getting caught up in the rush as the Union army retreated through Gettysburg with Bobby Lee hot behind them.

With no sign of Meade late on the afternoon of the June 30, I concluded that the battle was still two days away. Buford, with two brigades of cavalry, could probably push back Pettigrew's command. Meade would come up through Gettysburg and join Buford somewhere near Cashtown on July 1. The battle would open in earnest on July 2, and that would be the day Ol' Speedy would make his escape.

So as Jenny and I retired for the evening, I knew our time together was running out, but I still suspected we would have another night together. I did not, therefore, make any passionate farewell speeches, and as we drifted off to sleep together neither of us suspected what the morrow would bring.

CHAPTER 7

Jenny's house sat on the west side of Carlisle Street, facing east, and her bedroom was at the front of the house. Noises off the street entered her open bedroom window, but noises to the west were not so easily heard. And so it was, as the opening shots of the Battle of Gettysburg were fired on the morning of July 1, 1863, I dozed lazily in bed. I was aware that Jenny had gotten up and was making coffee downstairs, but I was drowsing in bed.

I remember it was an unseasonably cool breeze coming in through the window, and the vague thought that it smelled of rain outside crossed my mind, too. Jenny's bed was uncommonly comfortable, and I thought briefly that if it rained that might delay the battle even a day or two more, which would suit me fine. I felt very put upon that these armies should show up here in Gettysburg and disrupt my comfort.

What I did not realize was that it was Archer, Harry Heth and A.P. Hill who were coming into Gettysburg that morning. I cannot think of three bigger hot-heads in all of the Confederacy. Had I known these three were in charge, I'd have found the fastest horse in the livery and ridden as hard and fast as the thing would go in the opposite direction. [20]

"Good morning Jackson," Jenny said, coming into the bedroom with a tray of toast and butter and coffee for both of us. "It's a quiet morning. I stepped out of the house and walked down to the Diamond, and I saw some of Buford's cavalry still camped west of town off the Chambersburg Pike, but there was nothing else stirring."

"Meade will be up soon, I should think," I said. "By now Buford knows as well as everyone in Gettysburg that Lee is camped in the mountains to the west, and he'll have called up the army to meet them."

"You still think the best thing for us is to hide in the cellar?" Jenny asked me, sitting on the side of the bed and handing me a cup of coffee.

I had momentary qualms now, thinking that I might yet take her with me. But in the end, the soundness of not having her slow me down decided it for me. "Yes," I said. "If things around the city were to get hot, I believe the best place for us is in the cellar."

Jenny looked at me thoughtfully. "Do you have any qualms about not joining the army for the battle?" she asked.

"Which army?" I asked her, teasing.

She frowned. "Well, I suppose either army."

"No qualms," I said. "I've seen enough of the killing. I've had enough cannonballs shot at me. I've seen plenty of bayonets shining in blood. I feel fortunate to have survived so much of it, and I don't doubt that my luck will eventually run out. No, let the boys go and fight, and I'll be glad to hide in the cellar."

Just then, we heard shouting coming from the street outside. I got out of bed and looked out the open window. Two boys were running past, and I distinctly heard one calling to the other.

"Hurry up, Samuel, if you want to see the start of the battle!"

They were running north up Carlisle Street. I determined to pay them no mind, as I knew if there was going to be a battle it would obviously be west of town. But I should have understood that they were running north in an effort to get a good seat without being in the middle of the thing. [21]

"What was that?" Jenny asked me.

I returned to the bed and sat beside her. "Nothing more than a couple of boys with active imaginations," I said.

"No," Jenny said, and she put a hand on my arm to hush me, her head inclined as if she was trying to hear something. "No, Jack, I think I heard gun fire."

I listened myself, but heard nothing.

"Perhaps we should walk out to the Diamond and see if there is some news," Jenny suggested.

I stretched and yawned and considered letting her go alone, but I'd seen a trace of concern come over her face, and it was enough to make me a little worried, too.

I dressed myself in my civilian clothes and buckled on my Colt revolver. I put on my slouch hat. But then a thought occurred to me. If I was going to make my way away from the town, it might do me good to have a uniform or two in which to do it. So I put on my Yankee coat and, though it was too warm by far, I covered that over with a light colored linen duster. I rolled up my Confederate coat, too, and shoved it into a traveling bag I found at the bottom of Jenny's wardrobe.

"Are you planning to go somewhere?" she asked when I came back downstairs.

"Ah, ye never know what we might find out there, and I just want to make sure I'm ready," I told her.

Jenny cut her eyes suspiciously at me, and I think she must have known that I had flight in mind. But she said nothing, and together we walked out of the house and started out for the Diamond.

Buford's troops had camped on the outskirts of town to the north and west, but as we walked out into the streets we found no lack of activity among the Union cavalry in the streets. Mostly they were riding at a full gallop, some south and some into the town, and I could only assume they were delivering messages.

The activity reminded me instantly of those two awful days in Monterrey in September of '46 when Mexicans were standing on rooftops and shooting down into the street and couriers were dashing about the city with messages to retreat or advance.

"This doesn't look good," I said to Jenny.

There were plenty of civilians out in the streets, too, most of them just loitering and watching, waiting for something to happen.

We were not quite to the Diamond when I heard the first boom of cannon.

"That's cannon fire!" Jenny exclaimed, catching me at the elbow.

And now, I heard too the reports of musketry. Not far from town a battle was breaking out. [22]

As we came into the Diamond there was a growing crowd of civilians rushing to the same place, all in want of information just the same as us. I looked out Chambersburg Street and there saw a horrific sight: out on the road, not a mile from town, the cavalry was dismounted all across Seminary Ridge. The ridge was named because that's where the Seminary was located. It was a north-south running ridge and one of several ridges rippling away from Gettysburg out to the west.

Huddles of horses could be seen where two or three men were charged with holding the mounts while their mates were spread out atop the farther ridge, McPherson's Ridge. Those men on the farther ridge, who we could only barely see, had their carbines pointed west. Buford's cannon, and I did not see more than a couple of them, were being brought to the field, but I could also see puffs of earth as Confederate cannon fire burst near the Union troops and even behind them on the nearer of the two ridges.

"My Lord," I said to Jenny. "The Rebels are pushing this way!"

"Henry! Henry!" Jenny called, seeing young Henry Jacobs rushing down the road. Henry, seeing us, ran to where we were standing.

"It's starting!" he exclaimed, eyes wide with excitement. I could have told him he'd soon lose his enthusiasm, but he'd have not believed me. I thought of the people from Washington D.C. who had ventured out in buggies, the women carrying parasols and the men toting picnic baskets, to see that first battle at Manassas. They thought they were going for entertainment, but soon found themselves witnesses to the horrors of war. Young Henry, too, believed it was entertainment coming his way. He would learn differently.

"Where's your father Henry?" Jenny asked.

"He's gone to teach class, but I cannot imagine they will be doing much learning today!"

I'll confess that my memory is at times cloudy as I look back on those days of the Battle of Gettysburg. Moments I recall with supreme clarity, but other moments are a jumbled haze of confusion and soldiers and citizens rushing this way and that. If we stood there in the Diamond watching for five minutes or forty-five minutes, I could not tell you with any certainty. I remember at one point I decided to relieve myself of the traveling bag. I looked around for a spot where I might stash it, and decided to wedge it into one of the crooks made by the branches of one of the trees that lined the street. I recall that I had to reach up, almost standing on my toes, to get it into the crook of the tree, and I thought I could be relatively assured that if I needed it I would find it in that place, as most men were not tall enough to reach it. It never occurred to me that any number of men on the street that day were mounted and might easily snatch the thing from its height while atop a horse, nor did I bother to think that a child with a stick would easily push it out of its spot. But when Heth's cannon are firing in proximity to you and Union cavalry are all about the place, you do not always think thoroughly. So it was there that I stashed my Confederate captain's coat, and how I came to find it again later in the very place where I most needed it is beyond my knowledge.

For a while, Henry stood with us, trying as we were to catch glimpses of the Union troopers out on McPherson Ridge, but eventually he said he was going home. It did not occur to me that he was going home for a better view, or I'd have joined him.

"Everything depends on their ability to hold those Confederates back," I said to Jenny. "If the Confederates are able to push Buford's men back into the town, then likely as not it will be a disaster for us."

"At what point should we flee to the cellar?" she asked.

"When we see the fronts of those Yankee cavalrymen instead of their backs, it will be time to get to the cellar," I told her.

I was considering abandoning my plans to flee the town. The thing was closer already than I imagined it being, and I could not believe that Pettigrew was so easily pushing his way east against two brigades of cavalry. Of course, I did not know then that it was Heth's entire division on the opposite ridge, for from my vantage point I could not see a thing beyond McPherson's Ridge.

"I need a better look," I said to Jenny. "I know nothing of what's happening beyond that ridge."

"The cupola at the Seminary," she said. "That would provide the best view."

The Lutheran Seminary was west of town, just south of the Chambersburg Pike. It sat among trees on Seminary Ridge. I was reluctant to go in that direction, for we were seeing an occasional cannon shell burst on Seminary Ridge. But my need to understand what was happening beyond those hills was too pressing.

"I'm going to go there," I said to Jenny.

"I'm coming with you," she said.

You and I both know that it was too dangerous a place for a woman to be, but I could not bear the idea of going alone, and so I readily agreed to her company.

We did not go by way of the road. Instead, as we got to the edge of town, we started out across the fields and through the trees up the hill to the Seminary. In the valley between the school and the seminary several tents had been erected and a field hospital was already established. Even this early in the battle wounded were being brought back in ambulances or, if they were able, walking back on their own. We saw a man with blood streaming down his face and into his eyes stumble as he tried to make his way to the hospital, and another man – who appeared to be in shock – holding his left arm against his torso with his right hand, and that seemed to be nearly all that was keeping his arm in place for there was such a wound above the elbow that I could not see anything connecting the lower portion of his arm to the upper.

There was a fair amount of activity at the school when we reached it. What students remained at the school were gathered in the yard outside the school's main building, and they seemed undecided as to what they should do. There must have been two dozen mounted Yanks there in the school grounds as well, some waiting for messages and others riding up to deliver messages.

We were closer to the shooting now, and it was obvious to me that what had started as a light skirmish had now escalated considerably. Though we were east of the Seminary and had not yet achieved any sort of view of the battlefield, the boom of cannon was coming with more rapid succession, and the distant rattle of musketry and rifle fire was now an every-present refrain. Oh, not far on the other side of this big brick building, hell was breaking loose.

I should have expected half the officers in Buford's brigades would be gathered here at the Seminary, but I would be damned if their presence would deter me from my desire to get a decent look at what was taking place. I needed to know, you understand, because my personal safety depended on my seeing what was happening. If the Rebels were coming on and Buford was to be broken any time soon, then I'd be huddled with Jenny in her basement and praying to the Lord that a shell didn't crash the house down on top of us. But if Buford was holding fast, then Ol' Speedy was going to find a horse and gallop off to Philadelphia lightning quick.

"This is no place for a civilian and a lady," a lieutenant said to us as we started for the door of the seminary.

"I'm no civilian and she's no lady," I snarled at him. And with that, I stripped myself of the linen duster and tossed it on the ground. "I'm a major in this army, and I'll decide what is and is not a place for me."

The lieutenant looked doubtful, but he mumbled some apology and stepped out of my way.

While we were occupied in attempting to get past the lieutenant and into the building, a group of riders came up from behind us. I paid them no mind, initially.

I took Jenny by the hand and started to lead her up the steps into the Seminary, but just then there was a chaotic clatter coming from inside the building and I was nearly knocked aside as John Buford came bounding down the steps in a rush. B'God, the man was almost cracking a smile as he came past me.

"Reynolds is here!" he proclaimed to a group of mounted staff officers. "Infantry is coming up the road from the south! He's kept his word and is nearly in the town! Quickly, spread the word to our boys that the infantry is here and they must hold fast just a little while longer!"

Immediately a couple of the staff officers broke away from the group and rode off toward the sounds of fighting.

Buford was standing six feet from me, and he'd not noticed one of the men in the group that had just ridden up walking up to him. But I noticed the man now, and recognized him right away.

"What is the matter, John?" General Reynolds said to Buford.

I'd known John Reynolds in the early days of the war, and I'll say that he was among the more competent generals in the Army of the Potomac. When I first heard that Meade had replaced Hooker, I thought it should have been Reynolds who was given the job. Of course, when I heard that Hooker had replaced Burnside, I thought then that Reynolds, and not Hooker, should have been given the job. He was a tall man, like myself, and as well built. Reynolds was a decade or so older than me, but he kept a youngish appearance with short black hair and a well-trimmed black beard untouched by gray. His thin face was always tan and the corners of his eyes were wrinkled – both from being in the sun. He had dark, penetrating eyes and a small nose. On this day he was wearing his blue coat with the straps that marked him as a major general, and when the time came, this would cause him to draw the attention of Rebel sharpshooters.

Buford wheeled around, spotted Reynolds, and I thought for a moment the stern cavalryman would throw his arms around Reynolds. But Buford regained his composure and growled, "Hell's to pay."

Well, if I wasn't already unnerved, this pronouncement from Buford was enough to finish the job. My belly began to rumble loudly.

Buford led Reynolds into the Seminary where the two men went together to the cupola. Jenny and I chose to stand by and wait our turn, and pretty quick they were back down in the yard. Reynolds issued orders to one of his staff men to get to Meade and let him know that the battle was happening now, and then Reynolds himself rode back to his corps to speed along the infantry. [23]

Now I took my chance, and Jenny and I went into the Seminary. We climbed the steps to the third floor, and then we both ascended the ladder into the cupola.

I looked west to see the battle taking place, and the first thing I realized was that Pettigrew had not come alone.

Out to the west, spread along the road to Cashtown, was Rebel infantry everywhere. It was Hill's corps with Heth's men engaged in the fighting. There were so many Confederates within view that I could not understand how they had not already swept Buford's brigades from the ridges and overrun the city. But from my new vantage point, I could see that the thing was nearly done. Buford's cavalry was falling back, fighting for every inch of ground but giving it up by the yard. I thought they might break even as I watched.

The sounds of music – if I recall correctly, it was "The Girl I Left Behind Me" – caught my attention, and I turned to the east and saw Reynolds' men advancing. The band was marching, but the lead divisions were breaking away at the run, cutting across fields, knocking down fences and getting to the battle as quick as they could. Even as I watched, a group of them had gotten up to the white picket fence running along the yard of the Seminary and were knocking it over to allow those behind them free passage. I could see Reynolds, too, leading a company up toward the Cashtown Road.

And now all my hopes depended on these boys in blue. If they could push hard enough and fast enough, they could bolster the stand Buford's cavalry had made and keep the Confederates out of Gettysburg. That's what I was depending upon. A battle to the west – and the farther west the better – kept me safe in the city.

But if Reynolds' infantry was too late, if Heth had forced the foothold he needed to enter Gettysburg, the battle might well be fought on top of me.

"It's going to be a close thing," I said, looking at Jenny for the first time since we'd entered the cupola. She was standing rigid, her face pale, and her gaze was cast off to the west. There was horror on her face. "Are you all right?"

"They'll be in the town in the hour," Jenny breathed. "They're sweeping the Union from the field, and then there is nothing to stop them from entering Gettysburg."

"Maybe not," I said. "Reynolds' infantry is coming at the run."

"They're too late," she said.

Just then we heard a commotion below us, and I saw that Doctor Jacobs was ascending the ladder.

"Major Speed!" he said, his eyes wide with excitement. "I believe the battle has commenced!"

Up the ladder behind him was coming a junior officer, and it was about to be a tight squeeze there in the cupola.

The lieutenant emerged at the top of the ladder, crowding in so that there were now four of us there. "This is Lieutenant Bonaparte of the Signal Corps," Jacobs announced. "I've been asked to instruct him from this vantage of the lay of the surrounding territory."

Bonaparte saluted so that I remembered I was wearing a major's coat, and I returned the salute. He looked Jenny over one time, but he did not say anything about our presence there in the cupola. I suppose because I outranked him he concluded that if I wanted to show off the battle to a local girl that was my right as a ranking officer.

I'll confess, I was impressed with Jacobs' instruction as he pointed out the important points of the territory surrounding Gettysburg. Though I'd been in the town for a number of weeks now and knew the heights by sight, I did not know them by name. My familiarity with Gettysburg and with what would become the battlefield, was greatly improved during Jacobs' instruction.

"Here to our west where the fighting is taking place, this is McPherson's Ridge there where your men are forming up. That creek between the two armies, that is Willoughby Run. We are now on Seminary Ridge. If you will face east, to the south there is Cemetery Hill and beyond that is Culp's Hill. You'll see that Cemetery Hill runs as a ridge to the south, and those two large hills there are Little Round Top and, beyond it to the south there, Sugarloaf." He used the local name for the big hill to the south, the highest point in Adams County, Pennsylvania, that would be remembered all these years later as Round Top. "These are the important heights around the town. Culp's Hill and Sugarloaf are the two highest points, and I would think that you would want to secure these immediately. The ridge from Cemetery Hill all the way to Little Round Top is a good ground, giving you a commanding presence over the valley there where the Emmitsburg Road is."

"The Emmitsburg Road," Bonaparte broke in, "that's the road there where the First Corps is marching up from the south?"

"That's right," Jacobs said.

"There's another road coming up from Taneytown," the lieutenant said. "We have men who are coming up from that direction. Where is that road?"

Jacobs peered out at Cemetery Ridge for a moment. "You cannot get a good look at the road from here, but it is there beyond Cemetery Ridge," he said. "You can see there" – and he pointed to a spot just south of town – "where the Tanneytown Road and Emmitsburg Road connect."

The lieutenant had a small journal in which he was making notes and drawing out sketches. He asked a few more questions to which Jacobs provided answers. Then he said, "Thank you sir. You've done a service to your country. This information will be invaluable to us. My advice to you, sir, would be that you now retire to your home. If you should see our soldiers retreating into the city, you would do well to get into your cellar."

Then, with a final salute to me and a tip of his hat to Jenny, the lieutenant was descending the ladder. I did not know if he was riding his information back to Meade or if it was going to Reynolds, but having paid close attention to all that Jacobs had said, I saw now how the battle would likely run. And except for the outcome – for even at that moment I expected the Confederates would be victorious – I was correct.

The Yanks would never be able to hold McPherson's Ridge. They would have to fall back south of town to the heights Jacobs pointed out: Culp's Hill, Cemetery Hill and Cemetery Ridge. They would establish there on those hills and along that ridge a battle line to shield and protect the remainder of Meade's army, which according to Lieutenant Bonaparte was coming up the road beyond Cemetery

Ridge.

Lee's army would establish its battle line along Seminary Ridge, b'God right where we were standing! Longstreet would insist that once the ridge was fortified the Southern army would then wait on Seminary Ridge for Meade to attack. The Yankees would cross those wheat fields between the two ridges to attack, and there all along the Emmitsburg Road the Confederates would annihilate them. I could see it play out in my mind as if I'd seen it a dozen times before. And, except that it had happened in other places, I had.

But that put all the fighting uncomfortably close to me.

The three of us stood there for some time in the cupola watching the fighting out on McPherson's Ridge. Presently, Jacobs announced, "I believe I will follow his advice and retire to my home. I am concerned over the safety of my family."

"God bless you Doctor Jacobs and keep you safe in this terrible time," Jenny said, squeezing his hands.

"And you, too, my dear."

Jacobs looked at me. "Will you be returning to your duties now, Major?"

"My duties?" I asked, caught off guard by his question. I'd been chewing it over in my mind if escape to the east was still possible or if Stuart had finally arrived out that way somewhere. "Oh, right. My duties. Yes, I suppose I should find Reynolds and see if there's any good use I can make of myself."

"Jenny, dear, if the Major is to take up his place in the fight, and if you find yourself afraid, you are welcome to join my family and myself in our home."

"Oh, thank you, Doctor Jacobs," Jenny said. "Do not be surprised if you hear my knock upon your door."

Jacobs shook my hand very firmly. "I do not envy you, Major Speed, but I am confident that with men such as yourself protecting us in the face of the Rebels that my town and my country are well defended!"

I gave him a wink and a slap on the back and told him to keep his head down as he made his way back to town, but I didn't see the point in correcting him in the error of his judgment. [24]

Jenny and I remained in the cupola, transfixed by the horror and drama that was taking place before us as if on the stage in some brutal and bloody theater.

Oh, I'd seen it before – hadn't I watched the whole of Fredericksburg take place before me in just the same fashion? Nevertheless, I found it difficult to avert my attention from the panorama of battle playing out below me.

The Yanks were moving into positions to provide relief to Buford's battered cavalry. Infantry and artillery were coming onto the field in a ceaseless wave. But it seemed that as fast as they could get into place, the Rebels were bringing them under fire, and we watched as all along the ridge, from the woods up toward the big hill to the north, blue coats were falling dead.

Presently, I was about to witness something I'd not seen before, and that was the death of the commander on the field.

I knew John Reynolds back from my days working for Pinkerton and McClellan, and of course at the Seven Days. Reynolds was a good and solid man. Now, he was as lunatic as any of the rest of 'em who like to lead from the front – and it was about to be the death of him – but he had a decent sense of humor at camp and a calmness of character that I rather liked. I'll tell you this, I wouldn't have taken a hundred Lloyd Tilghmans for one J. F. Reynolds. [25]

The Iron Brigade was cresting McPherson's Ridge to join in the battle, and there at the edge of McPherson's Woods I could see an officer atop a black horse, sword drawn, as he directed the men into place. By this time I had a pair of binoculars, either left by Dr. Jacobs or one of the officers who had been in the cupola, and I put them up to my eyes and trained them on the officer in the distance. It was J.F. Reynolds, leading from the front. The thought struck me right then that the senior Union man on the field was at the very front of the fighting, mounted on a fine looking black horse and wearing his major general shoulder straps that I could see clearly even from my distance, and if some Alabama sharpshooter didn't knock him off that horse then it was a missed opportunity for the Confederacy. What better way to win a battle than shoot down the commanding officer, particularly a good one like Reynolds?

"B'God, Reynolds ain't gonna see the end of this battle if someone doesn't convince him to back up a bit," I said to Jenny, and I pointed him out to her.

In my memory, when I think back to the very moment, I can hear above the den of battle the singular crack of the sharpshooter's rifle, though I know I could hear no such thing when I was there on the day. But I see it as clear in my mind now as I did then through those binoculars. Reynolds was turned in his saddle looking back toward the Seminary, perhaps looking for more reinforcements. The expression on his face was concern, he knew he needed more men or what he had in place would break at any moment. And then I heard that crack – oh, it may have been any number of rifles going off at that moment, or it may have simply been a trick of the imagination – and a red mist appeared in the back of Reynolds' head and suddenly his eye was gone. He fell from the saddle immediately, and I did not need to be there to know he was dead before he hit the ground.

I'd just pointed him out to Jenny, so that she was looking at him, too, as he fell.

"Oh no!" Jenny exclaimed. She gasped. "Was that Reynolds?" she asked, but there was no point in answering for she knew it as well as I did.

From my vantage point I could see little through the trees and in the valley beyond McPherson's Ridge, but I believe I was able to spot a Confederate sharpshooter perched in a treetop beyond Willoughby Run. I assume, if that's what I saw in that treetop and not a squirrel's nest, that I spotted the sharpshooter who got Reynolds for he was perfectly positioned to fire that shot. [26]

That's that for the Union, I thought. I'd always had a pretty high opinion of Doubleday and Hancock as generals, but I had no confidence in Meade and certainly not that damned Dan Sickles. Howard showed his worth at Chancellorsville. [27] I could not see now where the Union would conjure a general who might lead them to victory against Old Peter and Bobby Lee.

I also believed that with the commanding general killed, the immediate defense of McPherson's Ridge would soon give way, and that would lead the Confederates in a rush right up to Seminary Ridge where they'd find me wearing a Federal officer's coat and nothing but explanations to protect myself.

We watched for a few more moments as the battle continued on the other side of McPherson's Ridge, but at length I could stand no more of it.

"We'd better find a safer place to be than this place," I told Jenny.

I tied the binoculars to my belt, and together we descended the ladder and made our way out of the building. Outside all was hectic activity. Officers were everywhere issuing orders. Men were still coming up from the road and through the Seminary yard to get to the battle. Rebel prisoners were being led to the rear. Men with stretchers bearing wounded were making their way to the hospital tents that had been erected below the Seminary and in the town.

A man pressing a bloody bandage to his shoulder caught sight of Jenny as he walked past us. "Sir, it's apt to get mighty uncomfortable around here for a lady," he said. "She might want to find refuge in the town."

"Aye, that's just what I was thinking," I told him, and I took Jenny by the hand and we retraced our path through the yard and down the hill back into Gettysburg. Enough cannon shot was going over the Yankees on the front line and falling behind them along the Chambersburg Road that I felt uncomfortable about taking the road back.

My memories of the rest of that morning and the early afternoon are a bit confused, though I recall that we made our way back to the Diamond where half the town had gathered hoping for news.

I remember that at one point a Yankee officer rode through town with word that all citizens should evacuate, but on his heels was another officer who came through town demanding that all citizens seek immediate shelter for there was no time for evacuation.

Some folks ran to their homes either to pack and leave as the first officer recommended or to barricade themselves as the second one suggested. But Jenny and I were among those who stayed put.

I know we were at the Diamond when the German soldiers – Howard's men – came into town sometime late in the morning or very early in the afternoon, for their bands played German songs as they marched to the front. I do not recall if it was before or after the arrival of Howard's Germans that we went up to Pennsylvania College and attempted to see some of the fighting from the cupola there, but Howard had established his headquarters at the college, and the man hisself was in the cupola. We looked for a while from the third floor windows, but the vantage point was not ideal, so we were not long there before returning to the Diamond.

We passed Jenny's house on the way from Pennsylvania College to the Diamond, and we stopped there for food. I didn't know it then, but this would be the last time I would eat a descent meal for a couple of days, and later I would be very glad for the meal.

We were not long back at the Diamond when Jenny met a young man she knew who led us to the roof of one of the local dry goods stores, Foohkenstock Brothers or some such. There was an excellent observation deck on the roof, and for the first time since leaving the Seminary we were provided a clear view of the Federals marching up from the south and the activity taking place out on Seminary Ridge. [28]

It was early afternoon by now, for I can check the history books and know that my old friend from the Chancellorsville Wilderness, General Rodes, arrived at the field of battle at 1:30 p.m., and we were standing on the observation deck of the dry goods store when I saw the Rebel reinforcements arrive. [29]

North of the Chambersburg Road, Seminary Ridge and McPherson's Ridge converge into the large and commanding Oak Hill. I had not understood why neither army had yet secured this position. The Yankees were getting men into the front lines on McPherson's Ridge as quick as they could get them up, and there were none to spare, I suppose. But I felt certain the Rebels had sufficient troops to get to the top of Oak Hill.

But now, at precisely 1:30 in the afternoon, I noticed activity at the woods where the Mummasburg Road disappears from view northwest of the city. Batteries were being hastily installed, and they were pointing into Doubleday's flank.

"More Confederates are on the field now," I said to Jenny, and handed her my binoculars so that she could see the artillery as the first puffs of smoke began to appear.

"Our cause is lost," Jenny said.

Well, her cause was lost. Though I fought on both sides in that war and considered neither to mean much of anything to me, in those moments where I witnessed battle I always found myself silently cheering for the Confederacy – even when their guns were pointed in my direction. I suppose that was in part because these were my fellow Southerners, and I suppose it was in part to my loyalty to my wife, who was fiercely Southern in her sympathies.

"Aye," I said. "Likely as not this will be all it takes."

I didn't know then, of course, that it was Rodes coming to the field. I'd seen Jubal Early march off to York a couple days before, and we'd heard rumors that Ewell was up at Harrisburg, and it could have been either of them. In short order, Early would arrive on the Heidlersburg Road from the northeast, and the Confederates would have a large arc surrounding Gettysburg, tracing from west to north to east of the town.

You'll know all about the cruel work Iverson put his men to. We witnessed that slaughter as Robinson's New Yorkers [30] got behind a stone wall for cover and Iverson threw his North Carolinians at the death. Iverson is a great example of why you don't give command of men in battle to a man just because he's some damned politician's son. Not only was his judgment entirely flawed and his military ability inadequate, but I heard in camp after the battle that Iverson was drunk. [31]

The Yankees were all hidden down behind a stone wall. The Confederates had not bothered to send out skirmishers, but were advancing their entire battle line. I could see that the Confederate line was not long enough and would be overlapped on both flanks by the Yanks. But worse, I could see that the Yankees behind the stone wall laying in wait for those North Carolinians had them well outnumbered.

I couldn't see what Rodes could see and didn't know what was in Iverson's mind, but if I could have yelled loud enough I would have told those boys from North Carolina to turn around, run back up that hill they'd just marched down and not quit running 'til they got home. B'God it was going to be a slaughter, and how their generals didn't see it was beyond me.

I watched as Iverson's men kept coming on, and I even muttered under my breath for them to turn back or take cover – but they were coming across an open field and there was no cover for them to take. Why had they not sent out skirmishers and felt out the enemy? There were thousands of Yankees crouched down behind that wall, and the North Carolinians could see them no better than a blind man!

Presently, as the North Carolinians came within just a few feet of the wall, the Yankees stood and, as one massive body, let loose a volley. Before where there had been a line of hundreds of Confederates, there was now nothing.

"My Lord! It's slaughter!" I exclaimed, and drew Jenny's attention to it. She gasped when she saw what had taken place.

What survivors there were from the center gathered in a low spot in the wheat field, finding some measure of protection in the shallow. Others who survived the initial shock and explosion of violence were running for their lives back up Oak Hill. Some of the Yanks gave chase and captured maybe as many as two hundred prisoners. But there in front of the stone wall, all in a perfect line, were at least five hundred dead and dying. [32]

I sit here in the comfort of my old age, recollecting these terrible events I witnessed, and it still sends a shiver up my spine. Imagine, watching a thousand men walking together through a field, and in the flash of a second one half of them are dead. It was brutal work those New Yorkers did that day, but if the tables were turned the North Carolinians would have done no less to them.

You can call me a coward if you like, and I suppose that I am. But I remain alive to this day in part because I refused ever to allow myself to be led to the slaughter by incompetents like that damned Iverson. And do ye know, old Jeff Davis kept him from the court martial he deserved and before the war was done Davis gave Iverson a body of cavalry to lead.

Presently, I'd had enough and could watch no more. Even from the roof of the Foohkenstock building, we could see little of what was taking place on McPherson's Ridge beyond the Seminary, but as we descended the ladder from the roof, I thought I could hear renewed fighting out in that direction. Pettigrew was pressing harder.

It must have been coming on to three o'clock when I reached the bottom of the ladder. The last activity I'd witnessed was Iverson's disaster, and all through the town there were still Yankee infantry coming up to the front. I did not know that Early's men were even then coming down the Heidlersburg Road at a run, and where earlier I was confident in a Confederate victory I was now beginning to have doubts. Longstreet was nowhere to be seen. Not a single regimental flag I'd seen that morning belonged to the First Corps. I had little confidence in Ewell or Hill. Some of their division commanders, Heth, Pender and Rodes, for instance, were solid military men, but others – that rat Jubal Early chief among them – were misplaced in their commands. But even in the Second and Third Corps, most of the brigadiers were uncommon good fighters and outmatched any man the Yankees could bring to the field. Pettigrew and my old friend from Milledgeville, Thomas Doles, were as good at the brigadier level as you could want.

But without Longstreet on the field, I thought the scene I'd just witnessed with Iverson's brigade would be repeated again and again. Longstreet knew how to fight. Lure 'em in and let 'em crash against your guns. Longstreet would have never allowed those five hundred men to be reduced to nothingness.

"It appears that your Yankees will be pushing the Confederates back to Cashtown," I told Jenny when she reached the bottom of the ladder behind me.

"That was gruesome," she said, still pale and shaken from what we'd witnessed. "The hospital tents will be filling up soon," she said. I remembered what she had told me about working in a hospital before taking up spying, and I could tell she had the same terrible pit in her stomach that I was feeling at the moment. The fighting was a damned sight too close for my comfort, and I had no control over how it would affect me.

I believed flight was no option. There were too many troops around the city now. A man walking away from the battle risked being shot as a deserter. I considered commandeering a horse, posing as a Yankee messenger and riding south toward Meade. But what would I do once I was there? Surely Meade would have guards out rounding up stragglers and deserters – I'd be unlikely to get past them.

Cowering in Jenny's cellar appealed to my natural instincts. At that very moment, all I truly wanted to do was curl myself into a ball in a dark and protected corner and weep like a child for my poor luck in ever coming to this Pennsylvania town. But hiding in a cellar gave a man no mastery over his own fate. Should Lee begin to shell the city, mere chance would decide for me whether I might live or die. Would a cannonball crash into Jenny's house, or would it be the neighbor's home? Would it be Jenny's home that would crumble into the cellar, crushing anyone weeping in a corner, or would it be the house across the street?

Out in the open as we were, we might be exposed to the occasional wild shot, but as strange as it is to say, I felt safer in my current exposed condition. At least now I had some idea of what was taking place. If the thing got too hot, I could move farther from the action. If risking flight from the town was the only option, I could do that from the Diamond a good bit easier than I could from Jenny's cellar where I likely wouldn't even know I need to flee until it was too late.

We began to walk the two blocks north back to the Diamond. Despite orders issued earlier in the day for people to flee to the safety of their cellars, Jenny and I found a large crowd of civilians still gathered in the Diamond, some coming or going and others just waiting. There was all sorts of activity, too, as messengers were riding into the Diamond to take one road or another, either south or east depending on the target of their messages. Regiments were still coming up from the south and turning out the Chambersburg Road for the front while others traveled up Carlisle. We'd not been there long when an officer rode into the middle of the square and began shouting that he needed homes to use as hospitals.

"The churches and public buildings are filling up!" he shouted. "We need private residences for hospitals!"

And now Jenny stepped forward to him, her bottom lip bit to steel up her determination.

"I've worked as a nurse," she said. "You can use my home just up here."

The officer looked at a couple of privates who were on foot nearby. "You go with her," he said to one. "Then go and find Doctor Van Aernam and take him to the house!"

Jenny walked quickly back to me, and she threw her arms around me. "I must do what I can," she whispered in my ear. "God knows I've done worse. I know that soon we must separate, anyway. Please, Jackson, take care of yourself. Do whatever you must – run if you must! – but please stay alive. And when this is over, promise that you will come back to me."

I held her tightly to me for a moment. "I'll do what I must," I said, feeling sheepish in the face of her courage. Then I took her head in my hands and pressed her lips against mine. "I love you, Jenny Rakestraw," I said, "and I'll be back to see you soon."

Well, I didn't exactly love her, but you say things to women when cannonballs are bursting all about and their eyes are full of tears.

Jenny now led the privates up Carlisle Street toward her house, and I could only hope that she would be safe there. If the Confederates did come into the city, they would leave her be and not molest the wounded in her home. Likely as not, there'd be a few Southern boys having their arms or legs sawed off in her house as well.

CHAPTER 8

I stayed at the Diamond after Jenny left, feeling very alone and nervous, but to occupy myself and avoid coming under the gaze of any ranking officers, I stood in the middle of the intersection of roads and directed troops as they came up. If I saw any stragglers or men wandering about aimlessly, I abused them for cowards and sent them up to the front. Engaged in such activity, no one questioned why I wasn't up at the front myself, though I feel certain a fair few of the stragglers I shouted at cursed me as they went up to meet their deaths.

I was thus occupied for an hour or possibly closer to two, but presently all hell broke loose around me.

I walked out toward the edge of town to see if I could get some sense of the battle taking place beyond Seminary Ridge. It seemed to me that the concussion of the Confederate guns was suddenly closer, the sharp crack of the musketry more pronounced.

The first thing I saw was the Yankee cannons, hitched to their horse teams, breaking across the open fields toward Cemetery ridge south of town. I knew what it was even before I could form the words upon my lips: "It's a rout, b'God!" I shouted, and what Yankee soldiers were around me looked first to me, and then to the cannons bouncing across the fields.

And then the men came on like a flood. They seemed to have gathered at the Seminary, for so many of them poured like water through a funnel out of that little gathering of brick buildings and trees.

They were coming by the dozens, then the hundreds, and soon the entirety of Seminary Ridge seemed to be alive and at the run, like an avalanche. Blue coats were scrambling along the railroad, along the Chambersburg Road, through the fields east of the Seminary.

They were coming down the Mummasburg Road to the north.

They were rushing pell-mell to Cemetery Hill or into the town itself.

And now, I saw the Palmetto Flag coming through the trees around the Seminary. They were the front running Confederates in the chase to catch Yankee prisoners, and they were so far out ahead that they were even outdistancing hundreds of Yankees who were late to break and run.

The South Carolinians were coming straight at me, now, rushing toward Chambersburg Street and to the exact spot where I was standing. Others were coming into town farther north. But before the South Carolinians would get to me, I knew I would be crushed beneath the feet of the stampeding Yankees who even now were close enough that I could see the expressions of panic on their faces. Some were casting their muskets aside so as to prevent the weapons from impeding their flight, others clutched their guns to their breasts as if the weapon gave them the courage to run.

I knew that look. I'd seen it many times before. At Monterrey and Shiloh, I'd worn the expression myself. It's a look of horror and desperation and fear. The tide of panic rushing at me consumed me, and though I'd spent a nervous enough day skulking about in Gettysburg, my nervousness was replaced with absolute terror. My belly did summersaults on its way to my throat, I felt the clenching in my gut.

I turned to join the tide and let loose a massive fart that propelled me forward, and I ran as fast as I could go!

My first thought was to flee to Jenny's for safety, and I started out north across an open field where the railroad came out of town. I turned down the tracks, reasoning that they would deposit me in the town just down from Jenny's house, but I heard an almighty clang that brought me to a stop. A bullet had clattered against the rail in front of me. I looked off to my left and saw that a brigade of Southerners was making fast for the north of town, and one of those Southern bastards had fired a shot at me. There was no time to plead my Southern roots or to explain that the Yankee blue coat I wore was given to me by Jeff Davis and that he'd sent me here hisself, or near enough to here, and that I was on their side.

So I dashed south back into town, across Racehorse Alley and back to Chambersburg Street and there I turned back to the Diamond.

Now, though, Chambersburg Street was congested with fleeing Yanks. I dashed into the mass of runners and joined them as they raced to the Diamond.

There at the town square they began to filter through the streets of the town, some dashing south and others continuing eastward. But as Heth and Pender broke through in the west, Early was breaking through in the east, and those men who fled east soon found themselves facing other fleeing Yankees with pursuing Confederates. South was the only way they could run, and every private in the army saw what I'd seen that first day when I rode into Gettysburg: Safety could be found in the hills south of town. You'll know the places, Culp's Hill and Cemetery Hill – that's where most of those boys sought survival.

Some of the Yanks were banging their fists against doors of homes and demanding entrance so that they might hide themselves. Others were pushing open doors of stores and homes without bothering to ask.

At the Diamond I stopped. Chaos was all around me. It was thousands of 'em on the run, filling the streets, and I knew if I was going to survive I'd have to do better than just run with the mob. I needed to explore my natural cowardly instincts and seek the aid of a lifetime of running from trouble to find my way to safety.

I looked first this way and then that, trying to remember any place I'd seen in my strolls through town that might afford shelter.

Jenny's house was out of the question now. Those Southern boys who'd fired a shot at me would reach Carlisle Street somewhere near Jenny's home, and it would be a near run thing if I could get to Jenny's and seclude myself in her cellar before the Southerners got there.

Then I remembered my gray Captain's coat! It would be a simple issue of timing. I could snatch my coat out of the tree where I'd left it, step back against a building, and as the last of the Yankees passed me by I could simply change my coat and cheer on Johnny Reb to victory: "This way, boys! Shoot them Yankee bastards!"

I fought my way through the fleeing Yanks to the tree where I'd stashed the travel case with my coat, and to my astonishment and dismay the thing was gone. Even now I could hear the Rebel Yell and the thundering of their footfalls along the Chambersburg Road. They would be in the town and rushing at me within two minutes.

Panic overwhelmed me. I thought I'd come up with a plan to spare myself, but my plan was foiled by the missing coat. Now I fell in again with the thinning ranks of fleeing Yankees. I was at the back of the pack, and when I looked over my shoulder there were no longer panicked faces behind me running for their lives, but jubilant victors whose faces were contorted with blood lust. The hunt was on, and b'God if I didn't pick up my pace those boys would have me bayoneted to the ground.

There was nothing for it but to flee with the Yanks to the south. But when the cannon and musket are firing in my direction, I'm pretty fleet of foot. I was outpacing most of the bluecoats near me, leaving behind my position in the exposed rear and pushing my way back into the middle of the mob. Fleeing among the crowd, there were bodies behind me to absorb the musket balls and perhaps spare me. I came upon a Yankee cannon being unlimbered and readied to provide covering fire. I ran another ten yards when I heard the thing let off a shot with an almighty concussion that nearly knocked me over. This was not some enterprising artillery captain bringing order to the chaos, it was just more chaos. And I was certain that within a few minutes that cannon would be in the hands of the Confederates.

I turned down an alley and came out on another street, more full of fleeing Yanks than even the street before. The road was so choked that a man might have walked upon the tops of the heads of all those Northern boys from one side of the street to the other without ever having to touch the ground.

This was no place for me. Fast flight was impossible in this crowd. I cast about for some new direction in which to run. I could see citizens in their windows, some were even standing in their open doorways, watching with horror as the soldiers in whom they had placed their hopes were running for their own lives.

The men around me were in a disastrous state. Their faces were blackened with powder and dried blood. I don't think any other man in that street besides myself was without black, dried blood on him – his own or someone else's. I could easily spot those who were from artillery crews, for they had dried streams of blood coming from their ears where the concussion of firing time after time had shook their brains and made their heads leak. Many of the men had discarded their coats in the terrible humidity and were just in their shirts and trousers. Some were bandaged or had their arms in slings. Some leaned on others for support and without much examination it was easy to find the bleeding hole where they'd been shot. Among these were many men whose faces declared that though the body still moved the life was gone, and these men would be dead before the streets unclogged.

It was terrible, awful horror everywhere I looked. Intermingled with this were the scenes of absolute lunacy – the children of a family standing on their porch with buckets of water and tin dippers, offering water to the passing soldiers. So many stopped to accept the water that they jammed up the road even worse.

For a moment I could imagine the bitter contest I'd been hearing all day: The stuffiness of the humidity in among the trees; the heat from the sun and the guns; the advancing a few feet at a time and the falling back again; and now they'd run a mile or more and were packed in like fish in a barrel with their tormentors in pursuit, and yet they would stand still and wait for a drink of water.

Imagining it made it worse. I pushed through the crowd to another alley and broke into a run as soon as I was free from the crowd. This alley deposited me on another street, and as I rounded the corner at the trot, I could see the Rebels were just two blocks from me and still coming on. A handful of Yankees had rallied and were engaging them in a bitter hand-to-hand fight. As I looked over my shoulder I saw a Reb dash in a Yank's brains with the butt of his rifle, and that provided the motivation my legs needed to move even faster.

I turned down another road and thought I was heading east, but I wasn't sure. I stopped to catch my breath at the entrance to an alley. At the intersection ahead, I could see the choked road. I could not go back into that crowd. Even now I could hear artillery in the town, the noise echoing off the buildings in terrible fashion. The Rebels had their artillery up, and I could only too clearly imagine what cannister would do to those unlucky souls trapped in a jammed up road full of Yankees.

I looked back to the road from which I had just come and my heart began to pound in my chest as I realized the men now running down that street were all dressed in butternut. All it would take was for one of those boys to turn down this side street, and I would be caught. I had no breath left for all the running I'd done, and I could see no escape.

To stay out of view of the passing Rebs, I stepped into the alley and then realized there was no way out. The alley ran the distance of the two buildings flanking it – houses, I suppose they were – and there was a large wooden fence at the end. There was nowhere left to run. Now, I sank to the ground and started to weep. Would there even be time to explain before they ran me through or bashed in my skull? Despair had overwhelmed me, and I wasn't even thinking about survival – I was just wondering what method they would employ to put me to an end. Would they shoot me or not waste the powder? Would they bash in my brains with the butt of a rifle or run me through with a bayonet. A memory of Monterrey, Mexico and Fort Teneria passed through my mind – fleeing Mexican soldiers running out the back with Speedy and a whole regiment of Mississippi Rifles charging in over the walls, stabbing those Mexicans in the back with our big Bowie knives as they tried to make their escape.

I sunk deeper in my despair with the realization that my own brutal actions in Mexico were on the verge of being repaid.

And do ye know, it was to Ashley Franks whom my thoughts now turned, that gorgeous married woman who wooed me when I was just a boy and led me astray. I damned her and that peach cobbler she plied against me. Had she not seduced me all those years ago, given me a thirst for beautiful women like her or Jenny Rakestraw, I'd have never found myself in Gettysburg. Likely, I'd have never found myself in this damnedable war at all.

As I sat there sobbing like a scolded child, I damned Ashley Franks for luring me into this hellish life.

But I had to admit, if it hadn't been for Ashley Franks I'd have never fled Scull Shoals. I'd have never met my lovely Eliza and been forced into marrying her. I'd have never gone to war in Mexico, never met Tecumseh Sherman with his stories of gold at Sutter's Mill. I'd have never gone to California with my young bride. I'd have never struck it rich.

Oh, aye, a licentious she-devil Ashley Franks may have been, batting her eyelids and plying me with one of the finest peach cobblers I've ever tasted, but when I considered all that came from it, I had to confess it weren't all so bad.

I wiped my eyes on my blue sleeve and said out loud to meself, "Ol' Speedy, son, you didn't survive so many battles and so much violence by giving up so easily."

Presently I caught hold of myself. I stood back up, wiped my face a second time and began to think. First I stripped that damned Yankee coat off of me. Whatever else was going to happen, I was leaving Lincoln's army once again. I might be able to claim to be a civilian if the coat was nowhere to be seen. I started to run to the back of the alley where I intended to throw the coat, the binoculars and my Colt over the wooden fence, but as I made my way toward the fence I caught sight of something that stopped me in my tracks. It was sitting on the ground there in the alley with me. I'll confess, I stood there staring at it longer than I should have, for I could not believe what I was seeing.

There before mine weeping eyen was a leather traveling case absolutely identical in every way to the one I'd stashed in a tree back at the Diamond. A fresh round of musket fire some blocks away stirred me back into movement. I snatched up that case, unbuttoned its flap and to my astoundment and disbelief I found my old Southern uniform coat!

If fate offers me an opportunity for survival, I'm not one to question it, but of all the chance encounters I've had in my life, this was by far the most curious. How that case and my coat made it from the Diamond to this alley where I happened to stop for a breath and a cry remains to this day an honest-to-God mystery.

But b'God there it was and I wasn't going to question my good fortune any longer!

I pulled the Confederate coat from the bag and stuffed the Yankee coat inside it. I tossed the bag to the back of the alley, and then – after peering around each side to be sure no one was in the street – I stepped out of the alley a captain on Longstreet's staff again.

I walked in the direction where I'd seen the Confederates dash past, and just like that rejoined the Army of Northern Virginia.

I was startled by what I saw in the street. There were no Yankees in sight now, except the wounded and dead, and there were dozens upon dozens of Southern boys, but not one of them seemed to have any hurry in him. They were all lingering about, congratulating themselves on their victory.

"What are ye doing?" I asked the nearest ones. There were seven privates standing in a circle talking to each other.

"Waiting for orders, sir," one of 'em said.

I looked him over. Though his uniform was in tatters and sweat was running from his brow, there was nothing about him to suggest he'd been in battle all day – not like those Yankees I'd been running with.

"You boys don't think you should follow up on our success?" I asked them.

"Nobody's told us to advance farther than here," the private said.

"Where's your lieutenant?" I demanded.

"Up yonder," he said, nodding his head down the street. "He told us to wait here."

I shrugged and took off my slouch hat to wipe my brow. "Any of you boys got water?" I asked.

One of the privates handed me a canteen that was nearly full. I took a long drink from it. The water tasted of the dirty stream from which it had come, but it provided what I needed.

"You haven't had much of your water, son," I said to him. "You boys been fightin' all day?"

"We're with Pender," another one answered. "Mostly it was Heth's that was doin' the fighting out where we was. We just came on the field in time to chase them Yankees off that ridge up yonder."

"Well, thank'ee for the water," I said, taking another drink and then handing back the canteen. "Guess I'll be off. You boys don't know where the First Corps is, do ye?"

"They's back at Cashtown," one of them answered. "They ain't even come up yet."

"Perfect," I said.

And now I walked back down the streets I'd recently run in the opposite direction. There was still shooting here and there, and twice I came upon a small band of Yankees engaged in a stand against an entire company of Rebels, but both times I gave the fighting a wide berth, and I strolled through the town almost as leisurely as I had done with Jenny in the days previous.

Massive groups of Yankee prisoners were being led to the back – since the war I've seen the number put at 7,000, and I don't doubt it – and in many cases prisoners had little or no guard. They just wandered on their own toward the Confederacy's rear until someone took them under command.

I considered taking some of them as prisoners to that I might pass through the town without some busybody Confederate officer telling me to hurry to the front and whoop the Yankees on my own, but the last time I'd tried to shirk duty by taking command of prisoners that damned fool Stonewall Jackson deputized me to chase after Howard's Germans and it nearly got me killed in the process. Is it any wonder his own men shot him? [33]

But what struck me as odd was the Southern attitude. Stuart should have been riding the streets of Gettysburg whooping and hollering and shooting off pistols and taking hundreds or thousands more prisoners. The infantry should have been up and pressing the attack as the Yanks halted their retreat and congregated at the town cemetery. But none of that was happening. It was as if the battle had been fought ferociously, but now everyone was spent and ready to call it a day. But they weren't spent. Hadn't I just been handed a nearly full canteen? Those boys standing around chatting and laughing were fresh troops who had seen little or nothing of the battle so far this day.

I determined that if I could not make good my escape from the war, then the best I could do was get back to Longstreet – especially if he was all the way back at Cashtown – and rejoin his staff. As I wandered back down the street, passing small bands of Southern men lounging at their leisure, I noticed a riderless, black horse grazing in a yard. The beast was saddled up and looked very much like a cavalry horse. The animal didn't start as I approached it, so I took it by the reins. I noticed one side of the saddle was slick with blood, so I took the blanket off the back of the saddle and wiped the blood away. I looked the horse over and could find no injury to the beast. I discarded the blanket there in the yard and mounted the horse, and now I was making my way back to Longstreet on a good cavalry horse. In the leather of the saddle was pressed a "U.S." Some Yankee cavalryman had been shot off his horse so that my legs might be spared as I went off in search of my friend Old Peter.

I rode into the Diamond, which an hour before had been crammed full of fleeing Yankees, and found it was now Confederates in gray and butternut, or in many cases just their shirts and britches, who occupied the town square.

Right away I noticed two knots of men on horseback, and I recognized in one of them was Ewell astride a horse and seeking shade under a tree. With him were other generals and staff officers. I was told that Ewell's wooden leg was hit by a bullet while he was at the square, but if that happened I did not witness it.

The other knot of men on horseback were staff officers, captains and majors. I recognized Jimmy Smith, one of Ewell's aides, among these men.

"What time is it, Jim?" I asked, riding up to the group of mounted officers.

Captain Smith looked at me for a long moment, and then recognition hit his face. "My Lord, if it isn't Jack Speed!" he exclaimed, a broad grin coming to his lips. "Why, Speedy, I thought the First Corps was back at Cashtown."

"General Longstreet sent me for'ard to see what was what up here," I said. "How come y'all ain't pressing them Yanks south of town?"

Now Smith's grin disappeared. Though he was Ewell's aide, he was also a veteran who remembered Stonewall. He shook his head and said only, "It's a shame Jackson ain't here."

I looked over at Ewell's knot of men again and realized the old general was sitting under that shade tree waiting for the recently deceased Stonewall Jackson to send him orders. He'd just secured a pretty fair victory, as best as I could tell, and he didn't know what to do with it.

"Where's Stuart?" I asked. "Why ain't he rounding up prisoners? Seems to me that's the sort of thing he'd enjoy being able to do now that all the hard work is done."

The infantry officers sitting around me got a chuckle out of my jab at the cavalry, but Jim wasn't laughing when he answered me. "Nobody knows where Stuart is. I'm surprised you didn't know that. He's been missing almost since we left Virginia." Then Jim looked down at my horse and saddle, and he wrinkled up his brow. "Say, Speed, are you riding a Yankee cavalry horse?"

"Mine was shot from under me," I said. It was just a little bit of a lie I told as explanation for why I was on a Yankee horse, but do you know it became something of a legend? Among Ewell's brigades were the Georgia boys under General George Doles. Doles was my age and from Milledgeville, and I knew him pretty well as we were in the local chapter of the Knights of the Golden Circle together. We'd often smoked cigars and played cards together in the room above my dry goods store where the KGC met. Had I been at home in Milledgeville when war broke out rather than saving Lincoln's life in Baltimore, I would have been in command of Doles' brigade instead of him, and what a disaster that might have been for the Twelfth Georgia!

Well, Jimmy Smith knew that Doles and I knew each other, and at some point, probably later that night, he happened to mention to Doles that he'd seen me. Doles wrote a pretty flowery letter home to his soon-to-be widow who showed it to my Eliza, and I received a letter from Eliza months after the battle gushing about her pride in how I'd been at the front at Gettysburg even while my own First Corps was in the back, and how all the hens of Milledgeville were talking about Ol' Speedy having his horse shot from under him.

Doles' widow showed me the letter after the war, and do ye know, he made me sound quite impressive: "I have heard that Captain Jack Speed was involved in the fighting of July 1 though he is on Longstreet's staff and Longstreet was not involved on that day. Brave Speedy had ridden forward on Longstreet's orders to observe the action at Gettysburg, and he was evidently involved in the fiercest of the fighting for he had a horse shot from under him. I am not privy to the particulars, but after losing he horse he managed to take a Federal cavalryman's horse away from him! What a tremendous warrior for our state Old Jack Speed is! I thank our Lord in Heaven that Captain Speed was not wounded in the action. I am proud to call him and friend and a fellow Georgian! I only wish he was an officer in my brigade!"

Well, that was Doles believing everything he heard. He met his end at Cold Harbor, which is one more reason I'm glad he had command of his brigade and not me.

"What time is it, Jim?" I asked, wondering if I had time enough to ride back toward Cashtown and the rear of the army before dark.

"Just a little after five o'clock," he said.

"Well then, I'm off to see if I can find Old Peter," I said. "Say, you boys may want to hurry your men along. Them Yankees are broken and battered on that hill south of town. If you get on now, you can end this thing today and the First Corps won't have to fight tomorrow! Fact is, you boys press a little harder, and the First Corps and I will ride into Washington D.C. in a couple of days and we can all be home before the first freeze."

Smith nodded agreement, cast his eyes over at Ewell and shrugged helplessness. [34]

I started toward the Chambersburg Pike, but here at the Diamond I could look up Carlisle Street to where Jenny's house was. I turned the horse back north, and rode the couple of blocks up toward Jenny's home.

The door was wide open, and in the front parlor I could see the activity of a makeshift hospital. Women whom I did not recognize were dressing wounded men, and from an upstairs bedroom I could hear a man crying out. I could not see Jenny from the open door.

Up and down the streets, Rebels were kicking in doors and harassing citizens in their search for hiding Yanks.

Now I issued my first orders given on the field at Gettysburg. I found two privates who were sitting on their rears eating food they'd pilfered.

"You two boys," I said, riding up to them. "You see that house there?"

They looked over at Jenny's house where I was pointing. "You step up to that front door, and you stand guard on that house. These are orders straight from General Ewell hisself. You prevent any man from going into that house who doesn't have business there. No matter what else happens tonight or tomorrow, as long as the Army of Northern Virginia is here at Gettysburg, you two are standing guard at that door." Now I looked menacing at them and raised my voice to put fear in 'em. "And b'God if I ride past here and catch either of you sleeping or off pissing somewhere or in any way failing to protect that hospital there, I promise you I will have you shot by a firing squad while you're hanging by your necks!"

I guess they took me seriously, for they grabbed up the food they had and both of 'em rushed over to the steps leading up to Jenny's front porch.

Satisfied that I had done what I could to provide for her safety, I now started down the Chambersburg Pike in search of Longstreet.

CHAPTER 9

Riding out the Chambersburg Road I was shaken to my core by what I saw. On both sides of the road the dead were everywhere. Yankees and Southerners alike. The fields were also still littered with wounded, though stretcher bearers and ambulances were already at work. Field hospitals were being set up, and the Seminary where I'd been earlier in the day, had already been turned into a hospital. It was all ghastly business. The dead were like leaves scattered by the wind. In places there were one or two to be seen out in an open field, but in other places, at the foot of Oak Hill, where Iverson's North Carolinians met disaster, the dead were in piles as if they had been raked to the spot.

The wounded were more gruesome than the dead, for they were forever moaning for water or relief. Some of the men were dragging the wounded to shade. Others were giving them canteens. Though two hours or more had passed since the Yankees' rout, most of the Southern army present on the field was down in the town, arresting prisoners and contemplating Ewell's reluctance to seize the heights south of Gettysburg.

Without knowing it, I had ridden right past Lee's headquarters and was beyond McPherson's Ridge, over near Willoughby Run. I was riding right through the area where the worst of the fighting had taken place. Passing me, going into town, were Ewell's wagons, some of the artillery, stragglers who were slow in coming up for one reason or another, and the wagons of the press and sutlers and other assorted camp followers. The road was so very crowded that I found it easier, riding against the flow as I was, to ride off to the side of the road.

My intention was to ride back toward Cashtown, avoid General James Longstreet, find the rear of the army and allow it to pass me by. It would be the easiest thing, now that I was dressed as one of 'em, to just let the Army of Northern Virginia pass and once they were gone I'd be able to turn north and make good my plan to get north of the war. At Chambersburg I could shed my Confederate coat for once and for all, ride north to Harrisburg and if Stuart hadn't torn up the tracks I could catch a train for Philadelphia and surely keep myself well ahead of Bobby Lee and his army. In Philadelphia a train could take me to New York.

What I did not know was that Lee had already established his headquarters in a rock house just off the Chambersburg Road near the Seminary. And as was his practice, Old Peter had ridden in advance of his army to be with the Southern commander, and various members of Longstreet's staff were still riding up, with the First Corps behind Ewell's wagon trains.

I was trotting along, there near Willoughby Run, trying hard not to see the devastation around me, when I heard a voice call out, "Ho! Captain Speed! My God, man, where have you been?"

My heart dropped into my stomach as I saw Mox Sorrel. He'd been riding along on the road, but at the sight of me he left the road and was now riding toward me.

"Mox," I said, trying to hide my disappointment. "Just headed to the rear to give Old Pete what information I have," I said. "Been down at the front, don't ye know. Better be on my way, don't want to miss the general!"

But Major Sorrel was already up beside me and he took my reins in his hand. "No, no, Speedy, Peter is up ahead of me here, already speaking with Gen'l Lee. Ride with me, it's just a ways up yonder, and while we wait you can tell me of your adventures these past few weeks!"

It's no secret I was fond of Longstreet and I liked the men of his staff pretty fair, too. Mox Sorrel was a good man, a good soldier, and a superb aide to Longstreet. When, after the war, Longstreet finally decided to defend himself against that lying Jubal Early's accusations, he wrote to both me and Moxley asking for any papers we might have that would assist him in recording an accurate history of the First Corps. Well, I was no use to him other than jotting down a few memories, because what records I had I'd burned in my effort to forget the entire blasted experience. But Moxley had all kinds of papers and visited with Old Peter often as the War Horse wrote "From Manassass to Appomattox: Memoirs of the Civil War in America."

Well, even though I was almost no help to him, Old Peter was still kind enough to send me a signed copy of the book: "To Ol' Speedy, my dear friend and comrade in the recent great conflict, for your service on my staff in the great struggle recounted in these pages and for your continued friendship since the close of those hostilities, I am forever indebted." Nice enough words, no doubt, but I can't help but think he'd have at least mentioned me in the pages if I'd been more help to him in the writing of it. I was at his side as much as Mox Sorrel was during a good bit of the war, and you'll notice if you read it that Moxley's name is on almost every damned page, and Longstreet fails to mention me even once. I'm a bit bitter about it, if you want to know the truth, but I also know that I never did anything Old Peter would have thought worth mentioning. He was probably worried that if he mentioned the few times he caught me skedaddling to the rear I might have found it embarrassing, so I suppose to him the favor was in not bringing my name into it.

"Well, Mox, there ain't much to tell," I said. "I've been trying to rejoin the army here, but had to come up through the entire Army of the Potomac to get to ye. I got caught in the town here when the fighting started this morning and have been trying to get clear of the shooting all day. It weren't until them Yankees ran that I was able to rejoin you boys."

"Speed," Sorrel said, looking down at my saddle. "You're riding a Yankee cavalryman's horse."

"Oh, aye," I said, and I gave 'im a version of the lie I'd told Jimmy Smith. "As soon as the Confederates started running into the town, I drew out my pistol and helped with the charge. When I saw this 'ere riderless horse, I thought I might do a better job of leading the boys if I was mounted."

"And how is it in the town?" Sorrel asked me as we rode back toward Lee's headquarters.

"Well, we chased them Yanks clear out of the town, but now they're all crowded on a hill over yonder," I said, pointing in the general direction of Cemetery Hill, although we could not see it from where we were. "If Ewell will press them before dark, I think it's reasonable to expect that our way to Washington will be pretty clear in the morning."

Now an idea struck me. Maybe I could make some excuse to Sorrel to continue my ride to the back. "What's the Corps' order of march, Mox?" I asked him.

"Hood, McLaws and Pickett in the rear," Moxley said.

"B'God, George Pickett," I said. "I've been meaning to talk to him about something. Maybe I should ride to the rear and see him now," I suggested.

"No, no, Speed," Moxley said. "Just come along with me. Old Peter won't be long. He'll want to see you himself. I hear nothing that sounds like battle coming from the town," Sorrel said. I listened, and he was right. There was the occasional musket shot or cannon booming, but there was obviously no fighting in earnest below us. "Did you say Ewell is attacking that hill?"

"Naw," I said. "I talked to Jimmy Smith, and he says Ewell don't want to attack without orders."

Mox spat at the ground. "Damnation," he said. "Ewell was never going to be the man to replace Jackson." [35]

We rode up to the house where Lee had made his headquarters, a pretty little place built of stone and situated just off the road. We dismounted and stood around for a while waiting and talking when eventually the door to the house opened and Lee and Longstreet walked out onto the front porch. Lee, always with a soldierly bearing, looked a bit unsteady to me. Longstreet, a great mountain of a man, looked typically disheveled.

"Gen'l Lee a'right?" I asked Sorrel.

"I don't think he's feeling his best," Sorrel said under his breath. "He camped in a cherry orchard over in Chambersburg. I think today he is marching at the quick step, if you know what I mean." [36]

I nodded knowingly, but I thought nothing of it. From the lowliest private even up to the highest general, the Virginia Quick Step got all of us at one time or another. If that's what caused Bobby Lee to lose his mind and order that charge, I'll confess he had the worst case of it I've ever seen. My opinion has always been That Bobby Lee was just too bull headed and he had his dander up.

Presently, Longstreet concluded his interview with Lee and mounted his horse. He rode out to the road where he found me and Moxley, and at the sight of me his big bearded face broke into a wide grin. [37]

After a brief examination, Longstreet declared, "My Lord, you are a sight! I am glad to see you healthy and whole."

"Speed was leading the charge down in the town when the Yanks broke and ran," Moxley informed him.

"Ah, well, it weren't exactly like that," I said, attempting to sound humble and leave Longstreet with the impression that I had, in fact, led the charge.

"Killed a Yankee cavalryman and took his horse," Moxley teased.

"Well, I found his horse," I grinned, and gave Longstreet a wink to let him think what he wanted.

And that's how reputations are made. Good old Moxley Sorrel exaggerated what I'd told him, I laughed it off with humble modesty and it got fixed in Old Peter's mind that I was at the front of the rout. Before the battle was out, Lo Armistead and Pickett both congratulated me on my part in the first day's fighting, and Bobby Lee hisself once introduced me as the man who chased the Iron Brigade out of McPherson's Woods. Of course, I couldn't help but note when I read it that Longstreet didn't bother to put that story in his book, either.

Longstreet was riding out along the ridge south of the Seminary to survey the ground, and Moxley and I rode alongside him. As we did, I gave him an accounting of what I'd seen in Gettysburg, the situation on Cemetery Hill and Ewell's reluctance to move against the hill. When he discovered that I had been in Gettysburg for "a number of days," as I termed it, he quickly asked me about the lay of the land.

From a spot on the ridge south of the Seminary, I pointed out to him everything that I knew of the town and the Emmitsburg Road to the south, allowing the example of Doctor Jacobs to assist me. Even as dusk fell all around us, we could still see the long ridge between Cemetery Hill and the two Round Tops.

"There's a road over on the back of that ridge, and behind those hills," I explained, "and I understand that's where Meade's army is coming up from."

Longstreet, who was able to look at a ground and immediately see whether it contained virtues for battle, looked up and down from Cemetery Hill to Round Top several times.

"That's good ground across the way there," he said. "If Ewell hasn't chased him off of there, Meade holds an excellent position. We could defend here along this ridge, but I wonder what would happen if we were to move to the enemy's left and position ourselves between the Army of the Potomac and Washington D.C."

"We know what would happen," Mox said. "Meade's masters in the capital would compel him to attack us."

"Yes," Longstreet mused. "Yes, I suppose they would. And if we could find good ground and be prepared for that attack, we would surely be able to take him apart in pieces. There would be nothing left, then, to prevent us from marching on Washington. B'God, Speedy, we could have this thing done in a matter of weeks!"

"Might be home before the first freeze," I commented.

Old Peter continued to look at the ground held by the Yankees, and the more he did the more he became convinced that working our way around Meade's left was the proper plan. On the evening of the first day at Gettysburg, from the very moment he rode up to where he could see the battlefield, Longstreet was in no mood to charge against Meade's position.

And then he suddenly exploded in anger, "B'God if we had the cavalry we would know what's what! Where is that damned Stuart? How is an army supposed to fight when it is blind?"

I looked questioningly at Mox. Captain Smith had made me

aware that Stuart's cavalry was no where to be found, but I did not realize until then the extent to which Stuart had left the army blind, and the bitterness that was being felt toward Stuart. You'll know all the stories, but some of the generals, Old Peter among 'em, were tossing around the idea of court-martialing Stuart for his dereliction. Here we were in Pennsylvania, with the Army of the Potomac in front of us, and the cavalry might as well have been in Europe or California for all the good it was doing. The cavalry, you understand, is the eyes of the army. An army on the march knows only what is over the next hill because it has skirmishers thrown out in front of it, but two hills over is the complete unknown. And so a cavalry must ride the perimeter of the army, feel out the enemy from time to time in minor engagements, and constantly report back. If Stuart had been doing his duty rather than off being Stuart, Lee would have known that Meade had left camp, crossed the Potomac and was within reach of Gettysburg before Pettigrew ever came to town looking for shoes. Stuart would have been there even now and able to tell Lee that the entire Yankee army would be on the field the next day. [38]

As it was, Lee only knew what was over on that next hill.

What none of us knew, as Old Pete, Mox and I stood looking out there at Cemetery Ridge in the growing dusk, was that looking back at us was Win Hancock, one of the best damned generals in either army, and Meade had put Hancock in command of the field, even though there were already men on that other ridge who had seniority over him. Oh, if it was Howard and Sickles and that lot in charge of things, we'd have been just fine. We'd have chased the Yankees off the heights south of Gettysburg, captured a quarter of them, killed a quarter of them and the other half would have been too scared and too poorly led to do anything but run. But Hancock the Superb, don't ye know, was over on the other ridge.

Of course, I'm here today to tell the story because he was.

"My Corps is back at Cashtown still making its way here," Longstreet said. "We'll ride back to that place and camp and see what we might do about hurrying along our men."

Whether I wanted to be or not, I was now back in the Army of Northern Virginia's First Corps, but at least I found myself on the general's staff and not in among the ranks of the men who would soon find themselves assaulting the hills across the way. Or so I thought.

It was late in the evening by the time we met with the front elements of the First Corps somewhere between Gettysburg and Cashtown, and we set up Longstreet's headquarters at that place while his corps continued to march past us. There were a fair number of newspapermen and foreign observers and others camping near Longstreet, and I recall a bottle of whiskey being passed around and some poker playing. After the deaths of his children, Old Peter wasn't much for the whiskey drinking or the poker anymore, though there was a time when he'd have been among the best at games around the campfire. This night, though, he retired to his tent early while the rest of us enjoyed ourselves. [39]

By now, word of the Confederate victory had drifted back among the ranks of the First Corps, and though the men were marching at night and moving at a dismally slow pace, there was a strong feeling among everyone, from the officers in the camp to the men marching past, that our invasion of the North would soon produce a conquering victory and an end to the war. I recall the regimental bands making a great racket as they came through, playing various songs, some of which I recognized and others I did not. Dixie was common enough, as was Bonny Blue Flag, but there were others, too, that were favorites of the army. Spirits were high among the men. If there was a disappointment felt by any of them, it was that the First Corps had missed out on the great battle at Gettysburg. Little did they know.

Though it wasn't where I wanted to be, I recall not minding too much that I was in camp. Mox and the Texan Goree and the rest of them were all good fellows, and I enjoyed their company. The staff of the First Corps formed a coterie of good fellowship that I've not enjoyed on many other occasions, and the night of the first of July, 1863, we were at the height of our camaraderie. I suppose the relaxed air, the lack of formality and the generally good feelings – prompted by one victory after another – compares favorably to my time with the Texas Rangers in Mexico. It's an odd thing for me to say, but were it not for the men on the opposite hill forever shooting at me, I'd have enjoyed serving in the army pretty well.

Old Peter himself was in a dark mood that would only grow darker over the next two days. He'd told me and Mox on our ride back to Cashtown that Lee had not yet formed a battle plan, but Peter was worried the old man would attack.

"Meade has a strong position, and I do not foresee victory for us if we try to knock him off of that ridge," he'd said. "We should have pressed this evening when the opportunity was there."

But none of this meant anything to me. I'd served in both the Federal and the Southern armies, had friends in both – if you can ever truly be friends with these maniacs who relish war the way they all did – and other than a couple of dower slaves who had outlived their usefulness, I didn't own any slaves myself or care a whit whether or not others did. When one side or the other lost, I couldn't see how it would have much impact on me personally. My only concern, now that I was back with the army, was in seeing myself well away from the shooting, and I figured being back with Longstreet was as safe as things would be for me.

Presently, however, events were transpiring to put me right in the thickest of the fighting, and had I been killed I'd have never forgiven Old Peter for his part in it.

After spending the last few weeks sleeping in Jenny's bed, I found the borrowed bedroll in the stuffiness of the canvas tent I shared that night with Moxley to be a poor substitute. A rock in my back kept me forever awake, so that after a couple of hours I'd had no sleep at all when Old Peter was up and calling for a horse. Longstreet rose early in the morning with the stars still out and no blueness of dawn yet in the sky.

I suppose he'd had as sleepless a night as I'd suffered, but Moxley was as well rested as a man can be before battle, for if it was not the rock keeping me awake it was Mox's incessant snoring.

There was time enough for a poor breakfast and poorer coffee (I'd been spoiled living with Jenny!), and then Old Peter, with we members of his staff in tow, set out for Lee's headquarters again.

I recall that it was still dark when Longstreet went into the little stone house where Lee had set up the headquarters for the Army of

Northern Virginia. Moxley went with him, but the quarters were too cramped, and the rest of the staff remained outside.

When Old Pete met with the commanding general, Bobby Lee had still not made up his mind what to do about the Yankees. Peter again pressed him to swing to Meade's left, but you'll know that Lee famously responded, "The enemy is there and that's where I'll fight 'im."

Well, volumes have been written and said since the war, mostly by Early and Pendleton who are both despicable liars. If you're wondering, there was no order for a morning attack. Most of the First Corps wasn't even up to the battle yet. If Lee had issued an order for a morning attack, it would have been me, Old Peter, Mox and Goree charging through the Peach Orchard at the entrenched Yankee army, and just the four of us probably wouldn't have been enough.

Even then, Longstreet couldn't stand the sight of Early, so he didn't accompany Bobby Lee to the barn north of town where Ewell had set up his headquarters. Instead, Old Pete rode down Seminary Ridge a ways, and then he sent me farther on. Though no order was issued, Peter knew that Lee was thinking to attack with the First Corps against Meade's left, and he was anticipating the order when he told me to ride south over near the rocky hilltop to reconnoiter the enemy's left flank.

"Be careful," Longstreet told me, for it was still dark. "We have skirmishers posted in that direction, and you should take care not to sneak up on them and get yourself shot."

Riding around in the dark with the enemy so near and our own pickets feeling skittish is no duty I care to have, so I didn't make much of my reconnoitering, at least not while it was still dark. What I did, instead, was ride a ways along the road in front of the Seminary feeling for some way to get south of the two armies. At no point during the entire battle did the thought of flight ever leave my mind, and being ordered off by myself seemed like the best time to slip away.

It was Pitzer's Woods where I was riding, to the southwest of town. To my west, somewhere in the woods, were the Confederate pickets, and off to my left, up on the hill, was the Third Corps of the Army of the Potomac, led by that maniac Devil Dan Sickles. I didn't know then, as I moseyed around in the woods, that I would soon come under that man's glare again.

My association with Dan Sickles began a couple of years before the war. He'd tried to murder me aboard a train because he suspected, rightly enough, that I'd come to grips with his lovely young wife. Not long after that, in '59, he'd done in Phil Key for the same reason, and when I read in *Harper's* about Sickles' trial it sent cold chills up my spine to know how close I'd come to sharing Phil Key's fate. [40]

I cannot say how long I was in the woods, perhaps two hours, but dawn had come on while I was still riding about on deer paths. At first light, I found our pickets set up in the woods, and I hailed them so they wouldn't shoot me and then rode over and spent some time with the men. They were all Alabamians serving in Anderson's Division, and they were all alone and wondering what was what when I found them. [41]

Hill's Corps, having come in late in the day of July 1, was fronting Cemetery Hill, and they must have been three miles away, so these skirmishers had been positioned in the woods completely alone and with no contact to the main body of the army since some time in the late afternoon or evening of the prior day.

Just now they were lighting their fires for breakfast, and I didn't mind at all having some of their biscuits, bacon and coffee with them, and they didn't mind sharing for I was able to provide 'em with gossip from headquarters.

I sat with a sergeant named Jube Elmore. He was from the hill town of Mentone, Alabama, he told me, just across the border from Summerville, Georgia. He'd taken the time over breakfast to show me a tiny daguerreotype of his wife and two daughters that he carried with me.

"It's been hard on them without me there," he told me. "Prices on everything are high, and there ain't enough men at home to care for the livestock or harvest the fields. We got to win this thing here in

Pennsylvania so me an' all these boys can get home and take care o' our families."

Jube was near to my age. He was a hulking man. I was taller than most and stronger built, but Jube Elmore made me look small. He must have been six foot three and weighed more than two hundred pounds. I wondered at how the company cook could keep him fed and still feed the rest of the company when rations ran short. Elmore's daughters in the daguerreotype were little girls, but judging from him and the image of his wife, I suspected they would not have remained small for long. "I ain't seen 'em since '61," he mused as I handed him back the picture. "Can't imagine how big they've got."

As you'll see presently, for good reason Jube Elmore sticks out in my mind all these years later.

But most of the boys around the campfire, Jube too, were less interested in the goings-on back home and more interested in what news I could provide about our army's present situation.

"It looks like we'll be attacking soon enough," I told them. "The First Corps is coming up and will occupy these woods here, and my guess is that Gen'l Lee will send Ewell against the two hills in front of him and send the First Corps against the ridge across the way there." I announced all of this as if I was an expert on Bobby Lee's thinking, but from what I'd gathered from Longstreet I felt that I understood well enough the tactical situation.

Though there was light enough to see by, and even from the woods we could see the tops of Little Round Top and Round Top, there was a mist in the hollow that prevented us from seeing anything of Cemetery Ridge where the Army of the Potomac was holding ground. Nevertheless, we all seemed to have an intuition that the ground across the way was a stronghold for the enemy. It would be too much to say that the boys in Lee's army were looking through the mist at Cemetery Ridge with trepidation, but they seemed to understand that whatever orders were issued they were going to have rough work in front of them.

But on the morning of the second day at Gettysburg, there was still an atmosphere of superiority among the Army of Northern

Virginia.

"We whipped 'em yesterday and them Yankees tucked tail and ran," Jube said to me as I sipped the nearly boiling coffee he'd offered me. "We'll knock 'em off that ridge, yonder. Them boys'll be runnin' all the way to Washington D.C. before this day is done."

If there were any misgivings about the coming battle here in Pitzer's Woods, it was that they might not see the action. These were Hill's men, set up in the woods as skirmishers to be certain no Yankees came up into our flank. But the main body of Hill's Corps was facing the center of Meade's army on Cemetery Hill, well away from these boys. If an order for Ewell to charge was given any time during the morning, they would have no opportunity to rejoin their corps and get involved in it.

"Are they gonna bring the First Corps over here to these woods so that we can get back up with General Ewell?" one private asked me. "We been sittin' over here all night and if they's gonna go after them Yanks up there on them hills, we don't wanna be still in these woods."

For my part, I never have been able to understand how a man can remain calm knowing that at some point during the day he would be asked to dash into the fire of the enemy's muskets and cannons, running the whole way, and if he's lucky enough to get within striking distance engage in hand-to-hand combat with desperate and dangerous men. I felt a greater kinship with Howard's Germans who turned and ran at Chancellorsville than I did with these Southern boys who were worried they might not get into the charge up Cemetery Hill. I've spent a fair portion of my life marching with armies and trying desperately – and too often unsuccessfully – to avoid those sorts of charges. But these Alabamians were genuinely nervous that they might be left out of the thing.

Well, I was there as a captain on a general's staff, so I did my part for the Cause and attempted to cheer them.

"Don't ye worry one bit about that, boys," I told 'em. "There's blue-bellies enough for all of us up there on that ridge!"

The boys gathered around me, a couple dozen of them I suppose, cheered at that, so I gave 'em a little more. "We'll all get our chance at 'em, I can promise ye. 'Less o'course them Yanks get to runnin' too fast and we can't catch 'em!"

Oh, they loved that. I suppose most all of them would be dead before the day was out, or so grievously injured that they would wish they were dead. But they all cheered now at the thought of running Yankees and getting in at the death, and I left them all in good spirits with the promise that Longstreet would soon be up and they would be allowed to go and reunite with their own corps.

Now I mounted again and rode slowly through the woods along trails trampled down by animals and local youth. At points the woods were so thick that I had to dismount and lead the horse. I went south, generally following parallel to the Emmitsburg Road, and I traveled with great caution for I was now south of our skirmishers and there could be Yankees anywhere.

The Emmitsburg Road cuts right through Pitzer's Woods, and by the time I finally came within sight of some Yankee skirmishers sitting around in a wide clearing, I had crossed over the road. When I saw them, my stomach dropped and I thought certain I would be captured, but I realized they weren't keeping much of a watch. I was already dismounted, and they'd not seen me, so I took a good look at them: I know now it must have been the remnants of Buford's Cavalry, and there wasn't much left there. They'd not seen me because these men were beaten by exhaustion. They'd been used up entirely on the first day. Even when Reynolds and then Howard came up, Buford's cavalry remained engaged in the battle for all of the rest of the day. I supposed they'd been ordered here to protect Meade's farthest left flank in an effort to give them some rest. They weren't truly guarding anything that I could see, but simply existing in this place.

Most of 'em were still asleep, though by now the sun had been up for a couple of hours. Those who were awake were not keeping guard. They were talking among themselves, playing cards, eating here or there. But they were unfit for any more duty.

Nevertheless, I knew they had me blocked from a southward escape. They might be all used up, but they were still good enough to catch one rider all by hisself trying to flee the battle.

Still dismounted, I decided instead to lead my horse back to the north, back toward our skirmishers and away from the Yankee cavalry. If I was going to slip away from the Battle of Gettysburg, it was not going to be to the south.

CHAPTER 10

I remember thinking that it seemed strange to me I'd not yet crossed back over the Emmitsburg Road. Using the road as the dividing line, the no-man's land, between the two armies, I was currently still on the Union side of the battle lines. But, as cautious as I thought I was being, it never bothered me that much that I'd not crossed back over to the Confederacy's side. I was taking it easy, moving slowly through the woods. For one thing, I did not want to sneak up on some pickets – Confederate or Union – and have them start shooting at me. For another, the more I loitered about in these woods the better the chance that the First Corps would get up to the front and make its charge without Ol' Speedy anywhere nearby. If I played the thing right, I figured I could spend the entirety of the day here in Pitzer's Woods listening to the shots being traded back and forth, and come dusk I'd ride into camp and ask Old Pete which side won.

So in that frame of mind, time and distance were of little concern to me. I did think about it, wondering where the road was and why I'd not yet come to it, but I did not give it the consideration I should have. I was aimlessly loitering and not being nearly as careful as I thought I was being.

Walking my horse through the woods, I found a wide path and decided to follow that. The morning was wearing on. The fog was thoroughly burned off, and an oppressive humidity had settled in the woods. Everything was damp from the recent rains, and if you've ever spent time in a Georgia forest on a wet summer day, you'll know the humidity I'm talking about – it's a wet heat that clings to everything and makes you sweat. I remember clearly thinking that those woods felt more like home than home did.

I couldn't tell you what time it was when I came out of the woods. I thought it was damned odd that I'd not found my way to the

Emmitsburg Road, and I was now passingly concerned that I'd somehow gotten myself lost. But the important thing to me was that I could see neither Confederate skirmishers nor Yankee infantry, and so I was at my leisure.

Now clear of the woods I could see how I had become turned around. Rather than wandering to the northwest and back toward Longstreet, I'd drifted in the woods and followed this path to the east. Above me now were the Round Tops – the big one that the locals called Sugarloaf was rising up over me with its steep angles, and the smaller one, Little Round Top, was to my northeast. To my right, between me and the two prominent hills, was the wooded valley of Plum Run, or as we who fought there would call it, Bloody Run. And not far from my location – though it was obscured from my view by a wood – was the Devil's Den, those enormous boulders where such terrible fighting would soon take place.

Ahead of me at some distance still was a small rise covered in peach trees. Again, I could not see it, but I know now there was a field of golden wheat to the east of that. You'll know the famous names: The Peach Orchard and the Wheat Field and the bloody carnage that would soon take place there. But from my vantage point, I could see no army. The Army of the Potomac was still up along Cemetery Ridge, hidden from my view beyond Little Round Top. No Yanks were up on top of Little Round Top that I could see, though I suppose they must have already had a group of signalers up there. Likewise, Pitzer's Woods hid from my view the Confederates to the west, and though I did not know it then, Old Peter was off on his circuitous march and countermarch to get in position, still well away from Pitzer's Woods.

Of course I knew both armies were out there, but I couldn't see them. And I reasoned that if I couldn't see them then they couldn't see me, and I was safe enough.

The Emmitsburg Road exited Pitzer's Woods northwest of my present location to run north into Gettysburg just along the edge of the Peach Orchard. Seeing the road, and not seeing the Yankees, I determined that I would skirt the edge of the woods, return to the road and then re-enter the woods to ride back east to find Longstreet and, I hoped, the rear of Lee's army.

I knew that somewhere just beyond the ridge of peach trees the Union army was lurking, and so I decided at this moment I would adopt the strategies of my old friend from Mexico, that famous Texas Ranger and Confederate general and absolute madman who got hisself killed by rushing to the front at Pea Ridge. Ben McCulloch would have put on a bold front and rid his horse right past them Yanks, acting the whole while like it was just exactly the sort of thing he was supposed to be doing. I'd been with him in Mexico when we rode past Santa Anna's pickets in just the same fashion, and I decided to do the same now. [42]

Of course, what I did not know was that Devil Dan Sickles had his field glasses with him.

I stripped out of my captain's coat and stuffed it along the saddle straps of the Yankee cavalry horse I'd borrowed on the horse's left flank so that as I led the horse north it would be away from any Yankee eyes on our right. I was grateful to be out of the wool coat, for the heat was becoming increasingly oppressive as the day wore on. I went frequently to my canteen, desperate for some relief as I was perspiring every bit of water I could get into me. Still leading the horse rather than riding, I walked along the edge of the woods up toward the peach orchard and the Emmitsburg Road. It was a mile or so from where I first exited the woods to the peach orchard, and I took my time in making the trek. Deliberately, I picked my way along as if I was looking about for something among the boulders and rough ground, hoping that any Yankees who might see me would assume I was just a farmer looking for a calf that had wandered off.

It was a gamble. I was leading a good horse, and there weren't many farmers left in lower Pennsylvania with good horses. A particularly observant man would realize, too, that the saddle on my horse was no farmer's saddle. I still had my Colt on my belt, but I hoped that might go unnoticed.

Eventually, as I worked my way up the rise toward the peach trees, I could see the Army of the Potomac up ahead of me along Cemetery Ridge. There were thousands of 'em up there on that ridge, pulling guns into place or eating a meal at a campfire or still digging in. Cemetery Ridge dips into a low spot just before it connects with

Little Round Top, and this spot of the ridge was directly to the east of the peach orchard.

I tried deliberately not to look at 'em as I went, though I knew they were there. A couple hundred yards away from me was the entirety of the Third Corps on my right flank.

I should have kept going, kept up my charade of the farmer looking for his calf, but now I couldn't help myself. It was fear, don't ye know, that made me stop. I had a sudden sick feeling as my belly rumbled, and I was sure that somewhere along that ridge someone was taking a particular interest in me. So I stopped, and with my horse between me and the Army of the Potomac, I began to look along the ridge.

There were pockets of men standing all along that ridge so that it seemed the entirety of the ridge to my east was full of men, and I suppose it was. From what I could see, none appeared to be looking in my direction or paying me any mind at all. And why would they? Even if they realized I was a Reb, one man by hisself was nothing to concern an entire army.

But then my eyes landed on a small cluster of men. I suppose there were a dozen of 'em standing together in a crowd, and b'God they were looking directly at me. I could see that one man in the center of the group had field glasses trained upon me. There was something familiar about the man, about the way he stood, and I was now certain sure he was pointing directly at me and talking to the men around him.

It could have been anything. An artillery commander pointing to the spot where he wanted a particular gun to cover. Someone from the general's staff pointing to the spot where he thought Johnny Reb might make his charge. It could even be a local boy among the Northern army, pointing to the woods where he'd killed a big buck and telling his friends about it. There was no reason, truthfully, for this to make me especially nervous. And if Ben McCulloch had been present, he'd have advised me to put my head down and keep on going.

But I had that sick feeling in my gut that those field glasses were sizing me up.

Now, a wise man would have said, "Speedy, old son, hop on that horse and ride hell for leather into them woods and get clear of this business." But wisdom comes with experience, and apparently all my experiences had not yet made me wise enough. Rather than flee for safety, I did a damned fool thing. I lingered there. I unstrapped my own pair of field glasses and held them up so that I could better see that cluster of men. And of course, then the charade was done, for no Pennsylvania farmer would have had field glasses tied to his belt.

I peered through the glasses and quickly found the man who was looking through his glasses at me. The man was wearing a particularly nice, blue dress coat. He wore a foraging cap, but it wasn't the cap that caught my attention. The brass buttons on his coat were polished, and there at the shoulders were embroidered gold stars. B'God it was a general looking at me.

Seeing me looking back at him, he dropped his field glasses from his eyes, and with them out of the way, I was able to see the face: The bushy moustache, the pudgy eyes, the bit of whiskers below his bottom lip. It was Devil Dan Sickles, and I believed that madman had recognized me!

If ye ever read the papers in those days, you would have known all about Dan Sickles and the murder of Phil Key back before the war. Well, the truth was, Phil Key wasn't the first man outside of her marriage to come to grips with the lovely, young Mrs. Teresa Sickles. On a train ride to Washington D.C., she'd caught my eye, and if I'd not abandoned that train while it was at full steam and given my ankle an awful twisting in the process, Devil Dan would have had to claim temporary insanity in his defense of my murder. Temporary insanity – have ye ever heard of such a thing? Either a man's crazy or he's not, and there's naught temporary about it. [43]

The moment I recognized him, I saw that old blood lust return to the Devil's eyes. He suddenly became animated, pointing first in one direction, then in another and shouting out. I watched him, longer than I should have, as he ran about yelling. And then, quite suddenly, I realized what he was doing.

That maniac Sickles, who had by this time already abandoned his wife, was still carrying a grudge against me! Here, with the entirety of the Army of Northern Virginia in proximity, Devil Dan was sending troops out to kill me all because I'd gotten belly-to-belly with his wife years before while giving her a tour of the inside of a tobacco barn!

It was farcical, and the shock of it paralyzed me. Still with those glasses up to my face, I watched as Dan Sickles ordered men forward for the sole purpose of killing me. He was pointing at me and shouting, and beating his fist against the wind, and then I heard the crack of a rifle and a bullet pinged against a rock not far from where I stood.

I dropped the field glasses down to my side so that I had a better view of the whole Third Corps, and I realized that a group of men in green leggings and coats were all aiming rifles in my direction. B'God it was Berdan's Sharpshooters! I recognized them from the green uniforms they wore. That first bullet fired from a rifled long gun in my direction was all it took to shake me loose of my paralysis. Now I scurried up the back of my horse, turned it toward Pitzer's Woods, and spurred the thing forward just as I heard a whole volley of rifle cracks. Leaves and limbs in the woods in front of me jumped and split as a swarm of bullets passed by, but by a miracle nary a one of their shots had found my back.

B'God Berdan's Sharpshooters don't miss, I thought to myself as my horse entered the thick timber of the woods.

I looked back over my shoulder long enough to see that an entire regiment, along with the sharpshooters, was now moving forward at the double-step. Devil Dan, in his lust to see me dead, had sent an entire regiment after me. It was nothing more than lunacy, giving me to conclude that the insanity that resulted in Phil Key's death was neither temporary nor satiated. The way the pretty, young Teresa Sickles got around, it's a wonder Devil Dan didn't have the blood of half of Washington D.C. on his hands. [44]

Pitzer's Woods were thick with trees and underbrush here, and maneuvering a horse through it was all that I could do. But the bullets were flying thick through the trees, and I spurred the horse forward, leaning over to hug his neck so that I was a smaller target and to avoid crashing my head against low branches. Berdan's Sharpshooters knew their business, and even from distance and with the first trees of the woods providing some cover, I still could hear the whiz and snap of the bullets. As I pushed the horse first this way and then that in an effort to get deeper into the woods, I actually saw the bullets crash into trees nearby. It seemed that every few seconds there was a volley thick as a swarm of bees busting up the timber all about me.

At last, the horse burst through a tangle of underbrush and I could see movement up ahead of me. It was Jube Elmore the Alabamians I'd breakfasted with earlier in the day! Salvation!

"B'God the whole Union army is coming!" I called to them as my horse crashed through the woods and into their encampment.

Fear was making me dizzy, and I fell out of my saddle as I reached the skirmishers. It was Jube Elmore, the big sergeant with the little girls back in Mentone, Alabama, who lifted me to my feet.

"Captain Speed!" he said, picking me up. "What's up?"

"The damned Yanks!" I shouted at the man, terror and panic infiltrating my voice. "Get yer men into battle line right now, son!"

And to add emphasis to my pleas, we heard the crack of a volley some distance through the woods. Already Berdan's Sharpshooters and the infantry had brought their pursuit into Pitzer's Woods.

"Grab yer guns, boys!" Jube shouted. "There's bluebellies in these woods!"

And just like that, the skirmishers were rapidly loading their rifles. They'd not done much to dig themselves in overnight, and so now they were crouching behind trees and looking for targets.

"What's happened, Captain?" Jube Elmore asked me.

"They spotted me while I was reconnoitering," I said. "At least a regiment of the Third Corps and Berdan's Sharpshooters are coming through the woods after me."

"You sure it's an entire regiment and not just some pickets?" Jube asked.

"Course I'm sure," I told him. "I saw Devil Dan hisself!"

"Why would they send an entire regiment after a single man?" he asked.

Well, that was a good question, but I doubted that Jube Elmore would credit it if I gave him the truthful answer. They sent an entire regiment out after a single man because Dan Sickles is a lunatic, and if you're smart about it you won't ever get belly-to-belly with the man's wife in a tobacco barn, for Devil Dan Sickles is a vindictive bastard with a long memory. But that wasn't an answer that Jube Elmore would likely believe.

"You wouldn't believe me if I told you."

Having come into the woods chasing a single man and finding instead an enemy of unknown strength, the Yankees now got down behind trees and formed up for a fight. The sharpshooters knew their business, fighting Indian style from tree to tree. The infantry regiment followed their lead, and the Yankee lines firing into us were soon stretched longer than our own. I could see it would not be long before the Yanks would be able to wrap around us and envelope us.

Those Alabamians, though, weren't going to be easily outdone in a shooting fight in the woods. They returned fire with glee, glad to finally have something to do. Meanwhile, I crouched behind a thick oak and prayed the Confederates would drive the Yanks back before Dan Sickles brought the entire Third Corps into the woods seeking vengeance for the sullied reputation of his bride. Of course, blaming Ol' Speedy for Teresa Sickles' sullied reputation was absurd, for I was not the first nor the last to bespoil their marital vows. The old girl got around quite a bit, and Devil Dan warn't no angel hisself – running around with whores the way he did – so why he thought it was necessary to risk the life and limb of all his men just to come after me continues to puzzle me to this day. But such is the mind of the lunatic: – If Dan Sickles had been sane and a person could make sense out of the things he did, then Phil Key would still be among us to this day and Berdan's would not then have been chasing me around in the woods.

Now, I wasn't much interested in remaining in the Battle of

Pitzer's Woods, and it was my desire to continue my progress toward the rear, but Jube Elmore was one of the sergeants who took his business too seriously. As I cowered and prayed behind the trunk of an oak, Sergeant Elmore joined me. He seemed to think that having led the Yanks in among his men, I was now in some way obligated to join in the defense of the woods.

"Captain, you might want to load that pistol of yours and shoot back some," Elmore said. "We could use the help here."

For show, and nothing more, I reached pointed my Colt around the trunk of the oak tree and blindly fired off a shot in the direction of the oncoming Yankees. It was good enough for Sergeant Elmore, who now resumed his command and issued orders to his men to fire and reload, fire and reload, walking away down their meager line.

I chanced a glance around the oak to see how we were faring, and saw that the sharpshooters and their supporting regiment were still progressing toward us. We were just a handful of skirmishers against an entire regiment and Berdan's, who I rated to be some of the best fighting men in the Yankee army. We were soon to be overrun. Gunsmoke was starting to fill the wood, too, so that when our boys fired their muskets and rifles from a standing position their targets were obscured. From my vantage point, on my stomach and trying to make myself small behind that oak tree, I could see that Berdan's were kneeling or prone so that they could still clearly get a bead on their targets. Our small band of skirmishers was getting smaller. I saw one of our boys fall with a gut-shot. Another went down clutching his chest. B'God, I knew this was no place for me, oak tree or not, and I decided it was time for Ol' Speedy to seek his escape.

That Yankee cavalry horse I was riding was a good mount. Despite the increasing rate of fire and the noise there in the dense woods, my horse was not far away. I decided I'd clench my teeth, close my eyes and make a headlong dash for the horse and pray no Yankee bullet found my backside.

I took two deep breaths, trying to gather up the nerve, but just then, Sergeant Elmore returned to my side. He was breathing hard and I could see what looked like spots of blood across his face.

"You're the ranking officer here," he shouted over the sound of the gunfire. "The only officer with us is Lieutenant Farley there, and I'm afraid he's about to get us all kilt."

I looked down the line and saw Farley, waving a sword and shouting orders.

"We're soon to be overrun here, captain, and Lieutenant Farley is unwilling to fall back," Elmore shouted to me over the din of the firing. "Through the woods, a hundred yards or more, are the rest of our regiments. If we can get back to them, we'll have numerical superiority over this single regiment in front of us, and it will be no thing to drive them back."

I looked from Elmore to Farley. "Have ye tried to reason with him?" I asked. I knew what the Alabamian sergeant was asking me to do. He was asking me to use my authority over the lieutenant to order the skirmishers back. But I was unwilling, under any circumstances – even to order a retreat – to move in the direction of the young lieutenant. He was standing exposed to the Yankee sharpshooters, and engaging him in any sort of conversation would unnecessarily put me in the line of fire.

"I've tried," Elmore said, and I very nearly felt sorry for the situation he found himself in. His frustration was writ in the lines on his face. The poor sergeant was being undone by the only two officers available to him, one a fire-eating madman intent on sacrifice and glory, the other a petrified coward skulking behind a tree and praying for an chance to make a run. "If you'll issue the order, he'll obey it!"

I took another look at the lieutenant, waving his sword around, and I gave some thought to telling Elmore to send Farley to me so I could issue the order. But Providence intervened, and Elmore and I stared aghast as the lieutenant's body flung backwards, punched in the chest by a bullet that opened a tremendous gaping wound in his torso. He was spitting blood from his nose and mouth, but do ye know, there on his back with his final breaths leaving him, he still had his sword raised to Heaven as if intending to lead a charge.

As was often the case for me, witnessing the violence of someone else's death was enough of a jolt to stir me to action. I leapt from my hiding place and issued the order: "Retreat! For God's sake, get the hell back!"

I dashed forward, and in a leap of pure panic jumped aboard my cavalry horse and dug my spurs into his sides. "Go, damn you!" I cried out. All around me my Southern brothers were abandoning the fight and fleeing back through the woods, and it was my desperate desire to find myself in the front of them. The bullets crashed through the leaves and the trees all around us. The horse started to move but stumbled, snorted and fell forward, dumping me face first into a tree. Whether the horse was shot before or after I jumped on his back I couldn't say, but he'd been hit and had faltered under my weight.

Smashing my face into the tree dazed me. I grabbed hold of a branch to pull myself from the ground, but I couldn't find my feet. My head was swimming, and the buzzing in my ears deafened me to the noise all around.

And there was Sergeant Elmore swaying in and out of my sight and standing over me. Elmore's hands gripped my arms and he tried to pull me to my feet. He was speaking, but I could make nothing of what he was saying. I was only just aware of the fleeing Confederates around me, and in my dazed state I had neglected even to be afraid of the oncoming Yanks. And now Elmore hefted me up in one great movement like I was no more than a sack of potatoes, he placed me roughly on his shoulder and then the Alabamian sergeant began pushing his way past the branches and brambles in an effort to get me and him caught up to his fleeing men.

I had the presence of mind when Elmore slung me from the ground to clutch hold of my old slouch hat, and my Colt revolver was still in its holster on my belt, but I'd lost everything else. Even my coat was still on the felled horse, so I was only in my shirt and trousers. It's the little things that sometimes save a life in a pitched battle, and it would not be long before I'd be glad not to have salvaged that gray coat, for if I'd had it on later in the day some boy from Maine likely as not would have bayoneted me up on Round Top.

The big sergeant from Mentone saved my life. No doubt had Elmore not plucked me from the ground in my dazed state and dashed through the woods with me flung over his shoulder, I'd have met my end there at Gettysburg. Had Berdan's sharpshooters caught me up and taken me back to Sickles, I am certain sure that Devil Dan would have tied me to the open end of a cannon and split me in two with a Yankee ball.

We made slow work of it, but Elmore kept moving until we came to the lines of Anderson's regiments. I was beginning to get my senses back, and was aware that a brief but heavy contest raged before Berdan's men were willing to give ground and move back to their own lines. [45]

CHAPTER 11

I always got on with Fitz Hugh Lee, and I genuinely liked him reasonably well. He was your typical cavalryman, loving a charge as much as any other entertainment, and in that we could not have been more distant. But when it came to carousing and chasing lovely Southern belles who were impressed with a gray uniform, Fitz and I were well matched chums. And I can forgive Fitz, too, for the part he played in seeking to place the blame of the Lost Cause on Longstreet, because Fitz wanted to keep pristine Uncle Bobby's reputation.

But of the rest who sought to shield themselves for blame at the expense of Old Peter – Jube Early chief among them – I had no use for them either during or after the war. As far as I was concerned, Jubal Early should have taken the stairs years earlier. [46]

As you'll know, the loudest complaints against Longstreet accuse him of stalling on the second and third days at Gettysburg, and so much has been made of the various times each movement was made throughout those days. Pendleton and Early – "knights of the pen," as Pete called 'em – were both known liars and sought to enrich themselves and enhance their reputations by destroying Longstreet's.

Well, here's what I know of Gettysburg – Longstreet attacked when he was in place. Had Bobby Lee issued an order for a sunrise attack – as Pendleton and Early and the others claimed – the only infantry available to Longstreet to send at Meade's left would have been me and Sergeant Elmore, and what a poor attack we would have made with Elmore no doubt being shot through and me running in the other direction.

It was noon when Sickles spotted me there near Pitzer's Woods and sent Berdan's sharpshooters to kill me. Elmore and his pickets fought with Berdan's for a bit before Lieutenant Farley was killed and I ordered a retreat, and another half hour was spent trading shots with the Alabamians positioned deeper in Pitzer's Woods. By my reckoning, that puts Berdan's in the woods until fifteen minutes before one o'clock. At that point, Sickles had still not yet advanced into the Peach Orchard, and neither had Longstreet completed his marching and countermarching.

In fact, the first of Longstreet's Corps was only just then arriving at the battlefield, as I can clearly demonstrate. Had Longstreet been guilty of the stalling that Early accused him of, I would have had ample time to make my retreat and I'd have avoided the hell that awaited me, both on the second and third days.

The first of Longstreet's Corps to arrive in Pitzer's Woods – the stepping off point for Longstreet's attack – were some of Hood's scouts, and they heard the shooting but were not present for the engagement with Berdan's sharpshooters. If ye don't believe me, check the regimental histories. [47]

The biggest blunder of the second day was the decision by that fool Devil Dan Sickles to leave the good ground he had and advance the Third Corps into the Peach Orchard. Sickles all but handed Lee the opportunity for success with his straight-on charge, but if Old Peter had truly been issued orders to attack at dawn, Sickles would have still been up on Cemetery Ridge and in a better, more entrenched position – and what he would have done to us there Pickett would find out on the morrow.

So there you have it. Bobby Lee issued no order for a sunrise attack because twalked no infantry with which to attack. Lee knew the disposition of his army. The First Corps was still on its way on the night of the first day and morning of the second, and upon arrival at Gettysburg they were meandering around behind the lines trying to find a way to their position.

Now that I've outlived nearly every blasted senior officer of the Confederacy, may mine be the final word on it.

If ye want to find the blame, blame Ewell and Early for failing to follow them fleeing Yanks up Cemetery Hill on the first day. The entirety of the war could have been settled right then had we dispersed the Army of the Potomac and kept on going down the

Taneytown Road to Washington D.C. Or blame Bobby Lee, if ye like, for ignoring Longstreet's advice to ride around Meade's left rather than attack straight on. Just as we had at Chancellorsville, there was opportunity to get into Meade's side.

Or, if ye like, ye can blame Ol' Speedy for my part in Gettysburg. On the second day I had opportunity to issue orders that would have forever rewrit the history of Gettysburg and the Confederacy. And again, on the night of the second day, a word from me could have convinced Meade to abandon his position, and what might have happened then? Oh, in all the times Old Peter and I walked his muscadine hills and talked of Gettysburg, I never confessed my role in it, but on the second day, when I turned Yankee spy again in a desperate attempt to save my own hide, I doomed Bobby Lee's army, and as much as any man cemented the fate of the Confederacy.

At my age tis no use to think on't. I don't know why, because it's no business of mine, but my dander always gets up when I give thought to the slanders against Old Peter. And now Eliza, coming to my study and finding my face flushed, is making me go for a lie-down. I'll resume my story after supper.

CHAPTER 12

After making good our retreat, with me slung over his shoulder, Sergeant Elmore propped me up against a felled tree and was good enough to fetch me a canteen with some wet mud in it. Then he abandoned me so that he might report on his lieutenant's death and presumably rejoin the fight as Anderson's detached brigades fought off Sickles' assassins. I found myself alone again in relative safety, and despite my swimming head and sore face, I was quickly giving thought to how I might retreat to the rear of Lee's army.

I'd come forward under orders from Longstreet to make a reconnaissance of the Union's left and I had intended to find for myself a route of escape in that direction. But now, horseless, fatigued and nursing a bruised face, I believed that headquarters offered me the best opportunity at securing a safe position for the coming battle. My desire was to find a cot in a hospital tent right close to that house where Lee had set up his headquarters, but it was no use waiting on stretcher bearers to get me there. I might be caught waiting all day. Instead, I decided to get up and walk on my own, and that was my undoing.

I steadied myself upon the trunk of a tree and climbed to my feet to see how well my legs might work. As I released my hold on the tree trunk, I found my balance was reasonably well restored and other than a stinging in the face where I'd gone headlong from my fallen horse, I was in decent enough shape. So now I started to trace my way through the woods, heading roughly back in the direction where I'd last seen Old Peter and back to where I knew Bobby Lee's stone house headquarters was located.

But as the final shots of the brief engagement with Berdan's were still echoing through the woods, I could see a group of dismounted men leading their horses toward me. Even through the woods I could see that they were Southern officers, and I began to get a little nervous that my plan of sneaking to a rearward hospital might be interrupted. So I decided to swing wide of them and started off in another direction, but it was too late.

"Captain Speed?" a voice called out to me, and I saw the familiar face of Evander Law picking his way through the timber. Law was a number of years younger than me, the youngest general in the Confederacy, and a good looking young man until his face was turned into a mess at Cold Harbor. He was so young he was not yet able to grow a respectable beard on his cheeks, but he wore a thick patch of chin hair and some soft whiskers below his nose helped to frame his frowning lips.

Being on Longstreet's staff, I knew pretty well all his division generals – Hood, McLaws, Pickett – and counted them among my friends. I'd interacted at least a little with all the brigadiers, too, and knew some better than others. I'll say this about Law, because he was a young fellow – not yet even in his thirties by this time – we always got along pretty well. Prior to Fredericksburg, Law and I had even been partners on a few nights playing euchre by the fire. But when he had the falling out with Old Pete after Chickamauga, Law and I never had a kind word to each other again. But his Alabama brigade, and Law hisself for that matter, were among the bravest fighters in an army chocked full of brave men. I suppose if given no choice of charging into a battle, I'd just as soon do it with those Alabamians as any other men I ever fought with, short of the Texas Rangers. [48]

And now, while I was trying skulk off to the rear, it was those brave men who were coming into Pitzer's Woods in front of me.

"Law, is that you?" I asked, knowing damn good and well which bastard it was stepping into my way and reaching out his paw to shake mine.

"Hell, Speed, what's happened to your face?" Law asked, pumping my fist and examining my face up under my slouch hat.

"Horse was shot from under me," I said. "I went face first into a big oak tree. Just headed back now to have a lie down in a hospital tent."

I let go of Law's hand and attempted to step around him, but he caught me by the shoulder, still looking at my face.

"Hell, Speedy, you look fine to me. Just a bit scratched up. Come on now, the fun is about to start. The First Corps is making its way into the woods, and you won't want to miss what happens next. Old Pete will be here soon enough."

I shrugged Law's damned hand off my shoulder and again tried to walk around him. "I'm damned dizzy," I argued. "I took a good jarring. Probably be best if I tried to rest for a bit."

"No, Speed," Law insisted, almost pleading with me as if he was doing me a favor by convincing me to stay. "Today's the big day. Look here, we're still coming up. It will be an hour or more before everyone is in place. Come on with me, now, and let's go have a look at what we're facing."

By now Law's staff had gathered round – all men who knew me by reputation. By the time of Gettysburg, I was pretty well known among most of the officers in the First Corps, not just for my exploits in Mexico but for what I'd done at Seven Pines to save Richmond. By the afternoon of the second day at Gettysburg, already most of 'em had heard rumors of how on the first day I'd unhorsed a Yankee cavalryman and led the charge through the streets of the town. It was all untrue, as ye know, but I had a reputation for being a firebrand. And now, everyone was looking to see if the brave Jackson Speed had turned coward and was trying to shirk his duty. It's harder than ye might think, in a crowd of men who have never known fear, to cower in the rear to avoid the fight.

Well, if for nothing more than appearance's sake, I was willing to walk a ways with Law. He'd said it hisself, we still had more than an hour before the First Corps would be in position and ready to set off, and that was plenty of time, I reasoned, to still find some safe spot from which to observe the battle.

Even as we stood there, the first elements of Law's division were coming through the woods and spreading out. They looked exhausted.

"We've been marching through most of the night, and this morning we marched first one way and then back the way we came,"

Law told me. "General Longstreet is in a rare state."

"How so?"

"Our guide had no idea where he was going. We walked back behind the ridge to the west trying to find some route where we could not be seen by the Yanks. We started out behind McLaws' division, but by late morning Old Peter had issued an order to countermarch, so it turns out we beat McLaws here. Honestly, it's been a mess, Speed. I saw Mox Sorrel after General Longstreet issued the order to turn about, and Mox says Peter is furious."

"Well, a delay like that, marching and countermarching, it's sure to get him a bit riled."

"It's more than that," Law said. "Old Peter doesn't like the orders. He says we should be sweeping around to the south, coming into Meade's flank."

"Aye, that's right, Evan," I said. "I've been scouting for Longstreet all morning. There's some cavalry down to the south, but if you get up on those hills yonder there's nothing more than some signalers to stop you from pushing into Meade's flank. Longstreet has it right. If there's to be an attack today, we should move through these woods to the south and then strike out east and then north. We could get right into those bluebellies."

Law and I set off through the woods up to Anderson's pickets who were still bandaging scratches and nursing the wounded from their fight with Berdan's. I did not see Sergeant Elmore among them, which was fine with me for I didn't want him to mention in front of Law or his staff how I'd gotten prone behind a tree and wept for salvation.

We passed through their lines and advanced through the area where Berdan's had been. Truly it had been a heated engagement, more than I realized in my dazed state, for saplings were split by musket balls and bullets had pocked nearly every tree of decent size. There were a number of dead here, and some of our stretcher bearers were out fetching up the Yankee wounded.

As I stepped over a body, a wounded man on the ground not far away raised his hand up from the forest floor and pointed a bony finger.

"There!" he shouted. Law and I stopped our advance to look at him, and I was horrified to see that he was pointing directly at me. The one hand was pointing at me, the other was holding a bleeding wound in his stomach. His face was black with powder, and dirt was plastered across his cheek. His eyes already looked vacant, but there was no doubting that he had me fixed in whatever life was left in his stare.

Law walked over to him and knelt beside him, and despite my horror at having a dead man pointing at me and calling to me, I followed a few steps behind the brigade commander.

"What's that, son?" Law asked, though I noted that there was little difference in age between the general and the dying private.

"He's the one," the private said, his voice getting caught in his throat so that he was barely audible. "He's the one we was sent to kill."

Law looked back over his shoulder at me, then back to the private. There was confusion all over Evander's face.

"What's that?" Law asked him.

"That one there," the boy said, still fixing me with his eyes and pointing at me with that bony finger. "General said to not come back without him. Wanted him dead or captured. That one there."

"What general?" Law asked.

"General Sickles. He said to bring that one back."

Law looked around for some stretcher bearers. "Come here and y'all take this man to a hospital," Law said to them, unable to leave the Yank to die alone. Then he looked back to me. "What's that all about, Speed?"

Well, there was no use in telling the story, though I'd now heard absolute confirmation that Dan Sickles had sent Berdan's Sharpshooters and an entire regiment to their deaths for the sole purpose of trying to assassinate me.

"Ravings," I told Law. "Ravings of a dying man. I suspect the man couldn't even see me. He's just rambling as he breathes his last."

Law frowned at me for a bit, but then he shrugged his shoulders and we resumed our walk through the woods. We had a small detachment with us, now, several men with rifles at the ready picking their way through the woods in front of us to be sure there weren't any remnants of Berdan's Sharpshooters sitting in the woods looking for a general to pick off.

"Damned odd behavior," Law said. "What the devil do you think he was on about? He was pointing at you like he recognized you."

"Well, I'd been out scouting when the Yanks across the way caught sight of me," I said. "Perhaps Sickles sent them after me to prevent me from providing the information of my reconnaissance."

Law took off his hat and scratched his head, thinking on it. "Seems strange that Sickles would engage such a large group to go after one scout. Why not just send some cavalry after ye?"

"Evan, if it was possible for a sane man to understand the mind of a Yankee politician, I suspect this war would have already reached its conclusion."

Oh, Evander Law liked that bit of jest well enough. He guffawed and slapped me on the back. "I suppose you're right about that Ol' Speedy," he laughed. "I suppose so. Well, let's go see what our Yankee politician is doing now!"

We hiked through the rest of the woods, and at the tree line we stopped and looked across the valley from Seminary Ridge to Cemetery Ridge.

"Jesus," Law blasphemed when he got his first sight of the Yankee position. "Speed, we're supposed to charge into that?"

Law took off his hat and wiped his brow, all the while keeping his eyes on the ridge across the way. Any officer in the First Corps understood well the defensive fight. Longstreet was a master at choosing ground and letting an enemy hurl himself against us. So Law could see at a glance that Meade had chosen good ground.

"You scouted out some of this?" Law said to me after a while.

"This morning," I said. I pointed out the way Pitzer's woods curved down to the south and showed him where the Emmitsburg Road came out. I pointed to roughly the spot where I'd been near the foot of Big Roundtop.

"That hill there, that's Sugarloaf," I said, using the local name for the big hill. "The one there with all the trees cut from it, that's where the Yankee signal is set up. As best as I could tell, Sickles is positioned directly across from us, beyond that peach orchard, and the Yankee line extends along that ridge and up to Cemetery Hill there."

Law looked for a long while longer. At length he pointed down toward the big hills. "Is Sickles' left anchored there on those hills, or is he down here below the hills?"

"All I saw was the signal up on the cleared hill. That's Little Round Top, there. From what I could see, there weren't no Yankee infantry up there. Sickles appears to me to be anchored where the ridge begins to turn into the hill."

"And south of us in the woods, did you say there was some cavalry down there?"

"Used up cavalry was all I saw. Most of 'em were dead of exhaustion and sleeping off yesterday's fighting. Honestly, they ain't standing any kind of picket duty or protecting the flank. It looked to me like they were done with the battle and retreating to the rear, and that's just as far as they got."

Law nodded slowly. I could see him working out the same plan of attack as Longstreet had. Hell, it was the same plan I would have come up with myself. That Bobby Lee was determined to attack head on rather than trying to get into Meade's left flank can only be put down to the fact that he'd not yet traveled this far to the south. He hadn't really seen what was in front of him, nor had he considered the mile-long charge from Pitzer's Woods to Cemetery Ridge. The Yanks would see us coming the moment we stepped off from the woods. They'd have all the time they wanted to site their cannon and load their muskets.

"It does seem there is a better way," Law said, more to hisself than to me.

Just as he said it, Law cocked his head and pointed an ear in the direction of the peach orchard. "Do you hear bugles?" he asked.

I inclined my head a bit forward and snatched my slouch hat off my head thinking I might hear better. "May be," I said. "No, wait, I think I do. Bugles and drums."

The noise was growing louder from across the way.

Cemetery Ridge was higher than the peach orchard. I know some have tried to claim it was not. But it's true that the orchard did sit on a bit of high ground in the valley between our position in Pitzer's Woods and Sickles' position on Cemetery Ridge. As a result, we did not have an excellent view immediately, but as the bugles and drums grew louder, Law and I were able to see the smart lines of Yankees forming up and advancing, their flags held high in the summer afternoon breeze, their muskets up against their shoulders. Everyone who saw it was forced to remark on what a fine and orderly advancement it was – parade ground perfect – and the credit for such an impressive march in proximity to the enemy has always been given to Sickles. But I knew better. I'd been with Pinkerton and Little Mac when these boys of the Army of the Potomac learned their business – drilling over and over again so that they were marching in their sleep. Sickles' Third Corps did a fine bit of parade ground marching that afternoon, and it was a spectacle to witness, but the credit is misplaced when given to Sickles for such a fine looking movement. That was all on McClellan. [49]

But seeing that the Third Corps was now advancing in our direction, it was not the smartness with which they stepped forward that I was thinking about. My bowels were rumbling with dread, for it seemed that Devil Dan had decided to throw the entire Corps after me. "B'God, he's bringing the entire Corps after me," I said out loud.

"What's that?" Law asked.

"Do you think they mean to attack?" I said.

Law watched in amazement. "Surely not." But with each beat of the drum the Third Corps of the Army of the Potomac was getting nearer. Cannon and caissons were coming forward, lines of infantry were coming forward, flanked by small bands of cavalry. They were cutting the distance between the two armies from a mile to just a few hundred yards. And as we watched, the infantry began to move into a line of battle, the artillery unlimbered and the Third Corps of the Army of the Potomac was taking up a position from which the First Corps of the Army of Northern Virginia would be able to reduce it by pieces.

"It appears that General Sickles has moved into that peach orchard," Law said, but it was less a statement of fact than it was a question of disbelief.

"I believe he has," I responded. "That's what happens when you make a New York politician a general."

Law and I could see clearly that the Yankee's Third Corps had marched to a position which would ensure its destruction, and at the same time the instrument of that destruction was coming into position in Pitzer's Woods. It was then John Bell Hood joined me and Law at the edge of the wood.

Sam Hood was born in Tennessee but in the regular army before the war he became a full-fledged Texian with all the faults such a thing possesses. Hood loved nothing better than to throw his men at a wall of enemy shot, and he'd rush right in with them. Consider the damage he did to his officers at Gaines' Mill. My recollection is that Hood was about my age, but with a long face made longer by his shovel beard, and I always thought he looked a good bit older. Hood was a cavalryman at heart, and he could not help himself but lead a charge. Around the campfire, I liked Sam well enough, but his desire to see the men under his command get themselves killed was too much for me to stomach, and up until Gettysburg, I always felt it was divine Providence that I'd never found myself attached to Hood's Division. [50]

"Hang on now," Hood said, walking up to where Law and I were watching Devil Dan Sickles. He looked up and down Cemetery Ridge and then had one of his staff officers hand him a roughly sketched map. Hood examined the map and then looked at the Yankee lines again. "I say Evan, the enemy's position don't correspond a'tall with the orders I received this morning from Gen'l Lee. What the devil's happened here?"

At this point Law and Hood began to discuss the changing situation on the battlefield. Hood's staff and a few of Law's began to gather around, and I took the opportunity to walk a few yards away and stand by myself. What ye never want as generals and officers begin talking is to be too nearby, for as soon as some damnedable job is required to be done, one of them is sure to cast his gaze in your direction and expect you to be all too excited to do it.

All through the woods the Army of Northern Virginia's First Corps was gathering up behind us, preparing to step off into the valley and charge the Yanks. Hood's men, and Law's, were continuing farther south than our present location, and it was McLaws' division that was filling the woods behind us.

It must have been three o'clock by then. Sickles was in the Peach Orchard, Hood and McLaws were in the woods and moving to their staging points. And now Sam Hood was conniving to try to send me to my grave.

"Captain Speed!" Hood called to me. He walked toward me with one of his staff men and a few other men I did not know. "General Law says you've reconnoitered some of the area to our south?"

Suspecting where Hood's thoughts were leading him, I hemmed and hawed a bit. "Well, you know Sam, I walked about a bit, but I couldn't say I really did much reconnoitering."

"That's fine," Hood said. "I want you to go with Lieutenant Pinckney here and see what you can determine about the enemy up on those hills, yonder." Hood pointed over toward the Round Tops. "Now that General Sickles has seen fit to move, we need to know what it is we are getting into. Gen'l Lee wants us to move north up the road there, but it looks to me like we will be unnecessarily exposing our flanks to the enemy if we proceed as ordered. Unless I'm mistaken, I believe there is a better way to the south."

"Ah, well, Sam, I had my horse shot out from under me earlier, and I ain't even got a canteen. I can't imagine trying to move about in this heat with no water."

Hood snatched the canteen out of the hands of one of his aides and handed it to me. "There now, you're watered, so there's nothing stopping you. I need you to go with Lieutenant Pinckney."

"Well, Sam, I was just thinking that with the battle imminent I should find General Longstreet and return my services to him. You know Old Peter likes to have his staff with him come battle time."

Hood stamped his foot and punched the fist of one hand into the palm of the other. "Dammit, Speed, we do not have time for worrying about who belongs to which staff. Take Lieutenant Pinckney and these men here with you and see what's what down on Meade's left. Get down there fast and then get back and report to me."

Well, once Sam Hood goes to stamping his foot there's not much use in arguing. I looked over at Lieutenant Pinckney and sized him up as the typical sort of Texian who knows no caution, and I thought he was just the sort of fool to get us both killed.

"Let's go, then," I said, determined that if the shooting started I would abandon the young lieutenant to his fate and hurry myself back to rejoin the staff of Lee's Warhorse. For the second time on this damned day I was being sent off to scout out Meade's flank. The first time I'd had an entire regiment sent to assassinate me, and I was not looking forward to what would await me on my second trip. [51]

If I'd loitered about in Pitzer's Woods and taken my time on my first reconnoitering, there was going to be none of it this time. Lieutenant Pinckney and his men were determined that we were going to scout out Meade's left flank on the double step and return our information to Hood in short order. We kept close to the tree line so that we could keep our bearings about us. As we got well south of the peach orchard and came near the big hill – Round Top as history calls it – we were nearing the spot where I'd earlier seen the cavalry relaxing. But they were gone now, and what I realized then was if Old Peter still wanted to get south of Meade and position our army between the Army of the Potomac and Washington D.C. – if he still wanted to pick a good ground and let Meade come at us as Lincoln and Halleck would insist – there was now nothing to the south to either prevent such a movement or raise an alarm among the Yankees.

Little Round Top had been cleared of timber, and though it was the shorter of the two southern hills, because it was clear it had attracted Meade as the right place to position the Yankee signal company. But as we stood at the edge of the woods looking up at the position, Pinckney was more interested in the bigger of the two hills. It was still heavily wooded, but even so it had the true commanding view of the field.

"That hill there," Pinckney said to me, "were you up it this morning?"

"Naw," I said. "I was near the base, but I did not go up the hill."

"Were there bluebellies around the base?" he asked me.

"Not this morning, but that was before Sickles sent his men forward. There's big boulders all around the base and a small creek running through there, too."

Pinckney gave Round Top a long look, and then he looked at his pocket watch. "I believe there is time for us to reach the summit and return our information to General Hood before the First Corps is in position to attack," he said. "If we hurry," he added.

"We cannot see from here if that hill is occupied," I pointed out. "Would it not be better to return with the information we have rather than risk being captured?"

Pinckney scoffed, as you might expect he would being a Texian and young and only a lieutenant and full of piss and vinegar. Oh, if he survived the battle I didn't doubt that he'd one day be made a general.

"Come on now," he said, and though I outranked him, I found myself following his orders against my better judgment.

When I visited Gettysburg and the grandchildren wanted me to show them Sugarloaf, or "Big Round Top," as they liked to call it, I pointed to the hill from the Emmitsburg Road and said, "Aye, your grandpappy climbed that hill twice on July the Second of Sixty-Three," but I did not attempt to take them to the top so they could see the view. Little Round Top was easy enough to walk up, but Sugarloaf was nearly impossible to summit, even when I was a young man and strong. The sides were steep and in the heat of the afternoon with the humidity high, it was dreadful work trying to climb the hill.

We were forced to drag ourselves up rocky inclines by grabbing hold of bushes that grew in the crevices and pulling ourselves up. I was in my shirtsleeves, but Pinckney and the other five men in our small group all wore their wool coats, and I was astounded that they did not pass out in the heat. We paused periodically, hiding behind boulders or trees, to drink from our canteens. As we climbed, we were able to see that Sickles had occupied with the smallest of forces the rocky area down at the base of Round Top, but we had not encountered any Yankees on the hill itself.

At length we reached near enough to the summit but had worked ourselves nearly all the way round to the east side of the mountain, and what we saw there took even me by surprise. I remember clearly that we were working our way slowly through the crevices of some of the large rock outcroppings that littered the sides of Sugarloaf. Pinckney was above me, he'd come to a ledge where no trees obscured his view. I was wedged in the crevice, pushing against one side with my feet and the other side with my back and trying to reach for a hold where I might pull myself higher toward the ledge when I heard Lieutenant Pinckney calling to me.

"Captain Speed," he said in kind of a loud whisper, and there was such an urgency to his voice that I half expected we'd wandered into a nest of Yankees. "I need you up here with me, Captain Speed." And with that, Pinckney reached over the side of the ledge and took hold of my hand and wrenched me to the top of the ledge. I swung a foot up and scrambled my way onto the ledge with him. I was on the ground on my back. Pinckney was in a squat now, his back to me, and he was looking out to the east. I rolled over and picked myself up to my knees so that I could see what had him so excited.

The Emmitsburg Road ran from the southwest into Gettysburg on the west side of the Round Tops and Cemetery Ridge. Opposite it, the Taneytown Road ran from the southeast into Gettysburg on the east side of the Yankee's position. We were now the first Confederates of the battle to have a commanding view of the Taneytown Road, and what we saw was enough to make your blood run cold.

Stretched out below us were Yankee supplies as far as the eye could see. All around the eastern base of Round Top, the Yanks had parked their wagons. Why, there was enough artillery – should it be confiscated by some enterprising Southern cavalry officer – to pound the North into submission, enough packets of lead and powder to shoot every Yankee north of the Mason-Dixon line twice, rations to last the army for months, shoes and clothes and anything else we might want, and all of it with virtually no guard at all.

Farther up we could see plenty of reserves being held so that they could move quickly along interior lines. I suppose this was the Army of the Potomac's Fifth Corps we were looking at, the men who I would soon be facing on the slope of Little Round Top. But they were not entrenched, they were just milling about and waiting for orders to move.

Me, what I saw was death waiting to be unleashed. Meade had twenty thousand more men at Gettysburg than Lee, and upon seeing the reserves waiting to be rushed into the battle, I was counting all twenty-thousand of 'em one at a time, and with each man I counted I saw my own death. But Pinckney saw something else, and he whispered it at me in hushed tones as if Meade hisself might hear my conspiratorial Confederate if he spoke up.

"If General Longstreet were to come around the side of this mountain," he said, "we could have those trains – all those supplies – without even a fight. And we could make a stab into the enemy's flank, as we did at Chancellorsville. An enveloping move to the south is all it would take. Am I mistaken, Captain?"

The rest of our small band were joining us on the ledge, and they were all in awe just as Pinckney was.

Well, as I previously stated, I was looking at it differently from the rest of 'em, but the lieutenant was right enough. I shrugged my shoulders. "Aye," I acknowledge. "I suppose so. Ain't no Yanks to the south to see us coming. A quick movement, don't let Meade have opportunity to respond, perhaps combined with a feint to his front. Oh, likely enough it would do the trick." And, true enough, when I looked at it like that, I did think Pinckney was right.

"We must get word back to General Hood quickly," Pinckney said. "I want to continue to the summit and make certain there are no bluebellies up in the woods on the top of this hill, but I should think this information is important enough that we should let General Hood know now. I'll detail a couple of my men to go back."

Now that was a duty I was prepared to undertake. "Hold on, lieutenant," I said. "This information is too valuable, too important by far, to trust to a couple of privates. Choose two of your men to come with me, but I'll be taking this message back to General Hood."

For the first time, Pinckney took his eyes off the Union wagons and gave me a suspicious look. I laughed and slapped him on the shoulder. "Oh, don't ye worry, lieutenant – I'll let General Hood know for sure that you were the man who spotted the enemy's weakness. The credit will go to where it is deserved."

Pinckney grasped my hand and shook it vigorously. "Thank you Captain Speed!" he said, but I loosed myself from his grip and started back down through the crevice even before he'd detailed two of his men to follow me. Getting off that mountain and back to the rear of our army was my urgent priority, damn the credit for finding the enemy's flank and damn Pinckney for being worried about which of us might receive the credit if the thing was pulled off. Oh, you could be certain sure when Jeff Davis looked to bestow laurels upon the man who spotted the Yankee weakness at Gettysburg, I'd arrange it so that those laurels fell to one Captain Jackson Speed, and Lieutenant Pinckney be damned.

Going down Round Top was not much easier than coming up it, but it was certainly faster. We were able to leap some of the boulders that we'd struggled to climb, and through the woods we very nearly tumbled from tree to tree until the ground began to level out and we were able to break into a run through the woods and back toward Hood. If Lieutenant Pinckney had been able to track our progress back to Sam, no doubt he'd have shed a tear at Ol' Speedy's enthusiasm to get the vital information in the hands of a general who might make use of it, but he'd have been mistaken as to the source of my ardor. No, I knew there were Yanks creeping around at the foot of Round Top, and I wanted to put as much distance between me and them as I could before they caught sight of me and decided to finish the job Berdan's Sharpshooters had started. [52]

CHAPTER 13

It was less than an hour, but not much less, when I found Hood again. His entire division had managed to get into Pitzer's Woods and was now fronting Round Top, so once I was back in Pitzer's Woods I did not have far to go to find him. Law was there with him, along with several of their staff officers. I stepped in front of the two Texian privates that Lieutenant Pinckney had sent back with me and made certain sure that Sam Hood got his information from me. If this should prove to be the turning point, the point at which the Confederacy should smash the Army of the Potomac and set its sights upon Washington D.C., it would be forever remembered that Jackson Speed's reconnaissance provided the vital bit of information. Damn Lieutenant Pinckney. I was the ranking officer, wasn't I?

"What did you find, Speed?" Hood asked me, forgoing all formalities and trying to hurry me up.

I'd just risked my neck climbing boulders and skirting the enemy on his behalf, and for my own amusement I decided to feed him the information with a tea spoon. "Well, Sam, we followed the woods down to the south and found no Yankees penetrating the woods. Then we circled around to the base of the big hill yonder. It's damned difficult getting up it, Sam, but we managed to climb up to the top. Big rock outcroppings that ye have to scale, difficult terrain all the way up. But, it can be managed. You'll know I was at Monterrey in Mexico with some of your fellow Texians back in '47, and those boys managed to get up those cliffs to attack Fort Libertad. Now, Sam, I'll tell you what, that was damned tough going, that was."

If he'd been familiar with my service in Mexico, Sam Hood would have known I had no part in scaling the cliffs to Fort Libertad and instead was chasing around in the streets of Monterrey with a blood thirsty lunatic colonel answering to the name of Jefferson Davis, but Hood had no interest in Monterrey.

"Yes, yes, Speed," Hood said, his face behind his beard growing red with impatience. "But what did you see of the enemy's position?"

"Ah, well, Sam. From this side of the mountain we were able to see how Sickles has aligned his men down near the base of the hills. There's a creek running through there, and he's got a battery positioned near that creek. There's also some huge rock outcroppings – ye might be able to see them from here – and there's Yanks all in among them rocks."

"Can we get into their flank?" Hood asked, and no doubt he was thinking of Stonewall Jackson's envelopment of Howard's Germans at Chancellorsville and imagining himself as the next hero of the Confederacy.

"Oh, aye, Sam. I'm sure that you could. You can follow the woods here and swing around to the south and then cut along that creek in between the big mountain and the rocks yonder."

Hood was calculating his flanking maneuver, so I decided now was the time to drop the important bit.

"But that's not the really impressive thing we saw," I said, and Sam Hood's eyes grew big as saucers.

"Tell me, Speed," he said, clearly praying that whatever I said next would give him a clue to Meade's undoing and his own everlasting glory.

"We found a ledge, it'll be around on the southeast side of the mountain there. Ye can't see it from here. But it gave us a good view, and we were able to see the enemy pretty well. There's a road running south over on the other side of the mountain, sort of parallels this Emmitsburg Road here. All his supply trains are parked at the base of the mountain, almost without guard. And that road leads straight into Meade's rear. It looks as if he's got another Corps held in reserve, but a quick action could take them almost completely unawares."

Hood licked his lips, then ran his gauntleted hand over his mouth. He was drooling, imagining it.

"Them trains would make a pretty good prize, Sam, and they could be had without too much trouble. But it's the rear of Meade's army that's the real treasure."

Hood looked me up and down, obviously trying to decide if I knew what I was talking about. He took a look next at the two Texians Pinckney had sent back with me, and both of them voiced their confirmation that what I'd said was in line with the message Pinckney had given 'em.

Now I played my trump card. Hood was about to step off into battle. Whatever happened next, the fighting was going to be damned rough, and Ol' Speedy wanted no part in it. I'd been near enough to it on the previous day. What I wanted was to find Old Peter and get myself near to him, and I expected Hood to present me with my opportunity. "If I were you, Sam, I'd be sending a messenger off to General Longstreet straight away to tell him what's what and get your orders changed."

Hood was agitated. Anyone could see that if he followed his orders and turned his men up the Emmitsburg Road it could lead to disaster. Hood's men would be exposed to enfilade fire from Sickles' Third Corps. But Sam could also see from the information I'd given him that there was an alternative – a flanking attack, a rout of the enemy! Though we were just a couple of months from Chancellorsville, already Stonewall Jackson's memory was being treated like a Southern Deity, and Sam Hood, standing there in Pitzer's Woods on July 2, 1863, had visions of becoming a deity in his own right. He could outshine Jackson right here and now.

Hood turned to one of his messengers. "Go to Gen'l Longstreet and tell him what ye've heard," he said. "Go and tell him to amend our orders and allow me to make a southern movement to attack the flank and rear of the enemy!"

Well, that was damned unlucky for me, for that was the assignment I'd wished for. I was as agitated as Sam Hood, but for other reasons. I could have wept. I'd done my part. I'd risked life and limb scouting out these woods and the big hill, not once but twice. I hadn't slept hardly at all and the last of the food I'd consumed had been hours before. I was exhausted, my face ached from tumbling into the tree, my limbs were exhausted from climbing up Round Top and then back down, and all I wanted to do was lie in a ball on the ground and cry for how poorly I was being used by this damned army.

I turned up my canteen and drank the tiniest trickle of water left in the bottom of it and got a mouthful of mud behind the trickle. And now I was out of water.

Hood had turned away and was giving out orders to his other messengers who were all dashing off one way or another.

"Sam, I'm going to find a drink of water," I said. "I'm parched."

"Like Hell!" Hood declared. "Evan Law is my far right. You go to him now and tell him everything you saw. He must know what opportunity is in front of him!"

"Ah, Sam, I'm done in. I ain't ate, my canteen is empty, I've been running around these woods all day – I need a lie down, Sam. My arms ache from the climbing and my face is sore as hell. I'm exhausted. Surely someone else can go along to Evan and tell him what's what."

Hood's wrath was visible as his face took on a deep scarlet color. Even his beard seemed to grow red. He took me by the arm and walked me a few feet away from his staff officers and the others around, and as we walked he spoke right into my face, spitting the words at me: "Listen here, Speed. I don't need grumbling now. We are all tired, we've all marched through the night, we all need something to eat. But the enemy is in front of us and has presented us with an opportunity for victory. D'ye hear me, Speed? Victory!" He shook my arm forcefully at the word. "Victory for the South, victory for the Confederacy, victory for our way of life! Now is the time and here is the place. We have him, Speed. We have Meade, and behind that Yankee bastard we have Lincoln. But we will not take him by loitering or delaying or whining about water or sore arms. Now I'm telling you to go along to Law. And when ye've told him what ye have to say, offer your services as a guide for his right flank."

I started to complain, but Hood still had me by the arm, and when I opened my mouth to argue, he jerked my arm pretty rough and said, "Not another damned word from your mouth, Jack Speed, or I'll court martial you and see you spend the rest of this war in a prison camp. How would ye like that?"

I'd heard horror stories of the conditions at the prison camps, and I knew Sam Hood wasn't making idle threats.

It was a tense moment there with Hood. Nobody, not even a man who fears battle as much as me, wants to get a reputation for cowardly behavior, so I tried to play it off. "Sure, Sam. No need to get feisty. Just this knock I took on the head earlier, that's all. I'm off to find Evan and see what we can do about getting into Meade's flank."

"That's right," Hood said, his red beard cracking open into a smile that was as menacing as his grimace. "Today, we win glory!"

Well, that was the last I saw of Hood before he was wounded, and good riddance to that Texas bastard. Like most all the rest of them, he was a good sort around the campfire, playing cards and sharing stories, but on the cusp of battle he was a madman, and his lust for glory made him all too willing to pile body upon body. And if my body was among those added to the pile, Sam Hood wouldn't lose sleep over that. I had no desire now to go find Law, but shedding myself of Hood's company seemed the thing to do at the moment.

Just then the guns started to fire. I couldn't now say whether it was Hood's guns behind us or Sickles' guns in front of us that got the thing started off, but balls were now being lobbed back and forth, and the battle of the second day at Gettysburg was set to get underway. [53]

CHAPTER 14

It took me no time to find Evander Law. Throughout the woods men who had marched and counter-marched all through the early morning hours and afternoons were now lying on their knapsacks seeking a big of rest as the cannons thundered in front and behind them, so if you wanted to find an officer of any rank, he'd be in among the only knot of men still on their feet. Indeed, as I skirted the edge of the wood, ducking my head each time I heard a cannon boom, I found Law surrounded by his staff officer.

I told him all I knew of the Yankee position, and shouting over the thunder of the cannon fire, I let him know that Hood had sent a messenger to Longstreet seeking an amendment to the original orders.

Hearing my story, Law was now chomping at the bit. If you care to, I'd encourage you to find somewhere a list of the officers killed or grievously wounded at Gettysburg. That list would be well longer than your arm, I'd wager. Dozens of them, on both sides, killed or maimed. And that is the madness of war. All these men fighting, desperate to achieve some measure of glory, but to what purpose? The mention of Stonewall Jackson's name even today will bring a tear to the eye of any old veteran who served under him or any old woman who can recall the Old South, but what damned bit of good did it do him? He died an early death after Chancellorsville so that his name might be remembered for a generation or, perhaps, two?

Contrast me, if you will. As I walk about town now in my old age, the youngsters all crowd around to hear Ol' Speedy tell stories of the war. Important men, if they know I'm in town and think I might donate to their campaign, invite me to dinner or toast me at parties. Didn't young Teddy Roosevelt sit in awe of your's truly and toast to my bravery? Oh, aye he did. And there's still any number of women who encounter me and give me that look that says, "Oh, the old veteran, what I might let him do to me if he were twenty – nay! – ten years younger." I've lived a long and full life and without the least bit of valiant effort have still achieved all the glory a man ever needs, and all I ever did was my damnedest to stay out of the thick of it.

Now which of us would you rather be? Stonewall Jackson, whose name may be a bit better known than my own, moldering in one grave for two score years while his arm molders in the other, or Jackie Speed, whose conquests up hills and into valleys never known to Stonewall continued for decades after that man's death? Oh, aye, if ye're a smart man, ye'd rather be me.

And that's what I never understood about these madmen like Law, or Hood, or Jackson – especially Jackson. They rushed to get theirselves killed all for some fool notion of notoriety. Oh, I'm sure if Stonewall'd had his preference he would have won his glory solely on the bodies of the men who fought under his command and not sacrificed his own limb nor life, but I knew the man, and I knew that to achieve his desire for glory he didn't mind if the expense was his future.

They all talked about glory as if it were a thing. "Today," they would tell you with a sneer on their lips, "we charge into glory!" Aye, you charge into glory, I'll be over here hiding under this log. Let me know how many men ye get killed, unless ye're among 'em yourself, and when I join ye in hell in fifty years I'll recount for ye all the times your young widow bounced upon my knees.

The trouble with them all, and what made all these maniacs so damned uncomfortable to be around, was they expected you to be as thrilled with sacrificing your life for their glory as they were to have you sacrifice your life for their glory.

Well, I wanted no part in it, so I complained to Law about my aching head.

"Look 'ere Evan, much as I'd like to go blazing into Meade's flank with you, shooting up all them Yanks and what not, I took a pretty good spill from my horse earlier, bashed up my face, as ye can see, and I was thinking maybe I should go somewhere for a lie down. So you be a good lad and save some of them Yankee bastards for me. I'm sure I'll be fit as a fiddle tomorrow."

But Law wasn't even hearing me. We were walking along the edge of Pitzer's Woods, the cannons booming both in our front and rear as Sickles' artillery traded shots with Longstreet's artillery, and Law was making the final preparations for his advance.

At the very south end of the army, Lee's right flank, we found an Alabama regiment, the Fifteenth Alabama under the command of Colonel Billy Oates. They were gathered up near a farmhouse on the edge of the woods from which point they would be making their attack. [54]

The men had not long been in position when Law and I arrived. Law quickly introduced me to Billy Oates and told Oates I was to serve as his guide. Given the opportunity, Law told him, Oates should move against Meade's flank. Law and Hood both, Longstreet too, I suppose, believed Meade's flank was exposed and could be got at. Bobby Lee, though, thought the right thing to do was to move along the Emmitsburg Road for a frontal attack, drive Meade from the top of Cemetery Ridge and scatter the Army of the Potomac.

In defense of Lee, who everyone believes was right anyway, I'll say that every Johnny Reb on that field at three o'clock on the afternoon of July the Second believed that with the slightest bit of pressure the Yanks would tuck tail and run like a kicked puppy. Lee's plans for a frontal attack, therefore, made a certain tactical sense.

Longstreet wanted to bring the whole of the Army of Northern Virginia to the south of Meade's army, dig in and let them Yanks come at us. Just as they had at Fredericksburg, an entrenched Army of Northern Virginia would certainly have cut the Federals to pieces. And the Yanks would have had to come at us, for we would have been between the Army of the Potomac and Washington D.C. – and that was always Lincoln's greatest fear, that his army would get turned and the Confederates would have been able to lay siege to Washington and Jeff Davis would have been in a position to sue for peace.

But with the way things stood on the afternoon of the Second, Evan Law saw better than anyone how to win the day, and as we stood there on the precipice of Pitzer's Woods, preparing to launch Lee's attack, Law was looking at me and Billy Oates to do it for him.

And we damn near did.

The three of us, Law, Oates and me, stood at the edge of Pitzer's Woods shouting our strategy over the roar of the cannon fire.

"Captain Speed will serve as your guide," Law told Oates. "He has seen the enemy's flank from that hill. Tell me again, Speedy, what's up on the big hill there?"

"Nothing is there," I said. "On the lower hill, the rocky one cleared of trees there, Meade has some signals and nothing else. Now that Sickles has advanced forward, Meade's reserves are spread out across the ridge. From the lower hill, there, you could move directly into his flank."

"Right," Law said to Oates. "That's what I want. Go up between those two hills there, move to the top of the lower hill – what's it called, Speed?"

"Little Round Top," I said.

"Get to the top of Little Round Top and then push through Meade's flank. Roll them up, Oates, and let us win this day!"

Oates looked at me from under the brim of his foraging cap and seemed to be sizing me up, maybe trying to determine if I was cut out to be a part of the Fifteenth Alabama. Well, I was a big man and healthy enough, and for anyone unaware of my cowardly nature, I looked like just the man you'd want marching into battle beside you, so I suppose Billy Oates was pleased enough with what he saw.

"You stay close to me, Captain," he said. "You get me to the right position, and I vow there is nothing that can stop me from getting into the Yankee flank."

Well, Billy Oates was a determined man, and I suppose he was close to being correct. But the Fifteenth Alabama – maybe the toughest regiment in all of the Army of Northern Virginia – had not yet met Joshua Chamberlain and the Twentieth Maine.

As Old Peter's staff officer, I knew a fair number of the

regimental colonels, either by sight or by reputation, but I'd not before met nor heard of Oates. But it did not matter whether we were meeting for the first time or had shared a campfire dozens of times, for I knew all I needed to know about him already.

Oates was a young man, good looking with long hair and a full beard, and sharp, penetrating eyes. He didn't seem the type to be bothered much by thought or contemplation, but quick to dash forward with pistol firing and sword waving.

If it's true that the First Corps of the Army of Northern Virginia was the hardest fighting Corps in Lee's army, and I believe it was, Hood's Division was the hardest fighting Division and Law's Brigade – made up of Alabamians – was the hardest fighting Brigade in our Army. No man rose to be colonel in a brigade of that reputation without being a careless fool. A smart man who kept hisself and his men alive would never make a regimental commander in Law's brigade.

So as a man came around to collect my canteen to take back to a well at a farmhouse behind our lines, I knew that if I was to survive the second day at Gettysburg I was going to have to find a way – and soon – to extricate myself from Colonel Oates' Fifteenth Alabama Regiment.

And now the drums were drumming and the bugles blaring and we were stepping off out of Pitzer's Woods – six hundred of us or more – the Fifteenth Alabama off to whip Meade so that Evan Law, John Hood, Old Peter and Bobby Lee could all receive the thanks from Jeff Davis and the laurels of our new nation. We were the far right of Lee's line, and because the commander had ordered an attack en echelon, we were the first to step out. The remainder of Law's brigade, then the rest of Hood's Division, were to follow us, and then it would be the whole of Lee's army – thirty thousand or more all along Seminary Ridge and curling up around the base of Cemetery Hill on the outskirts of the town – would step forward.

I'd done it before, in Mexico and in this war, stepped off with an army on the verge of charging into battle, and I can tell you it's a frightful business. I suppose there were plenty along that line who stepped out with courage, ready to do their part. Others, perhaps with the confidence of youth, who had not learned their lesson in our previous battles, stepped forward with conviction. But all I knew as the army moved forward was dread and fear. My legs didn't want to move, my stomach was in my throat, my thoughts were of my wife, my children, my home, the comfort of Jenny Rakestraw's bed – anything far away from this maddening hell as I desperately tried not to think of the minie ball that was sure to be spilling my insides momentarily.

I was sick with fear, but forward I went because when an army around you sets off, there seems no other way.

As we left the woods and started across a clearing toward the big hill in front of us, the ground was ragged and broken with rocks. No obvious formation could be maintained. We lacked the martial beauty of Sickles' Third Corps as it advanced into the Peach Orchard, but the Army of Northern Virginia was never a pretty thing.

"It's late in the afternoon for an attack," Oates said to me, his sword held high so that his men would always form up on him. "But when them Yanks yonder hear the lusty Rebel Yell, I believe they will make our work plenty short so that we might be finished by nightfall. What do you think, Captain Speed, how far will Gen'l Lee expect us to chase them?"

In response, I only swallowed hard in an effort to keep what little there was in my stomach from coming up. I was a big man, an easy target, and I was walking along side the regiment's colonel at the front of the line with the color guard just to my right. My God! I was sure to be among the first ones shot. My throat was so dry and I was choking in the dust we were kicking up, so I reached down for my canteen to give myself a drink.

"Tarnation, Oates," I said. "Your boys never returned with my water. Give us a drink, old son."

Oates patted his own hip where his canteen might have hung. He then looked over his shoulder at his men. "We appear to be marching into battle without benefit of water," Oates said.

I looked back over my shoulder and, indeed, I could not locate a canteen among any in the regiment.

"Perhaps we should go back and wait for the water," I suggested, but Oates merely scoffed at the notion. But I was thinking quick: "Would you like for me to go back and find the water boys and hurry them to the regiment?"

"There's no time for that now, Speed," Oates said. "We'll press forward and hope they catch us up soon."

We had advanced some distance, following skirmishers who were pushed out in front of us, when the dirt around us began to kick up and I heard a sickening "thunk" of a bullet hitting flesh behind me. I turned reflexively and saw a man five paces from me slumping back into the arms of his comrades, going down with a wound to his stomach.

I looked around and saw that the fire was coming from sharpshooters at a farm not far in front of us. I slumped my shoulders and ducked my head and tried to make myself small. Oates began to wheel the regiment to the right to avoid them, but it was slow work to move six hundred men, and the bullets continued to threaten. Some of the skirmishers up in front of us returned the fire, but the sharpshooters were shooting from behind walls and fences, and our skirmishers could do no more than compel the sharpshooters to sometimes duck their heads.

With the Yankee sharpshooters making a nuisance of themselves, Oates began to hurry us along. With boulders and stands of trees littering the way, the terrain was difficult to move over and our ranks began to break apart as we entered a wood at the base of Sugarloaf – the big hill that would be known to history as Round Top. We were back, roughly, on the trail that I'd followed earlier with Hood's Lieutenant Pinckney.

We crossed a small creek where I paused just long enough to splash some cool water into my mouth. This was Plum Run, and in an hour's time it would be running red with blood. Oates' men behind me had no luxury of a drink from the creek, for they soon kicked up so much mud that it was too poor even for a taste.

Beyond the creek, I spotted what looked like the approach Pinckney and I had taken up the hillside.

"Here," I said to Oates, pointing at the rocky cliffs of the big hill. "We can make our way up the hill here."

I suppose we'd passed beyond the spot where Pinckney and I had climbed the hill, for we were pushed farther to the east than I realized. The going was tougher, too. Here we were, six hundred men climbing hand over hand up a rocky incline with Yankee sharpshooters plinking the rock all around us. At every opportunity where I could find a ledge to stop and catch my breath, I did so, hugging the rock in front of me to be sure I wasn't exposed and an easy target for the sharpshooters. We had to scramble up that hillside, pulling ourselves up bodily by grabbing hold to tiny saplings growing between the boulders or finding crevices to wedge ourselves into and through which we could further our ascent.

Oates was as bad as the damned sharpshooters, for he was constantly sniping at me.

"Here, Speed," he would say, "keep moving. We must get to the summit."

"Come along, Speed, faster, we've got to beat the Yankees."

"Are you sure this is the way you came, Captain Speed?"

"For God's sake, Speed, get out from under that rock and continue climbing!"

At some point, I suppose, someone sent some number of men to chase off the sharpshooters, for I do recall that during our ascent we were no longer being shot at. I recall, also, being grateful that I was not toting a long gun and was not overburdened with a haversack or much equipment, for the climb was so difficult that I truly do not know how those boys of the Fifteenth Alabama made it.

But I'd have given all my gold in California for a drink of cool spring water.

By now, of course, I had lost my coat and was wearing only civilian britches and a cotton shirt with the sleeves rolled up. Even so, the heat was so oppressive and I was so parched that I could barely even give thought to my fears because of my exhaustion. Most of the other boys had on tattered butternut or gray uniform coats, though they left a fair number of those on the side of Sugarloaf. Every man among the Fifteenth Alabama was desperate for water, and by the time we crested the slope and found ourselves among the trees at the top of the big hill, we were suffering too much from exhaustion and thirst to do anything more than collapse.

But not Oates. Immediately he began surveying our vantage point.

As you'll know if you have even a passing familiarity with the Battle of Gettysburg, the timber from the western slope of Little Round Top had been harvested by a couple of brothers earlier in the year. Sugarloaf offered the highest vantage point of the battle, but it was heavily wooded and therefore was considered to be of little military value. But through the trees at the top, Oates had an unparalleled view of the battlefield. [55]

"My Lord, Captain Speed! Come and have a gander at this!" Oates called to me. I was sprawled on the ground and near to passing out. Scattered around me were others of Oates' Alabama regiment who were just as bad off as me, exhausted and suffering from thirst, but Oates took no heed of the fact that his men had been used up in the waterless climb.

"If it ain't a cool spring flowing from the earth, I've no desire to see it," I told him.

"I insist, Captain," Oates said, biting off the rank so as to make me understand he was issuing an order and not merely a request.

I struggled to get myself to my feet, and licked my lips with a dry tongue. "Not a spring, eh?" I said, looking about.

"It's Meade's army," Oates said, pointing through the trees.

And so it was. Below us was the summit of Little Round Top, empty of Yankees. Beyond that, though, were blue coats, like so many thousands of ants crawling over a giant, disturbed hill, upon Cemetery Ridge. We could see Sickles' Corps down to our left, and could see the remainder of Hood's army, shooting from among the giant boulders and pressing toward the Peach Orchard. We could see Meade's supply line and reinforcements down on the Taneytown Road off to our right. We could see his entrenched men on Cemetery

Hill and Culp's Hill and we could see all the way to the town of Gettysburg. To our left – off to the west – we could see the mountains twenty miles away where, just the day before, Oates and his men had been encamped. I even took note of the tiny white house just over the edge of Cemetery Ridge where there seemed to be an inordinate amount of activity. I did not know yet, of course, but that was Meade's headquarters, where I would soon play a vital role in handing Bobby Lee's army its most disastrous defeat.

Indeed, it was a glorious view, and – if I'd had a full canteen slung over my shoulder – it would have suited me to have stood there for what remained of the day and watched the battle play out. It would have made for a fine show. But the gleam in Oates' eye made me suspect there was little chance I was going to be left there in peace.

"Guns, Captain Speed," Oates said. "I need artillery. Half a dozen guns. Two guns. One gun! B'God, old son, but with one gun I could command the entirety of this battlefield! And the ascent up to the top of this mountain is such that a single company could defend it for days!"

"Oh, I don't know, Bill," I said. "All these trees are in your way."

"Look about you, Captain," Oates said. "These boys from Alabama know how to cut timber. We could have a field of fire cleared in under an hour."

Standing there at that moment, watching the advancing Confederates down upon the Emmitsburg Road and moving up through the boulders that would be known to history as Devil's Den, I could see that what Oates said had merit. A company working diligently could have a decent field of fire cut in half an hour. The men we had at our command could have easily held that big hill. The approaches from the east and south were steep and difficult – as we had just learned. We held the high ground on the easier approach, from Little Round Top, and could have beat back the entirety of the Army of the Potomac. Meanwhile, if we were able to haul by brute force a few guns – or even just a couple – up the side of that hill, a couple of gunners who knew their business could have blasted Meade's army to bits. Artillery from up on Sugarloaf combined with the infantry already engaged against Sickles – as I think back upon it now and remember the sight from up top of Round Top, I can tell you with absolute certainty that Colonel Oates had found the South's path to victory.

If you want to know when and where Gettysburg was lost for Bobby Lee, it wasn't on the third day with George Pickett's disastrous charge. I can tell you it was about three quarters of an hour past four o'clock in the afternoon of the second day.

"A word from you, Captain, and Longstreet will surely see the reason in it," Oates said. "I implore you, issue the order – as an officer on Longstreet's staff. They'll heed your judgment."

"You outrank me," I bristled.

"Yes, but General Longstreet won't give a thought to what I have to say, but you're his staff officer. He'll give more credit to his own captain than he will to a colonel he does not know."

That was probably true. Old Peter knew me well enough to know I had a good eye for ground, and I believe even in his perturbed state he would have acquiesced had I sent a message back informing him of our opportunity. And so I began to weigh my options. On the one hand, if we began cutting down trees and trying to haul artillery up the side of the mountain, we might easily catch the attention of Meade's reserves. And I could see them down there, behind Cemetery Ridge, thousands of them. It looked as if Meade had another full army just waiting in reserve. Those bluebellies might charge our position as soon as they saw the first trees fall, and while I didn't doubt that Oates could hold that position with the men at hand, I had no desire to be up on that hill when the Yankees decided to assault it or lob cannonballs upon the summit.

On the other hand, our orders were to lay into Meade's flank. If we did not stay on the hill, it was not charging Yankees I had to worry about, but it was Yankees behind entrenched positions firing at me as I was caught up in Oates' charge. And that was a far worse thing.

Oh! I was heartsick, for there were no good options for Ol' Speedy today! I'd been flung into the death of Gettysburg, and on this hilltop there seemed no salvation.

Oates stood gnawing on his bottom lip waiting for me to decide what I would do. No doubt he was correct – from this hilltop the battle might be won, and with victory every Southern belle would have one name upon her lips: "Colonel William Oates." He'd be made a general, no doubt. Perhaps a corps commander. Perhaps he'd be sent out west and given command of an army. Likely as not, a victory at Gettysburg would have meant victory for the South, and Oates might well have been the leading contender to be the third president of the Confederate States of America, right after our current president, Jeff Davis who would surely be followed by Bobby Lee hisself.

Meanwhile, I was only able to think of how I might convince him to continue his charge but leave me behind on this hill to wait for the battle to be over.

"Captain Speed," Oates implored. "We must hurry. We've gotten a late start to the day already. If you see the wisdom in attempting to hold this position and bring up artillery, we must do it before the moment is lost."

Still I said nothing. Was it possible that I might carry the message back to Longstreet myself, and in so doing remain behind the advancing army and keep myself safe? I considered it, but I remembered those sharpshooters. If they'd returned to their position near the barn, a single man would be a target for them as they would know I was carrying a message. No, I had no desire to try to get back to the bottom of that mountain by myself and get shot down by Yankee sharpshooters.

"Captain Speed?" Oates was nearly in tears waiting for my response.

But then the moment passed.

How he managed it I have no idea, but as I was trying to make up my mind how I might extricate myself from this perilous predicament and Oates was dancing on one foot and then the other waiting for me to say the word that might allow him to be the South's hero of Gettysburg, some captain from Law's staff appeared on the top of the hill on horseback! Had he shown up with a rope and ladder, I'd have believed it more. I'd climbed that hill twice already and used every bit of strength and energy I had hauling myself over boulders and pulling myself up by grabbing hold of roots and saplings, and here was a captain on horseback riding up to us as if we were in the flat land of Illinois. There must have been a path that I had overlooked, but I still cannot imagine how he appeared, mounted, at our side. [56]

"Colonel Oates! Can you explain why you have halted your men?" the captain demanded.

The captain's presence startled us both and I believe Oates was as astonished to be looking at the man's horse I was. I didn't recognize the captain, but Oates seemed to know him well enough.

Oates extended a hand toward his exhausted men, most of whom were still on their backs and trying to catch their breaths. "We have no water, Captain Terrell," Oates explained, "and my men are spent from the climb."

Terrell looked the men over and sniffed his disdain. I noticed strapped to his saddle was a canteen which I assumed to be full. "Mind if I get a drink, there, captain?" I asked, reaching toward the canteen. Terrell ignored me as I took a long drink of the water, then slung his canteen over my own shoulder.

"General Hood has been grievously injured," Terrell said. "General Law has risen to command the division. General Law has sent me to inform you that it is his desire to see you press your attack immediately."

Oates raised his eyebrows. "Look at this, Captain Terrell," he said, pointing north through the trees. "With just a bit of work, we could get some artillery up to the top of this hill. My men could begin felling trees now. In no time, we could have clear lanes of fire established, and from this position we command the entirety of the field! Please, please, please go back and have Law send us some guns! Even one gun! The day can be won from right here!"

Poor Billy Oates, he was in a state.

"Look here," Oates said, walking through the trees to gain a better vantage of the east where Meade's reserves and supply trains were. The captain dismounted, tied his horse to a branch, and followed. "The ascent here is sheer. There is no way the Yankees can climb to us." Now Oates marched us a few paces north where we could better see Little Round Top and the battle below us. "Only here, along this path between these two hills, could the enemy attempt to march to us, and the route is so narrow that only a few men could pass at a time. Easily – easily! – I could cover this position. It would be nothing to hold this hilltop! And with cannon, three or two or even just a single gun, we could tear into the enemy!"

Oates was frothing at the mouth, and he reminded me of my colonel at Monterrey, Jeff Davis, rushing his men into the death because he could taste victory. The difference now was that Oates was wanting to just hold ground, ground that could be easily held with minimal loss. The more he talked, the more I liked his plan. Why, if Oates got his way, I'd be able to hide behind a couple of the boulders in the rear while his men defended the summit and fired their cannons. Now that I considered it fully, I believed Oates had not only found a way to win the battle but had also found a safe location for me to sit the thing out.

"I believe the colonel is correct," I interjected. "I've been examining our position, and I can't see how it could be assailed by the enemy, and as you can plainly see, we could destroy the Yankee's ranks with cannon from here."

Terrell gave me a quizzical look. "Who are you?" he asked.

"This is Captain Speed of General Longstreet's staff!" Oates shouted. "He's on General Longstreet's staff! Surely his opinion of our current position outweighs orders given earlier!"

Terrell, though, was plainly unconvinced. He was one of these damned fool army men who only know the orders they've been given and cannot think with creativity. Terrell spit on the ground and shook his head, apparently deep in thought.

"I've just come up the side of this mountain on horseback," Terrell said slowly, "and I can tell ye it's a damned tricky climb. It would take engineers to figure how to get cannon up here quickly, and we haven't got the engineers or the time."

"Bobby Lee is an engineer," I remarked. "He could have it done.

He hauled them guns at Cerro Gordo." [57]

"General Lee," Terrell said, correcting my impudence. He spit on the ground and shook his head in further thought.

Oates danced from foot to foot. I nodded encouragement.

Finally, Terrell looked at me. "You're a captain on Longstreet's staff?"

"Aye."

"Do you have the authority to override his orders?"

Well, if ye put it like that. "I do not."

"Nor do I have the authority to override the orders of General Law. Or General Longstreet. I cannot argue against the advantage you have discovered on this hill, Colonel Oates, but I must insist that you press your men onto that hill."

And having said it, Captain Terrell extended his hand, pointing a long index finger down at Little Round Top. He was standing to my left, to the west, and the sun coming through the trees this late in the day cast him as nothing more than a back-lit silhouette, black with his finger pointing down at the lower hill, and for the world I believed he looked as if he was extending the touch of Death hisself, and I shuddered my fear.

"That hill," Terrell repeated. "That must be your objective. Get your men up and moving, Colonel, and press into Meade's left from that position yonder."

And like that, the South passed by its finest opportunity to win the day, win the battle, and likely as not, win the war. Two captains and a colonel who could all see the merit in the suggestion at hand, but not one of us with the courage to countermand Longstreet, who also did not have the courage to countermand Lee. Battles are won and lost in the details, and in this detail and on this day, we failed to win.

But winning and losing was of little concern for me. Terrell now mounted his horse and turned to ride back down to find Law with the message from Oates that Oates would advance his Alabama regiment into Meade's flank. With his back to us, I gave Captain Terrell a wave with his own canteen, grateful he'd forgotten to retrieve it from me.

"That hill below us is unoccupied," Oates said. "If we press quickly, we can occupy that hill and from there launch our attack into Meade's flank. Up!" he called to his exhausted men. "Up, boys! For Alabama! For the Confederacy!"

Oates drew his sword and pointed it along the path leading to Little Round Top. His color guard formed up. His sergeants got to work kicking the men off the ground. The lieutenants started counting their men to make sure there were no stragglers.

CHAPTER 15

Since the war, I've read that we missed occupying Little Round Top by less than a quarter of an hour. As I joined Oates and his Fifteenth Alabama on the path across the saddle from Round Top to Little Round Top, we were entirely sheltered from the battle by the woods around us. We could certainly hear that a battle was raging ahead of us, but we no longer had the view we'd had from the higher summit.

On the second day of the battle, I believe no other man at Gettysburg was so greatly gifted with opportunity and so greatly beset with misfortune as was Colonel Billy Oates. At the precipice of Round Top, he had the path to victory at his feet. And now, as we marched forward to Little Round Top, he was again marching to a prominent spot on the battlefield from which he could surely launch the sort of assault Stonewall had enjoyed two months earlier – a charge to roll up the flank, to secure victory, to achieve everlasting fame as his nation's savior.

Just as at Chancellorsville, I was at the front of the charge, marching along with Oates and his Alabama regiment on what was little more than a deer path winding its way through the woods in the saddle between the two southern prominences of Cemetery Ridge.

What we did not know was that already Meade's reserves from the Taneytown Road were hurrying up the other side of Little Round Top. If we'd had our canteens perhaps we would not have delayed so long in our exhaustion at the summit of Round Top. Perhaps those Alabama boys, with some water to wet their lips, would have been quicker in their step along that path. But we had no canteens, and though we did not know as we marched along that we were in a foot race, we would soon find out that we had lost the competition to be first on top of the hill.

I cannot say that my mind was at ease, for I was nearer the battle than I cared to be. However, I was not in a panic, either. From Round Top I had seen for myself that the place we intended to occupy was vacant of federal troops. Though I was being pressed forward against my will by this madman Oates who was furious over his lost opportunity and determined now more than ever to steal a second opportunity, I was formulating a plan to extricate myself from the Fifteenth Alabama. My orders had been to guide Colonel Oates up the mountain, but at no point had Law nor Hood nor Longstreet sent me to be slaughtered in the battle. Oates was up and over the mountain now, and my work was complete, my orders fulfilled. Once we were atop the shorter hill, I intended to explain to Colonel Oates that I had done every bit of my duty, and my place was now with Longstreet. I could have said as much from the top of Round Top, but the descent there was more difficult and the chance greater of encountering stray Yankee sharpshooters on my retreat.

No, once the Fifteenth Alabama was prepared to make its assault, Ol' Speedy would be making his retreat.

And so we made our way through the woods, over rocky and rough terrain, the men spread out on the path and on either side of it, in a ragged column of march. Oates was beside me at the head of the column, the color guard just behind us and, beyond our sight, the Yankees piling up rocks between trees and boulders so that when we came within musket shot they would be well hid from our view.

"You know, Colonel, I think I've managed to perform my duty here," I said, as we walked along. "I was thinking that I should probably return to General Longstreet's command and render what further services he sees fit."

Oates looked at me slantwise. "Well, you did get us up the backside of that mountain, for all the good it did," he said, and I could hear the bitterness in his voice at having had his opportunity taken from him. "If ye'd like to return to General Longstreet, I don't see no harm in it."

And as my old friend Allan Pinkerton would have said, there was my plan perfected. Oates was more agreeable than I'd have thought he would be, but I was truly of no value to him any longer.

We were not yet to the cleared part of the top of Little Round Top but were still marching along the deer path in the saddle of the two big hills when something ahead caught my eye.

"What's that?" I asked, stopping in my tracks and pointing through the woods and up the hill in front of us. Oates stopped, looking along my line of sight. The color guard stopped. Some of the men fanned out around us and stopped level with us.

"I don't see anything," Oates said.

"That's an entrenched position," I said, looking at the low wall of rocks piled between two boulders on a ledge ahead of us.

"Probably had pickets out here last night," Oates said. He started to walk forward, but my fear prevented me from moving. I reached out and took hold of his arm.

"No," I said. "No, I believe I saw something behind those rocks. I'm telling you, there's Yankees up ahead."

Now, if Billy Oates had known me better, he'd have realized that no one was better than Ol' Speedy at spotting and avoiding danger. But he didn't know me, and he scoffed at my warning.

"I think the captain is seeing ghosts," laughed a sergeant of the color guard.

Oates frowned at the sergeant and looked back up at the rock wall. "Sergeant O'Connor," he said, "let's keep the men moving."

But just then hell opened up on the Fifteenth Alabama, delivered by the rifles of the Twentieth Maine.

From behind the low wall, from around the boulders, and from behind what seemed like every tree in front of us smoke and fire exploded as muskets opened fire, sending a wall of lead at us that dropped the men around us at an alarming rate. I'd have probably been cut down as well, but before the first hammer fell on the first percussion cap, I'd already dropped to my belly and pressed myself into the earth.

"Alabama!" Oates shouted, his sword in the air, and all around our column men began rushing forward, loading their muskets and firing at will. Having survived the first volley by kissing the ground, I was determined that I would find better protection before the Yankees fired off their second volley. Without raising myself off the ground even an inch, I rolled off the deer path we'd been following and crawled on all fours to hide behind a big rock jutting up out of the ground.

Oates stood his ground, as did the color guard. Those Alabama boys behind us were fanning out and rushing forward now and returning fire. A second volley erupted from the hill above us and more men fell dead and wounded. Officers rushed about, attempting to put order to their ranks and get the men to spread out and form up something resembling a line of battle.

"Charge!" I heard Oates yell, and the order was repeated up and down the tattered line, and the men began to dash forward. All along the hill in front of us, Yankees appeared behind boulders and trees, shooting another devastating volley into our ranks.

I watched as the exhausted men of the Fifteenth Alabama pushed forward, covering about half the distance between our position and the Yankees. But another volley from above us knocked the men back, and as one they seemed to retreat back to where they'd started from. The men regrouped, closing their ranks as best they could in the wooded, rough ground.

And then there was a hand upon my shoulder, rolling me over. "Captain Speed?" Oates asked. "Are you hit, sir?"

"I think I must be," I said, wanting nothing more than to be left alone. Oates looked me over and saw that I was unhurt. "You've only stumbled to the ground," he insisted. "I need officers now! To your feet, man! We must restore order to the men and make another charge!"

Another volley cut through the air, raining leaves and broken limbs down upon Oates and me. That damned Alabama colonel lifted me up to my feet, and I saw in his eyes the crazed look of a madman with the blood lust upon him. Oates had been working himself into a terrible state of desire, and now that the moment was here he'd gone stark raving.

"We must push the enemy in front of us off this hill!" he shouted at me over the noise of the shooting. "This hill is our position, and we shall occupy it presently! I have already lost officers, and I need you now to help me lead my men for'ard!"

I said something to him about Old Peter and a general needing his staff officers, but the maniac slapped me across the face. "This is no time to show cowardice, Captain Speed! Men must be courageous!"

He'd lost his sword, and now Oates drew out his pistol. For a moment, I thought the maniac would shoot me, but instead he raised up the revolver like it was his missing sword.

"For Alabama! For the Confederacy! Charge!"

And I was caught up in it. It was that damned Sergeant O'Connor, who'd laughed at me for seeing ghosts, who took hold of my elbow and dragged me forward now.

"The fun's just starting now, Captain!" he hollered, and he was showing me a grin like we were dashing off to a dance.

I stumbled over branches and rocks and men rushed forward past us, carrying me and Sergeant O'Connor with them and closer to the line of Yankees now leveling their muskets at us, and I saw the flash and explosion of fire and smoke as the muskets again unleashed hell, and I could hear the balls ripping the air as they slid past us to tear up branches and cut through leaves and burst chests and smash skulls, and I cried out in terror, but that damned sergeant kept hauling me forward until at last the line that had rushed past us wavered and receded like the wave of an ocean, broken against the sand and rolling back into the sea. And we rolled back with them.

And Oates was at my side again, and with him a number of his remaining officers. Our men were fanned out and shooting randomly up the hill, and Oates was holding a council of war with musketry still crashing all about us.

"There!" he said, pointing at the Yankees. "Do you see them?" he asked the group at large. "Do you see them, Captain Speed?" I glanced forward but saw nothing more than death in front of me. "Do you see them moving among the trees, closing their ranks? They are giving up their flank, running back toward the main body."

I looked again, and indeed I could see it. As we charged forward and shot down some of the Yanks, others slid back to close the ranks. And in doing so, they were shortening their line. A shorter line gave us an opportunity for envelopment.

"We can move to our right and then swing back to the left," Oates said. "Do you see?" The other officers answered him in the affirmative, some still looking to try to find what he was on about. Terror had so gripped me, that even if I'd wanted to utter a response I could not form words. But Oates looked directly at me, waiting for a response. "Do you see them, Captain Speed?"

"Damnation, man, what do you want? I see them. I see them," I answered.

"Return to your companies. As you do, move along our line. Let the men know. We shall advance forward at our right, turn back to the left and get into their flank and in behind them. We shall issue an enfilading fire and we shall chase them off our hill! Do you understand?"

Again, his officers answered in the affirmative. But for my part, I had nothing to say. I had no company to return to, and I'd be damned if I was moving along the front of the line to issue orders to men I didn't command.

"Go and tell the men," Oates said. "Quickly now!"

The officers dispersed, but I held my ground. "Captain Speed," Oates said, looking thunder at me. "I am in need of your assistance. We have lost many officers already. I need you to help us spread the word so that we might move the men in concert with each other."

"Aye, I'll let 'em know," I told him.

Oates left me, moving down along his line to the left. "You heard him sergeant?" I asked O'Connor. "Go and tell the men."

O'Connor, sniffing out my cowardice, grunted disgust at me, but he did as he was told. And I put my back against a large oak tree and took a breath. My hand fell to my side and brushed against the metal canteen I'd taken off Captain Terrell. Remembering its presence, I took it up and had a drink. It was still mostly full. As I went to replace it on my belt, I realized to my horror that at my feet was a wounded lieutenant. He'd ripped open his own coat and his white shirt was covered in blood. His face was blackened from powder. He was looking desperation at the canteen in my hand.

"Can I have a drink, sir?" he asked, and there was a rasp to his voice, and I could barely hear him above the din of the battle. Like the rest of the Fifteenth Alabama, he'd not had a drink since we'd been in Pitzer's Woods.

I slid down the tree trunk to sit on the ground, careful to keep my back against the tree to keep myself safe. The boy tried to lift his hand to take the canteen but it would not move. I put the canteen to his lip and poured a little of the water into his mouth.

"I'm gut shot," he said. I realized one of his hands was resting on his belly, a finger still inside the wound where he'd felt it out. "I'm Lieutenant Cody," he said. "You'll tell Colonel Oates I've been mortally wounded?"

"I'll tell him," I said.

"You're lucky to have your canteen," he said. "Neither I nor my men had our canteens returned to us."

I gave him another sip from Terrell's canteen.

"We've just got to push them Yanks off that ledge up yonder," he said. "They'll run. They always run. Trouble is, ain't none of these boys got enough spit to give a good Rebel Yell."

He tried to give a smile at that, but he only grimaced.

"The pain's awful bad," he said. "I sure wish I wasn't dying on Northern soil. I wish I could get back home. I'd like to see my paw again. You tell Colonel Oates to write to my paw, tell him I died like a brave man? He'll be so disappointed I'm dead."

Now, talking about his father, the water I'd fed him was leaking out of his eyes.

"I'll tell him," I said. I thought about giving him another drink, but I decided it would be wasted on this boy with his leaky eyes and instead would save it for myself.

"Don't tell my paw I cried," Lieutenant Cody told me, and that was the last thought he had on this earth.

It was a sorrowful thing, for sure, but better Lieutenant Cody receive that mortal wound than Captain Speed. Down the hill below me men were hiding behind trees, clutching at their wounds, dying or preparing to die. I wouldn't be able to make my way past them to try to secure myself a spot in the rear without some meddlesome sergeant or captain clutching me by the arm again. My best option was to stay here with the recently deceased Lieutenant Cody, let the next charge pass by me, and then perhaps I could make a dash back down the deer path and find a boulder to hide behind.

But now Oates was beside me again, and the color guard was following him so that the Yankees shooting at will were targeting us, and under my breath I cursed that madman for putting me back in immediate jeopardy.

"Are the orders issued, Captain Speed?" Oates demanded.

"Aye," I said. "And Lieutenant Cody here wants you to write to his paw and let the old man know his son died bravely."

Crouched over me, Oates spared a moment to look at the young lieutenant's lifeless face. "We shall make certain he did not die in vain. Up now, Captain! Up and let's make this charge again!"

Oates has written that we made five charges in an hour and a half. To me, it seemed we must have made more than a dozen charges up that hill. Whether this was the Fifteenth Alabama's third or fourth charge, I cannot say, but with Oates at my side and Lieutenant Cody's final words weighing heavily on my mind, I know that this was my second charge at the ledge.

We charged again, this time following the route Oates had picked out for us, swinging first to our right and up the hill, and then cutting back to the left to attempt a flanking maneuver on Meade's far left.

There was nothing for it. I was caught up in the charge and could neither hide nor run, and so I drew my Colt and fired some number of blind shots forward and into the Yankee ranks, praying to God that if there was a man among them drawing a bead on me that my wild shots might find their way into him before he had time to pull his trigger.

And now Oates' strategy took effect.

"Forward men! To the ledge!" Oates called out above the noise of the firing guns. "Push them from that ledge!"

The men obeyed, pausing only to fire or load their guns as we made a shooting charge into the Yankee flank. The bluebellies returned fire with destructive effect, but we pushed them out from behind their stone wall, out from behind the boulders and out from behind the trees. In ones and twos and then in groups of half a dozen or more, they retreated up the hill, firing as they went.

An officer near us went down and I heard him call out for his mother. [58]

For a moment, just a brief moment, it seemed that Oates' gamble had achieved its desired effect. In that moment it seemed that we had won the battle and pushed the enemy off of its defensive position. The men paused in that moment. Some slapped each other on the backs, others grinned their success at one another. The smart ones reloaded their weapons.

And then the moment was gone, for those Maine Yankees rallied and charged back at us. We were in no way ready to receive them, and in a heart's beat they were upon us, some coming at us with bayonets and others coming at us shooting. Again, I dropped to the ground and prayed to God that the Alabama boys would be strong enough to drive the Yankees back before some damned fool buried his bayonet in my back.

I looked up in time to see Oates standing on the rock ledge and firing into the oncoming Yankees, and then I realized that the Yanks were again retreating. Now we had driven them from their position and beat them back from a charge. In the lull that followed, I got to my feet, fired another pistol shot up the hill, and then congratulated Billy Oates for his successful campaign.

"B'God Billy, we licked 'em!" I shouted at him, and Oates' blackened face broke into a smile.

"Indeed we did, Captain Speed!" And the daft fool slapped me on the shoulder and said, "I thank the Lord you were with us this day, for I could not have accomplished it without your assistance!"

I stood there with him as Oates began receiving reports from his officers, and none of what they had to say was good. Whole companies were reduced to just a handful of men. Some of the officers reported that they had no ammunition. I recall clearly a lieutenant holding out a single paper wad of ammunition and informing Oates this was the last shot available to what remained of his entire company.

At length, Oates held another council of war with his officers.

"We cannot hold this position," he said. "We are low on ammunition and must now prepare to retreat. If we had just one more regiment, another company, even, we could pursue our success. But we have suffered grievous injury and are without the means to continue the fight. We must withdraw."

That was the first sensible thing I'd heard this man say, and I was already prepared to lead the Fifteenth Alabama back to Pitzer's Woods in the quickest route I could find.

"Pass the word!" Oates called out so that his men might hear him. "We're withdrawing to the base of this hill! We must pull back and re-supply!"

Now the color guard was up around us again, and Sergeant O'Connor with them. "Colonel, sir, it may not be quite over," O'Connor said. Something in his voice filled me with dread, and so I looked up toward the top of the hill, and to my horror I saw that the Yankees were coming back.

"Oh, Jesus!" I shouted, and it was neither blasphemy nor a curse I uttered, but a sincere prayer for deliverance.

Coming at me at an uncontrolled downhill run was a Yankee private, his gun with its bayonet held straight out in front of him. He was twenty yards away, and then fifteen, and I could see that his eyes were fixed upon my chest where he intended to bury that damned steel blade jutting out so brutally from his leveled musket. I cocked my revolver and fired my last shot of the day, and I watched as the force of it threw the man backwards, the musket disappeared from his hands as his arms and legs sprawled out like a giant bird.

But there were others running shoulder to shoulder with him, and they were still coming on, and I took a step backward, my foot landing on a loose rock in that low wall the Yankees had thrown up, and when the rock broke free of the wall, I stumbled backwards and fell over myself. I dropped my revolver as I went over and crashed against the ground with an almighty shudder.

Above me, Oates was shooting his revolver at men who were within arms reach of him. O'Connor was struggling with a blue-coated Yankee. It was hand-to-hand fighting, men bashing each other with their muskets and wrestling each other to the ground. They were swinging bayonets at one another. Some men were fighting with knives while others punched at each other. It was terrible, desperate fighting and as bad as any I've ever experienced, which is really saying something, for I've been in some of the worst scrimmages ever fought on American soil.

I scrambled to my feet, prepared to make the run Oates had already ordered, but all around me was confusion. There were Yankees ahead of me and behind me. The flags of the color guard were waving in my face. I saw a blue-coated arm reach up to grasp the Alabama flag, and a strange thought struck me – the coat was the same color as the flag. I saw a flash of steel as O'Connor brought down his sword and brained the Yankee trying to take the flag.

Confederates were fleeing the field. I could see them running, stumbling, falling down the hillside, desperate to get away from the hoard of oncoming blue. Some were being bayoneted in the back; others were surrendering. Just a moment ago I had congratulated Oates on his victory, and now his men were dissolving into flight.

If ye're thinking of judging me for what I did next, you can save your vile superiority. If ye weren't up on that hill that day, ye don't know how bad it was. Oates led a regiment of six hundred men toward the summit of Little Round Top, and when the remainder gathered at the bottom of the hill there were nearly four hundred dead, wounded, missing or captured who had been left behind on the side of Little Round Top. The regiment was reduced to a mere two hundred thirsty, broken men. And among those dead was Oates' own brother.

So say what ye will, but Ol' Speedy survived it.

I drew the Bowie knife from my belt and in one slash I cut the Alabama flag off its staff. It didn't matter to a soul, for as I was cutting down that flag, the flag bearer was receiving a slash of his own from a Yankee bayonet. The boy fell mortally wounded at my feet.

Quickly, I wrapped that flag around me, so that at just a glance, those Yankees would think I was wearing a coat resembling their own, and now I turned around and looked at the fleeing Alabamians running down the hill, and I hollered out, "That's it boys! For Abraham Lincoln! For the Negroes! Chase those damned rebels into hell."

And I started walking backwards, back up the hill, so that I might blend in with the Maine boys charging forward.

And as I picked my way backwards into the lines of the Yankees, I sang for all I was worth: "Mine eyes have seen the Glory of the coming of the Lord, He is trampling out the vintage where the grapes of wrath are stored; He hath loosed the fateful lightning of his terrible swift sword – John Brown's body lies moldering, don't ye know." [59]

CHAPTER 16

Billy Oates and his Alabamians were fled well down the hill before my ruse was discovered, and I was shortly escorted by a couple of Yankee privates who kept jabbing at me with their bayonets to a man they kept referring to as "the kernel" but who proved to be Colonel Chamberlain of the Twentieth Maine.

"Kernel Chamberlain, sir, this 'ere prisoner says he's one of our spies," one of my captors explained.

Chamberlain looked exhausted. He wore a big, bushy moustache and tired blue eyes and a uniform that looked impeccable despite the trials it had just been through.

"A Union spy?" Chamberlain asked, looking me over.

Wadded in my hand was the Alabama flag I'd covered myself with.

"That's correct, sir. I was Pinkerton's right hand, a personal friend of Abraham Lincoln – saved his life in Baltimore back in '61, don't ye know – and I've been marching as a spy in Lee's army since it left Virginia," I told Chamberlain. "I captured this 'ere flag from the fleeing enemy."

Chamberlain squinted at me and furrowed his brow. Of all the things he might have expected to find on this hill in Pennsylvania, he very clearly was not expecting a man claiming to be a Yankee spy fresh from Bobby Lee's army and presenting him an Alabama flag as the spoils of war.

"I'm not really certain what to say," Chamberlain admitted, looking between my captors for guidance. "Do you have any papers supporting your claim?"

I smiled and gave him a wink. "No, sir, I'm afraid I do not. In the spy business, we've found it's best not to tote papers around announcing our true purpose."

Chamberlain frowned at me.

"If I may, sir," I said.

"Yes, please," Chamberlain said, desperate for me to offer him a way out of this inconvenient mess I'd created for him.

"Perhaps you might pass this problem along to someone else who better knows what to do with me. As I'm sure you understand, the information I have from General Lee's army could prove to be of a certain importance to General Meade, considering the proximity of the Army of Northern Virginia to our present location."

"Yes," Chamberlain said, still looking at me with uncertainty. "I can see how information from the rebel army might be useful."

"Perhaps one or two of your men might escort me to whichever general is nearest to our present location and in command of the field," I said. "Most of 'em know me and can vouch for me."

Chamberlain's brow relaxed a bit and he gave me a slight nod. I knew now that I was safe. It could have gone either way. If Chamberlain were the overly suspicious type, or just a blood-thirsty maniac, he might well have had me shot on the spot. But I'd bluffed my way through it. Of course, it wasn't entirely a bluff. I had, after all, saved Lincoln and it was true, too, that I'd worked for Pinkerton at the start of the war and served the Union as a spy. In fact, I suppose the argument could be made that I was simply resuming my former duties. For that matter, if you carried the argument far enough along its natural course, one might make the case that I had never abandoned my former duties and had, all this time, been spying for the Union and had just now finally turned up to report. However the argument went, all that mattered to me was that no one shot me.

"Yes," Chamberlain said. "I think that would be appropriate." He looked around and found the man he was looking for, calling to him to get his attention. "Sergeant! Sergeant, please come here. This man was captured among the rebels. He claims that he is a spy for the Union and has information for General Meade. I want you to pick two men to go with you, and escort this man to General Sickles. Allow him to take his flag, there, and he can present that to the general."

Now I swallowed hard. "Dan Sickles, eh? Isn't there a general nearer to us than Sickles?" I asked.

"General Sickles," Chamberlain repeated.

It would take a good bit more skill at bluffing than even I possessed to convince Dan Sickles not to shoot me on sight, but my immediate danger now was that Oates would pick up a couple fresh regiments and charge back up the hill, beaten though he was. My immediate desire was to get away from the shooting, and I trusted to Providence that I would find a way to avoid a confrontation with Dan Sickles. Providence, of course, would provide.

The sergeant was wary of me, but the privates were decent enough now that Chamberlain had acquiesced to send me up the chain of command, and thankfully they stopped jabbing me with their bayonets as we marched back up the hill to the summit of Little Round Top.

Though the hill was difficult enough to walk up in places, it was nothing like the exhausting climb up Round Top. Chamberlain's Yankee privates were as spent as I was, and the pace we set was not particularly difficult, though we moved through the woods and to the bald summit of Little Round Top too fast for my liking. I needed time to catch my breath and to think of some way of avoiding disaster, for when my escorts got me up to Devil Dan Sickles, I could expect nothing good to come from that interview.

As we came out of the woods at the top of the hill, I now had a new vision of the battle and how it had progressed in the ninety minutes or so since we had last seen it from the height of Round Top.

Though we had felt entirely alone fighting against the Twentieth Maine in the woods of Little Round Top, I could now see that there were other Confederates who had also attacked and been in the woods on that hill with us. Like Oates' men, they'd been beaten down the hillside to the area of the large boulders known forever as Devil's Den. Rebel sharpshooters down among those boulders were still sending Minie balls up into the Federal ranks, and the Yankees were returning fire.

On the western slope of Little Round Top, the cleared face of it, lines of Confederates were still trying to advance up the hill among the boulders and stumps, and Yankees were pushed well down the slope attempting to forestall their advance.

My escort and I kept well back from the front lines, but all around us was activity as reinforcements and stretcher bearers with wounded and men bearing cases of ammunition rushed about. Farther down the field, about half a mile along Cemetery Ridge, I could see that McLaws' men had pushed into the Peach Orchard where I'd last seen Sickles and dislodged the Yankees there. It had every appearance of having been a rout of the Third Corps in the Peach Orchard.

I could not see much of the detail of the battle taking place down in the Wheat Field or the surrounding woods, but the noise was such that I could tell it was damned hot business and death was being delivered in gruesome fashion. Frequently we heard the whistle of incoming artillery, and my escort and I would pause to duck our heads before moving on. As the crow flies, Devil Dan Sickles was not even a full mile from our starting point on Little Round Top, but we could not move in a straight line, and the terrain was not convenient for walking. I delayed at every opportunity – stumbling and pausing to squeeze my ankle as if I'd turned it, stopping to look out across the field as a fresh barrage of artillery was sent flying one way or another, standing to take a drink from my borrowed canteen. I was in no hurry to get in front of that maniac Sickles and have me ordered shot or hung or whatever disaster he'd have in mind for me.

The field below us was ever changing. Even as we passed off of Little Round Top and began walking the crest of Cemetery Ridge, I could see Federals of Sickles' Third Corps retreating from the untenable position Sickles had marched them into earlier in the day. Below us, coming through the woods, Yankees were retreating into the creek – Plum Run – and Confederates were giving them the Rebel Yell as they pursued. Truly, it was a terrifying thing to be on this side of that Rebel Yell, even up on the crest of Cemetery Ridge and away from the fighting.

But Meade had men who were still not yet engaged in the battle, and reinforcements were marching past us to shore up the gaps on Cemetery Ridge left by Sickles' ill-advised advance into the Peach Orchard. And those boys in butternut were exhausted and low on ammunition. They must have felt that every time they shot a Yankee down two more came in to take his place – and their math would have been nearly correct.

I'll tell you something else, and I only know it because I'd switched sides in the middle of the battle. Hood's men and McLaw's men and all the other men assaulting the Union position, they all started the day with the belief that they could push forward against the Federals, shoot 'em up a bit and shake them loose from the hills. They all believed before the day was over the Federals would tuck tail and run, and they believed it because they'd seen it happen so many times. Certainly, it's true that the Third Corps retreated out of the Peach Orchard as a skeleton of what it had been at dawn, and those Yankee boys ran like everyone expected them to. But up here on the ridge, the only running I saw was from men running into the fray – Federal bluebellies running to secure their position and close up their ranks.

If Bobby Lee's vision of victory was determined on the Yankee army fleeing from its ground at Gettysburg, and I believe that it was, I could have told him on that afternoon that there would be no victory on this field.

It wasn't Meade who lit the fire under the Yankees. As a general, Meade's only use was in being so indecisive that his subordinates were forced to make his decisions for him, and he was lucky to have one or two subordinates who were smart enough to make good decisions.

Perhaps, instead of being well-led, it was pride that drove them Yanks forward.

Before, but especially after Chancellorsville, their own newspapermen were ridiculing the Army of the Potomac as cowards who knew only how to run and not how to fight. But here they were, making good use of their inside lines and rushing forward instead of back. They had a confidence I'd never seen when Little Mac was in charge back when they strutted about just fine until someone started shooting at them. Excluding the Third Corps that had been destroyed because Sickles was a fool, the Yankees all around appeared to conduct themselves with an air of determination.

As I realized what was taking place around me, I turned to look at my escorts. They'd fought just as hard as Oates' men over on Little Round Top. They taken our charges and charged in return. They'd come at us with bayonets – a hard enough thing for any man to do. And it had been Billy Oates' Alabamians who had been the ones to fall head over ass back down the mountainside. Hood's Division, Law's brigade – the sons of Texas and Alabama and Georgia – these were the best fighting men the Confederacy had, and as I considered it, I began to realize that I'd not just seen them fall back, but I'd seen them get whipped.

It had not yet reached its conclusion, but I could already see that the day was lost to the Confederacy. I wondered if Lee had men enough to win the battle on the morrow.

All of this I noted as a casual observer with a professional eye. But I had concerns of a personal nature that were more pressing. There was no wondering what greeting I would receive from Devil Dan, and before my escort got me to him, I had to find some way to save myself.

"Y'all boys are from Maine?" I asked my escort.

"That's right," said the suspicious sergeant.

"What corps are ye in?"

"Fifth Corps," the sergeant said.

"So why would ye're colonel be sending me to Dan Sickles?" It was a question I was asking more to myself than to my escort, for no sergeant can ever say why a colonel has done one thing or another. I ran through my memory of the hierarchy of the Army of the Potomac. It had been some time since I'd been with the Federal army, and the way Lincoln changed commanding generals it was impossible to say who had been moved to which brigade, division or corps. But my recollection was that Meade hisself was formerly the commanding general of the Fifth Corps, and Meade having just been promoted to command of the entire army, there must be some new man in charge of the Fifth Corps. "Who's in charge of the Fifth Corps these days?" I asked.

"General Sykes," the sergeant said.

"Oh!" I exclaimed, satisfied that I now had my answer. "Tardy George!"

Sykes' division of regular army infantry at times – such as at Gaines' Mill – distinguished itself as a brave and effective fighting unit, but anyone who met Tardy George Sykes would know it was due entirely to their own ingenuity and not that of their commander. Like so many others in the Union army, Tardy George – some folks called him Slow Trot – was neither a good general nor a bad general. He was just a general. I believe Sam Grant once referred to him as "lackluster," and that about summed up Tardy George. He just existed as a general in the army and nobody much cared whether he came or went.

As I realized what had transpired during my brief meeting with the Maine colonel, I was forced into a grudging appreciation for Chamberlain. Chamberlain understood that if I did indeed have valuable information for Meade, it would take Tardy George days to work up the initiative to get me in front of Meade. So rather than send me to his own corps commander, he was sending me to the closest man he thought capable of making use of me. What Chamberlain lacked was not good sense, but a complete understanding of the entirety of the circumstances. Yes, Tardy George could not be relied upon to make a quick and judicious decision, but Devil Dan – even on this momentous day – was more interested in doing honor to his marriage bed by gut-shooting the man who'd defiled it.

As we advanced along the crest of Cemetery Ridge, the artillery from behind Pitzer's Woods was getting thicker and the activity of the Union men was also picking up. We came to an east-west running road that traveled from the Emmitsburg Road, through the Wheat Field, crossed up and over Cemetery Ridge where we were and connected to the Tanneytown Road on the east of Cemetery Ridge. The Yankees were pushing men down the road at the run, rushing them to get to the hole opened up in the line where the Third Corps had recently been.

With cannon shot falling all around us and bluebellies running about, the sergeant decided it would be better to keep me in a place and go off on his own to locate the general. He told the privates to stay with me.

He walked a few paces away and found an officer engaged in directing the reserve troops down the road and to the front line.

"Point me to the command of the Third Corps," I heard the sergeant shout to the officer over the din of the blasting cannon and the horses toting carts and the men running every which way.

The officer stopped what he was doing to stare aghast at the sergeant.

"There is no command of the Third Corps," he said, and for a moment I thought that officer might dissolve into tears. "Where in hell have you been?"

The sergeant lamely pointed to the south, to the direction of Little Round Top. "I've been on the left," he said.

The officer shook his head. "There is no Third Corps," he said. "The entire corps is gone, decimated, destroyed. They were caught among the peach trees and the rebels rolled over them. They're all gone."

The sergeant looked up the road toward the Peach Orchard, disbelief showing on his face. "The entire Third Corps is gone?" he asked.

A group of three men walking past us caught my attention. They were heading to the rear, moving slow, leaning on one another. One of them, the one on the right, had a bloody shirt tied around his head, covering a wound. The man on the left of the group was limping on a leg that had blood stains running down from a hole in his thigh. He was using his musket as a crutch. The man in the middle had his arms draped around the shoulders of the other two men. His hip had been shot away so that one leg simply dangled. The men on either side of him were supporting his weight, holding his arms around their shoulders. I wasn't even sure he was still alive. As I looked, I realized that there were hundreds of them, limping, staggering, stumbling – all making the trek back to the rear to seek out an ambulance or a stretcher or just a place in the shade away from the heat where they could die with some bit of comfort. Their faces bore the hollow look of corpses. Not a man among them passing by us was whole – every man was covered in blood, most with visible, ghastly wounds. Whatever McLaws had wrought on the Third Corps must have been devastating.

But passing them in the other direction, going to the front, were the fresh men full of determination, the men whose pride would not allow the Confederates to advance.

"Who's in charge of the field?" the sergeant asked. "Is General Sickles present?"

The officer shrugged his ignorance.

As if in answer to the question, though, a team of stretcher bearers were now coming by. What caught my attention was the man on the stretcher, with a lit cigar clutched in his teeth and he was waving his hat to the crushed men all around him.

He looked a damn fool, but then I realized who the damn fool was just about the time his eyes fell on me.

"You!" he shouted at me, and he actually rolled off his stretcher, attempting to stand on a leg that had been shattered by a cannon ball and would no longer support him. He fell on his face in the dirt. "You!" he shouted at me again, raising himself up off the ground and he followed it up with a string of expletives and unintelligible oaths, so that the privates holding me captive became uncomfortable and began shifting about on their feet.

There was an entire retinue of men following Sickles' stretcher bearers, his staff officers I suppose, and rather than attempting to make sense of why he was gibbering on, they busied themselves with trying to get him calmed down and back on the stretcher.

The man we sought, Devil Dan Sickles, was there on the ground in front of us shouting about someone getting his sword and vowing murder.

No one paid heed to the ravings of the maimed lunatic, and they soon had Sickles back on the stretcher, and were toting him away while he continued to demand his sword and demand satisfaction for his tarnished marriage bed. My guess is they all assumed he was delirious and thinking of poor Phil Key.

But the commotion had garnered the attention of a group of mounted men who now turned their horses in our direction. In the middle of the group of horsemen I saw a familiar face – the thick moustache, the long chin beard, the prominent nose, the searching eyes. Oh, I could have wept with joy having seen the maimed Dan Sickles carried off the field on a stretcher and then seeing my deliverance riding up to me with a smile on his face.

Providence provides.

Win Hancock reined in his horse and dismounted right in front of me.

Hancock exclaimed, "My Lord, Ol' Speedy – I did not expect to see you in this place and on this day!" And do ye know, he grabbed me up in an embrace like we were the best of chums. That put my suspicious sergeant and the two privates in my escort at ease.

"Win, I've brought you a gift from the fighting," I said, and I handed him the Alabama flag. "Took it off some of the men of Longstreet's First Corps on that hill down to our south."

Hancock looked over his shoulder at Little Round Top.

"Are we holding on our left?" he asked.

"Oh, aye, your Maine boys chased them rebels right off the hill. You can be proud of their service today."

Despite his fondness for me, General Win Hancock was one of the few truly intelligent generals in the Army of the Potomac, and the thing I liked best about Hancock was that he never once attempted to force me into the death. Even Old Peter, who was the closest thing I had to a friend in either army, had sent me forward more times than I cared to remember. But Win Hancock never pointed to an entrenched army and said, "Speedy, go and make a charge at those fellows and see if they are able to shoot you dead."

I'd known Hancock since Little Mac first started organizing the Army of the Potomac early in '61. At the time, Hancock was the army's quartermaster general. Working for Pinkerton, I had little enough to do most of the time, and so I found myself frequently going down to the quartermaster to secure various supplies to make army life more pleasant for me and Pinkerton.

Win was good enough to give the commander of special services and his major a couple of nice walled, canvas tents. We never wanted for fresh beef, and one evening when I had a hankering for cathead biscuits and sausage gravy, Win provided a cast iron skillet of the size necessary to feed my appetite, he came up with a quantity of lard and flour, buttermilk and even sausage so I could make a decent gravy. You couldn't find a good plate of biscuits and gravy in the entire Union army, not like you could find at home in the South, and I was not above making my own if I had to.

Win stood around chatting while I cooked, and he helped me dispose of the evidence, and after that Win and I had biscuits and gravy together nearly every Tuesday night until the army left camp and started for Manassass.

So if he hugged me like a brother, I suppose I shouldn't have been too surprised, for it's hard not to feel a close connection to a man who's made you cathead biscuits once a week for some number of months. And, you'll know too that Hancock and Reynolds were good pals, and with Reynolds being killed on the first day, I suppose Hancock was glad to see a friend alive.

But now Win's attention was on the battle in front of us.

"It's touch and go here," Hancock said. "That damned maniac Sickles has extended our lines too far forward, though I'll confess he did it in grand style. But now the entire Third Corps has been knocked backwards, and I'm trying to plug this gap before your Southern friends across the valley there split this army in two."

Hancock had little use for Sickles or the rest of the politician generals. Hancock was a graduate of the Military Academy and a professional soldier, and unlike the politicians, he knew his business.

"So what has brought you to the front? Still engaged in special services?"

"Oh, aye, Win, still spying for Lincoln."

And just like that, I found myself again attached to the Army of the Potomac. I'd fled the war, deserted if you want to call it that, and come here to this tiny town in Pennsylvania in the hopes of escaping the war, and in the course of a day found myself again fighting not just in one army but in the other as well.

Now Hancock got down to business. He turned my Alabama flag over to one of his staff officers and made one of his men go and find me an officer's coat so I didn't get shot as a straggler or a rebel. He also had someone scare up a revolver for me, just in case our lines were overrun and I had to defend myself. And in a few moments he got the best information I could provide.

You'll wonder how a man goes from fighting with one army to providing the other army information about the first and keeps his conscience clean, but I can tell you I've never had any qualms about it. So long as I was not dead or starving in an infested prison, my conscience never troubled me. Ye see, I didn't start this war, nor did I have any care to be in it, and if I was going to be forever forced back into the fray, my only concern was seeing myself safely out when it was over. Lincoln and Davis, Bobby Lee and Meade – they were the architects of all this death and mayhem, and Ol' Speedy just wanted to be shed of it.

So if my safety and well being depended upon telling Hancock what I knew of Bobby Lee's army – or at least some of what I knew – then that caused me no pangs of regret.

Besides, it was nothing he wouldn't know soon enough, anyway. Too many rebels had been taken prisoner in the fighting all along the line, and prisoners were always questioned as to what brigade they were in, and that information was always passed along to the commanding generals.

I gave Hancock the disposition of Lee's army – from Lee's right to left, Hood and McLaws, Anderson and Pender, Rodes in the town with Early and Johnson wrapping around Meade's right flank on Cemetery and Culp's hills. I gave him my best estimates of the size of Lee's army – employing my old trick during my days of spying for Pinkerton of doubling the size of some regiments and adding an extra ten thousand men here and there. By the time I was done, Hancock was convinced he was facing an army nearly twice the size of the actual Army of Northern Virginia. I found it surprising that Hancock had almost no intelligence to make him doubt the troop counts I provided. Meade had come hunting Lee in Pennsylvania without any idea of the consistency of his prey.

More regiments were coming forward in columns to plug the hole Sickles had left in the center of the Union line. Directly in front of us a regiment of Irish Catholics received absolution from a priest who served as their chaplain, and seeing those sons of Erin in their green coats and with their green flag, I was reminded of my old company from Mexico – the Jasper Greens of Savannah who only did battle with a bunch of mountain boys from Marietta on the deck of steamer. I wondered if these Yankee Irishmen were as prone to drinking as the Southern version.

After getting me a blue coat, one of Hancock's men also found a horse that had lost its rider, and I mounted up with Win and the rest of his staff. We occasionally were threatened by a stray cannonball, but the fighting was taking place forward of our position, and I felt as safe as I had on Marye's Heights where I'd watched the Federal bluebellies destroy themselves against the entrenched Confederates overlooking Fredericksburg.

Wounded and broken men were passing us in retreat, but the regiments and brigades coming up in support were filled with the confidence and pride I had seen in the men from the Twentieth Maine and those positioned all along Little Round Top and Cemetery Ridge. These were also fresh men. They'd come up in reserve in the night and had brief rest. They'd not seen any of the fighting of the previous day, nor had they been involved when Sickles and the Third Corps were destroyed. Aye, these were fresh Yankee troops moving forward against Confederates who had marched through the night and all through the morning and had already been engaged in heavy fighting to dislodge Sickles.

From our vantage point, we could see Barksdale's charge give way at the Plum Run line, and though the Union losses in killed, captured and wounded were severe, as the sun got lower on the horizon to touch the tops of the mountains to the west, it became obvious that the Southern engine was running out of steam.

Perhaps if Pickett had been forward and engaged or if Early had attacked Culp's Hill, and thus prevented Hancock from bringing fresh troops to Meade's center. Perhaps if Oates and I had gotten artillery to the summit of Round Top or had full canteens to keep his men moving so that we might have beat Chamberlain to Little Round top. Perhaps if a dozen little things or a couple big things had gone differently. But in the end, Longstreet didn't have the troops he needed to knock the Yankees off the ridge, and the Yankees – suffering from poor leadership, though they were – had men to spare. Those men, too, had something to prove, and Gettysburg was the ground where they intended to prove it.

As the Army of Northern Virginia broke itself against the line formed along Plum Run – the line Sickles should have held to begin with rather than advancing into the Peach Orchard – I recalled the first time I rode up the Emmitsburg Road into Gettysburg – less than a month ago, though now it seemed like a lifetime ago. I recalled looking at the two big hills to the south, the ridge running from the two hills to the north and connecting with Cemetery Hill. I recalled thinking at the time that it was good ground to hold, good ground to defend. As Meade proved, even an incompetent commander could win a battle on the right piece of property, and anyone interested in studying how battles are won and lost should bear in mind that the property where Meade won on the Second and Third days of July, 1863 was ground chosen for him by John Reynolds on the First of July of '63. If you're looking for the victor at Gettysburg, you'd be misplaced in naming Meade. Reynolds, dead though he was, rushed to Gettysburg, held off the Confederate Army and told his men what ground to hold. Reynolds picked the spot and all Meade did was not abandon it.

But anyone interested in surviving a war should bear in mind that Reynolds – who did his duty and saved Lincoln's Union – was dead. I, on the other hand, was already formulating a plan for escaping Gettysburg.

As the battle fizzled in front of us, it heated up to the north. At Cemetery Hill and Culp's Hill we could hear the guns blaring as Ewell finally engaged the enemy in his front. I witnessed none of it, and can offer no opinion beyond what can be read in the history books. But I'll say that if Ewell and Early had attacked in concert with Longstreet – as Lee had wanted in his ordered echelon attack – I cannot understand how they could not have penetrated the Union line at Meade's right. Many of those reinforcements that Meade and Hancock pushed to the south to defend Little Round Top and to plug the hole left by Sickles in Meade's center came from Culp's Hill. The Federal line there was thin enough that Ewell and Early should have been able to press their advantage.

CHAPTER 17

"General Meade wants to move the army to the south, establish a defensive position at a place called Pipe Creek and wait for Lee to attack," Hancock said to me.

It was nearing midnight. I'd not slept for two days nor had I eaten anything since that morning when Sergeant Elmore had shared his breakfast with me. I'd hoped that some officer in Hancock's staff would light a campfire and cook us up some supper, but none of them seemed to have any matches. So with a rumbling belly, I followed Hancock around as he issued orders, shored up Meade's weak center, pushed fresh reinforcements hither and thither, and I stood about grateful for my health as Win received reports of Union losses.

The losses were terrific. Killed and wounded from one end of Meade's line to the other, Hancock believed, totaled more than nine thousand men.

"We lost another nine thousand yesterday," Hancock said to me. "Nearly twenty thousand men killed or wounded, and beyond that are some unknown number of captured. We arrived here with eighty thousand, Speed, and we are now down to less than sixty thousand. And based on the numbers you have provided me, we could well be facing an Army of Northern Virginia as strong as seventy thousand, depending on their casualties."

Oh, aye, if Lee had ever had seventy thousand men he'd already have occupied Washington D.C. Based on all I'd seen of his losses on the first and second days of the battle, I estimated Lee's army to be something less than forty thousand. Hancock didn't know it because I'd lied about Lee's numbers, but the Federals still had a massive advantage in numbers of men.

And now Meade was calling a council of war in the hopes of getting permission from his subordinates to withdraw. Only the

Union generals were so adept at retreating on the cusp of victory.

But for my plan to succeed, I needed George Gordon Meade and the Army of the Potomac to stand still and not move an inch.

What I reasoned after the sun went down on the second day of the battle was this: Lee had gotten the attack he wanted, the attack Longstreet had advised against, and he'd suffered terribly. Now Longstreet would make Lee see sense, and the Confederates would withdraw. They'd come from the mountains to the west. There was still strength enough in the Army of Northern Virginia – I believed – that it could salvage its Pennsylvania campaign. I knew Old Peter well enough to know his advice to Lee would be to fall back to the mountains at Cashtown and establish a defensive position. Lincoln and Halleck would demand that Meade press and attack – it was well known in the North as well as the South that Lincoln was desperate for a general who would attack. In no way would Lincoln accept dithering now. If Meade did not attack, Lincoln would replace him immediately with some general who would press the enemy. And then, in an entrenched position in those mountains at Cashtown, on good ground of their choosing, Lee and Longstreet could destroy the Army of the Potomac.

That is what I believed would happen. Never did I imagine after the brutal beating they took attacking such excellent ground – the beating I witnessed on Little Round Top and Cemetery Ridge – would Lee ever conceive another charge against Cemetery Ridge.

Assuming the Confederates would move west, I needed Meade to stay where he was for the next day. If he then pursued Lee west or if he moved closer to Washington D.C. to protect the capital, that didn't matter to me. I needed Meade to stay just one more day, because Jackson Speed was about to make his run to the east.

And so I fed Hancock the story I needed him to believe.

"Retreat to Pipe Creek?" I demanded, making out like I was incredulous at such a notion.

"Meade's chief of staff, Butterfield, he drew up the retreat orders earlier today before the battle began. There's a creek to the southeast, Pipe Creek. It's good ground to establish a defensive line. I believe that General Meade thinks we can better protect the capital from that position."

"B'God Win, ye've got the best ground I've ever seen right here. If ye want to fight a battle, hold this position. Ye saw for yourself how your army held it today."

Win let out a deep breath of frustration and shook his head sadly. "I agree with you, Speed."

"So convince Meade to stay," I said.

And on the spot, I came up with the lie that kept Meade at Gettysburg and destroyed the hopes of the Southern Nation. "I heard Lee and Longstreet talking last night, as they planned out today's battle. They agreed that if their assault failed, they would hold their position with a skeleton force while retreating back to the west, to Cashtown. Don't ye understand, Win, if Meade retreats, he'll expose his rear to Confederate attack. But if ye'll hold here, by morning Lee will start his withdrawal. Late in the morning you can attack Lee's position and find more than half his army gone. Destroy his rearguard, and then follow up his retreat and you can take Lee's rear. It's that easy, Win, but it will never happen if Meade retreats. If Lee see's Meade's ass end, he'll kick it for sure!"

In the dim light of the moon and the campfires dotting Cemetery Ridge, I could see the clockworks in Hancock's brain turning. What I said made sense to him.

"Come along, Speedy," Hancock said. "You come to this council of war and tell General Meade these things you've told me. Perhaps you can make him see sense." [60]

The small white house where Meade had set up his headquarters was behind Cemetery Ridge near the back side of Cemetery Hill and positioned close to both the Taneytown Road and the Baltimore Pike. I rode there with Hancock and his staff. Among those in the council of war, I recognized Slocum and Sedgwick, Howard and Sykes, Meade hisself, of course, but there were others there as well, and some of them I did not recognize. There were not much more than a dozen of us crowded into the room, and Hancock had me stand back in a corner of the room so that I was wedged back behind a table with a flickering candle on it.

Staff officers from all of the corps commanders were there, crowded around the house. The most senior of those officers pushed their way onto the tiny front porch and vied for position at the doorway hoping to hear what was happening. Others were farther back in the crowd, depending on word to spread back to them as to what was being discussed.

Hancock sat at a table, as did Sykes and Slocum. Butterfield also sat at the table, taking notes on what was said. Meade stood in the center of the room. A couple of generals sat on the ground. A wounded general, a man I did not recognize, reclined on a poorly constructed bed behind Meade.

"First I will say this," Meade said when all were gathered and the council opened, "I intend to govern the conduct of the Army of the Potomac by the decision made here tonight by this council of war."

Well, that – for Meade – was the most important part out of the way. Now, no matter how things fell out, Meade personally was absolved of responsibility. That's what comes of a president and a secretary of war inserting theirselves into the conduct of the war as Lincoln and Halleck had: – the generals are less interested in achieving victory on a field as they are in abdicating responsibility so as to avoid the wrath of their political masters.

You notice, never did Lee call together his subordinates and say to them, "Whatever happens next ain't my responsibility, no y'all tell me what to do." No, for better or worse, Lee was his own master and Davis stayed pretty well out of his way. That's not to say Davis still couldn't interfere and dash Lee's hopes – as he was about to do.

Interestingly, the biggest fear any of the Yankee generals had was that Lee would make a flanking movement to the south. They feared that Lee would either attack into their flank or, once between Meade and Washington D.C. establish a defensive position and force Meade to attack. One man among them in particular, perhaps it was John Newton, commanding the First Corps, was particularly concerned about this possibility. You'll note, their biggest fear was precisely the plan that Old Peter had urged Lee to adopt.

Slocum was adamant. "We must stay and fight," he said.

"The Army of the Potomac has already retreated too much," Win Hancock said. "I am in agreement with General Slocum that we must stand our ground."

I noted that the wounded man on the bed had fallen asleep, and I considered it an excellent option. By now, exhaustion had completely overcome me. But I knew that I was too near the death and must keep myself awake and my wits sharp long enough to get clear of Gettysburg, and for my plan of personal salvation to succeed, I must now convince Meade that his army needed to remain here.

The council of war was prolonged a bit when a cavalryman came in with some captured letters that indicated that Lee would not be receiving support from Beauregard. I was not aware of it then, but I've come to understand sense that Lee's invasion plans included a plan for PGT Beauregard to come north with whatever men could be found to make it appear that two armies were invading. Lee's idea was that a second army would force Meade to split the Army of the Potomac and in so doing make the Army of the Potomac more vulnerable.

The dispatches were first given to Butterfield who handed them to Meade. While Meade read, Butterfield summarized the contents of the dispatches.

"It seems that General Lee had intended for a second army to invade, and the information contained within these dispatches shows that Mister Davis in Richmond has declined to send that army. General Lee's Army of Northern Virginia is all we may expect to find here in Pennsylvania."

Hancock now took his moment. "General Meade, I've brought with me an officer who I believe can provide information we may find valuable to this proceeding." It was always uncomfortable in those days to discuss spy work, for many of the officers in both armies were opposed to spies and viewed the work they did as unsavory and ungentlemanly. Lee would not tolerate a spy in his presence, making exceptions for me because, technically, I was on Longstreet's staff and an officer in the army. But the smart ones – Longstreet and Hancock among 'em – understood the value of information. Nevertheless, Hancock was reluctant to outright call me a spy. Also, Hancock never asked and I never said under whose orders I was conducting myself. I suppose, since Pinkerton had been dismissed from service to the Union, I was dismissed as well. The truth of it was, I'd now served in the Confederacy for more than a year and had not had any contact with any Yankee officers. But Hancock also knew, or was led by me to believe, that Lincoln and I were personal friends, and I suppose that and those cathead biscuits was all Hancock needed to know about me. "Major Speed here has conducted special services for the army for since its formation under General MacClellan, and he has information fresh from our enemy. Major Speed, please give an accounting to General Meade of the information you shared with me today."

Now all but the sleeping man on the bed turned their attention to the corner of the room where I was crammed in behind the candle, and I understood that this was my moment to convince Meade to stay put so that I might make my escape from the battle. So I gave them all my best Speedy grin and laid out my story.

"Well, sir, I happened to be in a position to overhear a conversation between generals Longstreet and Lee," I said. A couple of the men in the room who didn't know me sat up now, looking astonishment at each other. "Based on their discussion, and the results of today's fighting, it is my belief that in the morning Lee will begin his withdrawal west to Cashtown. He'll leave a rearguard as a ruse, attempting to make you hold your position, but if you attack in the late morning, you'll be able to smash through the rearguard and catch Lee in retreat."

Hancock was nodding. Slocum, I could tell, liked the idea. Sedgwick was licking his lips at the thought of attacking a retreating Southern army. I wasn't sure that I'd convinced all of the others, so I decided to push my proposal.

"Even if they've changed their minds, general, you lose nothing by holding your ground here. If Lee were to attempt another attack, the ground you hold here is ideal for fighting a defensive action."

Meade scoffed at the statement, rolling his eyes and shaking his head.

"This is no place to fight a battle," Meade said.

Well, his attitude astonished me. I could not have imagined better ground on which to fight a defensive action. Though his losses were staggering, Meade had won the day, and he didn't even seem to realize it. Lee had attacked him and he had held his ground. If Meade lost anything, it was only Sickles' salient that was lost. Had Sickles held his original position, Meade's losses would likely have been insignificant compared to the losses Lee would have suffered.

"But of course it is!" I countered. "B'God, man, you hold the high ground on either flank. You have interior lines through which you can rapidly support any point that Lee might threaten. Any attack Lee could make – either on the flanks or in your center – would require Lee to fight up hill against entrenched positions. How could you possibly believe this is not good ground? Even if Lee does not abandon his position and expose himself to you, all you have to do is just hold this spot against him. Why, any fool could win a battle on this ground."

Meade glared at me, furious that I would question him in such a way in front of his generals. But my speech had achieved its purpose. I could see all his corps commanders considering what I'd said. Hancock and Slocum both nodded agreement. And Meade, because he was unfit for the command he held, did not challenge me. Any self-respecting army commander would have had me in irons for talking to him in such a way.

"I propose we make a vote," Meade said. "General Butterfield will provide you with slips of paper."

And so they all wrote their choice on the slips of paper, and when Meade was done counting the votes he announced the council's decision. "Well, gentlemen, it is settled," he said. "We will remain here."

I could have shouted for joy. The council broke up pretty quick so that every commanding general could return to their men and prepare for the next day's fighting.

Now that Meade's army was staying put, I had only to extricate myself from Hancock's company and make a run to the east. In my calculations, I figured by now most of the cavalry would be close to the fighting, and I knew it would be a near run thing getting through the cavalry and beyond the shooting, but I believed that was my only opportunity now to escape the butchery.

Win and I walked outside the small house where Meade had his headquarters, and Hancock's staff officers were already mounted and holding our horses. Hancock and I mounted our horses, and I stepped mine over to his.

"Listen, Win, it's been a real treat seeing you, and I'm pleased I was able to provide some assistance here tonight. But I'm here on orders that come from higher up than you or even General Meade, and my duty is not yet done."

Hancock nodded. Back in '61, I'd allowed him to believe by my own implications that I was on good terms with Lincoln – and I suppose I was, having saved his life – and if I now implied that I was acting under direct orders from Lincoln, Hancock was prejudiced to believe that.

"I understand, Speed," he said, and he reached out his hand to give mine a shake. "I wish you Godspeed, Major, and I hope that we'll soon be reunited."

"Oh, aye, I'm sure we'll see each other soon enough."

CHAPTER 18

It would not do to try to ride a horse through the Yankee lines and past the Confederate lines, and so I knew I would soon have to go on foot. But for the moment I was so weary that I decided to ride the horse as far as I could.

I had no exact plan at this point, just a vague notion that if the armies would both stay in Gettysburg I would get away from this place, and because I thought it less likely that either army would move northeast, that was the direction I chose to go. I rode the horse over the back of Cemetery Ridge and down to the Taneytown Road, through a field and over to the Baltimore Pike, and there I found the Federals' teamsters and ammunition wagons. Some of the men were eating, some were sleeping, some were sitting around campfires wondering how long it would be before Bobby Lee's army chased the Yankees out of this place and they had to run for their lives.

The wagons' horse teams were all tied up, and I left my horse in among them.

As I passed through the teamsters, I soon found myself in among some of Slocum's troops holding Meade's right against Lee's left, and facing General Edward Johnson's division of Ewell's corps, Lee's army.

In the dark I was neither challenged nor questioned and I passed from the teamsters and into Slocum's lines with no more trouble than stumbling over branches and rocks as I picked out a path through the dark woods.

"Coming to fill your canteen, sir?" a private asked me when I ran into a group of about two dozen bluebellies.

"That's right, son. Have you got a creek up here?"

"There's a spring where some of the boys have been taking their canteens, sir," he replied. "Will we withdraw tonight, sir?"

"Withdraw?" I asked, and for a moment I was concerned that Meade had somehow changed his mind and word had already reached the flank.

"I hear wagons rolling down on the pike," he explained.

I stopped for a moment and listened myself, and indeed, I could hear the noise of wagons moving along the Baltimore Pike, and as I listened, they did indeed seem to be moving away to the southeast. But I'd just come through the teamsters, and there were no wagons even hitched to horses, much less wagons on the move. [61]

"I was just down among the teamsters with the ammunition trains," I told the private. "They were not moving, and I've attended the general's council of war where the decision was made to stay and fight on this ground. There will be no withdrawal, son."

"Thank God for that," the private said. "I'm fed up with running."

But we both stood there listening, even as the other men moved forward to the spring to fill their canteens.

"It does sound like wagons moving away from the field, though, doesn't it?" I said.

"Yes sir, it does," he said.

I suppose it was brought on by exhaustion or perhaps it was because I was consumed with fears of my own death and so I was given to such ideas, but then a morbid thought occurred to me: "Perhaps," I said, "it is the army of those who have died here today, advancing to the peace of Heaven."

My morbid imagination must have unnerved the private for he said, "Maybe so," in an uncertain tone and then started back through the woods to catch up with the others and fill his canteen.

I stood listening to the phantom army in retreat a while longer, and the noise filled me with dread. I had been down on the roads – both the Taneytown Road and the Baltimore Pike – and the wagons there were not moving. But clearly through the dark night I could hear the clear sounds of an army withdrawing from the field, and I was frozen to the spot for a long while, my morbid imagination churning my belly. But at last I shook off the exhaustion and these haunting noises.

"Speedy, son, you must leave this place," I said to myself, and I turned to follow the small company of men with their canteens.

As I moved through the woods, I could hear voices in front of me, and I followed them to the spring. There I found what I suppose may have been a unique feature in all of warfare: during the War of Northern Aggression, it was not uncommon when the fighting ceased for the men of the two armies to meet at a watering hole or a stream and converse. Down around Culp's Hill in the early morning hours of July 3, 1861, that watering hole was Spangler's Spring.

The men who'd spent the day shooting at one another, and expected to do it again in the morning, chatted pleasantly enough with each other – sharing jerky or tobacco, Yankees passing Northern newspapers across for Southern newspapers. Some of them teased each other. "We sho did whoop you boys today," one Southern braggart said, summoning forth howls and jeers.

"If you whooped us, how come you aren't occupying our hill?" a Yankee asked.

"We'll have it by noon tomorrow!" the Southern boy promised.

"So you think we'll fight tomorrow?" the Yankee asked, growing suddenly serious.

"We ain't goin' nowhere," the Southerner responded.

"Well, we aren't either," the Northerner promised.

"Then I guess it'll be a fight tomorrow," the Southerner said.

"We'll whoop you tomorrow then," the Yankee vowed.

I don't doubt that it was a scene repeated all over the battlefield that night in every place where two armies were close enough to talk. I'd witnessed the same thing at Fredericksburg, where the men sometimes called to one another across the Rappahannock during the long weeks of standoff.

Maybe the same thing occurred in Europe when two nations

went to war with each other, but I would expect language or hatred going back for generations would have prevented the exchange of pleasantries. But in Lincoln's war, where sometimes the opposing forces consisted of neighbors and cousins, and everyone spoke the same language, and many of the men could not articulate their reasons for fighting, opposing fighters frequently shared a smoke or a conversation or traded a bit of jerky for some coffee.

The officers didn't care for it. They feared that if the men befriended one another they might find it more difficult to shoot at each other the next day. I can say I never witnessed a man hesitate to shoot at the enemy on either side, and I fought in both the Eastern and Western theaters in a variety of armies. Of more concern, though, was the tendency for intelligence to be shared.

For instance, at Spangler's Spring I learned that J.E.B. Stuart – Lee's cavalry commander – and his men had at last returned to the Army of Northern Virginia. At last, Lee's army had its eyes and ears. The men of both armies also shared that neither army was moving from the field. By dawn, gossip would spread from Spangler's Spring to army headquarters and Lee and Meade both would know each other's secrets – or at least those secrets that were known to the men who conversed at watering holes. [62]

The men lingered, drinking from their canteens and then refilling them. All of them were carrying canteens back to the men in their companies, and they took their time to fill them.

I did not engage in the conversation. The men didn't talk to officers. The coat Hancock had found for me had the bars of a captain sewn into it, though officially I carried the rank of a major in the Federal army. Rather than talking with them, I stayed back a little ways, making as if I was filling my own canteen and listening to the gossip they shared.

I needed a plan. It wasn't as simple as just removing my coat, crossing to the other side of the spring and walking into the Confederate lines. I would be challenged coming back.

But as I considered my options, I decided that maybe it was that easy.

Gathered at Spangler's Spring there were two dozen Yankees filling canteens and at least that many rebels. They were paying no attention to me, so I took a few steps down the small stream created by the spring. They still weren't bothering to look at me, so I stepped back into the woods a step, then two steps, then I stepped behind a tree. As far as I could see in the moonlight, not one of them – not Jonny Reb or Billy Yank – had even glanced in my direction.

Quietly, I slid out of the Yankee captain's coat and laid it noiselessly onto the ground. Now I stepped back to the stream. Then I took a step over it. Then I took two steps closer to the group of men, bent over and let the water run into my canteen.

Now the rebels started to walk away, and I got in behind them, walking with them as if I had always been a member of their party. And just like that, a Yankee officer had disappeared inside a group of Southern water carriers.

We walked past the pickets who paid us no mind, and once behind the lines, the Confederates went with their load of canteens to join their regiment. For my part, I just kept walking through the woods. I passed through a place where there had been some fighting, for there were dead lying among the trees. I carefully picked my way past the corpses, but when I came upon one who was wearing a tattered gray coat, I decided to strip him of it. If I was going to be passing along behind the Confederate lines, I wanted to at least look like one of them.

In the span of just a few hours I had managed to pass first from one army into the next and then from that army back into the other. If it sounds like it was easy, well, it was and it wasn't. It was damned unnerving, I can say that. On Little Round Top, my life depended upon quick thinking, a likeness in the color of the Alabama flag and the Yankee coat and the hand of Providence giving Ol' Speedy more than a little help. If a cannonball had not skipped across the field of Gettysburg and smashed Devil Dan Sickles' leg to bits, your faithful biographer would likely have been tied to the violent end of a cannon and left with a great big hole where his rumbling bowels had once been. Sickles was that sort of vengeful bastard. There were fewer bullets flying by far when I rejoined the Confederacy in the early morning hours of July 3, but it would be difficult to overstate the fear every footfall held as I picked my way through the dark woods knowing that Yankee muskets behind me and Confederate muskets ahead of me might well fire into any noise that sounded like a man walking in the dark.

Johnson's men were on Culp's Hill down near the base, facing Slocum's men who were entrenched farther up the slope. As I pushed farther down the hill and behind Johnson's lines, I came down off of Culp's Hill and into a valley where a big creek ran. There was still some activity as stretcher bearers were bringing the wounded out of the woods. The stretcher bearers were moving north along the creek, and so I decided to follow their route. Soon I came to the place where a bridge on the Hanover Road crossed over the creek, and I went up the slope to the road.

On the Hanover Road I found Johnson's wagon train with ammunition and supplies. Though plenty of men were sleeping along the side of the road, enough men were moving about that no one took any interest in me. What I noticed was that here, where there should have been cannon, there was none. Ewell, on Lee's far left, seemed to have no artillery available to him. It was curious, and I wondered how Ewell would dislodge the Federals on Culp's Hill without it.

I had a decision to make. My first plan had been to simply walk off to the east, away from both armies. I'd convinced Meade to stay where he was, and east was my way to safety. But I had new cause for concern. If what the men at the spring said was true and Stuart was returned to the army, I had to worry about Confederate cavalry patrols, and they'd be looking for stragglers and especially deserters. A deserter might well be shot on sight.

I was exhausted and could not think straight. It now must have been some time between three and four o'clock in the morning. I'd not eaten, I'd not slept, I'd endured terrible physical labors in climbing Round Top not once but twice, I'd been engaged in what felt like the hottest action of the war, and now I just needed food and sleep.

Too exhausted to think or make a decision, I stood vacillating on the Hanover Road.

I tried to clear my head and weigh my options. East to Hanover would get me away from the fighting, but if I was arrested by cavalry from either army and could not bluff my way out of it, I could be shot as a deserter. But I could also not stay here in Gettysburg. If the fighting of the second day was bad, there was no doubt that the fighting of the third day would be worse. I could try to get back into the town. There the townsfolk believed me to be a Yankee officer. Surely they would hide me and keep me safe, and I knew that Lee would never bombard the town. There, in the town, I might find safety.

But if the fortunes of battle changed, the fighting might well come back into the town, and I could find myself yet again caught in the crossfire.

I'd found myself in this same predicament too many times, and there never was a good choice. What I knew for certain was that if the battle was raging in Gettysburg, then I needed to be away from that place. And so I decided that I would abandon the town, flee east as I had originally planned, and take my chances with the cavalry.

I began walking down the Hanover Road, past Johnson's trains and teamsters. At no point was I challenged, and in my stupor I was gaining in confidence. As I got east of the last of the wagons, I noticed some teamster had tied up his horses to a fence post off the road in a patch of grass, and owing almost entirely to my exhaustion, I decided I would take one of the horses and make my escape to the east faster than I could on foot.

I walked back and quiet as I could rummaged through some of the wagons until I found a blanket, saddle, bridle and tack stuffed in a corner of a wagon. It was all poor quality stuff, mostly cavalry gear that had been shot up or worn to bits. Some of the teamsters kept this sort of equipment where they could grab it quickly and ride off on one of their horses if a charge routed the soldiers in front of them and threatened to capture the wagon train. I wrapped all of it in the blanket to keep it quiet and then went out to where I'd seen the horses tied. With an eye constantly over my shoulder, I saddled a horse and mounted. In truth, I was amazed I'd managed to get atop the horse without being seen. Now I turned the horse east and started to ride to my salvation.

"Thief!" some damned fool behind me yelled. "He's stealing a horse! Deserter!"

Though I knew well enough the thief he was shouting about, I turned to look, and there I saw a teamster pointing at me. I put my heels into the horse's side and he began to gallop away down the Hanover Road. Being part of the wagon train, he was a big brute and slow as a mule. It wasn't the stealthy escape I'd planned, but the horse seemed willing enough to travel, and I believed my salvation was at hand. But as the horse galloped down the Hanover Road, I could see shadows in front of me. Cavalry! And they'd heard the commotion and were moving to block the road ahead.

"Halt there!" a man called from the group in front of me. The horse and I continued down the road with the mounted men growing larger by the second, and we were now close enough that I could see half a dozen riders with pistols leveled in my direction. "Halt or we will fire!" a man shouted.

I slowed and pulled on the rein to turn the horse, and as we started back down the Hanover Road toward the wagon train and back toward Gettysburg, I heard the explosion of their revolvers behind me as the cavalrymen fired a volley at me. The horse did not stumble and I knew I'd not been hit, and I thanked the Lord that the men were poor shots.

The wagons were too cramped along the road and the teamster's shouts had roused men all around the wagon trains. What had seemed an easy escape just moments ago had turned into a terrible debacle. Now the teamster was running forward, attempting to catch me and the horse with his bare hands, and other wagon drivers were joining him, their arms outstretched toward me as I rode back into the crowd they'd formed. They spooked the horse, and he started bucking and kicking.

In a moment, I felt and almighty crushing in my chest as the horse threw me and I landed sprawled on my back with all the air rushing out of me.

One of the teamsters was on top of me now, holding me, while another landed a punch in my face. And the cavalrymen who had shot were galloping down the road.

"Hold him!" some man shouted, and I felt myself being jerked from the ground and men had hold of my arms, bending them behind my back. I coughed and spat, trying to get my breath back.

Now the cavalry was on me, four men led by a lieutenant who was demanding to know what the hell I'd been thinking.

"Courier," I said through my coughing. I forced out the words despite the rough manner in which they were handling me. "General Longstreet."

"He's a damned horse thief!" one of the teamsters said.

"Just borrowing the horse," I wheezed.

The teamster, who had determined himself to be my prosecutor, said, "He's a deserter and a horse thief. You should shoot him dead now."

"I'm a courier for Longstreet," I said. "I have a message for the general."

"Longstreet ain't in that direction," the wise lieutenant noted.

I took as deep a breath as I could. I wondered if I'd broken ribs on my fall. "I'm all turned around in this town," I said. "I'm carrying a message for General Longstreet, and it's imperative I get to him."

"Why didn't you announce yourself as a courier when you rode toward our picket?" the wise lieutenant asked, and I was beginning to wonder if I wasn't facing two prosecutors and I hoped there wasn't an executioner in the lot, as well.

"You were shooting at me," I said. "I thought maybe you was Yankee cavalry. I told you, I'm all turned about. Will you please have these men release me? I can barely breathe."

The lieutenant, now dismounted, looked me over. "My God, have you been shot?" he asked.

"What?" I asked, panicked that one of their bullets had struck me. The lieutenant was looking at my chest, and I looked down to see what he'd seen. In the growing light of dawn, I realized that the coat I'd stolen was dark with blood over the left breast, except for the spot where a ball had torn away the fabric and there was a hole. Well, I knew I'd taken the coat off a dead man, but I did not realize the coat bore the evidence.

"It's nothing," I said. "I lost my coat and found this one. What's important now is that you men release me so that I can get my message to Longstreet."

The lieutenant plainly did not believe me, nor did the teamsters. But I could read in his face a bit of concern that if I was telling the truth and had an important message, he wasn't going to be the man to prevent that message from being delivered.

I did not know what was to happen to me next. Perhaps the prosecuting teamster was going to get his way and I would be shot. Probably the cavalry officer intended to arrest me as a deserter. My hope was that he'd put a horse under me and send me off to Longstreet, though I doubted that would happen.

But whatever was to come, I was saved – for the moment, at least – by a revolver fired into the air. You can check the history books and learn that the shooter was the Yankee Brigadier General John Geary. It was just a muffled shot in the distance, but it was undoubtedly a pistol shot we heard. [63]

For a moment we all turned our heads towards Culp's Hill from whence the shot had come. But a second later, it seemed that the whole hillside erupted as a thunderous volley was let loose. From our position on the Hanover Road we could see the muzzle flashes through the trees. They came from far enough up the hill, that I knew it was a Yankee volley being fired down at Johnson's men.

"Tarnation!" the cavalry lieutenant exclaimed. "It's starting early today!"

The teamsters now turned loose of me. I stumbled and nearly fell forward, but was caught by the lieutenant. He held me up. "The truth now," he said, and he looked directly into my face so that I could smell the tobacco on his breath. "Are you a deserter, or are you carrying a message for General Longstreet?"

I put on as convincing a face as I could muster. "I'm a member of Longstreet's staff," I said – and by opening with the truth, perhaps I made my case more convincing. "I'm Captain Jackson Speed. I'm carrying a message for the general, and it is imperative that I get that message to him."

The musketry on the hill behind us immediately became more fierce as the Rebs returned the volley. The lieutenant was indecisive.

"This road takes you back into the town – that direction," he said, pointing. "You'll find Longstreet is that way. If I see you on this road again today, behind our lines and moving east, I will shoot you dead. D'ye understand that?"

"I do," I said. "But I'm telling the truth. I'm on Longstreet's staff."

"Very well, then go and deliver your message." The lieutenant turned to get back on his horse.

"A horse?" I suggested, but he turned around with a snap and stared rage at me.

"Not on your life," he said.

With the first shots of the third day of battle erupting to my left and the blueness of dawn coming on, I turned west and started to walk down the Hanover Road back into the town of Gettysburg.

I'd received such a scare – first from the cavalry firing a volley at me and then from the teamsters snatching hold of me – that I made up my mind to just go and find Old Peter. My will to flee had left me. Longstreet had thrown me in at the death once in this damned battle, and I believed I could trust him not to do it again. I would go and watch the third day of Gettysburg from Longstreet's side, and come what may, I would stay with the Army of Northern Virginia until I found myself a better opportunity to escape.

CHAPTER 19

I wandered along the Hanover Road back toward Gettysburg, and I was as morose and dejected as I could be. I was sore in my ribs and my face ached and my limbs were stiff and exhausted, I was scared beyond reason. With each step I took the fighting seemed to be getting more intense behind me up on Culp's Hill, and if I hadn't been so worn out, I'd have run down the Hanover Road just to get more distance between me and that fighting.

I suppose there were stragglers along the road, more of Ewell's wagon trains, the trash that always has a way of piling up behind an army, perhaps there were pickets and cavalry even along this stretch of road that took me behind Ewell's lines on Cemetery Ridge. But I did not see any of it. I felt completely alone walking along that road, and when I recall the scene in my mind I have an image of myself in the dim light of the early morning walking a road as alone and deserted as I.

I had traversed the entirety of the battlefield – from the very far south end at Round Top and Little Round Top up Cemetery Ridge to Lee's farthest point on his left at Culp's Hill. I had endured some of the roughest fighting any man would see in this war on Little Round Top. I felt lost, and my unhappy predicament seemed to have no conclusion that did not involve me getting killed in this damned Yankee town.

"Why did I ever come here?" I asked myself out loud, and then I had to grin at myself when I remembered the reason. Like a damned fool, I'd come here for Jenny Rakestraw, and now my mind drifted to that beautiful frame. Even now, in my old age, I can say with honesty that I've never yet encountered a woman worth dying for, but I've come across a few that were worth enduring hardship for. Today, knowing that I survived Gettysburg, I can say Jenny Rakestraw was worth all I endured on her behalf. Smooth, flawless skin. Beautiful blonde locks that fell about her face in the sweetest curls a man ever saw. Those lovely green eyes, and those high sitting, pretty pert teats of hers. Oh, aye, I suppose even on the morning of July 3, 1863, I thought that Jenny Rakestraw was worthy of every bit of violence I'd endured for her. I felt my pace pick up a little. By the time I entered the town of Gettysburg, there was a spring returning to my step.

The month I'd spent with Jenny Rakestraw here in Gettysburg was one of the most pleasant times of my life, and certainly those were the best weeks I'd spent in this God forsaken, damnedable war.

I found the streets of Gettysburg nearly deserted. Here and there, families gathered on a front porch listening to the sounds of battle, their faces in the growing light of morning betraying their terror at the resumption of the guns to the south.

I paid no attention to the small groups of Gettysburg's citizens, though I might well have recognized and even known some of them. But I suspected that they would not recognize me, covered in dirt and another man's blood on his Confederate gray coat, and I supposed my face was probably black from the powder.

So even though my thoughts were on Jenny, I was startled when a woman called out my name from a front porch.

"Jackson! Oh my, Jackson! Is that you?"

I looked around and saw a woman dashing forward from the porch of a nearby brick house. I recognized her without fully seeing her in the gloom. She was wearing a homespun blouse and skirt, her clothes covered with a white apron with some sort of dark pattern on it. Her blonde curls were tied up in a bun, but I could tell it was Jenny Rakestraw rushing toward me.

She flung herself into me. When she wrapped her arms around me and squeezed me into a hug, I yelped with the pain.

"Jackson are you hurt?" she said, taking a step back and looking at me. "Oh my Lord! You've been shot!"

"No, no, Jenny," I said, and I slid my arms out of the coat and dropped it onto the dirt road. "I borrowed another man's coat," I told her. "He was no longer in need of it."

"But you're hurt?" she said, looking at the way I was holding myself.

"I took a tumble off a horse," I said. "I might have broke some ribs."

Jenny took me by the hand and started to lead me to the house where she'd come from.

"They've set up a hospital here," Jenny said. "Come in here."

I had no interest in arguing the point, and so I allowed Jenny to lead me up to the house where we pushed past other women who gawked at Jenny and me, I'm sure trying to understand why she had rushed forward to embrace a Confederate. We walked first into a parlor where men were laid out on a sofa and on the rug on the floor. There must have been nearly a dozen men, all with sheets over them, lying in the room. They were all bandaged. Some looked at us, others were asleep. One of the men, to me, looked suspiciously like he was beyond the need of the services of a makeshift hospital.

Candles were lit throughout the house. The place smelled foul. Death had happened here. Limbs had been sawn here. It was a grim place, and I wondered how a person could ever live here again. I wondered, too, if Jenny's home was as awful as this one, but I knew it must have been.

From the parlor we walked deeper into the house to a bedroom. Again, there were two men on the small bed – too small for the two of them, really. Both men were unconscious, and I realized that they both had also recently had a leg sawed off.

"Here," Jenny said, and she reached for a basket full of strips of cloth. "Take off your shirt and let me bandage your ribs."

As she turned to me, I realized that the there was no embroidered pattern on the front of her apron. It was just a plain white apron. Instead, what I had seen outside in the dim light of early morning were stains of blood on the apron. Before I took my shirt off, I untied the bow at the front of the apron, pulled its straps that were wrapped around her, and then lifted it over her head.

"I cannot bare to look at you wearing the stains of this battle," I said to her.

She looked at me with a sad face so that I thought she might cry, but it seemed she could muster no more tears.

Jenny began wrapping the bandages around my torso, wrapping them tightly and tying them off. "We have fresh water," she said. "I'll get you some water." She talked as she worked. "I was so worried about you, Jackson. I nursed the wounded as they brought them into my house. Then I went out to some hospital tents they set up in the road and nursed the wounded there. As more and more hospitals opened in tents or buildings, I kept moving from one to the next. Keep your arms in the air, Jackson, so I can finish this. I kept thinking I could find you. I kept thinking they would bring you to one of the hospitals. When the hospital I was working at filled – whether it was in a house or a tent – I would move to the next one hoping to find you. I thought if you were wounded on the field and I could find you that I would stay with you and take care of you. Protect you if the armies came back into the town. You were all I could think of, and my prayers that I would find you again are what kept me going."

She tied off another bandage. She was facing me, and now she slid her arms around me again, burying her face into my bare chest. But she did not squeeze, she just held me in her arms. Though it caused me pain, I'd held my arms in the air while she did her work, but now I dropped them and put them around Jenny, holding her with one arm across her shoulders and my other hand firmly in the small of her back.

"Where have you been?" she whispered into my chest.

I had to think to remember. "It's been so long since I slept," I said to her. "I got caught in the charge when the rebels entered the town. From there, I worked my way back toward Cashtown where I ran into Longstreet, and I spent the morning yesterday – God, was it just yesterday? – with Old Peter. Then I scouted south of town, down around Sugarloaf and through the wood."

"Pitzer's Woods," Jenny said.

"I think that's right," I said. "And when the charge was made, I was on Lee's right wing. I made the charge up Sugarloaf, then across to Little Round Top. I was caught up in a horrendous fight. I was captured by the Yankees, but convinced them that I was a Union spy. It was true enough, I suppose. And then I was with Hancock, and in Meade's council of war. And just an hour or two ago I crossed back across the lines and now I am here."

She kept her face pressed against my chest and moved her hands up to my shoulders where she could pull me a little tighter without causing me pain.

"I do not know that I can ever let you go," she said.

"I don't want you to," I said.

The hand that was in the small of her back, I worked it a little lower, giving her a squeeze, and with her face pressed against my chest, I could feel her cheeks rise as she smiled. "Oh, Jackson, you do not quit, do you?"

"I ain't dead, Jenny," I said. "Just banged up a bit."

"Not here," she said. "But I know a place."

Jenny handed me my shirt soiled with dirt and sweat and other men's blood so that I could put it back on. Then she took me by the hand again, leading me back through the rooms of this house turned hospital and out into the street. We could hear the guns on Culp's Hill and Cemetery Hill. We crossed the empty street and Jenny led me down another road. There, at the end of the block, were a number of walled canvas tents. No guard was nearby.

"Some rebel general set these up yesterday morning and no one has been back since then," Jenny explained. "I kept expecting them to establish a hospital here, but they never did."

She picked a tent and lifted the flap door and held it open for me to walk in.

A general's tent is a decent place as far as army lodgings go. The posts stand tall enough that I did not need to stoop once inside. A wood-framed cot had been set up and there was a blanket rolled up at the foot of the cot.

"Here," Jenny said, following me inside, and now we came

together in another embrace, she kissing my neck and me clawing at her rear and pulling her thigh so that her leg was pressed up against me. We kissed and collapsed onto the cot together, and I pulled at her blouse to get it over her head.

I could have wept tears of passion as I took her breasts in my hands, working those beautiful red nipples in between fingers until they were like tiny red cherries. Jenny moaned and cried out and took my head in her hands and kissed my forehead. There was a fervor there between us I'd not experienced in such a long time. It was as if I had slipped into some sort of trance, a surreal daze of ecstasy, so that everything beyond the canvas walls of the tent seemed to melt away from existence and there was only Jenny and me and our bodies and her breath and her hands and her pert teat in my hand and her beautiful round rump in the other. I reached up and pulled at her hair, pulling it out of the bun and allowing her golden hair to fall down around our faces so that it tickled my nose. Jenny laughed when I blew one of her curls out of my face. "If you didn't want it tickling your face, why'd you undo the bun?" she asked.

I smacked her rear and bit her lip, and our bodies rocked back and forth on a general's cot, and Jenny giggled and then gasped and I could no longer hear the music of the guns nor could I smell the death beyond the tent.

When I was living with Jenny in Richmond in the spring of '63, there had been an explosion at a munitions manufactory. The employees of the manufactory, all young Irish immigrant girls whose hands were small and worked well for loading bullets were burned in terrible fashion. Though I've seen maimed and broken and destroyed bodies on battlefields from the Atlantic to the Pacific, there was never a battlefield more gruesome than the human destruction wrought by that explosion. It's one thing to see a man who recently had a gun in his hand with his insides leaking out, but it's another thing entirely to see young girls burned and bloodied.

To cleanse my mind of the horror, I'd taken Jenny that night, hoping that the pleasure I found in her arms would alleviate the dreadfulness of what I'd witnessed. I suppose that for Jenny, that morning in the general's tent was very much the same sort of release.

She'd seen too much and needed to forget.

I was happy to do what I could to oblige.

Perhaps we fell asleep there on the cot, or maybe we were merely drowsing. Jenny, missing her blouse and skirt, was lying against my broken ribs. Other than my bandages, I wore nothing. One of us had pulled the general's blanket up over us. If we had fallen asleep, we were not asleep long for there was still only a blue light of dawn outside when the tent flap opened.

The figure entering the tent was in full uniform and wore a foraging cap. He did not see us in the darkness of the tent. He stepped to a camp desk in the corner of the tent opposite the cot. I felt Jenny's body stiffen when she realized we were not alone, but, smart girl that she was, she did not jump or make a noise.

The officer – for only officers in the Confederate army had full uniforms – rummaged through the camp desk, at last finding what he was looking for, and he turned and left the tent, leaving the flap open behind him. He stood outside the tent, and from his posture I could guess that he was attempting to read a paper he'd taken off the camp desk.

"Is that it or not?" I heard someone ask him.

"I can't make out any of the writing," the man outside the tent said. "It's too dark for me to read this."

"I'll get a candle from this house," the other man said.

I squeezed Jenny's hand to get her attention and then whispered to her, "Quickly, grab your blouse and go out the back of the tent."

Jenny brushed her lips against my cheek. "Come back to me," she said.

"I swear I will," I whispered back.

And now she quietly slid out from under the blanket, bent over to pick up her garments and crawled out of the tent flap in the back. I watched her as she went, taking one last look at her near-perfect backside, and I could have wept for I knew it would be the last time I saw it.

I reached over the side of the cot and snatched my trousers from the ground and slid them on, then I laid back on the cot and pulled the blanket back up over me. In a moment, I would be caught, but for just a few seconds longer I needed to rest.

I heard the men outside talking again, and I could see the flicker of candle light.

"This ain't it," one of the men said. "Glad I went and got a candle."

Now they were both coming into the tent, the candle light glowing bright against the canvas walls.

"What in God's name?" one of the men exclaimed, and I felt a crash as the man kicked the wooden frame of the cot. "Who the hell are you?"

I shot up off the cot like a madman.

"Kick a cot I'm lying on again," I raged, "and it will be the last thing you ever kick!"

I was playing a gambit. I'd seen enough of the man who entered the tent to know he was young, and the uniform he wore led me to believe he could not be more than a lieutenant. So I decided to try to bully, rather than bluff, my way out of this mess. Now, with the light of the candle giving me vision, I could see both men were just boys, and both were lieutenants.

"What is your name, son?" I demanded. "I'll have you digging latrines as a private before this war is over!"

Both of the boys withered in front of me, and I must have been a terrible sight. Ever since I was just a teen, I was a big man, tall and well built. I towered over these two lieutenants. My face was black with powder, my ribs were bandaged. I must have looked terrifying to them.

"We're getting papers from the general's desk," one of the lieutenants stuttered.

"At his request," the other added.

"Oh, aye, 'at his request,'" I mocked, and in the tiny confines of the tent I took a step toward them. I could be an intimidating sight when I wanted to be. "Did the general also request you disturb the captain sleeping on his cot? Did the general also request you kick a wounded man?" They could both plainly see the bandages on my torso. "A couple of damned couriers, I'll wager! Riding about on your damned horses! Where were the two of you yesterday when I was charging up that hill to the south and every Billy Yank in Pennsylvania was aiming his damned musket at me? Probably taking a nap, knowing how you couriers behave!"

The one holding the candle bristled at my accusations, but Ol' Speedy wasn't done yet. I made myself big, moving about in the tent, turning and bending over to grab my shirt, my belt and holster and my boots. Both lieutenants had to back up again to get away from me, and now they were pressed up against the canvas wall of the tent.

"I've not slept in two days," I thundered. "The general was good enough to let me use his tent and cot to try to catch a few minutes of sleep, knowing full well I'll be making another charge today, and you two come in here kicking hell out of my cot! If I did not have business at headquarters, I swear to God above that I would have you court-martialed and hung!"

And with my gun, belt, shirt and boots in a bundle in my arms, I walked through the open flap of the tent.

I did not stop until I was a couple of blocks farther along, and then I pulled on my boots and put on my shirt and my belt. I checked the gun to be sure it was loaded. After bullying those lieutenants, I was feeling a bit of confidence and thought maybe I'd shoot the next man who disturbed my rest.

I kept walking, going generally south and west out of town. Perhaps it was now five o'clock in the morning, perhaps even a bit later than that. The blue of the first morning light began to turn bright. The sun would soon be up. The guns on Cemetery Hill and Culp's Hill were still going. A full and fierce battle was being waged in the early morning on Lee's far left.

I walked out through the fields leading up toward the Seminary. I was going to find Longstreet and hoped that I would be able to watch whatever remained of the Battle of Gettysburg from his side. I knew Longstreet well enough to know that there was little chance he would take pity on me and tell me to go have a lie-down in his tent, but if I was lucky, he'd provide me with a horse and I could sleep in the saddle. Having gotten a brief taste of what it would be like to close my eyes and drift away, I was ready to do the thing officially, even if I had to do it from a saddle.

CHAPTER 20

I cannot recall the time, but it was still early enough. They say that the fighting on Culp's and Cemetery hills ended sometime around eleven o'clock that morning, and it was well before then. I'd wandered our lines near the Seminary, not far from Lee's headquarters, asking officers if they could point me to Longstreet. The sun was now rising, but a fog was hanging low in the valley between the two armies. When I did finally find Longstreet, he was surrounded by members of his staff and was looking through the trees on Seminary Ridge across the valley at Meade's army.

"The enemy holds a strong position," I heard Longstreet say to Mox Sorrel. "I wonder if we will be so fortunate as to have them press forward, as they did yesterday."

Longstreet handed his binoculars to Mox, and that's when the big, ruffled general saw me standing there in front of him.

"Howdy Speed," Old Peter said. He did not look surprised to see me, nor did he appear very enthusiastic to have the evidence before him that I'd survived the previous day's battle. "I don't mind telling you, I was concerned when I heard that you did not make the retreat with Colonel Oates yesterday. But I never lost hope nor confidence that you would soon reappear here at my side. If any man is capable of surviving, you are certainly that man."

Well, I was gratified to know Old Peter had been asking for me and spared a thought to my health. He'd lost thousands of men over the past two days, and I was gratified to be among those he gave specific consideration to.

Old Peter now turned his large frame in my direction and pointed his shovel beard at me. "Tell me, Captain Speed, how close were we yesterday?"

"Close, Pete," I said.

"What would have made the difference?" he asked.

"A regiment, maybe. When we went up the side of the shorter of the two hills, we overran the Yankee's positions. We lacked ammunition and men to finish the job. The Yanks retreated, but then they charged, coming at us with bayonets. Another regiment, more ammunition, it could have made the difference. The Yankees captured me, and I learned that they were entirely out of ammunition. If every man of ours on that hill would've had another round or two, we could've finished the job. Or if we'd had sufficient reinforcements to absorb their charge, we could've finished the job. As it was, we did not have enough of either."

Peter nodded but made no remark. I was not delivering news to him; he already knew how close we'd been and what would have made the difference. Then, "Captured, huh?"

"Yes, sir."

"But you managed to get away?"

"I did."

"And what can you tell me, having been behind our enemy's lines?"

"Meade is making good use of his interior lines yesterday. Well, not Meade, exactly. Win Hancock was the man making the decisions. He shifted troops effectively yesterday afternoon. When you broke Sickles in that Peach Orchard, Hancock moved men from Meade's right wing onto that ridge, over yonder. I can tell you, too, the Yankees ain't looking to run this time. They're a determined army."

"Because we're in a Northern state?"

"I think they're just tired of being referred to as cowards," I said.

Old Peter looked grim. Looking back on it now and knowing how it all turned out, Longstreet seemed to possess the clairvoyance to already know how the day would end.

"We pressed hard here on Meade's center," Longstreet told me. "We knocked the Third Corps out of that Peach Orchard and chased them to the creek, but reinforcements established a strong line at the creek and we did not penetrate. That would be Hancock's doing."

"I saw the reinforcements marching forward," I said.

"General Lee believes that the fighting on the flanks last night and this morning has forced Meade to weaken his center. He believes a direct assault on the center will dislodge our enemy from his position. General Pickett's division is being brought forward for the purpose of making that charge at Meade's center. Tell me, Captain Speed, what are your thoughts on that plan of battle?"

Well, my thought was that we should probably turn around and march back to Virginia and see if we couldn't get the politicians to work this out and end the war, but I doubted very much that either Lee or Meade or Jeff Davis or Abe Lincoln were going to agree with me.

"My thought, General Longstreet, is that I would very much like to have the Army of Northern Virginia occupying that ground over there and let Meade come at us."

Longstreet's big face broke into a smile, and I saw a gleam in his eye. He nodded and looked at Mox. "Captain Speed would make a fine army commander, don't you think, Mox?"

Sorrel slapped me on the shoulder. "I'm happy to have you back here with us, Speedy," Mox said. "Though I do not know that I would want the captain trading places with General Lee."

Mox and I were good chums and got along particularly well at the campfire, but I always wondered if he knew me too well.

"I'll need you, today, my old friend," Longstreet said, and they were the words I was desperate to hear.

"Oh, aye. I'm a bit tired, a bit banged up, but I'll be right here by your side," I said. I was about to add that I needed a horse and saddle, and if it wouldn't be too much to get a pillow, also, that would be appreciated.

Longstreet wagged his beard at me. "No. No. I lost too many officers yesterday, Speed. Our ranks are woefully lacking. I'll want you in the afternoon's attack."

I opened my mouth to make a protest, but at that moment a cheer went up among the nearby men, and I turned to see the commanding general riding his gray horse toward us.

I could have sobbed, and very nearly did. It was cruel in the extreme. I'd been battered and ill used by the Yankees on the previous day. Longstreet knew I had been engaged in the fighting on the First day and had been in hot action on the Second day – b'God I'd even been captured and escaped the enemy! – and still Old Peter – my friend! – was threatening to send me back into the death.

But now Lee was up, dismounting his horse to stand with Longstreet, and Mox and I stepped back.

"For God's sake, Mox, isn't there a piece of bacon in this army? I have not eaten in twenty-four hours."

"Come along, Speed, let's see if we can't get you some victuals."

"Mox, it's insanity that Peter would expect me to be engaged today," I said. "I've not slept. I've not eaten." I pulled my shirt out of my belt and lifted it to show him my bandaged torso. "For God's sake, Moxley, I've broken my damned ribs. Surely he cannot be serious. Besides, Pickett was not engaged yesterday. He's suffered no losses. If Longstreet is looking to fill holes in his ranks, Pickett has no holes that need to be filled. What of Hood's division?"

"Law is division commander now. Hood was injured yesterday," Mox said. "They are to hold our defensive line from the base of the hill to the Peach Orchard."

"That's where the holes are!" I said, reasoning that if I had to be used I would rather hold a defensive position than make a charge.

Mox smiled pity at me, but offered no more succor than that weak smile. "Speedy, I sympathize with you, honestly I do. But you know how Pete is about George. He's probably sending you to keep Pickett from getting lost on his way to the enemy. Let's get you some nourishment and maybe you can catch some sleep before the army is engaged. We still have some hours yet." [64]

We walked farther behind Seminary Ridge where we found some of the men gathered around campfires, and Moxley, following his nose, brought me to a fire where they were cooking up some beans and salt pork. The men around the campfire begrudgingly gave me a plate of beans and a spoon, and Mox sat with me while I ate.

"I'll confess to you, Speed, I'm a bit envious," Mox said while I ate. "I watched you go off with Hood yesterday, and I hear you come back this morning talking of being captured and escaping the enemy. And I'm jealous at the adventures you have. I cannot imagine how thrilling it must be to be you."

Over a mouthful of beans I told him, "You're welcome to take my place today." Mox only laughed as if I was joking.

I'd just finished eating the beans and pork and was thinking of now borrowing a blanket when Mox tapped me on my arm. "Pickett's here, we must go."

Indeed, a great commotion was being made over my shoulder, and when I turned to look I saw Pickett with his great golden locks of curly hair, looking prim and proper on his horse, riding up to the spot where Mox and I had left Lee and Longstreet.

The way Sorrel followed me around that morning, I believe to this day he intended to prevent me from slipping off to the rear. Together, we went back up to where the generals were gathered and found Lee and Longstreet to be engaged in conversation. Longstreet's attitude seemed to be hostile and Lee, always fatherly and forgiving with all his generals, accepted it.

"Great God!" Old Peter exclaimed, and bore the look of frustration of a man seeking to argue against a rock wall. "Look, General Lee, at the insurmountable difficulty between our line and that of the Yankees – the steep hills, the tiers of artillery, the fences, the heavy skirmish line. And then we'll have to fight their infantry against their batteries. Our men will have to charge into grapeshot! Look at the ground we'll have to charge over, nearly a mile of that open ground there!" Longstreet's big thick arm extended out to point at the valley between the two armies. "We will be facing canister and shrapnel!"

Lee did not look at the ground. Instead, he kept his eyes on Longstreet. The patient father with the petulant child. Lee smiled at his subordinate. "The enemy is there, General Longstreet, and I am going to strike him." [65]

Longstreet rolled his massive head around on his shoulders in frustration. He sighed heavily. Lee remained composed.

Those who witnessed it, even Pickett who would be asked to make that charge into the Yankee canister and would be shattered by it, always remembered the scene in the same way: Longstreet having a tantrum, Lee remaining patient and steadfast. And to a man, all the witnesses described it as such. But consider for a moment: Perhaps it was Lee who was having the childish tantrum, calm though it was, and Longstreet who offered the fatherly advice. Longstreet was, after all, the one who argued the correct position – and had been arguing the correct position since the first day of this battle.

Lee could not be moved from his decision: Charge and charge and charge again. But Lee was wrong. The charges were disastrous. Longstreet, even now, argued in favor of moving around the enemy's flank, and he was correct. Maneuvering was what Lee's army needed to do. The Yankees had to be dislodged from that ridge, and no charge would do that. If Lee's foray into Pennsylvania would find any success, he had to lure Meade off of that ridge and deceive him into a trap. It could be done – even now with the guns raging on Culp's Hill – it could still be done. But the child was refusing to budge, throwing a tantrum in his own way, and the father – who by rank must succumb to the wishes of the child – did the only thing left to him to do: Longstreet obeyed orders.

"General Pickett," he said, seeing George standing off to the side. "Are your men forward?"

Mox, who forever took care of details and that's what made him an excellent chief of staff, managed to find me not only a horse but also a clean shirt and coat. He gave me a purse full of bullets to go with the Yankee Colt revolver Hancock had supplied me with, and a full canteen, for which I was thankful.

"I've got a decent hat here for you, too," Sorrel said, holding up a gray cavalry hat. I removed my own brown slouch hat, the one that had seen me through so much, and examined it. Indeed, it was rough looking with stains and dirt and an unfortunate tear in the brim, but I replaced my cover with a grin.

"Mox, I've got an affinity for this old slouch hat."

"Suit yourself, Speed." Now Moxley unbuckled his belt and slid his sword and scabbard off of his belt. "I couldn't find a spare sword for you, but I thought you might take mine." He handed over the sword to me, and I drew it from the scabbard. I'd always preferred the slightly longer dragoon blade of the cavalry sword over the blade of the infantry officer – if I could keep my enemies an extra three inches away from me, so much the better – but it was a generous and compassionate offer from Sorrel, and I took the sword with gratitude. More times than I cared to remember, my father's old cavalry sword had saved my life, and if I was going to have to make this damned charge beside George Pickett, stinking of all that oil he put in his beard, then I didn't mind being as well armed as possible.

"It's a good sword, Moxley. Thank you for it."

I suppose Moxley was trying to make me feel the part – putting me in a fresh uniform, getting me a sword for my belt and plenty of ammunition for my revolver. Perhaps he thought if I was fitted out as an infantry officer, I would also act like an infantry officer. But the uniform and sword did nothing to qualm my rumbling belly, and having had the beans and salt pork, I knew it was not hunger that now disrupted my bowels. Fear had once again gripped me.

But my ability to flee was impeded – Mox kept close to me throughout the morning and gave me no opportunity to leave the army. I asked repeatedly if orders did not have to be taken to one location or another, but some other courier was always found. When I realized I had no field glasses with which to better view the enemy, Mox loaned me his own. At no point in the morning did Sorrel allow me beyond his reach. It seemed that if Longstreet wanted me to tend to Pickett during the charge, Moxley Sorrel understood that it would be left to him to tend to me prior to the charge.

Lee and Longstreet and Pickett rode the lines of Pickett's men, and the staffs of all three generals rode with them. At various points during the morning, particularly as the fog burned away with the daylight and the heat and humidity increased, Lee would stop and point to a specific spot on the horizon and issue orders to Longstreet. Often, the trees were so thick that we were forced to dismount and lead our horses through the woods. At other times, we would ride out in front of the woods, and as the fog burned away, when we did this we were within sight of the enemy across the way.

Perhaps if I'd had sleep at some point in the last two days I might have been successful at finding some way to escape Sorrel's watchful gaze, but I was too exhausted and too cloudy of mind to think thoroughly. And so sheepishly I followed the generals around on their inspection of the men and the battlefield.

We made a large group. At some point General A.P. Hill joined us. Two of his divisions – Heth's and Pender's, now under Pettigrew and Trimble – were to be attached to the First Corps to go with Pickett's division in making the charge.

With so many generals and their staffs riding about in front of the lines, each time the Yankee gunners saw us they would lob a cannonball in our direction. Those shots came to nothing, but for me those cannonballs seemed to give weight to Longstreet's warnings of canister. As the morning wore on and my part in this insane charge neared, each thunder of cannon from across the way made me wonder if that was the canon that would fire the grapeshot that would make me dissolve into a spray of bloody mist.

My one hope was in Longstreet – the same man who was sending me to an early grave. He had not yet given up his argument against the charge.

I believe now the guns on Culp's Hill had finally stopped. Johnson's fight on Lee's left had concluded. We could assume that it had not ended favorably for Johnson, for if it had, we'd see all of Meade's army fleeing directly at us. But there was no rout on the far end of Culp's Hill.

The noon sun was in the sky. The day was plenty warm, and I had by now unbuttoned the coat Mox had given to me.

"General Lee," Longstreet said. "With the two divisions of General Hill's Corps combined with Pickett's, I will have fifteen thousand men. Entrenched on that ridge there are at least forty thousand with batteries and interior lines from which they can draw reinforcements."

Longstreet hung his head and would not look directly at Lee. He sounded tired and defeated. "General, I have served in the army my entire life, have been a soldier from the ranks to the position I now hold. I have been in all kinds of engagements, from two or three soldiers to an entire corps. And I believe I am correct in saying that there was never fifteen thousand men who could successfully assault that ridge being held by forty thousand."

For two days, Longstreet had argued against assaulting the Union position. He'd made his objections as strenuously as he could, and each time Lee rejected his chief lieutenant's pleas. There was little fight left in Longstreet, but he believed so strongly against it, that he could not help but make a final objection. Even so, when Longstreet carried out the orders given him, there were those among Lee's generals who blamed Longstreet for the disaster.

"Sir, I believe if we were to make a flanking maneuver and draw the enemy out –"

But Lee cut him off.

"No," Lee said, and now the patient father, if that's the role Lee played, was out of patience. There was a bite of anger in his voice. "I am going to take them where they are, there on that ridge."

Lee now turned his horse to ride away, and I saw a fury on his face that I'd not ever seen before, leastways not toward Longstreet. "The attack must succeed," he said. [66]

Longstreet frowned and dropped his eyes to the ground, his head hung in resignation. But if Old Peter was dispirited, it was nothing to the way I felt.

A little while later I found myself on a rise behind the trees of Seminary Ridge. I was sitting my mount beside Longstreet. Mox Sorrel was a little ways behind us, still watching me.

"Do you see that large tree in the distance, the one shaped like an umbrella?" Longstreet asked me. I squinted at the spot where he pointed to. "That is your objective," Longstreet said. "You must keep General Pickett focused toward that tree. Do not allow him to wander. Keep him moving in the direction of his objective. When you cross the Emmitsburg Road you will find yourself in a swale and you should be protected from enemy fire there. When you reach the top of the slope, though, there is a fence. You must get through that fence as quickly as possible, and at that point it should be a charge at the double step. You must close that distance as quickly as possible to limit casualties. Break into a run and give 'em the old Rebel Yell. With luck, it will shake those Yankees loose." [67]

I listened to him, but I barely heard him. He was directing me to my death, and I could pay no attention to him.

"Peter, my ribs are sore as can be," I complained. "Perhaps I should retire to one of the hospital tents."

"Not now, Speedy," Longstreet said, frowning at me. "Now, I need you to guide George. You know how he can sometimes be."

I suppose I should have been flattered. Longstreet was sending along one of his favorites to keep a watchful eye and corrective hand on one of his favorites. Longstreet had known Pickett all the way back to West Point, and though most of us considered Pickett a laughable caricature of the – what was it Sorrel had called him? – "carpet knight," Longstreet thought highly of his division commander. But he knew that Pickett needed careful handling – why he thought I was the man to handle him, I'll never understand.

CHAPTER 21

A few famous notes went back and forth between Longstreet and the commander of the artillery, but I was no longer present when this took place. By this time, Longstreet and I had already gone to instruct Pickett in the attack, and Longstreet left me with George while he went back to the position from which he would command this unfolding disaster. [68]

Pickett's men were positioned in a point on Seminary Ridge that was well wooded and provided some cover from the view of the Federals on the opposite ridge. George and I stayed near the edge of the wood, waiting for the bombardment that was to begin at any moment. At some point I believe I fell asleep standing on my feet. But Pickett was in a rare state of excitement. He believed he had been gifted a wonderful opportunity for achieving glory, and I remember him telling me that he intended to dedicate his victory to "The love of my heart, the stars in my sky, my Sallie," and then he showed me a photograph of the woman who was to receive the honor of the dedication.

She was lovely, no doubt, and if I'd not been vacillating between desperate fear and extreme exhaustion, perhaps I would have admired her enough to start thinking about how I might get George to invite me over for Sunday supper some time, but I didn't even have a thought for a pretty woman at that point.

The giddy general at my side seemed unable to perceive what was so obvious to the rest of us – there would be no victory here today. Pickett's confidence, I believe, came from Lee. He assumed his commander infallible, and if Lee ordered the charge it was because Lee believed it would succeed.

Longstreet's chief of artillery, Colonel Alexander, rode up to see Pickett at about that time.

"What time is it, colonel?" I asked.

"It's half an hour past noon, Speed." Now he addressed George. "General, what are your thoughts on the assault against the ridge?"

Pickett, animated as hell, bounced up and down and swore that this was to be the finest charge of the war, that here on this field the South would win a victory that might well bring about the end of the war. Pickett overflowed with enthusiasm, swearing his men were fresh and eager for the fight.

Alexander took a look at the valley through which we were about to charge.

"I'll give you the best chance for success that I can, general," he said.

"You soften 'em up a bit, and we'll finish 'em off," Pickett promised.

Alexander nodded and rode back to his guns.

"It shall be a grand victory today, Captain Speed!" Pickett said to me. "The order of march has robbed me of distinction too many times, but finally today I'm to be given a glorious opportunity. I am glad you will be here with me to share in that glory!"

"Oh, George, stuff it," I said, my rage at being so unjustly treated by Longstreet finally boiling over. "We are marching to disaster, George. Any damned fool can see that. Them Yankees are entrenched, they are double our number plus another ten thousand, and with his interior lines, Meade can send ten thousand more if they are needed. And it's Win Hancock over on that ridge. Hancock the Superb, George. Do you think Hancock will allow us to knock him off that ridge?"

Pickett was aghast, and I believe he was going to slap me, or offer to arrest me or draw his sword and challenge me, but whatever he was going to say was lost, for just in front of us, an explosion erupted as Alexander's signal gun fired.

The explosion of the signal gun so caught me off guard that I dropped to my belly and burrowed my face into the dirt.

All through the woods behind me, Pickett's men, lying against the ground so that the Yankees would not see them moving about through the trees, gave a laugh.

"What's wrong, captain?" some fool called out. "Never heard a canon shoot before?"

Laughter rippled through the woods, but I ignored the men. I was too exhausted even for my pride. And do ye know, I was on the cusp of making one of the most disastrous charges in all of military history, but I wasn't nearly as scared as I might have expected. Oh, certainly, lying in the dirt my bowels were exploding and adding to the thunderous volley of the bombardment, but the fear that usually gripped me on the precipice of battle was not there in the way I might have expected. Instead, it had been replaced by an absolute rage – I was furious with Lee for refusing to pay heed to Old Peter's good advice; I was furious with Longstreet for insisting that I become George Pickett's nursemaid; I was furious with Pickett for being so inept that he needed someone to hold his hand to be able to find a big tree in an open field; I was furious with Mox Sorrel for watching me all morning so that I had no opportunity to sneak off and hide; but most of all I was furious with that damned teamster who had raised the alarm when I was just about to escape from Gettysburg forever.

Sixty seconds after the first gun, a second gun exploded, but I was already on the ground for this one, and thank God that I was. With the second signal gun, there was an almighty explosion of violence as Alexander let loose all his guns, shaking the earth and sending out such an enormous concussion that it seemed the air itself had exploded. The disastrous assault that would be forever known as Pickett's Charge was about to begin.

Almost immediately, the Yankee guns across the valley returned the salute, and the cannonade from both sides was unendurable.

All through the tree line on Seminary Ridge the men were hidden, but Alexander's guns were out in front of the trees on the downward slope of Seminary Ridge. So when the Yankee gunners returned fire, they were targeting our artillery. The balls, of course, overshot the artillery and crashed into the trees, or they skipped across the open field, past our guns, and into the woods to dance across the men.

A big bombardment will shake your brains with the earth bouncing and the concussion ripping through the air, but with the Yankees returning fire, we were suffering through two massive bombardments. Cannonballs ripped through the trees where we were hiding. Branches snapped and fell at their impact. Trunks exploded in a crash of splinters, and entire trees were toppled. The men who had laughed at me were silent now. I guessed most of them were praying to God for deliverance, and some were probably thinking of their mothers.

I've read that Alexander was firing two balls every second, and sometimes as many as six a second.

It was a horrendous thing. The noise of the cannons across the way combining with the shocking thunder of our own cannons, and the unceasing explosions sent a pounding through the body so strong I thought my chest would burst. If it went on an hour or five hours I couldn't tell you, but with my body and my face depressed against the dirt it seemed to me it must have gone on for week.

Though I kept my face buried into the earth, I did look up at one point to see how Pickett was taking it all. I confess, I so detested the man at the moment that I hoped to see him hugging the earth with me, maybe weeping for his mother. But do ye know what the damned fool was doing? Pickett was engaged in writing one of his damned love letters to Sallie. I'd seen the photograph of her, and she was a stunning beauty, no doubt. But at the moment of death, only a fool would leisurely find the words for such a letter.

There were those among us who laughed and joked as the shells burst into the tree line. Others stood or walked about. Some smoked their pipes or sipped from their bottles or, if they had any, ate some bread or bacon.

But not so with Jackie Speed. I pressed myself against the ground as hard as I could, and I wept, not so much perhaps for what was happening for I do not remember thinking that I would be killed or maimed in the barrage of cannon fire. But I wept for what was coming. Most of those boys in the woods with me – even those who like me were flat against the ground and calling for their mamas – hadn't seen what we were going to be asked to do, but I'd been in the fighting of the day before, I had seen Meade's lines and the determination of his men. Longstreet may have lacked confidence, but I was certain sure of how this day would end.

I do not know how long it had been since it started, but the bombardment of the Yankees and their responding cannonade had been going on for some extended period – a quarter of an hour, perhaps longer – when there was a brief lull in the shooting.

Not far from where I was hugging the earth I heard a soldier shout out: "Run little hare!" Without lifting my body, I turned my head and saw some of the boys laughing as a rabbit darted out of its hole and charged for the rear. "If I was a hare, I'd run, too!" the soldier called after it.

The boys around him all laughed at that, but to me it sounded like solid advice worth following.

I now turned my head a bit to look at the Yankee lines in time to see a cannonball, fired short by a Yankee gun, skipping across the golden hay covered field in front of me. I watched in horror, realizing that the ball was skipping in a straight line directly toward me. The ball took a bounce and shot upward, striking the top of the tree under which I was lying, and twigs and splinters rained down all around me, thunking off the top of my slouch hat.

At length the Union bombardment seemed to sputter. They were no longer shooting with the same ferocity. It seemed from where we were, with our own guns still blasting hell out of Cemetery Ridge, that our artillery must have chased some number of the Yankee guns off the ridge or, better yet, knocked them out of existence.

"Where are you going?" Pickett demanded as I got up into a crouch.

"I'm going to find Longstreet and convince him to see sense," I said.

Pickett made no argument. Instead, he stood up with me. "Yes," he said. "I'll go with you. I've written Sallie a letter and, if – if, oh how terrible a word – if the worst should befall me, I want to be sure in the knowledge that she has received my final missive to her."

I had to wonder if George Pickett even realized there was a war about, or if to him it was all just a dramatic backdrop to the romantic play that was his life.

With Pickett following, I dashed from tree to tree, terrified that the Yankees would resume their bombardment and I would have my head shot away, until I came to where our horses were tied. I looked my horse over to be sure it had not been hit, then mounted him and started to ride toward the rear. I was aware of Pickett behind me, but he wasn't the horseman I was, and I set a quick pace, taking a zigzag route in case the Yankees picked up the pace of their guns again. I hunched forward and buried my face into the horse's neck, trying to make myself small for fear one of the cannonballs being fired behind me might find its way to me through the woods.

I've never experienced a cannonade to match it. More shot and shell was thrown down range by both armies than in any other artillery fight before or since. But it's a fact, in an artillery bombardment, whether you live or die, is all a result of chance and luck. If you want proof, consider the example of Win Hancock over on the other ridge. He rode is horse about on that ridge with balls bouncing and exploding all around him. But he was never shot off his horse nor maimed. [69]

When I found him, Longstreet was seated on an old split-rail fence located across the road that ran south below the Seminary. He looked as dejected as I felt. His staff officers and a host of couriers were nearby, but all were giving him his space. Anyone who did not know him might have thought he was sulking at being reprimanded by Lee, but if that was the case he would not have tried to push the issue after Lee first rejected his proposal. No, I believe Old Peter had already gone into mourning for the men who were not yet dead.

Longstreet's reputation has become tarnished since the war. At the hands of Early, and even Fitz Hugh Lee, the old guard publicly blamed Longstreet for the loss at Gettysburg, and it was all lies meant to shield themselves – or in Fitz's case, his uncle – from the blame they rightly deserved. But find me some old veteran from the First Corps today and mention Old Peter to him, and the veteran will shed a tear and tell you that never was there a general who took better care of his men.

Longstreet wasn't sulking. Longstreet was mourning. And if I didn't think I was among those he was mourning, he'd have had my sympathy. But as it was, Peter knew the charge was death, and he was sending me into it.

I rode straight up to him, preparing my speech in my mind. I had reasoned arguments to make. None of these men even knew me, I was going to tell him. If Pickett fell, it would serve better to have one of their own captains as the man next to him, for that man would be familiar to them, someone who had earned their respect, someone who might have a better chance of getting them to follow into what was sure to be hell. I intended to tell Old Peter that I could serve better by remaining here with him as a courier. My horsemanship was well known, and surely Longstreet would see that if Pickett's line needed correcting, mounted, I could dash to him and deliver the message to straighten out.

Oh, certainly serving as a courier was as dangerous as joining in the march, but if Old Peter relented and allowed me to remain with him, there was the chance that no message would need sending and I might not even be called upon. Or, if he did turn to me and say, "Speedy, ride up there to George and ask him direct his march a bit to the left," well, I could mount my horse and dash off in the wrong direction and never find myself in the charge, and when all was said and done I'd just ride up to Longstreet and confess that through the smoke and the carnage and the shooting I never did find Pickett. Or, if Pickett were killed (which was likely as not), I'd just report that I delivered the message to the corpse.

But I never had the opportunity to plead my case.

Pickett had caught me up, and now he stepped his horse in front of me, between me and Longstreet. Pickett saluted, and though Longstreet looked directly at his division commander, he said nothing.

I dared not speak. Even when he told me that all his children had died during the previous winter, Longstreet did not look so grave. In that moment, I was more afraid of questioning Longstreet than I was of charging against the entrenched Yankees. [70]

And even though the cannons still thundered, we heard the beat of the hooves as a courier rode up to us.

"General Pickett," he said. "I've been trying to find you. I have a message from Colonel Alexander!"

The courier handed the message to Pickett who opened the folded piece of paper and read it. I stepped my horse up beside his and read over his shoulder. "If you are coming at all, you must come immediately or I cannot give you proper support," the message said. "The enemy's fire has not slackened materially, and at least eighteen guns are still firing from the Cemetery itself."

But even as I read the message, I could tell that the Yankee's cannonade was slackening.

Hood stepped his horse forward and leaned down to hand the message to Longstreet, who read it.

Then, a second courier rode up. He saluted, "General Pickett – a message from Colonel Alexander!"

I watched as Pickett opened the message and again read over his shoulder. "For God's sake, come quick! The eighteen guns are gone!"

"General," Pickett said, handing the second message to Longstreet. "Shall I lead my division on?" [71]

I've known a hundred or more of these madmen generals – maniacs who were all too willing to throw any number of men at the death so long as it raised up their own banner. A few were willing to rush into the death for their own glory, but most of them I ever knew were more pleased to stay behind the lines and send ten thousand men to the death, all for some fool's notion of honor. No one has yet been able to explain to me what is honorable or glorious about ordering other men to die on your behalf.

But Old Peter was not among them. Here he was, on the verge of sending fifteen thousand men to their deaths, and Old Peter was grief-stricken. He could not utter the order to charge. Instead, he simply closed his eyes and dropped his head in a nod of assent. And I could see the gleam of a tear roll down his cheek.

Pickett turned to go, but then he stopped and took out his pencil and the envelope addressed to his sweetheart. He jotted some last note and turned his horse back to Longstreet, handing him the envelope. As Longstreet looked up to take the envelope, I could see that his cheeks and beard were wet with his tears.

Now Pickett rode off to join his men.

Old Peter looked at me. He shook his massive head sadly and dropped his eyes to the ground. "I'm sorry Speedy," he said to the dirt at his feet. "I would have preferred it another way."

I opened my mouth to protest, but Mox Sorrel was now up with us, pushing his horse in between me and Longstreet.

"Better go, Speed," Sorrel said. "Pickett's going to need you now. Go and do what you can to bring those boys from the First Corps back to us."

"For God's sake, Mox, what can I do?" I whined at him.

"Help Pickett, Speed. Help him be the general they need now. Come on Speedy, it's just one more adventure for you."

I sighed heavily and spat on the ground and shook my head in consternation. "Damnation Mox," I said, but I had no argument left to make, not in front of Old Peter, anyways. "I hate this war."

But I turned the damned horse and followed in Pickett's tracks, wondering if maybe I should have writ Eliza a love letter.

CHAPTER 22

Pickett had the drums and bugles going by the time I got back to him. His men were getting up now, shouldering their rifles, giving one last check to their satchels for ammunition.

"Be certain you have your canteens, boys!" I called out, remembering my thirst from the day before.

Dick Garnett, one of Pickett's brigadiers, was there, smoking a cigar. He was bundled up in a big overcoat, which I found to be damned odd in that brutal heat. [72]

"Any final instructions?" Garnett asked Pickett.

"No Dick," Pickett said. "Nothing I can remember."

"Make good time crossing the valley," I said to Garnett, remembering Sorrel's caution to me earlier. "It's going to be hell over yonder. We'll be exposed in the valley. As you cross the road, you'll be down a slight hill that will provide a little cover. When you top the hill, make your charge there. The Yanks are down behind a rock wall. That umbrella-shaped tree you can see, that's about where the rock wall is. The plan is to get in their ranks on the other side of that rock wall, converge on that tree and split Meade in the middle." [73]

Garnett bit the cigar and nodded his head to me. "Thanks, Speed. I'll greet you on the other side of the wall, then." Well, you'll know Dick never greeted me again.

There were no natural barriers between us and the Union line on Cemetery Ridge. Behind the Peach Orchard and the Wheat Field, where I'd witnessed the fighting of the previous day from the Union line, was the Plum Run creek, but it did not extend so far north. In essence, except for a farmhouse, the road and a couple of fences, there was nothing that would stop us from running directly into the canister and musket shot from the Yankees.

Now Pickett turned to face his men and made an address to them. I don't remember the words he used – something about Virginia, I suppose – but he didn't waste any time with his speech. "Virginia! Let's go let those Yankees shoot us up," or something of that nature was all he had to say.

And with those words of encouragement, Pickett's division stepped off, passing through the line of guns and down the eastern slope of Seminary Ridge and into a field of tall hay. As they came out of the woods, the color guard unfurled their flags. One of the bands, still inside the trees, opened up the march with "Dixie." The smoke from the cannonade – which I'm told lasted longer than an hour and a half – hung so thick in the valley that the sun was blotted from the sky, and the Yanks surely had trouble seeing us for we could barely see them. When I came out of the woods, my first thought was that the artillery had knocked the Yankees off Cemetery Ridge, for I could see nothing of our enemy. But as the smoke began to dissipate some, I could see their flags, showing that the ridge was still occupied with regiment upon regiment.

I was trying to decide if it was better to stay near Pickett, as Longstreet wanted, or get farther away from him for fear that sharpshooters would target an officer. At length, I decided to stay close to Pickett. I reasoned that Fate tends to be a cruel mistress, and most often she strikes down the generals who best know their business – where was Reynolds? If Fate held true, I believed she would spare Pickett.

It was a good choice I'd made, too, and if Fate hadn't intervened to try to get me killed, I might well have come out of Pickett's Charge as unscathed as the man hisself. If you look at the lists of casualties, you'll notice right away that every man in gray who went into the battle mounted was either killed or wounded or had his horse shot from under him. The exception was Pickett, and the entirety of his staff. Had I been fortunate enough to remain with George throughout the conflict that afternoon, I'd have avoided the terror of that charge and only been a witness to the slaughter. But Fate did intervene.

I don't know if you ever had the chance to see those Southern boys fall in, form up, dress line and advance into real battle, but it was never as much a military drill as it was a very large gang of armed men bustling in to slaughter their enemy. And once the Rebel Yell was let loose, only chaos and confusion and death followed. Off the parade ground, no officer could get even a single Rebel soldier to advance with anything amounting to order.

I'd seen Little Mac in '61 drill his Yankee troops to perfection, and in the intervening years I'd seen those men break and run on almost every field where they were committed.

I ain't saying that well-drilled men will break or that disorder and chaos are what carries battles, but when it came to those boys in butternut, when they were engaged with their enemy, they fought as individuals and ignored nearly everything their officers had ever told 'em. All the officers of the Confederacy could have survived the thing, had they chosen to, by simply pointing to a spot in the distance and telling their men, "You go up yonder and kill everything you can find." And their men would have done it and no need for the officers to lead or follow.

But the lack of military discipline that ordinarily accompanied this army did not exist on that third day at Gettysburg. They looked like a European army, forming up in their lines of battle, dressing their lines, closing their ranks and marching forward. Even when the cannonballs started to fly into their midst, killing five or ten at a time, even under the tremendous pressure of being shot at from both flanks and the front, they held their order across that mile-long valley. When the cannon shot crashed through their ranks and dropped five men here and eight men there and a dozen men there, the officers shouted out their orders and the boys looked right, felt with their left and closed up their ranks like professional soldiers.

After more than two hard years, these farm boys who were so good at killing their enemy had finally turned into soldiers.

Had Pickett and Pettigrew simply turned them loose and told them to dash across that field and up that hill and kill all them bluecoats, maybe it would have been different. Maybe if they hadn't had to stand for that abuse from the Yankee cannons, those boys could have crossed that field quicker and routed their enemy – as they'd done so many times before. I don't know. Old Peter never thought so. Everyone but Lee and Pickett thought the thing was damned folly from the start, but since Bobby Lee was the one making the decisions it didn't matter what any of the rest of us thought.

To my horror, though, I was soon to find myself in among 'em.

Today, as an old man with a fine home and a fine family and lots of grandchildren and great-grandchildren, I can view their actions with a certain professional detachment, but there was no detachment when the first blast of cannon shot came from Little Round Top and bounced into our lines.

The guns we thought, prayed, our artillery had silenced were now suddenly alive and sending death into our ranks. A shot crashed into our right flank, fired from Little Round Top. A hole opened up, but the men did their duty and closed ranks and kept marching. Now another battery sent a solid shell into the ranks – this time the shot came from Cemetery Ridge – and again the ball bounced through our ranks, dropping more men. Again, they closed ranks and kept marching.

I sat my horse, watching. Pickett was riding in circles there on the open slope of Seminary Ridge. When he saw his right flank start to go wide, he sent his brother to straighten them out. I moved my horse a bit away from him in the hopes that he would not be sending me to straighten the next group. As I watched the cannon shot ripping into the ranks in that valley of death, I had no desire to get nearer than I was.

But the right flank never corrected itself, and soon disaster was upon Pickett's division.

We had remained on the slope of Seminary Ridge as we watched the division advance toward the Emmitsburg Road. Cannon, firing solid shot and then canister as our boys got closer, was dissolving our line. Now, on the right, where Lang and Wilcox should have been, Kemper was about to meet destruction.

A Federal regiment on Kemper's right stepped out of the Union line, turned so that they were facing into Kemper's exposed flank, and fired volley after crushing volley into his exposed side. The regiments of Lang and Wilcox, which should have been there to protect Kemper, had gotten lost in the thick smoke and from the moment they set off from Seminary Ridge were always going in the wrong direction.

"I can stand no more," Pickett said angrily, and he charged out into the valley. His staff officers followed at a gallop, and my damned horse – without any urging from me – followed along with the others.

Out here in the exposed valley, fear gripped me, and I hugged the horse's neck as shot exploded through the air all around me. Pickett and his staff were making for the safety of the farm in the middle of the field. Seeing it, and seeing that it had a stone foundation that would offer protection even from the cannonballs being fired into the valley, I charged ahead, passing by his staff and passing by Pickett hisself.

There were already men gathered at the farm house, stragglers and wounded, using it for shelter, but I rode right up so that horse and rider were pressed against the stone foundation of the house. My horse nearly stepped on a wounded man who was leaning against the house, but he was unconscious, possibly dead, and I was less concerned about his health than I was about getting myself pressed up against that stone wall as much as possible. If I could have dissolved myself into the thing I would have.

Now Pickett and his staff caught up to me. Pickett reined in his horse as he reached me. He did not immediately direct his horse behind the house, but instead held his ground where he could get a look at the battle. His staff were squeezed behind the building with me.

"Kemper is imperiled!" Pickett yelled. "Captain Bright! Ride back, quickly, and tell General Longstreet that I cannot hold without reinforcements!"

I breathed a sigh of relief as one of Pickett's staff men directed his horse away from our group and began riding back toward Seminary Ridge. Better Captain Bright be out there exposed than Captain Speed, I thought.

"Captain Speed!" Pickett yelled to me, and I looked dread at him. "Ride to General Armistead. Inform him that General Kemper is imperiled, tell him to press forward with all possible speed!"

"George, Lo Armistead is all the way up there, near to the Union line. Surely you can't expect me to ride that far forward?"

"Now Speedy!" Pickett yelled, and he was not chastising my hesitancy but simply trying to urge me to move quickly.

"Hurry captain!" one of his staff men yelled at me, and I was sure the man was telling me to go before Pickett sent him instead.

There was nothing for it. With Pickett giving me a direct order out here on the field, I'd have been shot dead if I'd have refused. I'd delivered messages in the midst of hot battles before, so I buried my spurs into the horse's side, put my head against his neck, and charged out into the hellish storm ahead of me.

In moments I was even with the rear of Armistead's column, and I could see his color guard up in front of me. I charged forward. A solid shot from a cannon came flying through the ranks, tearing the hindquarter from my horse. The horse screamed and went down, sending me ass over head into the dirt. The beast kicked and screamed an awful noise, and some generous soul put a bullet into its head.

Though I had not been touched by the shell nor even hurt much in my fall, I cried out and stayed on the ground with my face in the soil. The truth was, with my dander up in the midst of the fighting, my broken ribs weren't even troubling me as they should have been after taking another spill from a horse. But whether I was hurting or not, panic had gripped me.

"Cap'n," a sergeant yelled at me and came running over, taking me under the arm and twisting me so that he could look at me. "Are ye hit?"

"No, blast it!" I raged at him.

Had he left me alone I might have laid there in the tall wheat for a day or two days until a burying party came to get me. Then I'd tell them it appeared as if I'd recovered and at that point I would have gone on about my business. But the damned sergeant, being the imbecilic helpful sort, pulled me up to my feet and, to make certain I was looking my best for whatever Yankee shot me dead, the damned oaf actually brushed the dirt from my uniform.

"Leave off with that," I told him. "I have a message for General Armistead."

The sergeant pointed toward the color guard. "That'll be Gen'l Armistead, there."

I now ran through the ranks, pushing men out of my way and leaping past others. I wanted to deliver the message and be gone.

"Lo!" I called out to Armistead. "Lo Armistead! I've a message from George!"

The mounted general to whom I was running and shouting turned in his saddle to look at me, and when he did, I could see that it was Kemper and not Armistead. "Kemper!" I said. "Your flank is exposed, old son! The Yankees are pouring it into your side!"

"I am well aware of that Captain Speed," Kemper said, and he was angry as hell. "I am here at this moment to ask General Armistead to hurry his attack!"

I dropped my shoulders in defeat – I'd nearly been killed on completely unnecessary orders. Pickett wanted Armistead to quicken his pace, but Kemper wanted it even more and had come back on his own to make the same request I'd been sent to make.

Now I turned and tried to make my way back through Armistead's ranks, but it was slow going trying to push through the men, and I found myself getting caught up in their march, and I was being pushed down the line toward the center of the advancing column. For a moment the column stopped, and I could not determine the cause. And then I head the explosions as two massive volleys were let loose – one from Armistead's column and a returning volley from the Yanks high up on the ridge. And now Armistead's column broke into a run, and I found myself being dragged forward in the rush. The mass of bodies pushing toward Cemetery Ridge prevented me from making a retreat, and now it was forcing me forward at the run. We crossed over the Emmitsburg Road and over fence posts that had been knocked down by the men in front of us, but intermingled with the posts from the fence were dead and dying men who'd been caught by the fence and had been easy victims for the Yankees on the ridge.

I could now finally see Armistead. Lo was not mounted but was on foot, and he had put his black hat atop his sword and was commanding the men to concentrate on him as he ran forward at the Yankee line.

And now, just as the first of Armistead's men reached the rock wall, all along the wall, Yankees suddenly appeared, standing up from behind the wall, and they fired a sickening volley into our ranks. Around me the Rebel Yell went up, and the men rushed forward with that chilling Yell issuing forth, and though I was terrified, I was swept forward with the tide, and there was naught I could do about it. I realized that my own voice – though more a panicked scream than a yell – was joining in with the others, and a witness might have thought I had turned maniac with the rest of 'em.

There was a point where the rock wall made a 90 degree turn back up Cemetery Ridge. The spot has come to be known as "the Angle," and it was to this spot that Armistead was leading his men. I was completely caught by the mad rush, being pushed and dragged forward by fools who did not have the good sense to turn back.

I stumbled and fell, but as some ass behind me picked me up to my feet, I looked forward and saw three men get hit by canister fired at no more than ten yards. In one moment the men were there, bayonets pointing forward, and in an instant they were gone. All that remained of them was a red mist that hung in the air like bloody cigar smoke.

"Oh, Jesus!" I screamed. "I can not do this again!"

With no other thought but self-preservation, I drew my Colt revolver and began firing into the battery that had erased those men from existence. My only thought was to kill those gunners before they fired their damnedable grape shot at me. At least two of my shots told, dropping Yankees manning the cannon, and then I thumbed back the hammer and squeezed the trigger and the gun clicked on a spent round. I dropped to a knee as men rushed about me, charging those last few steps to get beyond the rock wall, and I reloaded the gun. This was the first time I'd used the Yankee revolver given to me by Hancock – my God! this was Hancock's corps we were assaulting, and Armistead right there! – and even in the hell that was taking place all about me, I noted how worthwhile it was to not have to use percussion caps with shaking hands. [74]

Having reloaded my revolver, I resumed my part in the battle, shooting at the battery that had destroyed the three men in front of me. As quick as I'd loaded it, I emptied the rounds in the revolver. Again, I dropped to my knee and reloaded the thing. This time, even though I did not have to fool with the percussion caps, my hands were shaking so badly that I still dropped several of the encased bullets on the ground as I tried to reload the weapon. [75]

I'll confess it was cowardice that pushed me forward. Here, just feet away from the rock wall, from the Union line, I did not want Armistead's entire column to advance and leave me behind – I would be too easy a target for the muskets still sending lead sheets into our ranks. Likewise, I could have no thought for retreat – a sharpshooter would find great sport in gunning down a man running away, or perhaps some damned lieutenant of Armistead's brigade would shoot me down if I sought to withdraw. Either way, a lone target fleeing through that valley would surely be killed.

And there, in the heat and thickness of the battle, with no tree to hide behind, it seemed that the only way to survive was to kill the enemy and chase him from his position. And so with only a thought to self-preservation in my mind, I lent my support to that cause.

I got up off my knee and charged forward with Armistead's men. Now I was more selective in my targets, only shooting the revolver when I was confident I would hit my target. I dropped three more men before the chambers were again empty.

Now I was inside the rock wall, and from what I could see, the Yankees were in full retreat. But I witnessed a cannon blast that destroyed every bit of a dozen men – dissolving them into vapor – and then the Yankees were rushing forward to meet us. I holstered the revolver and drew out Mox Sorrel's sword. Everything was chaos and smoke and fists and swords and muskets and bayonets. There was too much activity for any man to even understand what was happening, and so all I or any other man there at the angle could do was engage the enemy that was nearest him.

A bluebelly in front of me was about to bayonet a Southern boy who was on the ground. I ran the sword into the Yankee's belly all the way to the hilt. He dropped his rifle and fell backwards, dragging sword and me with him. I had to jerk the sword several times to dislodge it from his gut. When it finally came loose, I staggered sideways, knocking my head against the spoked wheel of one of the guns. The knock I took to my head dazed me. I sensed more than saw a man beside me, and I slashed with the sword, feeling it cut into his flesh. Whether he was Yankee or Confederate, I never knew, but the man dropped to the ground and rolled in agony. I staggered but did not fall.

Aching and confused from hitting my head against the wagon wheel, I clutched Mox's sword in my fist and swung it wildly, unable to focus on the events around me.

A voice calling to me through the fog of my head was saying, "Drop Speedy! Drop to the ground! Play possum, old son!" I knew the voice was the sane, working part of my brain telling me what to do.

But my knees would not buckle. And now in my line of sight was a blue coat, and the man wearing it had his musket held by the muzzle like a club, and he was raising it up to dash in my brains with the butt of the gun. So I shoved Mox's blade upwards, running him through the throat. The Yankee choked on blood and dropped his gun, grabbing at his wounded neck, and the sword slid out of his throat as he stumbled to the ground. I pressed forward into the fight.

I saw Armistead up in front of me. His black hat that had been the guidon for his men was now pushed down his sword to the hilt, and the thought ran through my mind that poor Lo's bald head would now get a terrible sunburn because his hat was ruined.

"It's the Philadelphia brigade!" Armistead shouted, turning to look at his men. "Give them the cold steel!"

Lo put his hand on the barrel of a cannon, pushing it to try to turn it so that we might operate their own gun against the Yankees. But then I saw his body shake as he was hit with shots, maybe four or five shots all at once, and Lewis Armistead was slumping into death.

I had thought the Yanks were doing the smart thing and running for safety, but now it seemed that they were charging back down the ridge to meet us. By now I had staggered unmolested farther up the field of battle, passing by the spot where Armistead lay dead. The smoke was so thick and the fighting around me so fierce and the knock on my head so violent that everything was confusion in my mind. I was desperate for some relief. In my dazed and frightened state I saw just a few yards in front of me the umbrella shaped tree. For some reason, that umbrella shaped tree took on a majestic quality in my imagination. It represented to me safety, for it was the objective pointed out to me by Old Peter. I think I must have believed that the rest of the Army of Northern Virginia would soon join me at that tree, and so that was where I would find safety in numbers. I now made a dash, hollering as loudly as I could and swinging Mox's sword at anything that might try to prevent me from getting to the tree.

I was breathless and exhausted by the time my hand touched the trunk of the tree, and for a moment I believed I had secured the safety I sought, for what I found under that tree was an immediate relief from the unrelenting heat. It must have been ten degrees cooler there in the shade of that big oak, and its trunk felt strong and protective under the palm of my hand. I leaned against the tree and caught my breath.

And now my head began to clear and I was able to look about some and take stock of the situation. Armistead was dead. The Yankees I'd seen fleeing the field must have regrouped, for they had charged back into the fight. [77] All along the wall and in among the Yankee artillery it was hot, brutal hand-to-hand fighting, and men were falling dead everywhere. I could hear Yankees yelling "Fredericksburg!" and I understood their taunt: – They were remembering when they had charged our entrenched troops the previous December and been shattered by us. Now, Gettysburg was Fredericksburg in reverse. It was the Confederacy destroying itself against the Federals' entrenched positions.

And here was I, at the umbrella shaped tree that Longstreet had promised was our objective, yet no other Johnny Reb was here with me.

It was the jeers of the Yankees, calling "Fredericksburg!" and the recollection of the ghostly white bodies on that field the next morning that stirred me from my exhausted and stunned inactivity. I had lingered too long at this tree and must escape.

My first thought was to once again shed my Confederate coat, perhaps lie down at the base of the tree, and when the shooting was done, whether I was taken for a Union man or a Confederate, I would beg to be taken to Hancock and let him offer me protection.

I was, for a moment, alone at the High Tide of the Confederacy.

This umbrella shaped tree marked the spot that proved to be the farthest penetration any Southern man would make into the enemy line on that third day at the Battle of Gettysburg, the farthest point of Bobby Lee's foray into the Northern States, the closest the Confederacy would come to victory. For more than two years, the Tide of the Confederacy had rolled ever forward, coming farther and farther up the beach toward nationhood. But here at this tree just south of Gettysburg, with me, behind Union lines and in the midst of a terrible fight, the Tide of the Confederacy would pause and then begin to recede. Never again would the Confederacy come this close, and Ol' Jackie Speed was the man standing at the very farthest tip. And I was contemplating dropping my coat and switching sides.

But then a better plan occurred to me. I decided I would just step out from behind the tree and snatch up the closest Yankee and surrender to him. Then I would beg to be taken to Hancock and avoid a Yankee prison.

And that was my intention when I stepped out from behind the umbrella shaped tree, Mox's sword still clutched in my hand, but I was too late. Now coming up around me was the rest of the Confederacy's Tide, beaten and battered with no officer to command them and nothing driving them forward but their desperate desire to kill Yankees. There were a dozen, and then another two dozen, joining me up around the tree, and with them they brought bluebellies by the scores, and they were all fighting with fists and clubs and bayonets.

Some damned Yankee officer now caught sight of me, and seeing that I had no man to grapple with, he decided to charge me, the point of his sword extended toward me as he rushed at me, screaming like a man possessed. Even now I can recall in my mind his maniac face, his mouth opened in a scream of hatred, his face, though shaded by the brim of his hat, red with heat and fury.

Oh! It was a terrifying sight, and I thought the blade of his sword looked three feet wide as he came charging at me to run me through.

I screamed and jumped back behind the tree, and now it was a child's game of catch me if you can, that Yankee officer slashing at the trunk of the tree as I danced around it to stay clear of his blade. He was hell bent on killing me, and I saw no escape, so I danced and maneuvered until he caught his blade in the trunk of the tree, and in the moment it took for him to jerk the thing loose, I stepped forward and gutted the bastard, pushing the blade of Mox's sword into his belly and the slashing the thing out so that I opened up a frightful wound. The Yankee grabbed at the innards spilling out of his gut and tried to stuff them back in, and now I gave him a good hard kick so that he fell to the ground to molest me no more.

The small band of Confederates who had joined me under the tree were leaderless, and being the only officer still standing, I decided to order a retreat. I reasoned that I was less likely to be shot in the back if there were a couple dozen other targets near me.

"For God's sake, we must get the hell out of here!" I shouted, and the panic in my voice convinced the men.

We all turned back toward Seminary Ridge and began to run.

There was still disastrous fighting taking place at the rock wall and the canon where Armistead was dead, and my hopes of a clear path back to the safety of Pitzer's Woods and Longstreet were dashed by a line of bluebellies standing in our way and waiting to receive us.

Those Yanks set about my retreating companions with a passion, swinging their muskets like clubs, but Johnny Reb hadn't learned how to run, and my small band of Confederates stopped their flight to give as good as they got. I now fell to my hands and knees to crawl through the mass of fighting men.

I still had Mox's sword clutched in my fist, and I gave a couple of them Yanks a slash on their thighs to remember me by, and in doing so I helped some of my fellow Confederates come out the other side of the fight. One of them helped me to my feet, and we were ready to continue our run.

Pettigrew's men were all intermingled with Armistead's men, now, and we'd been ten minutes or more on the Yank's side of the rock wall engaged in bitter hand-to-hand combat.

Even now, there was no clear path of retreat. Yankees were everywhere, swinging their damned muskets or fighting with bayonets.

And now an almighty crash against my head sent me sprawling to the ground.

Stunned, I looked up and saw some blue-coated bastard standing over me with his musket gripped in his hands. The cowardly son of a bitch had clubbed me from my blind side, swinging that musket around to crash into my forehead. He'd knocked my old slouch hat off my head and opened up a gash that was leaking blood into my eyes and all but blinding me. And now he was standing over me preparing to finish me off. Dazed though I was, I still knew how to survive, and I slashed at the only part of him I could reach with Mox's sword. A line of red opened up across his hips and groin in the wake of the sword tip, and the Yank dropped the musket and grabbed at himself, swearing and cussing before fainting to the ground.

That knock to my head was tremendous. My mind was swimming and I could not find the sky to know which way was up. I knew I must get to my feet and run, but it seemed when I tried to stand I kept knocking my head against the ground.

Four Southern boys lined up in front of me and fired a volley. Then one of them took me by the arm and started to drag me farther along my route of retreat. I looked up at him as he pulled me along. He was so young, that at first I thought he was a woman, and I recalled the lovely Kate Cherry dressed as a Union soldier and kissing me.

"Oh, Kate, darling," I said to the young Confederate boy. "Shall we go and have a lie down under that tree, yonder?"

"I ain't Kate," the boy said to me. "We cannot stay here, Captain."

He continued to drag me back away from the Yankees. I saw what seemed like ten thousand Yanks rushing down the slope of Cemetery Ridge, and I thought what an appropriately named place this was for it would soon be full of graves.

I was too big and the boy was too small and we were making poor time in our retreat. He lunged forward in spurts, dragging my arms so that I thought he would jerk them from their sockets.

And then the boy dragging me was shot in the chest, and he stumbled and fell, sprawled on the ground ahead of me. I crawled up to him to be sure he wasn't Kate Cherry. Now my brain was clearing enough that I could see he was just some dumb child of the South who had followed his brothers, maybe his paw, too, into this terrible war.

"Come on, son," I said. "Gather your strength. Get me back across that field and to our lines."

"I think this is the end for us, Captain," he said to me, and his voice was choked with blood. He was just a boy, not old enough to shave. His face was dirty, his hair was wild and he looked rail thin. I looked at his wound. Blood was issuing out of a frightening hole in his shoulder. By the time I looked back into his face, he was lifeless.

"Like hell," I answered. "The end of you, but Ol' Speedy can get out of this yet!"

It was sheer instinct for survival and nothing more that allowed me to get myself upright, for my head was still swimming and there was only weakness where I should have found arms and legs. But the boy's words had roused in me the last bit of strength I could muster.

I was weak and exhausted and sore, but I was too scared to die. I stood into a crouch, and I lifted the body of the boy who'd pulled me out of the Angle. I wrapped his arms around my neck and held them there so that his lifeless body hung down behind me, covering my back. And dragging him like that, like a heavy cape, I began my long, terrible trek through the tall hay and back across the valley.

As I went, a musket ball smashed into the back of the boy dangling off my back. The force of it knocked me over, face first, and the boy sprawled on the ground where I dropped him. For a moment the breath was knocked out of me, but I choked and sputtered until I was breathing again. Then I dragged the boy back over my shoulders, got up into a crouch again, and continued staggering back across the valley.

Another shot struck the boy on my back, but this one shattered his leg and did not knock me to the ground. I stepped over dead and dying men as I crossed back over the field. Around me other men were fleeing – it was now a rout at the Angle. Armistead's broken and shattered men were everywhere. Some were running past me – running for their lives. Some were walking in their pride because they refused to run. Some were stumbling along, carrying their friends or their cousins or their brothers. Some were crawling, too wounded or too exhausted to walk or run. But all around me the devastated and crushed men of Pickett's division were retreating. The battle raged on behind us as first Pettigrew and then Trimble followed in Armistead's footsteps and destroyed themselves against the Federal wall on Cemetery Ridge.

The lifeless body had saved me once, maybe twice, and I refused to drop it and take my chances that another musket ball might find my back as I crossed the valley. But the boy was awkward to carry, and I was exhausted, and so I was not among the first retreating Confederates to reach our lines.

It seemed an eternity as I stumbled across the field, but eventually I found myself climbing the slope of Seminary Ridge. Ahead of me was an officer mounted on a gray horse. Whether it was because I was exhausted or dazed, I did not immediately recognize the officer, but when his soft voice called to me, I knew immediately that it was the army's commander.

"Are you injured, son?" Bobby Lee asked me.

"I don't know, sir," I said. "I feel injured."

"You have a wound on your head," he said.

"Yes sir," I answered.

Lee stepped his horse toward me a few paces. "This man you're carrying," he said. "I believe he has passed, son."

"Has he?" I asked.

Now Lee looked at me askance. "Captain Speed?" he asked.

"Aye, sir," I said.

"Why don't you put this boy down, Captain? Should you not be with General Longstreet's staff?"

I dropped down to my knees and rolled the dead boy off my shoulders. After such a long walk with him on my back, and now being relieved of his weight, I felt that I could have jumped up and run. There was a cool sensation across my shoulders where I'd been carrying the boy, the air catching the wet blood he'd left all over my back. Not wanting Lee to understand that I'd had him draped across my shoulders as a shield against Yankee sharpshooters, I examined the body, purely for Lee's benefit.

"He is dead, sir. We were engaged in the fighting, there at the rock wall. He dragged me out of it and then he was shot. I thought maybe I could get him back here to a surgeon."

Upon hearing my pitiful story, Lee hung his head. "This is all my fault, Captain Speed. All my fault. Please now, go and find General Longstreet. We must do what we can to gather our army and prepare in case those men yonder decide to try to attack us while we are weakened. Go and find General Longstreet. I will see that your friend receives a burial."

"Aye, sir," I said. "Don't be too hard on yourself, General Lee. All of this, it's just what men like you do."

"Thank you, Captain Speed," Bobby Lee said. "I appreciate your words, son."

The old man missed my point, so I shook my head in disgust and struggled to my feet and staggered back up towards the woods. At the line of artillery, Longstreet's was the first face I saw, and the big bear threw his arms around me and nearly crushed my ribs in an embrace.

"I thank God you have come safely back to us, Captain Speed!" he said. "Have you been shot?"

"I don't think so Peter, but my ribs are still broke from this morning. Would you mind easing up on me a bit?"

Mox Sorrel was coming up now. "Lord, Speed, your head, old son. Did they shoot you in the head?"

I reached up and felt the place where that Yank had tried to brain me and realized that blood was still running freely all down the side of my face.

"Mox, I'm sorry, but I lost your sword," I said.

Sorrel looked disappointed, but he merely frowned and shrugged. "I killed two or three Yanks with it, though," I said. "If that makes it better."

Moxley smiled. "Glad to know you put it to good use. It must have been hell up in that place, Speedy."

I tried to put on a stoic aspect to impress them with my bravery, and through the throbbing pain of my head wound I attempted to consider some speech that might get repeated in their memoirs or their letters home. But at that moment my legs gave way and I dropped to the ground, and I stretched out on my back and the exhaustion that had been burdening me all through the day finally won, and I closed my eyes and whatever was to happen next was going to have to do it without me.

CHAPTER 23

Some cavalry skirmishes were fought in the late afternoon of July 3, but I slept through any of that. Longstreet had stretcher bearers take me to his tent and lay me out on his cot. A doctor stitched up my head. I slept through all of that, as well.

At some point in the night, Sorrel woke me and explained that the army was preparing to move out. We were withdrawing back to Virginia. Our foray North had reached its conclusion. I could hear a hard rain hammering against the canvas tent and for a moment could imagine what hell it must be for those still dying on the battlefield.

"I can arrange to put you in an ambulance," Sorrel said. "The wounded are to leave in the morning."

"Oh, no," I said, for I'd seen how they crammed the wounded into those wagons and knew what a frightful journey that would be through the rain soaked roads of Pennsylvania. "Find me a horse, Mox. I'll ride out of here."

Sorrel patted my shoulder. "I owe you an apology, Ol' Speedy, friend. Yesterday, I honestly thought you were shirking. I thought you were trying to get out of the duty of keeping up with Pickett. I thought you'd seen what that charge was going to be like – the same as all of us could see what it was going to be – and that you tried to shirk. I even made some comment about it to Old Peter. He was quick to defend you though, Speed. And when I saw you coming back from the battle, all beat to hell and trying to save that poor boy you had on your back." Mox was lost for words. "Truthfully, Speed, I'm ashamed of myself."

"No hard feelings, Mox," I said. And doing my best to make him feel worse for spotting me as a coward, I added, "I'm truly sorry that I did not bring you back your sword. I'll get you a new one as soon as we're in Richmond."

Sorrel sniffed, and in the dark tent I could not see if it was the rain giving him the sniffles or if he was weeping at his shame and my courage. Poor old Mox Sorrel, he spotted me for a coward, and because I was lucky enough to survive Pickett's Charge, he now had to offer me an apology.

"You're a good man, Speed. You showed me your bandaged ribs yesterday, told me you'd not slept and hadn't eaten. We all knew you'd conducted yourself with nothing but bravery the day before, up on those hills with Colonel Oates. And still, I had the gall to doubt you."

"Really Mox," I said. "I don't want you to give it another thought. What's important now is that we keep the army whole and get back to Virginia."

Mox sniffed again. His voice cracked when he said, "I'll go and see if I can't find you a good horse."

A flash of lightning lit the shadows in the tent, and for a moment I could see Sorrel, seated on a cracker box, in silhouette. Then the thunder shook the sky.

"We tempted Fate coming here to Pennsylvania," Sorrel said. "I wonder if we wouldn't have been better off staying on the Rappahannock. Every time the Yanks tried to cross it we beat them back. Coming here now feels like a mistake."

"Oh, aye," I answered. "Coming to Gettysburg was about the worst thing I've ever done."

Another lightning bolt. More thunder. Even the canvas now was starting to drip.

"Longstreet was right about that charge," Sorrel said. "It should have never been ordered."

"That's true, too, Mox."

"But I don't think any man has ever regretted being right more than Old Peter does now."

On July the Fourth, the rain slackened in the morning, only to return in the afternoon. Meade did not move from his position, and

Lee was able to get the wounded started back for Virginia.

I didn't move far from Longstreet's cot, though the tent was drenched along with everything else.

I toyed with the idea of trying to make my way into Gettysburg to find Jenny Rakestraw, but in the end I did not feel well enough. I was still exhausted, my head ached and my ribs were sore and my legs were too stiff to carry me.

At some point during the day an older man sought me out and found me resting on Longstreet's cot. He was part of Armistead's brigade and explained to me that when he enlisted all three of his sons had enlisted with him. There in the wet tent, he told me it was his son's body I'd brought back from the fight, and he thanked me for bringing his son back to him.

"I am told you're the officer who carried my son's body back," he said. "I was able to bury my son, and for that I'm grateful to you, sir. Everyone in our company is talking about it, about how an officer on Gen'l Longstreet's staff carried my dead son back to me."

I had little desire to talk to the man, for he was overcome with sadness at the loss of the boy. Nevertheless, I did the thing I thought Old Peter would have wanted done. "He died well," I said. "We were beyond the rock wall, inside the Yankee lines, right there with General Armistead. The fighting was hot, and when I was injured, your son dragged me out of the fray. There was a general retreat, and we were starting to make our way back when he was shot."

I remembered that the man had seen his son's body. "He was shot at least twice, maybe a couple more times. I picked him up, hoping to get him back to a doctor. But I could not move fast enough across that valley to save him."

The man shook his head sadly. "Thank you for bringing him back. I'm glad to know he will not be buried in no damned Yankee grave. His maw couldn't have stood that."

On July the Fifth, Longstreet's Corps – what was left of it – withdrew to the west behind Hill's Corps. It rained on us the entire way. I mourned the loss of my old slouch hat, left behind at the Angle, but Mox had found me a Confederate gray hat, the kind worn by the cavalry, and it suited me well enough and kept the rain off my face, or, I suppose, would have done so if the rain had not been so torrential and so persistent.

We arrived at the Potomac a couple of days later, but the river was so swollen we could not immediately cross. Even though Lee was defeated and limping away, Meade refused to follow immediately. With our back to the Potomac, Lee constructed defensive works to protect the army until the river went down enough that we could cross it. By the time the Army of the Potomac finally caught up to us, Lee was ready to make the crossing back into Virginia.

Throughout the withdrawal, I avoided anything amounting to difficult work. My bandaged ribs, which a doctor re-bandaged a couple of times during the retreat, and stitched up head served to keep me on the injured list. And I think, too, Longstreet felt bad for forcing me to make that charge with Pickett, and to make it up to me he allowed me to shirk for a while.

I'd seen every bit of the battle, and I'd seen it from both sides.

Lee won the first day, without question. The Yankees were in a rout by sunset, and it was only Reynolds – who by that time was well dead – who had saved the day for them by establishing Cemetery Hill and Cemetery Ridge as the army's rally point.

Though he achieved no tactical advantage, I would also say that Lee won the second day. At several points along his line he nearly achieved complete victory on the second day. But in the long run, Lee could less afford the losses of the second day than Meade, and so perhaps Meade was the true victor on July the Second. Probably, when you calculate all of the implications of the second day's fighting at Gettysburg, it would have to go down as a draw.

But on the third day, there is no question who won. Meade broke an entire division and two brigades from another division. Lee left the field having been whipped pretty good.

But do ye know, all throughout that retreat I heard boys saying again and again what a great victory we had scored in Pennsylvania. Men who had fought in the battle – even men who had been in Pickett's Charge and should have known better – left Gettysburg convinced that Lee was infallible and Meade had been taught a terrible lesson.

It's remarkable to me that Lee's men had such confidence in him that even when they were the ones getting whipped, they still believed Lee had scored a major victory at Gettysburg.

I never argued with them then, and I won't argue with them now. There's plenty of blame to go around for the Confederate's loss at Gettysburg. Ewell and Early could have, and should have, pressed the advantage we had on the first day. Their failures were the most egregious, in my mind. We lacked sufficient reinforcements on the second day to follow up the victories we achieved.

But in the end, we should have never fought the battles on the second and third day. We should have maneuvered Meade off that ground. Weeks before the battle took place, as I first rode up the Emmitsburg Road in search of Jenny Rakestraw, I could see that Cemetery Ridge, with the book ends of Culp's and Cemetery hills to the north and Little Roundtop and Sugarloaf to the south, was excellent ground for winning a battle.

But I wouldn't say that out loud, not then and not now. Longstreet was the goat of Gettysburg so that Lee could continue to be the hero of the Confederacy.

Banged up the way I was, that ride away from Gettysburg in the rain was terrible to endure, but when I wanted to complain, I reminded myself that mounted on a horse, as uncomfortable as it was, I was better off than I would have been crammed into a wagon with half a dozen other wounded men forever moaning and crying out, their gangrenous wounds stinking up the stuffy, covered wagon. No, I'd take a jarring in my ribs and a pounding in my head atop a horse over those hellish conditions any day.

When I have returned to Gettysburg in the years after the war, taking my children and grandchildren, I have looked among the faces of the women I have passed on the streets to see if I could recognize the blonde haired woman whose beauty led me to desert my way into the Bloodiest Battle ever fought on American soil, but I have never seen Jenny Rakestraw since the morning of the third day, when together we slipped into a general's tent and slipped out of the reality of that terrible time.

I do not think Bobby Lee ever came to understand my words as I returned from the terrible carnage of his disastrous charge. But what I intended for him to hear was this: All the blame for the carnage and destruction of lives and property at Gettysburg could be laid at his feet. When he directed his troops and planned his attacks, Lee could not comprehend that men who bled, men who dreamed, men who died were part of his plans. He only ever saw us as numbers to be pushed around on a battlefield. He could no more help the destruction he wrought than a dog could help pissing on its master's shoes. I'd always had contempt for Lee, and those madmen like him who sought glory on the graves of other men, but as I crossed back over that Valley of Death between Cemetery Ridge and Seminary Ridge, toting the body of that poor damned boy on my back, I hated Bobby Lee. But he could not understand that, either.

EPILOGUE

About two months after the war was over, not long before I went back out West, I found myself dozing in my study at home in Madison when a knock to the door roused me. It was a warm afternoon, but the windows were all open and a soft breeze was coming through, and I vividly recall a feeling of contentment in finally achieving the sort of pleasant peacefulness I'd dreamt of for four years.

When I got to the door, I was alarmed to find a young private in Yankee uniform standing on my porch, shifting from one foot to the other as he waited. No doubt he was more than a bit nervous to be walking around in Georgia dressed all in blue without an army to support him. There were still plenty of men out West to whom the word surrender held no meaning, and the blue and gray there were still shooting at each other. There may well have been a few of those renegades running around in Georgia, as well, so you'll understand his nervousness.

When I first saw him, I instinctively thought he must be trouble. I wondered if the politicians in Washington D.C. had decided to start arresting Confederate officers after all. So I decided I'd put on a pretty strong front, and if he seemed intent to putting chains on me then I'd make a dash for the back door and find Courage in the stable.

"What do ye want, boy?" I demanded as I opened the door.

"Are you Major Jackson Speed of the United States Army?"

I jumped in fright and looked first left and then right to make sure none of my neighbors had heard him.

"Silence your tongue, fool," I hissed at him. "Don't ye know where ye are? You can't be about here accusing folks of having served in the Yankee army."

The boy, sensing my fear and being none too comfortable hisself, went pale and looked around to make sure no one was coming after us.

"Yes, sir," he whispered to me. "Sorry, sir." Then continuing in a whisper, he asked it again: "Are you Major Speed, sir?"

"What do ye want?" I asked, frowning at him.

"I've a package here, sir, for Major Speed. It's from the War Department, sir. It's been sitting around for some time, and I guess they finally decided to see that you got it." And he extended his hand to show me a small box tied in twine with an envelope stuck in the twine. The writing on the envelope said simply: "Maj. Jackson Speed, United States Army, Madison, Georgia."

Seeing my name attached to the U.S. Army on that envelope made my stomach drop. If that damned fool private had shown that envelope to any of my neighbors, they'd be tying my neck to the highest branch they could find. I looked up and down the street one more time to be sure no mob was marching to the house with nooses and torches.

I snatched the box from his hand. "You be gone now," I hissed at him, "before the neighbors start talking."

"Yes, sir," he said, and the boy wasted no time in getting down off my porch and hurrying back down the road.

Curious, I intended to take the box back into my study and open it in private, but Eliza called to me from the parlor: "Jackson, was that a Yankee soldier on our porch?"

"It was, darling," I said.

"What on earth was that filth doing at our door?" she demanded, and there was more than a little tinge of hatred in her voice.

"Ah," I stuttered, searching for an answer, "well, it seems he was looking for General Tecumseh Sherman. Says he heard the man was in Georgia and wondered if I might know where to find him."

Now she raged, "Oh! Jackson Speed! Do not use that devil's name in my house ever again or you will find yourself sleeping under the porch with the dogs!"

I laughed so that she would know I was only kidding with her, but Eliza did not return the laugh. Nevertheless, mentioning Sherman had had its effect, for she was no longer asking about the Yankee private who'd been on the porch. Thank God she'd not heard him address me as a Yankee officer, or a mob of neighbors set on hanging me would have seemed like salvation.

Now I went into my study and sat down at my desk. I took a knife and cut the twine, then used it to slice open the envelope.

I gave a start when I glanced at the signature on the letter, for the man who had signed this letter was now dead and in a grave in Springfield, Illinois. Abe Lincoln had written to me from the great beyond. But the date on the letter was almost a year old. The letter had been written just a month after Gettysburg.

"To Maj. Jackson Speed," it began. "Dear Sir:

"I have spent a portion of the day with General Hancock, with whom I am told you are acquainted, and he has provided me with a list of names of certain individuals whom he believes acquitted themselves admirably on the recent field in Pennsylvania, and of whom the General and others familiar with the events of those days believe special recognition is deserved.

"I must confess that it came somewhat as a surprise to me to discover among those names one with whom I was already familiar. I inquired further and was told that on the second day of that great struggle, Major Speed, who was not detached with any portion of the Army of the Potomac so far as the War Department is able to perceive, captured a battle flag belonging to an Alabama regiment among the rebels. Further, I am informed from General Hancock, that this same Major Speed provided invaluable evidence at a counsel of war on the evening of the second day of that battle, and this evidence was used, in part, to convince General Meade, his staff, and his corps commanders that they should make a stand on that field.

"Further inquiry on my part brought confirmation from General Hancock that the Major Speed in question was yourself, the major who was once attached to Mr. Pinkerton's special group.

"Some effort has been made in the following days to determine your whereabouts, but unfortunately the War Department has been unable to locate you.

"Enclosed please find my thanks and the thanks of our Republic for the services you rendered on that day in Pennsylvania. No doubt, you are currently engaged in continuing to render services, though to whom and for what purpose, I cannot imagine. Perhaps, if we should both survive this present struggle, we might arrange a more fitting ceremony during which I can personally and formally present you with this Army Medal of Honor. I am sure at that time I should be glad to hear more of your exploits and discover to what ends you have been engaged in these intervening weeks.

"Until then, I remain, your president, Abraham Lincoln."

I had to chuckle when I read the old devil's letter. Abe had sized me up and knew me as well as I knew meself, and you could find throughout his missive the evidence that he didn't believe a wit of what Hancock told 'im.

I could see it all play out in mind: Lincoln seizing upon my name, demanding from Hancoock some evidence that I should receive an award, Win, quaking, no doubt, to have the commander in chief thundering at him. And it seemed Lincoln had put Stanton and the War Department through some trouble in trying to locate me and determine what the devil I was about.

But it was all true enough. I had, in essence, taken an Alabama flag and I'd counseled Meade and the others to stay put, hadn't I? Never was it my intention that they should stay there and slaughter Pickett or win the field, as they say, but b'God I'd pleaded the case pretty hard.

So maybe Lincoln gave me the honors without ever believing they were deserved, and maybe they weren't deserved, but I had done the things they said I had done.

I opened the box and took a look at the medal. It was a pretty thing – a red, white and blue ribbon attached to a gold star with an image of some war goddess or another holding a shield against a man with snakes in his hands. Above the star was an eagle with a cavalry sword clutched in its talons and crossed cannon barrels below the eagle. So the cavalry and artillery were represented, but I did not see where the shoeless and hungry infantryman had any representation.

No doubt there were boys without arms and legs wearing the things with pride or mothers who had put the medal in a place of honor and were shedding tears for lost sons every time they passed by the thing.

Well, war is a terrible thing, there ain't no doubt about it, and I was always plenty glad that all them other mothers and wives were shedding tears, and my Eliza was in the parlor ranting about Yankees and Tecumseh Sherman rather than wearing a black dress and veil.

I gave the letter another read and chuckled again. Truth was, Lincoln was as much a rascal as me, and if he'd not been besieged by the trappings and troubles of the office of the presidency, I suppose we'd have gotten along pretty well.

But when I was done reading it, I folded the letter back up and put it inside the box with the medal. Then I went to my old locker and stuck the box way down deep inside where it would go forever unnoticed by my redheaded, fire-eating, Yankee-hating wife. It wouldn't do for my beautiful Eliza to find such damning evidence that I'd been cavorting with Yankees. No, the Army Medal of Honor would not be adorning my walls nor placed with care upon my mantel. [78]

I drew a cigar from the box on my desk and lit it, and then I leaned back in my chair and put my feet up on my desk.

The war was over then, and I believed at the time that I'd survived the worst that life could give me and would now be enjoying my remaining years in comfort, leisure and peace. The breeze blew through the window, ruffling the curtains and scattering my cigar smoke.

Lincoln's letter made me think of Gettysburg, and that place always made me think of Jenny Rakestraw. I wondered what became of Jenny. My hope always was that after the war she found a man she could love, some man who would appreciate her. She was a rare gem and deserved a good life. I hope, too, that she left that place. I hope that she moved out west somewhere, to a place that was not haunted by the ghosts of Gettysburg.

the end

END NOTE: THE BATTLE OF GETTYSBURG

It would be impossible to encapsulate in a few paragraphs the effect of the Battle of Gettysburg or even to try to summarize it. Tens of thousands of pages by dozens upon dozens of writers of historical nonfiction have been printed on the subject, and one must assume that tens of thousands more pages will be printed in the future. Speed's recollections and impressions of the battle are accurate enough as far as one man's opinion goes, and those seeking to know more about the battle have any number of potential sources with which to improve their education.

An important point that Speed refers to often in his memoir about that battle is the perception that General James Longstreet, Lee's Warhorse, was somehow responsible for the Confederacy's loss. Unlike almost anyone else from his generation or from the South, Speed seems inclined to lay the blame at the feet of General Robert E. Lee. However, Speed was always quick to criticize most men who wore the stars of a general, and his opinions appear to be deeply rooted in his cowardice and ill feelings toward those who led armies, specifically armies to which he was attached.

Longstreet is one of the few exceptions among those generals who receive Speed's vitriol, and so their personal relationship and enduring friendship quite possibly colored Speed's opinions.

Throughout the remainder of his life, Longstreet was forced to defend himself against the accusations of Jubal Early, Fitzhugh Lee and others who claimed that Lee lost at Gettysburg because Longstreet was slow to obey orders.

This perception persisted in the South for most of the century following the War, though in the 1950s and 1960s, historians took a closer look at the historical record and largely absolved Longstreet of the blame. They found that the "orders" Longstreet failed to obey were likely never given – for instance, a dawn attack on the second day would have been impossible, for Longstreet's First Corps was still marching from Cashtown. Historians also found there was plenty of blame to be laid at the feet of those who criticized Longstreet – Ewell and Early were repeatedly in a position to do more to press their advantage against the Federal army and they failed to do so.

But to blame a Confederate general or all of the Confederate generals is to take away the credit due to the Army of the Potomac. There is little in the historical record to commend General George Meade as the commander who won Gettysburg. More accurately, he was the commander who did not lose Gettysburg.

As Speed points out, it was Meade's subordinates who won that battle. Brigadier Gen. John Buford's cavalry delayed the Confederate advance on McPherson Ridge. General John Reynolds, though killed early on the first day of the fighting, had selected the high ground south of Gettysburg where the Army of the Potomac would make its stand. General Winfield Hancock on the second day made use of his interior lines to repair the damage created by General Daniel Sickles (who inexplicably was gifted an Army Medal of Honor for his leadership at Gettysburg). Brigadier General Gouverneur Warren saw the danger at Little Round Top and Colonel Strong Vincent defended Meade's left flank.

All across the battlefield, from one end of Meade's famous fishhook to the other, men of every rank in an army known for its quickness to retreat did little things or enormous things to save the Union's position.

And finally, on the third day of the battle, Lee ordered a charge that should never have happened. The Union army's strength of numbers and supplies and an excellent position for fighting a defensive battle insured that before the first of Alexander's artillery fired, Lee was already beaten.

Confederates leaving the field did not know they had lost. Many later reported believing they had ventured into a Northern state and won a tremendous victory at Gettysburg.

Nevertheless, history has seen fit to mark Gettysburg as the "High Water Mark" or "High Tide" of the Confederacy. It represented the South's most confident time, Lee's farthest foray into Northern territory. Had the Army of Northern Virginia been successful at Gettysburg, it is possible that they would have turned on Washington D.C. Lincoln, who badly needed a victory to keep the citizens in the northern states from giving up on the war, might well have been forced into negotiating an end to the war.

The Battle of Gettysburg lives in our national conscience in a way no other Civil War battle does. Perhaps in the American memory, the only other battle that comes close is D-Day from World War II. Certainly the numbers of lives destroyed at Gettysburg make it one of the most terrible battles in American history – nearly 50,000 Americans killed, wounded or captured (3,155 Federals killed and 4,708 Confederates killed) – but there is something more that draws us, as a nation, to Gettysburg.

As editor of the Jackson Speed memoirs and an amateur historian, I believe it is this: Over the course of those three days, some of the best military minds of not just their generation but of any age met on a ground that seems almost perfectly suited for battle, and across the field men of both armies engaged in acts of courage that have been seldom rivaled in any war. In martial history, few battles are as grand and horribly magnificent as Gettysburg.

To those who are interested in learning more about this battle, I would strongly encourage a visit to the battlefield. It is America's most hallowed ground.

FOOTNOTES

[1] Who the staff officer might have been has been lost to history, however, Speed's story is confirmed by John Wills, owner of the Globe Inn. Wills seems to have taken great pride in the fact that his hotel was known among the Army of Northern Virginia, and after the war he many times told stories about the Rebels who visited his establishment. Wills claims that the Globe was often a stop by men whom he suspected to be Confederate spies in the days and weeks leading up to the battle of Gettysburg. He told the story that during the battle he saw a staff officer with Jubal Early, and when Wills questioned the man he tacitly confirmed that he'd eaten a meal at the Globe three weeks prior to the battle.

[2] Who the staff officer might have been has been lost to history, however, Speed's story is confirmed by John Wills, owner of the Globe Inn. Wills seems to have taken great pride in the fact that his hotel was known among the Army of Northern Virginia, and after the war he many times told stories about the Rebels who visited his establishment. Wills claims that the Globe was often a stop by men whom he suspected to be Confederate spies in the days and weeks leading up to the battle of Gettysburg. He told the story that during the battle he saw a staff officer with Jubal Early, and when Wills questioned the man he tacitly confirmed that he'd eaten a meal at the Globe three weeks prior to the battle.

[3] Alexander Buehler was the son of Samuel Buehler, a book merchant and druggist in Gettysburg. By the time of the war, the younger Buehler was being groomed to take over the store from his father. The store was a popular gathering place for the local college students and it was at this store where Jenny and Speed and many of the rest of Gettysburg's citizens picked up pieces of gossip in the days leading up to the battle.

[4] There was a fire in Emmitsburg, Maryland, in the early morning hours of June 16, 1863 that burned more than two dozen homes and left more than thirty families homeless. Other residents of Gettysburg

also reported seeing the flames – one report has them visible around midnight – and other Gettysburg citizens confirm that crowds gathered in the streets of Gettysburg and that the rumor quickly spread that the Army of Northern Virginia was burning Emmitsburg. Speed provides the only evidence that any members of the Home Guard rode to Emmitsburg, however other contemporary accounts of the event confirm that many Gettysburg residents left town in the night fearing that the Confederates were approaching Pennsylvania.

[5] Shiloh translated means "the place of peace." In a volume of his memoirs to be released after the current volume, Speed details his involvement in the Battle of Shiloh, and we know that this was the point where he first left the Union Army to join the Confederacy. On the first day of the battle, the South won a major victory with what amounted to a surprise attack against William T. Sherman and Ulysses S. Grant, but on the second day of the battle the Union army recaptured lost ground and drove the Confederacy off the battlefield.

[6] The story goes that General Hooker got his nickname due to a reporter's clerical error. The report contained a sentence that ended with the word "fighting" and the next sentence began with "Joe Hooker." As it was, the report seemed to indicate that Hooker was "Fighting Joe Hooker" and the nickname – however inappropriate – stuck. At the Battle of Chancellorsville, Hooker failed to push his advantage and ordered a halt to his troops' movements before Lee was engaged. As a result, Lee had time and space to send Stonewall Jackson on the flanking maneuver in which Speed was so instrumental.

[7] It seems likely that the Hagerstown man did indeed have good information. General Richard Ewell's corps was the lead division of the Army of Northern Virginia in its invasion north, and on June 15, Ewell began the crossing at Williamsport. To say, though, that this was the "main body" of the army is a gross exaggeration, though the man can hardly be blamed for being alarmed. On June 17, Generals Longstreet and Hill were barely on the move from their encampments at Culpeper and Fredericksburg, respectively. It was also not correct that the Army of the Potomac was standing still. By this time, Hooker

had abandoned his Falmouth encampment and was on the move toward Manassas where he intended to prevent Lee from turning east and engaging Washington, D.C. If Speed's memory is correct that this event took place on the afternoon of June 16 – the day after the Emmitsburg fire, then likely the Williamsport witness who provided the information saw Ewell's lead elements crossing the Potomac and sounded an immediate alarm.

[8] Speed is likely confusing the Seminary with Pennsylvania College, also in Gettysburg. Dr. Henry Louis Baugher was president of Pennsylvania College and had lost a son at the Battle of Shiloh in 1862. Baugher was adamant that his students avoid serving in the war and repeatedly instructed them not to join any local militia. Eventually, several of his students would join the 26th Pennsylvania Militia and would take part in the first skirmish on the outskirts of Gettysburg, a short-lived affair in which the 26th Pennsylvania's 743 men would nearly all be taken captive.

[9] General John C. Pemberton, commander of the Confederacy's Army of the Mississippi, in May of 1863 suffered severe losses against Union General Ulysses S. Grant in Mississippi. By this time, Pemberton was in Vicksburg and Grant had laid siege to that city. Coinciding with the Battle of Gettysburg, Pemberton realized his men could no longer hold out against Grant's siege on July 2, 1863 and Pemberton surrendered on the morning of July 4, 1862. Though Gettysburg is remembered as a major turning point in the war, the loss of Vicksburg was vital to the Confederacy because Grant's victory there essentially cut off the western states of the Confederacy and allowed Grant and Sherman to turn their attention east. Speed is correct that Jubal Early's Division of the Army of Northern Virginia arrived in Cashtown on Friday, June 26, 1863 and marched through the Town of Gettysburg on that day.

[10] It remains a point of interest that Lee's cavalry led by Jeb Stuart was in fact no where nearby. When Lee set out for Pennsylvania, Stuart and the cavalry were given orders to guard the Army of Northern Virginia's flank, and much has been made about the order and the way Stuart interpreted the order. Regardless, Stuart's cavalry

went to the east, at one point riding within sight of Washington D.C. and was always well to the east or north of Lee's army as it moved into Pennsylvania. At the time, the cavalry was the eyes and ears of an army, and Lee was left blind and deaf without word from Stuart for much of the Pennsylvania Campaign.

[11] The 26th Pennsylvania Militia, consisting of 743 men recruited by W.W. Jennings, included 21 students from Pennsylvania College. Dr. Henry Louis Baugher vehemently urged his students not to join the emergency militia, perhaps motivated by the loss of his son at Shiloh the year before. Most of the men were captured and immediately paroled.

[12] Though JEB Stuart's cavalry was largely away from the main body of the Confederate army during the Pennsylvania Campaign, the 35th Battalion under the command of Elijah White of Loudon County, Virginia, was assigned to one of Jubal Early's brigades. White's Battalion was the one riding through Gettysburg on this day.

[13] Speed's recollections are accurate enough as far as they go. Other citizens of Gettysburg largely confirm the general tone of the interactions citizens had with Jubal Early's men as they marched through the town. The Confederates also allowed the citizens of Gettysburg to speak to and provide food to the 175 members of the emergency militia who had been taken prisoner. However, not all the encounters between Confederates and townspeople were quite so friendly. As White's cavalry first rode into town, they were in pursuit of Bell's volunteers. Private George Sandoe, one of Bell's cavalrymen, was chased down by White's cavalry and killed in the streets, giving him the unfortunate distinction in history as being the first soldier killed in Gettysburg. In some cases, homes were searched. The black people the Confederates found were taken prisoner and sent south. Some homes were vandalized. In at least one reported case, Southern soldiers poured black cherries over the floor of a house and then cut open a bed and spread the stuffing over the cherries and wrote on the wall "Done in retaliation for what was done in the south." That scene in particular is very reminiscent of some of the acts of vandalism (which were far more widespread) committed by troops in

Fredericksburg when the Northern army occupied that Southern city. On the whole, however, Gettysburg's citizenry reported little more than teasing – and many returned as good as they got – and in most cases of "requisitioning" the Southerners paid for the goods they took either in Confederate money that would have been useless to a Pennsylvanian or, remarkably, sometimes in silver coins. Speed is undoubtedly correct that the Army of Northern Virginia was in high spirits in those days before Gettysburg, as confirmed by numerous sources both among the Northern citizens who encountered them and their own recollections and those of their officers.

[14] The "someone" who was found was David Kendlehart, president of the town council, who was hiding in his home near the Diamond as soldiers throughout the city were seeking town officials to bring to Lieutenant General Early at the Diamond. Early issued a demand to Kendlehart for quantities of bacon, flour, onions, coffee, sugar, salt and 500 hats of any style. Early also demanded the town pay $10,000. Kendlehart said the town could not provide the quantities requested, but he did order the shops to open and that the citizens furnish whatever they could afford to give the Southerners. After dark, the 50-year-old Kendlehart snuck out of his home and fled the town.

[15] This conversation between Speed and Jenny took place on the morning of Saturday, June 27. During the day there would be a series of increasingly hostile telegrams between General Hooker and Lincoln's General-in-Chief Henry W. Halleck in the Federal War Department. The end result would be that before the day was out, James Hardie, assistant adjutant general of the Federal army, would depart Washington, D.C. by train to Frederick, Maryland, where the headquarters of the Army of the Potomac was presently located, with orders relieving Hooker of command and replacing him with George Meade, though the orders would not arrive until the early morning hours of June 28.

[16] Dr. Michael Jacobs was a professor of mathematics at Pennsylvania College, but was also an avid botanist who kept a daily journal of meteorological readings. His son Henry was 18-years-old at the time

of the battle.

[17] Speed is seldom kind to his contemporaries. It is remarkable that he thought so highly of James Longstreet, for with the possible exception of U.S. Grant, he seldom met a general in any army for whom he had a kind word. But his depiction of Henry Jacobs seems particularly unfair. Henry Jacobs was 18-years-old at the time of the Battle of Gettysburg, and both the younger and elder Jacobs left to posterity invaluable records of the events that took place at the time of the battle. Henry Jacobs was one of the first to publish a description of the battle from the point of view of a citizen of Gettysburg. Like his father, he became a college professor and eventually rose to the level of Dean of the Lutheran Theological Seminary in Gettysburg. Furthermore, Henry's sister Julia, 16-years-old at the time of the battle, became something of a heroine. During Lee's retreat, a picket of Confederate sharpshooters set up just down the street from the Jacobs' home and in front of the Jacobs family they fired on unsuspecting Union cavalry in an attempt to cover Lee's retreat. Having witnessed what her brother termed "murder," Julia stood in her family's front door and warned oncoming Union cavalrymen of the danger ahead. Realizing what she was doing, the Confederate sharpshooters turned their guns on her, but for as long as thirty minutes she continued to warn Federal troopers of the danger while the sharpshooters fired on her. Eventually, Union infantry came up and engaged the Confederates in a duel, and Julia, unharmed, was able to return to the safety of her home.

[18] Surely this is none other than sixty-nine year old John Burns, "the hero of Gettysburg." Burns, a veteran of the War of 1812, on the first day of the battle took up his antiquated Enfield rifle and joined the Federals fighting west of town on McPherson's Ridge. Burns fought with the Iron Brigade. Though he has become popular in legend, evidence suggests he was cantankerous – arguing with his neighbors and calling them cowards for not joining him in taking up arms against the invaders. He is said to have shot a mounted Confederate officer while fighting with the 7th Wisconsin, but he received a number of wounds, and when the Federals fled, Burns crawled away from his gun, buried his ammunition and swore that he'd not been

fighting when the Confederates captured him. A Confederate surgeon dressed his wounds and the Southerners carried him home.

[19] Speed's memoirs clear up a minor mystery that has lingered since the battle of Gettysburg. As he marched toward Gettysburg in search of shoes, General Pettigrew received information from three separate sources that a large force of Federals was in the vicinity of the town. Because he was under orders from Lee not to engage the enemy, Pettigrew halted the column and proceeded cautiously. Two of the sources of the information are known. Pettigrew himself talked to two of them. One of them was a local doctor with Southern sympathies who was paying a visit to a patient out on the Chambersburg Road when he came upon the advancing Southern column. The second was General Longstreet's spy Harrison who rode into Gettysburg to scout in advance of Pettigrew and then rode past Buford's advance cavalrymen into the Confederate column where he warned Pettigrew of Buford's approach south of town. But one of the sources has gone down in history as an unnamed local farmer who was believed to be a member of the Knights of the Golden Circle. This organization was formed largely from Southern veterans of the Mexican-American War. The group's ultimate ambition was to invade and conquer Mexico as well as islands in the Caribbean. Their hope was to have the Southern states secede from the Union and form a new country consisting of the South and these conquered lands. Texas Ranger and Confederate General Ben McCulloch, with whom Speed served in Mexico, was among the leaders of the Knights of the Golden Circle. In other volumes of his memoirs (specifically, Jackson Speed and the Blood Tubs), Speed mentions his involvement with the group but indicates his participation did not go beyond card playing, drinking and story telling. Through these memoirs we now know that Speed was the unnamed farmer who provided the warning that allowed the 47th North Carolina to avoid a Union ambush.

[20] Pettigrew on June 1 camped between Cashtown and Gettysburg. He rode back to Cashtown where he told Henry Heth and A.P. Hill, the Third Corps commander, of seeing Buford's cavalry ride into Gettysburg. Neither Heth nor Hill would credit that the Federals were anywhere near Gettysburg in force, believing the cavalry Pettigrew

saw was no more than an observation force. They decided that Heth would take his entire division to Gettysburg to get the shoes and chase off the cavalry. The march began in a drizzle at 5 a.m. July 1.

[21] This is likely Daniel Skelly and Samuel Anderson who went out the Mummasburg Road north of town early on the morning of July 1 where they climbed a tree to watch the first fighting of the morning.

[22] The first cannon shots were reported west of town, within about three miles, at around 8 a.m. on July 1, as Heth, after "feeling" what was in his front decided he faced only dismounted cavalry and concluded to sweep the Federals off McPherson's ridge. Union General John Reynolds was encamped just four miles from the Confederates, downstream of Marsh Creek, south of Gettysburg. Buford's intention was to hold the Southern army long enough for Reynolds' infantry – the left wing of Meade's army – to get forward.

[23] Speed's recollection of the meeting of Buford and Reynolds at the Seminary on the morning of July 1 is largely corroborated by G.B. Garrison, one of Buford's scouts and Captain Stephen Weld, Reynolds' aide-de-camp. The time was 8:35 a.m. Buford had been in the cupola and seen the line of Reynolds' infantry moving up the Emmitsburg Road. When the two met on the steps of the Seminary building, Reynolds questioned Buford about the situation and Buford famously answered, "Hell's to pay."

[24] Speed's recollection of his meeting with Dr. Jacobs and Lieutenant Bonaparte is nearly impossible to reconcile with the historical record. Dr. Jacobs' son Henry recalled that Dr. Jacobs did in fact survey the land with a Signal Corps officer by the name of Bonaparte, but Henry is very clear that this took place on the top floor, or perhaps in the cupola, of Pennsylvania College in the north section of Gettysburg and not the Lutheran Theological Seminary. Henry does not record that his father ever went so near to the fighting that morning as to be at the Seminary. It is possible that Speed and Jenny were at both the Lutheran Seminary and later at Pennsylvania College, or perhaps Dr. Jacobs and Lieutenant Bonaparte left the College and went to the Seminary for a better view.

[25] General John Fulton Reynolds was captured during the Seven Days Battle in June of 1862 but was exchanged on August 15 for Confederate General Lloyd Tilghman who was captured when he surrendered Fort Henry to Union forces under General U.S. Grant.

[26] Modern historians debate whether Reynolds was shot by a sharpshooter, a volley or perhaps even friendly fire. Speed's recollection does not clarify the issue, as even he has to question whether it was "a squirrel's nest" or a sharpshooter he saw in the trees.

[27] Union General O.O. Howard held the right flank of the Union Army at the Battle of Chancellorsville two months prior to the Battle of Gettysburg. His men, many of them German immigrants, were taken completely by surprise by Confederate General Stonewall Jackson's charge (which, ironically, Speed led) and ran, many of them over a mile, when the Confederates broke through the woods on their flank. Howard's Germans earned a poor reputation following their hasty retreat at Chancellorsville, and Howard himself received a fair amount of the blame.

[28] It was most probably the Fahnestock Store, and Daniel Skelly who led them to the observation deck. In personal narratives of the battle, Skelly recounts how he watched much of the battle in the morning and early afternoon from the observation deck on top of the store where he worked as a clerk (a store he would one day own) and that he also led General Howard to the observation deck. Skelly reports that Howard was on top of the store's observation deck when he first learned of Reynolds' death. Speed does not confirm it, but it was likely Skelly who woke him up that morning as he rushed up Carlisle Street looking for a point from which to watch the battle. Skelly found a tree to climb and stayed there in the first hour or so of the battle until cannon shot came too near, and then he retired to the store's observation deck.

[29] Confederate General Robert E. Rodes led the flanking charge at Chancellorsville that routed Union General Howard's men. Speed was also at the front of that attack – attempting to escape the duty Stonewall Jackson had assigned him of leading Rodes' men through the woods and into the Union flank. For more on this, see Volume III of the Jackson Speed Memoirs: Jackson Speed on the Orange Turnpike.

[30] Speed refers to the Union men behind the stone wall as "New Yorkers," but in fact there were regiments from New York, Maine, Massachusetts and Pennsylvania.

[31] Brigadier General Alfred Iverson Jr. was a veteran of Mexico and had attended the military institute of Tuskegee, Alabama. In 1855, when Jefferson Davis was Secretary of War and Iverson's father was a U.S. senator, Davis appointed Iverson a first lieutenant in the U.S. First Cavalry. Speed is not the only person to make the charge that Iverson was intoxicated on the first day at Gettysburg, and whether or not the charge that Iverson was "off hiding somewhere" is accurate, Iverson certainly did not go with his men as they set out across open fields to assail the enemy line. From June 27 to June 30, Rodes was in Carlisle, Pennsylvania, where Iverson had been stationed prior to the war. The men found a significant quantity of government whisky, and many of the men indulged to excess. Iverson himself reunited with old friends from his time there. There were many accusations that men from the brigadier general down were still showing the effects of too much alcohol on the first day at Gettysburg.

[32] Speed's numbers are accurate enough, and probably as accurate as any available. Regimental reports from the day are lost, however later records have it that 1,470 men and officers marched against the stone wall and 512 were killed or wounded and another 308 were missing. As many as 200 were taken prisoner as Union men at one end of the battle line rushed out to catch the fleeing Southerners, but those 200 were re-taken later in the day. There was controversy at the time. Iverson, who did not go forward with the attack, claimed he saw men raising a white flag, and word spread that an entire North Carolina regiment surrendered. Later, when confronted with the fact that some

500 of his men were lying dead in a straight line of battle, Iverson exonerated the men. Iverson himself was soon relieved of command, but he was never to lose the shadow of responsibility for the Confederate disaster on Oak Hill. Lee's pioneers dug shallow graves in the field and buried the North Carolinians in common graves. To this day, the graves are known as "Iverson's Pits." Rodes recalled later that after the first day's fighting he was riding behind his line and saw what he thought was an entire regiment lying down in the rear to escape the fighting. He rode to them, and then realized it was an entire regiment of dead from Iverson's brigade.

[33] The incident Speed refers to happened during the Battle of Chancellorsville and is chronicled in Volume III of his memoirs, Jackson Speed on the Orange Turnpike. During that battle, General Jackson with some of his officers had advanced forward after dark to do some reconnaissance. When he was returning to the Rebel lines, skirmishers fired upon the group believing they were Federals. Jackson was shot several times and wounded. He lost an arm as a result of his injuries, but initially it was believed he would survive. While recuperating, he came down with pneumonia and died.

[34] Speed notes here what historians have debated for 150 years: What if Ewell had pressed his advantage? There were still two hours of daylight, and the general feeling among all the Confederates now in the town of Gettysburg was that they would soon make a charge on Cemetery Hill. Among the most vocal to Ewell about pressing their advantage was Major General Isaac Ridgeway Trimble, who served on Ewell's staff. Trimble rode forward to examine the situation at Cemetery Hill and Culp's Hill. He urged Ewell to attack, but Ewell declined because he had received no orders from Lee to do so. Trimble begged first for a division and then a brigade and said he would take Culp's Hill if granted the troops. Finally, he asked, "Give me a good regiment and I will engage to take the hill!" When Ewell denied even this, Trimble threw down his sword and swore that he would no longer serve under Ewell. But it was not just Trimble who saw the eminence and believed it should be occupied at once. The men themselves cheered for an advance, crying out, "Let's go on!" A common view held by those who have studied the issue is that both

Ewell and Early in the late afternoon of the first day were in position to take Culp's Hill, and possibly Cemetery Hill as well. Had they done so, Gettysburg would quite obviously have turned out differently as these Union positions proved to be critical on the second and third days of the battle. Speed notes, too, that Ewell had risen to command a corps after the death of Stonewall Jackson. Again, those who have studied the war often wonder what the outcome might have been if Jackson were still in command.

[35] Strictly speaking, no one was intended as a replacement for Stonewall Jackson. After Jackson's death, General Lee divided Jackson's Second Corps into two corps, the Second Corps under Ewell and the Third Corps under A. P. Hill.

[36] General Robert E. Lee's physical condition during the Gettysburg Campaign has been the subject of much historical debate. Clearly, he was not himself during the battle. Some modern historians have offered evidence supporting a theory that Lee suffered a mild heart attack prior to the battle. Some historical scholarship has blamed the raw cherries in the field where he camped at Chambersburg for giving him a case of diarrhea, known among the army as the "Virginia quick step."

[37] Longstreet marks the conclusion of his meeting with Lee at headquarters at 7 p.m. on the evening of July 1. Likely, Speed and Moxley Sorrel were waiting outside headquarters for at least an hour, assuming Captain Smith's time of 5 p.m. was correct and Speed had a slow ride from the Diamond to Lee's headquarters which was just beyond the town, opposite the Seminary on the Chambersburg Pike.

[38] It cannot be stated any better than what Speed says here. General JEB Stuart, the flashy cavalry officer, had been missing since the Army of Northern Virginia crossed the Potomac. Stuart had been east of the army, even on the outskirts of Washington D.C., and had done some damage to rail lines and telegraph lines, and he had captured some wagons. But what Lee needed was intelligence reporting the movements of his adversary. Had Stuart been present, perhaps Lee could have scouted the lay of the land south and east of Gettysburg

and given more credence to Longstreet's proposal of getting around Meade's flank, getting the Army of Northern Virginia between Meade and Washington D.C., and fighting a defensive battle.

[39] In the early months of 1862, a scarlet fever epidemic broke out in Richmond, Va., where Longstreet's wife Maria Louise was living with the couple's four children. In the matter of just eight days, scarlet fever took three of the four children. All of Longstreet's friends and associates said the general was devastated by the loss of his children and that his personality was forever altered.

[40] Speed details his first encounter with Daniel Sickles in "Jackson Speed and the Da Ponte Diamond," contained within Volume III of the Jackson Speed Memoirs. Union General Daniel Sickles was among the most colorful characters from the American Civil War. His affairs were numerous and famous: He was censured for escorting the prostitute Fanny White into the New York State Legislature and introduced the same woman to Queen Victoria of England; he had an affair with the Queen of Spain Isabella II after the war when he was serving as the United States Minister to Spain. Sickles was also the first person to successfully use temporary insanity as a defense against a murder charge. In 1859, after discovering that his wife Teresa Bagioli Sickles was having an affair with Philip Key, district attorney of Washington D.C. and the son of Francis Scott Key, Sickles gunned him down in Lafayette Square.

[41] For clarification purposes, these Alabama regiments Speed found on picket duty in Pitzer's Woods on the morning of the second day were from the Third Corps. They were under the command of Wilcox of Richard H. Anderson's Division of Hill's Third Corps and should not be confused with the Alabamians of George T. Anderson's brigade of Hood's Division of the First Corps. To add to the potential for confusion, Speed encounters both the Third Corps Alabamians and the First Corps Alabamians in Pitzer's Woods on the second day and, at least briefly, is involved with both groups of Alabamians during engagements during the course of the day.

[42] A Texas Ranger during the Mexican-American War and one of the leading figures in a movement to have the South secede from the Union, invade Mexico and Cuba and form a new nation, Ben McCulloch was a legend who lived up to his own myth. He was made a general in the Confederacy and died at the Battle of Pea Ridge (also known as the Battle of Elkhorn Tavern) in 1862. Famously, McCulloch on a scouting mission rode into Santa Anna's camp and escaped beyond the Mexican pickets, in part by acting as a rancher looking for a lost horse and walking in view of the pickets. Speed took part in McCulloch's famous ride into Santa Anna's camp, and recounts the adventure in Jackson Speed: The Hero of El Teneria.

[43] See "Jackson Speed and the Da Ponte Diamond" contained in Volume III of the Jackson Speed Memoirs. Dan Sickles, a Tammany Hall Democrat, had a colorful life before and after the war. In 1859, while serving as a Congressman from New York, Sickles discovered that his wife was having an affair with Philip Key, son of Francis Scott Key and district attorney for Washington D.C. Sickles shot Key several times, killing him, in LaFayette Square within sight of the White House. Sickles surrendered and was charged with murder, but in the first use of the plea of temporary insanity in the United States, Sickles was acquitted. Though Speed indicates Teresa Sickles had many lovers, outside of Philip Key and Jackson Speed himself, there is little indication that she participated in other affairs.

[44] Throughout the morning of the second day at Gettysburg, General Sickles worried over the position of his Third Corps on Meade's left. Though aligned along Cemetery Ridge with the rest of the Army of the Potomac, Sickles felt the ground he held was not superior to the high ground of the peach orchard in front of him. Around noon, well before the Confederate army was in position to launch its attack of the second day, Sickles sent Berdan's Sharpshooters, who wore a distinctive green uniform, and the Third Maine Regiment forward. Later in the day, against orders, Sickles advanced the entire Third Corps forward into the Peach Orchard. Those who witnessed the movement said later it was executed in grand style and something many of those present on the battlefield would never forget. Nevertheless, Sickles endangered his entire Corps and the whole of

Meade's left as a result of the movement.

[45] According to records from the battle, Anderson's three infantry regiments were 300 yards behind the skirmishers. The Maine Regiment and Berdan's Sharpshooters battled Anderson's infantry for twenty-five minutes before returning to Sickles, where they reported that they believed the main body of the Confederates was not in front of Culp's and Cemetery hills as the Union believed, but rather that they were located in Pitzer's Woods in front of Sickles. Though Longstreet's First Corps was on its way to the approximate location of Anderson's regiments in the woods, Longstreet was still well away from that location. It is worth noting that while historians have puzzled over Sickles' behavior on the second day at Gettysburg, only Jackson Speed makes the claim that Sickles advanced forward off of Cemetery Ridge first a regiment and then an entire Corps solely to enact revenge against Speed for having a brief affair with his then-ex wife Teresa Sickles. According to Longstreet, Anderson's infantry was sent to Pitzer's Woods to meet the advancing Maine Regiment and Berdan's Sharpshooters, but most other sources agree with Speed that the men had been left there over night to guard Lee's right flank.

[46] Speed's vehement defense of Longstreet is uncommon in his memoirs. Nearly every other commanding officer under whom he served, in any war or encounter, found nothing but contempt from Speed in his memoirs, but Speed often writes fondly of Longstreet and notes in his memoirs frequently that his friendship with Longstreet lasted until Longstreet's death. Speed also appears to kindle a deeper hatred for Jubal Early than he did for other generals, whom he despised almost universally as is illustrated in this reference "Jubal Early should have taken the stairs years earlier." Early died in 1894, at 77 years of age, after falling down a flight of stairs.

[47] Though there are certainly differing accounts, Speed's reckoning of time on the morning and early afternoon of the second day is largely supported by other sources. He is correct, too, that the first elements of the First Corps to arrive in Pitzer's Woods were Hood's skirmishers, and they did indeed hear the fighting between Anderson's regiments and Berdan's Sharpshooters. By the time

Hood's skirmishers reached Anderson's regiments, the brief engagement had concluded and Berdan's had retreated out of Pitzer's Woods.

[48] Brigadier General Evander McIvor Law, originally from South Carolina, was a graduate of the South Carolina Military Academy (now the Citadel) and for two years prior to the war taught history at Kings Mountain Military Academy. In 1860 he moved to Alabama to start a military high school, and at the outbreak of war joined the Alabama militia. He served as a brigadier general under Hood in Longstreet's First Corps. At Gettysburg, when Hood was injured, Law took over division command. Toward the end of the war, Law feuded with superior officers, including Longstreet, and Longstreet had Law arrested twice. Lee and Hood both intervened on Law's behalf and at Cold Harbor, Law was back in command of his brigade. There, though, he received a gunshot wound to the face that fractured his skull and injured his left eye. Speed identifies Law as the youngest general in the Confederacy, but this is inaccurate; Law was not even the youngest Confederate general at Gettysburg as Lieutenant General Ramseur was a year younger than Law.

[49] General George McClellan "Little Mac" to the Army of the Potomac that so adored him, was Lincoln's first in a long line of commanders of the army. At the start of the war, McClellan organized the Army of the Potomac and put an emphasis on drilling and preparations. Though Speed may be partly correct that the men of the Third Corps owed their training to McClellan, just as many of them who drilled under "The Young Napoleon" in 1861 would have been gone from the army (through expired enlistments, injuries, deaths and disease) by the summer of 1863.

[50] John Bell Hood, known as "Sam," was actually born in Kentucky – not in Tennessee as Speed claims. He was nearly expelled from West Point for excessive demerits and graduated near the bottom of his class. Prior to the Civil War, he served in the regular army in California and then Texas. When his native state of Kentucky remained neutral, Hood decided to fight for Texas and led what became known as Hood's Texas Brigade. He was known for

aggressiveness and was rated one of the best fighting generals in Lee's army. At the Battle of Gaines' Mill during the Seven Days Battle, Hood broke the Union line in a charge that resulted in every field officer – except Hood – being killed or wounded.

[51] Speed's recollections of his movements of this hour are nearly impossible to reconcile with the historical record. Hood would have dispatched Lieutenant Pinckney's reconnaissance at nearly the same time that Sickles began his forward movement off of Cemetery Ridge and into the Peach Orchard. Speed indicates that he and Law watched Sickles' entire movement together and they discussed that Sickles stopped in the Peach Orchard. For Speed to have been present with Law in Pitzer's Woods throughout the entirety of the Third Corps' march into the Peach Orchard, he could not have also been present with Pinckney during the reconnaissance. Most likely, Speed, Law and Hood saw the beginnings of Sickles' advance and he would have watched the remainder of it with Pinckney as they conducted the reconnaissance. It seems apparent, then, that Speed attributes some of his conversation with Law when it almost certainly must have been with Pinckney.

[52] Speed's recollection of Pinckney's reconnaissance corresponds with the official record; however, it is worth noting that neither Hood nor Pinckney make any mention of the captain from Longstreet's staff joining the reconnaissance. Hood recalls only that he sent Lieutenant Pinckney and five of Pinckney's men, and Pinckney reports only that he detailed two of his men to return to Hood with the information of Meade's supply trains parked at the eastern base of Round Top. As we now know, Lee refused Longstreet's requests to make a flanking movement around the base of Round Top, and so no laurels were bestowed for the reconnaissance, neither to Lieutenant Pinckney nor to Captain Speed.

[53] The artillery started sometime between three o'clock and four o'clock on the second day, by most accounts nearer to four o'clock. Most accounts of the battle agree that Hood's men, beginning with Law's brigade, stepped off to begin their charge at almost exactly four o'clock.

54 The 15th Alabama, commanded by Colonel William Oates, was actually in the middle of Law's Brigade, flanked on either side by two other Alabama regiments and not on the far right as Speed recalls. However, when the order to march was given, one of the regiments to Oates' right fell back in reserve while the other moved behind Oates and then to his left, so that by the time Law's Brigade was engaged in the battle, Oates' 15th Alabama had in fact become the far right of Lee's entire army.

55 In the autumn of 1862, the Weikert brothers who lived east of Little Roundtop had cut timber on the western face of the hillside (the side facing the Devil's Den) for winter firewood and to make a profit from the sale of timber. Neither Lee nor Meade knew of the narrow dirt road coming over Little Round Top and descending down the eastern slope on which the Weikert brothers carried the timber they cut.

56 As Colonel Oates halted his men at the summit of Round Top, Captain L. R. Terrell, General Law's assistant adjutant general, did climb to the top on horseback to inform Oates that Hood had been injured and that Law had taken command of the division and to press Oates to continue his attack. Like Speed, Oates recalled being stunned that Terrell had managed the astounding feat of getting to the summit of Round Top mounted on a horse.

57 At the Battle of Cerro Gordo during the Mexican-American War, Captain Robert E. Lee, supervising the army engineers, built roads and arranged for the movement of artillery over what Ulysses S. Grant would describe as "chasms ... where the walls were so steep that men could barely climb them. Animals could not."

58 Probably this officer was Captain Henry C. Brainard who fell near Colonel Oates. "Captain Brainard, one of the bravest and best officers in the regiment, in leading his company forward, fell, exclaiming, 'Oh God! That I could see my mother!' and instantly expired," Oates wrote of the incident.

[59] Speed here mixes the lyrics of two favorite songs among the Union army (both sung to the tune of the old southern folk hymn "Glory, Hallelujah"), "The Battle Hymn of the Republic" and "John Brown's Body."

[60] Speed's account lends confirmation to the unproven story that General Meade's Chief of Staff, General Daniel Butterfield, drew up plans for retreat on the afternoon of July 2, 1863, before Longstreet's attack began. Evidence suggests the plan for withdrawal was only in the event of emergency, and all the copies of the plan were destroyed within days of the battle. Having won a major victory, Meade had cause to not want it to be known publicly that he'd considered withdrawing. Telegraph messages Meade sent to Halleck before and during the battle on the second day indicated his intent was to hold his ground or attack and not to retreat. Nevertheless, the persistent charge that Meade considered withdrawing to the Pipe Creek line also finds support in the historical record. If Meade's mind was made up, there seems to have been little reason for Meade to have held his council of war late on the night of July 2.

[61] Many Union soldiers and Confederates, too, positioned in the vicinity of Culp's Hill reported that in the early morning hours of July 3 they could hear wagons moving away from the battle along the Baltimore Pike. The assumption among Confederates was that they would awake to find Meade's army gone. Union troops, too, said they believed they were withdrawing when they heard the wagons moving. There were, however, no wagon trains moving down the Baltimore Pike and the Union army certainly was not retreating. Despite the fact that it was widely reported by soldiers of both armies, no explanation has ever been found for the noise the soldiers heard, and to this day it remains a mystery of the Battle of Gettysburg.

[62] The legend of men from both armies meeting in peace at Spangler's Spring has largely been debunked by modern historians, and so it seems odd that Speed would recall conversations taking place at the spring if modern historians are correct. The legend of Spangler's

Spring is largely thought to have been a myth created after the war to help with reconciliation, to show that the two armies consisted of men who could converse during a pause in the battle. It was printed in newspapers and eventually accepted as truth (many historians prior to the modern period reported it as such in their histories of Gettysburg). There is a monument at the battlefield marking Spangler's Spring. It is possible that Speed's memory was affected by the legends which certainly existed prior to his writing of Volume IV of his memoirs.

[63] Brigadier General John Geary of Slocum's Corps of the Union Army of the Potomac at approximately 3:45 a.m. on July 3 began the battle of that day by firing a pistol into the air as a signal for his men on Culp's Hill to fire their first volley at the men of Johnson's brigade below them on the hill.

[64] General George Pickett was one of Longstreet's favorites, though the historical record left by Longstreet's chief of staff, Moxley Sorrel, suggests that Pickett was often too distracted by his famous love affair with the beautiful LaSalle Corbell. Sorrel wrote that Pickett would often abandon his post while the First Corps was at Suffolk to steal away in the middle of the night to see Corbell and would ask that Sorrel cover for him with General Longstreet. Sorrel also reports that in times of immediate danger, Longstreet would have his staff "give (Pickett) things very fully; indeed, sometimes stay with him to make sure he did not get astray."

[65] Speed and Pickett both record this exchange between Lee and Longstreet in almost the same language. Pickett put the meeting at eight o'clock in the morning, which generally corresponds with Speed's estimations of time, though Speed is certainly less exact.

[66] General Longstreet also recorded this final conversation with Lee before Pickett made his famous charge, and Speed's recollection corresponds almost verbatim with Longstreet's.

[67] In the 150 years since the Battle of Gettysburg, the objective has come to be known by historians of the battle as the "clump of trees." But at the time of the battle, the "clump of trees" between the Codori farm and the Bryan barn that was Pickett's objective was just one tall tree over several saplings and bushes running along a low stone wall.

[68] Unfairly, Longstreet at this late hour sought to abdicate responsibility for the charge by giving it to Col. E.P. Alexander, the commander of artillery for the First Corps. According to Lee's plan of battle, Alexander was to initiate a bombardment of Cemetery Ridge in the hopes of disabling the Union artillery and softening the infantry in advance of the Confederate attack. Longstreet sent a note to Alexander telling him to observe the bombardment, and if it did not drive the Federals from the ridge or "greatly demoralize him as to make our efforts pretty certain" then Longstreet preferred that Pickett not be given the signal to charge. Alexander, already concerned that he lacked the necessary ammunition to make such a sustained bombardment effective, responded with his own note, telling Longstreet that if there was an alternative to the assault he believed it should be "carefully considered" due to the short supply of ammunition. Further, Alexander said he would only be able to judge the effectiveness of his bombardment by the return fire of the Federals because the entrenched infantry was too difficult to see. Longstreet sent an immediate response, telling Alexander that he should make the decision as to when Pickett should make his assault based on the success of the bombardment. Alexander went to see Pickett before responding, and finding the general in high spirits and eager to make his attack – and believing that Lee's attack plan included sending the entire army forward and not just three divisions – Alexander decided that the attack should be pursued as planned. He wrote back to Longstreet a carefully worded note: "When our artillery fire is doing its best I shall advise General Pickett to advance." It was not the guarantee of success Longstreet had sought.

[69] As the story goes, Union General Hancock rode across Cemetery Ridge during the Confederate bombardment in an effort to inspire his men. One of his brigadiers called to him through the thunderous barrage, "General, the corps commander ought not to risk his life that

way." Hancock, still mounted, said back, "There are times when a corps commander's life does not count."

[70] In the early months of 1862, a scarlet fever epidemic broke out in Richmond, Va., where Longstreet's wife Maria Louise was living with the couple's four children. In the matter of just eight days, scarlet fever took three of the four children. Longstreet and his wife were so distressed at the loss of three of their four children that Pickett and LaSalle Corbell arranged for the funerals for the children.

[71] Pickett, who also recorded the meeting, remembers it differently from Speed. According to Pickett, it was not a question he asked, but a statement in the affirmative: "I shall lead my division on." Otherwise, Speed's recollection corresponds closely with Pickett's of this last meeting between the generals prior to the charge of the third day.

[72] General Garnett was ill at the time of the battle, though on July 3, 1861, he was in good spirits and the only visible indication that he was feeling poorly was that on the hot day – where the temperature was recorded in the high 80s but, with the humidity, felt more like 100 degrees – Garnett was wearing a heavy blue overcoat.

[73] In his own recollections, Pickett claims that he advised Garnett to make quick time across the valley, saying, "It's a hell of an ugly looking place over yonder." Considering the lack of faith Longstreet had in his general, one might assume that Pickett overheard Speed's speech to Garnett and, over the years, adopted it as his own.

[74] Win Hancock and Lewis Armistead (Lo to his friends) were longtime friends, perhaps the closest of friends to serve on different sides in the Civil War. Both men were wounded in Pickett's Charge, Armistead was mortally wounded. Their friendship was well known among their respective circles, and certainly Speed, considering his friendship with Hancock, would have been aware that the two men were intimate friends.

[75] It is unclear exactly what sort of revolver Hancock gave Speed, though most likely it was a Smith & Wesson Model 1, a gun so popular at the outbreak of the American Civil War that the company could not keep pace with the orders. Production of the Smith & Wesson Model 1 began in 1857 and it was the first commercially successful revolver to use rimfire cartridges rather than loose powder, ball and percussion cap. We know that through most of the first years of the war, Speed carried a Colt Navy revolver which would have required the user to stuff paper cartridges into the chambers and fix percussion caps on the nipples at the rear of the chambers.

[76] Though Armistead was shot several times, he did not die on the field. Wounded at the Angle, Armistead was taken by Union soldiers to a field hospital where he died two days later. Family friends secured the body and Armistead was buried in Baltimore.

[77] Speed is correct that a portion of the 71st Pennsylvania regiment positioned at the Angle fled up Cemetery Ridge. Brigadier General Alexander Webb halted the retreat and was eventually able to get the Pennsylvanians to counterattack along with other regiments that were in reserve.

[78] The Army Medal of Honor, today known as the Congressional Medal of Honor, was established during the American Civil War in 1863 to give special recognition to soldiers of the United States military who distinguished themselves "conspicuously by gallantry and intrepidity" in combat. Not including Jackson Speed, 64 Union soldiers at Gettysburg were awarded with the Medal of Honor.

Town of Gettysburg July, 1863

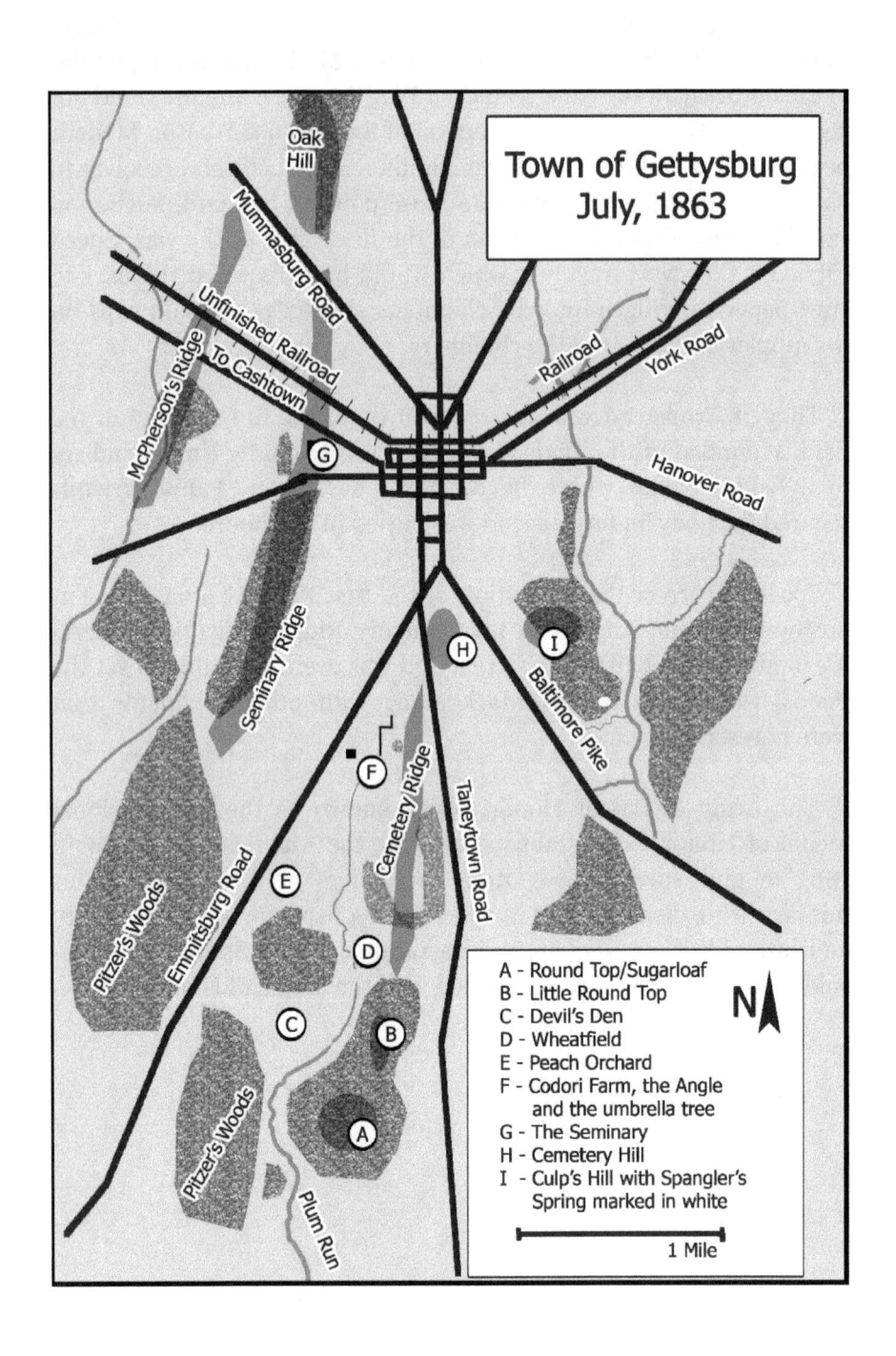

A - Round Top/Sugarloaf
B - Little Round Top
C - Devil's Den
D - Wheatfield
E - Peach Orchard
F - Codori Farm, the Angle and the umbrella tree
G - The Seminary
H - Cemetery Hill
I - Culp's Hill with Spangler's Spring marked in white

ABOUT THE AUTHOR

Robert Peecher is a writer and journalist. He is the author of the Jackson Speed Memoirs (a series of historical novels set during 19th Century America featuring the cowardly, womanizing Jackson Speed) and the Moses Calhoun Potboilers (a series of short stories about a hard-boiled Deputy Sheriff in rural Georgia who battles bumbling meth-heads and other miscreants). He lives in Bishop, Georgia, with his wife and three sons. To contact Rob or to keep current with his projects and new releases, please visit his website **robertpeecher.com**.

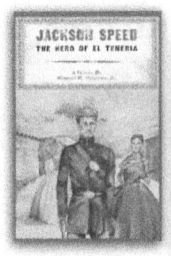

Titles by Robert Peecher

Jackson Speed:
The Hero of El Teneria
Volume I

Jackson Speed
and the Blood Tubs
Volume II

Jackson Speed
on the Orange Turnpike
Volume III

Jackson Speed
at the High Tide
Volume IV

Moses Calhoun
Girl Who Dreamed of Vegas

Moses Calhoun
The Missing Wife

Four Things My Wife
Hates About Mornings
& Other Collected Stories

robertpeecher.com